LOST GIRL

LOST GIRL A NOVEL

HALEY WARREN

imPRESS

MB

imPRESS Millennial Books
Greenville, SC

First imPRESS Millennial Books paperback edition June 2023

For information on imPRESS Millennial Books Consulting, please visit our website at www.impressmillennial.com or contact imPRESS Millennial at publisher@impressmillennial.com.

Printed in the United States of America

ISBN 9781778248320 (Paperback)

To all the other
Lost Girls out there,
may you find
yourself again.

Dear Reader,

Thank you so much for picking up this book. I hope you love the next chapter in Charlie's story. Before you start reading, I want you to be aware of a few things you'll find in this book.

This book mentions the death of a parent, suicide, and previous cheating.

As much as I would love you to read this book, you're more important.

Always take care of yourself.

Haley

LOST GIRL

CHAPTER ONE

David Kennedy was standing in the back of the lecture hall. His foot was kicked up against the stone wall, arms crossed over his chest, and that worn Tarheels hat I could pick out of any crowd turned backward on his head, with blond waves peeking out to curl gently over his ears. The words I was about to say to the students died on my tongue as I took him in, my eyes tracing the way his black t-shirt stretched over his broad shoulders and chest. Our eyes met momentarily, and he arched an eyebrow at me, the corner of his lips pulling up.

My heart somersaulted in my chest, and the familiar beat against my ribcage that happened every time I saw David started. It always sounded the same as it pulsed against my eardrums; it was always whispering the same word. *Home.* I knitted my eyebrows at him, sticking my lower lip out in confusion before turning back to the small group of my seminar students. I sat back against the desk in the center of the room, crossing my leather-booted feet at the ankles.

"As I was saying, papers are due next Friday. Physical copy in my office by 4 p.m." My cheeks burned, and I worked to keep my eyes trained on the students in front of me instead of wandering to David to see if he was still looking at me.

"Is it true your brother's engagement party to Noa Dahan is this weekend? I saw it in Vanity Fair," Devi, one of the senior students enrolled in the International Relations seminar on solving global issues I instructed, asked.

She leaned forward in her seat, propping her chin up on the palm of her hand, the other twirling her braided curls between her fingers like a schoolgirl.

I smiled tightly, folding my arms across my chest. My heart dropped for an entirely different reason, accompanied by the usual twinge of jealousy and pang of regret whenever Deacon's engagement was mentioned. Neither of these feelings had anything to do with my brother and everything to do with the man standing in the back of the lecture hall. It didn't help that Deacon was marrying one of the most famous supermodels in the world. Their impending nuptials and general bliss were shoved down my throat every time I turned on the television or walked by a newsstand.

"I regret encouraging socialization in this class now. But yes, that's why the seminar is canceled next week. I'll still be in Chicago. Any questions about your papers?"

"Will we get to see photos of the party? And your dress?" Devi continued, a small smirk playing on her face.

"I'm sure you'll see them in Vanity Fair as well. If there are no questions about your papers, you're all fine to leave for the day. Email me if you have any questions between now and then."

I gestured vaguely at the door at the back of the room before turning and walking to the other side of my desk. I took a deep breath, steeling myself for the inevitable when I would be left alone with David. The hum of conversation filled the room, and I dropped down in the worn leather chair that sat behind the desk. I made a show of gathering and stacking the papers I would need to take with me, watching from the corner of my eye as the students all began gathering their things and moving toward the exit.

But I wasn't focused on them.

I was watching David as he casually loped down the stairs, hands tucked into his pockets. My heart pulsed rapidly, and that familiar feeling of home wrapped around me. The closer David came, the farther down the stairs he walked, the more it felt like I was coming to the end of a long trip. I continued to look down, the words on the page blurring in front of me.

David stopped in front of my desk, the continued picture of casual elegance, when he swung the chair opposite me around and sat in it, folding his arms across the back. I flicked my gaze up from the blurred page. I could practically feel my heartbeat in my throat and despite my best efforts, my eyes roved over him hungrily. I drank in everything about him: the sharp planes of his face, the stubble lining his jaw that he never seemed to shave anymore, and the lines surrounding his eyes that betrayed the time that had elapsed since we first met. I hoped it meant he had things to laugh about, to smile about, things that made him happy—even if those things weren't me.

"Been awhile, Charlie." David smiled easily, leaning forward even farther. Those lines around his eyes crinkled, and I wanted to run my fingers over them. "You look great."

I looked down, not thinking there was anything particularly special about the crisp white shirt I tucked into a leather skirt this morning and paired with knee-high boots. But that was David. He always saw the things in me I couldn't; he always offered me what I would never deserve. I raised my eyes to meet his, my stomach plummeting when I caught a glint of sparkling honey in his eyes.

"You too," I whispered, continuing to trace every part of him.

The words hung in the air between us, growing thicker with every passing moment. The last time I saw David played out behind my eyes. I breathed in and out, not moving my eyes from his, feeling the condensation from that sweating glass I had been clutching like a lifeline, hearing the noises of the city all around us while I offered up the rest of my life spent in penance, and the "maybe" he offered me tinged with hope for something that never materialized.

Shaking my head, trying to knock those memories back into the hiding spaces I liked for them to stay, I felt a fake, moronic, Winchester smile slide into place.

"What are you doing here, David? Don't tell me you're enrolling."

A wry grin appeared on his face, and he took his hat off, running a hand through his hair before placing it back on. I felt a pang in my chest. It was such a distinct, David mannerism, and it was so at odds with the way he carried himself in the rest of his life.

"No, but if I had more professors like you, I might have considered a few more years in grad school. I missed my flight. I was going to just get on the next one, but Deacon said you were taking the jet home this afternoon? Is it alright with you if I catch a ride?"

My stomach dropped at the thought of being in close proximity with David for an extended period of time.

"Can you really *catch a ride* on a private jet? But, uh, sure, of course. I have a meeting with my supervisor shortly. Guillaume called me earlier to let me know he's landing at Teterboro at 5:15. Do you want to meet there?"

"No point driving separately, Charlie. I'll pick you up around 3?" David stood, his strong hand grabbing the back of the chair and swinging it back around again.

I arched an eyebrow, eyes skittering over the veins and calluses that adorned his hands. "You keep a car in Manhattan?"

"You never know when you might miss a flight and need to drive with your former girlfriend to a private airport." David knocked on the desk with his knuckles, his smile never faltering. "I'll see you later, Charlie."

"My address—"

"I know where you live. Thanks." He smiled at me one more time before turning away and walking back up the stairs.

He came to a sudden halt on the first landing, shoving his hands in his pockets before he looked back at me. "Tripp will be there."

The statement hung heavily in the air between us, sucking all the air out of the room—exactly like Tripp would have. I swallowed, and a pang of regret ate away at my insides. There was nothing I could say to change what those words meant to both of us.

"I know," I answered quietly.

David nodded, saying nothing in response, before looking away from me again and leaving me sitting there with nothing but my own failures pressing in on me.

I continued to stare at his retreating form, my heart in my throat as I watched him throw open the door to the lecture hall, sunlight illuminating his silhouette like he was some sort of angel on earth. And he was, at least to me, even if he was no longer mine.

CHAPTER TWO

For the second time that day, I was confronted with David leaning against something. His foot was kicked up against the wheel of a car I assumed was his but didn't recognize. I could have probably drawn a map of his old BMW with my eyes closed, could feel the leather against the back of my skin when I closed my eyes. But that wasn't this car. Predictably, my heart dropped, beat itself bloody against my ribcage before somersaulting and finding its place again where it continued to skip erratically in my chest.

The simple smile was secured on his face. I studied the way David leaned against his car, not a care in the world, somehow looking shockingly more beautiful against the deep gray paint of it. I cocked my head and peered around the front of the car, eyeing the corner of the flat black Audi emblem. I was sure it was an RS7, and I wrinkled my nose.

It seemed like a decidedly un-David car. But there he was, propped up against it. His shoe was probably scuffing the rim of his tire. A snort escaped my nose as I thought of what Deacon would do if someone placed the bottom of their shoe against his Bentley.

He extended his hand, holding his palm up and gesturing to the giant bag I was holding. I smiled awkwardly, neither of us saying anything as I deposited it in his hand and watched him walk around the car, setting it in the trunk, while I rocked back and forth on my heels. The telltale click of the car lock sounded, and I ducked inside, not wanting to stand outside amongst our own awkwardness any longer.

"So..." David began, clearing his throat and looking anywhere but at me, while we both settled into our respective seats.

The stiff leather of the passenger seat was warm from the early summer sun, and it burned the exposed skin of my shoulder blades.

"Are you going to tell me what dress you're wearing to the engagement party, or do I have to wait to find out from the Vanity Fair article like your students?" He asked.

I scoffed, sliding my sunglasses from the top of my head to cover my eyes. I was partly shielding myself from the sun, partly from David. I didn't have much of a poker face.

"Come on David, you know I won't get to dress myself. No, there will be a rack of Sabine-approved gowns waiting for me at the house."

Watching from the corner of my eye, David smiled fondly. "Should I be expecting you to make a grand entrance in something sequinned?"

"And take attention away from the bride-to-be?" I shook my head. "No, this is likely the one time Sabine will have selected something that might just allow me to fade into the background."

David opened his mouth to speak but closed it before bringing a hand to rub across his jaw as he merged into traffic. I could imagine the words he would have said to me once upon a time—that I could never fade into the background, that I was the most beautiful girl he had ever seen. It didn't matter that I found the chocolate color of my hair boring, that it was always hanging flat around my face, that my eyes were the only interesting thing about my face, and I had to share them with my brother. Forest Green Winchester eyes. Or, that I didn't like the straight bridge of my nose. David loved it. He loved all of me.

Silence fell between us, and I shifted uncomfortably. It felt heavy as it pressed against my skin and so out of place between the two of us. I turned away, looking pointedly out the window and watched aimlessly as people carried on with their lives outside. We drove past trees that were beginning to bloom and life carrying on without us together, while the silence continued to permeate every inch of the car. I scrambled for anything I could say to make it better, to erase the stain I left on us, when David spoke.

"Have you talked to Tripp at all?" He cleared his throat uncomfortably before continuing. "He still works at WH."

I whipped my head around, eyes widening behind my sunglasses at hearing Tripp's name spill from David's mouth. "I know he does. But that's Tripp. Only a cockroach could survive an apocalyptic event of that magnitude," I muttered, scratching at my neck, like that could stop the way my heart twisted at the mention of his name.

"So, have you talked to him?" David pressed.

"No. He's reached out a few times, but I've ignored him for the last year and a half," I answered, an apology ready to tumble from my lips, like another could possibly make a difference to David.

"He golfs with your dad pretty regularly," David said flatly, his eyes never leaving the streets in front of him.

I nodded, unsure why David would be bringing up Tripp. "I also know that. Leave it to Steven to befriend the man integral to my personal downfall."

"Steven?" David asked, ignoring the second half of my comment. "You don't call him 'dad' anymore?"

"Not really." I shrugged, my stomach tightening uncomfortably. "He's not much of a father to me."

I imagined there was a time when David would have comforted me, reached his hand across the car to grab my own and close the distance between us, to remind me of all the ways I was enough for him, even if I didn't feel enough for my father. But he said nothing, both hands gripping the steering wheel tightly, and the silence that had no business between us fell again. It stayed tight, like a noose around the neck of our former relationship for the rest of the drive and suffocated us the entire plane ride back to Chicago.

My father's house looked the same. Set far back from the road, the security gate was uncharacteristically wide open—no wrought iron gates sealed Steven's fortress today. The circular driveway was filled with large, nondescript white trucks that likely belonged to whatever vendors Noa selected for the engagement party. I recognized the name of the floral company—favored by Winchester Holdings for events—written across the side of one of the trucks in elegant, swirling script.

I could see the imposing stone pillars that surrounded the front door beyond the line of trucks, as the driver that picked us up at the Chicago Executive Airport pulled up neatly at the end, delivering me right to my father's doorstep. I could vaguely hear David thanking the driver before opening the door. Smiling politely, I offered my thanks before steeling myself and trying to quell the nausea rolling in my stomach. The thought of being this close to David—to my father—for an extended period of time, had the taste of bile rising in my throat. I spoke to my father only when required and only saw him when it was unavoidable. I hadn't seen him since an incredibly awkward dinner in the spring when he was passing through New York.

The front door swung open, revealing my brother. Deacon bounded down the steps like a child, his chocolate hair ruffled and unstyled as he opened his mouth in what I assumed was a bizarre shriek before jumping off the last step and tackling David into the side of one of the trucks.

I grimaced, pushing open my own door. "You're a thirty-one-year-old man, Deacon. Grow up."

I rolled my eyes as I exited the car. Deacon now had David in a headlock, hair spilling across his forehead.

"Hi, Charles." Deacon smiled before turning back to David, who looked like he was trying to flip Deacon over his back.

"Haven't seen your only sister in God knows how long, but okay, enjoy your wrestling match," I offered, chest tight as I started up the stone steps of my father's home.

"I saw you two weeks ago," Deacon wheezed. It looked like David had elbowed him in the abdomen. "I haven't seen David in almost a month."

I would have answered, but the door opened again, and though I knew better than to expect my father, a small seed of hope threatened to poke through the soil of my heart. Our relationship was perfunctory at this point—but there was a tiny child in me who wished he would come to greet me, to welcome me back home. But a different piece of my heart stood there.

Taylor stepped through the door, her arms wide, and a tiny, knowing smile on her face. Her blonde hair was piled on top of her head in a messy bun that my straight hair would never be able to achieve, and her brown eyes twinkled for me while she bounced back and forth on her feet. The disappointment of my father not deigning to show his face was quieted by the sight of her. She was my best friend in the entire world and aside from my brother, the only thing I really missed about my former life in Chicago.

"Hi," I whispered, tears pooling behind my eyes when I wrapped my arms around her. "You smell like an industrial cleaner or something."

A strangled laugh came from Taylor, and her arms tightened around me. "It's formaldehyde. I observed a patient's autopsy this morning. I came straight from the hospital. Deac told me you were coming with David, and I thought you might need a friend. Nothing like being forced to breathe the same air as your biggest regret for a few hours. How was the trip?"

Pulling away, I turned back to where Deacon and David were now standing talking like normal, backs turned to us before they made their way down one of the many stone pathways that spanned the grounds of the house.

"Silent. He couldn't fucking wait to get rid of me," I answered. "We barely spoke the entire plane ride. He only looked at me once when I choked on a sip of water. I think he would have debated letting me die right then and there had he not had you to answer to."

Taylor wrapped her arm around my shoulders, turning me toward the still open front door. "Don't worry about it. David is far too noble for that sort of thing. Come with me, I was helping Noa out back."

A bitter taste coated my mouth as I thought about the fact that Taylor was closer to my brother's fiancée than I was. I hardly knew anything about Noa, beyond the facts that were a matter of public record. I had spent a sum total of four hours alone with her. It wasn't that I didn't like Noa—she was fine and seemed more than nice enough. Deacon was enamored with her but looking at them always felt like I was staring at my own mistakes. All the things I could have had if I wasn't so fucked up. And she was just another reminder that everything had changed. Everything was different. I was no longer number one in Deacon's life, and I never would be again.

As Taylor and I crossed the threshold of my father's home, I closed the door gently behind me, and out of habit, I inhaled deeply. The house smelled the way it had for the better part of a decade—like my mother was never there at all.

At this point in my life, I had lost count of how many times the sprawling backyard of my father's home had played host to events like this, how many times it had been taken over by white tents, sprawling floral arrangements and catering or wait staff dressed in black ties. Today was no different, but instead of Rebecca, the WH publicist directing where everything should go, the world's foremost supermodel stood in the middle, organizing the scene like a conductor, a wide smile stretched across her perfect features.

Her hands were waving animatedly, the giant emerald cut diamond on her finger catching every ray of sunlight. When Deacon told me he was going to propose, I half-expected him to tell me he was using our mother's wedding ring, but I guess that would have been bad luck. I never knew what happened to it. The last time I saw it, I was watching my father stare at it silently after David left it at my feet. It was probably locked up in a vault somewhere, along with any other human emotion my father had ever felt.

Noa turned, a smile that portrayed only genuine happiness toward me stretched across her face. Her brown skin was bare, somehow flawless and sparkling in the sunlight—much like that giant diamond. Guilt bubbled in my stomach as a standard, fake Winchester smile fell into place on my own face. Despite how fake, how forced they always were, no one ever seemed to notice that a Winchester was probably never smiling on the inside. Noa spent most of her time in New York, and despite living in the same city, I hadn't once made an effort with her in fear I would somehow be forced to spend time with David. The only time I saw her was when Deacon came to visit.

"Charlie!" Noa continued to smile, features soft and bringing me in for a hug, while my arms hung limply at my sides. I noticed Taylor narrow her eyes at me, and I mechanically raised my arms and hugged her in return. "It's so great to see you. Deacon's so happy you came out a day early."

"Really?" I asked, arching my eyebrow and unable to stop myself. "He seemed far too busy wrestling with David to even notice I was here."

Noa's amber eyes glittered, and she continued to smile brightly, like Deacon's near constant childish behavior was endearing. I found myself staring at her eyes a moment longer. They were the subject of many headlines about her. Whereas David's eyes glinted with shades of honey or amber in and amongst the more common brown, Noa's are a light amber color. According to Vogue, it was incredibly rare and part of what made her so striking. She was still smiling when she spoke. "You know your brother. He's probably the most childish person I've ever met, but I love him."

"I have a theory Deacon stopped maturing around the time he hit puberty," Taylor offered, pushing me firmly toward the tent that would play host to the engagement party sat, taking up the majority of the yard.

"I'm not sure that would be backed by science, doctor." I stared at her pointedly as she narrowed her eyes at me.

I gestured toward the tent, turning to Noa with another dumb smile. "What can I do to help?"

She smiled, overlarge and genuine, too consumed with her own happiness to notice the discomfort that was practically radiating off my skin. "The staff have pretty much taken care of everything but come see how everything looks."

Walking down the gentle slope of the lawn to where it flattened out, I stared determinedly at my feet, putting one in front of the other. The stone ledge lining the edge of the lake encroached onto the periphery of my vision, and if I wasn't careful, I knew I would be able to see Tripp and me sitting out there, our backs to the house, my ridiculous dress trimmed in ostrich feathers, and our lips meeting for the first time in years. If an artist were to paint it, they would probably call it something like the beginning of my downfall. I could add that memory to the long list of ghosts haunting this house.

I followed Noa and Taylor into the tent, looking up to see a clear roof. The view of the stars would be unobstructed.

Noa moved forward to help a struggling server balance a box they were holding precariously on their forearm.

"It looks like Baz Luhrman threw up in here," I muttered under my breath to Taylor.

In a surprise to none of us, Deacon had become obsessed with his version of the Great Gatsby when it came out in 2013. It went as far as him asking our father to start investing in liquor.

"Be nice," she said through a tight smile. "The theme is the roaring twenties."

I turned to look at her, ensuring a moronic smile had taken up residence on my face. "You don't say?"

Taylor moved to step in front of me, a bony elbow finding its way to jab into my ribs. "Deacon always wanted to be Jay Gatsby."

"Jay Gatsby gets shot," I hissed, reaching up to pinch the back of her arm.

"Do you really think Deacon ever finished the book?" Taylor deadpanned before turning to Noa. "What can we do to help?"

I took a moment to take in what I was seeing. The entire side of the tent was taken up by tables covered in draped golden fabric that shimmered, weighed down by enormous towers of champagne coupes. Interspersed between the towers were large displays of white feathers, the plumes draping over ornate crystal vases. Scattered through the room between each table were tall, gold embossed wooden stands that were topped with assortments of white flowers, offset with twisted branches painted in gold that stuck out behind the bouquets. Each table for guests was circled by golden chairs with ivory padding, as opposed to the drink tables that were draped in ivory fabric. A giant display of white feathers took up the center, where they sat atop a black crystal riser. Gold-edged plates and drinkware sat in front of the place settings, with neat, silky black napkins placed on the top. There were tiny

15

bouquets of white roses surrounding the feather display in the middle of the table.

A grimace pulled on my lips as I imagined what monstrosity Sabine would dress me in now.

"Charlie?" Noa spoke, beckoning me and walking toward a smaller table I hadn't noticed before. It was pushed into the corner of the tent. "I want to show you something."

I glanced sideways at Taylor, eyebrows knit in confusion, and she shrugged her shoulders before turning to help a server unpack a box of champagne.

Noa stopped in front of the table, and I noticed her smile was replaced with a look of hesitancy, her fingers fidgeting with the seams of her white shirt. I opened my mouth to ask her what we were doing over here, what she wanted me to see, when I saw the photograph at the center of the table.

Photos of my mother were placed across the tiny surface, and it was clear whoever had put them there did so with care. A portrait of my mother I recognized from my father's office sat in the center, surrounded by other, smaller photos of the family I used to have through the years. There were some of her and my father from when they were young and photos from various family vacations. Strings of pearls were placed carefully across the table, wrapping around the photos almost lovingly before they came to circle three tall white candles placed in the back. A smaller, softer, display of feathers and flowers sat opposite it.

My eyes burned and I blinked, bringing my fingers to run along the frame of the middle portrait. "Where did you get all these?"

Noa moved closer to me, like she wanted to offer me comfort but didn't know how to. "I asked the staff to help me pick some out. I don't know. I just thought she should have a place here. Deacon never talks about her."

Her voice trailed off, and I turned to face her, knowing my eyes were red with unshed tears. Before I could think better of it, I reached forward to grab her hand in my own. Her eyes widened in surprise before a soft smile pulled on her lips. I studied her for a moment longer, our hands still grasped above the table, and I noticed the way she was looking at me. It wasn't a look I had ever received from my brother or father. She was looking at me like I was someone who might be missing someone, who might still be grieving after all these years. I opened my mouth to say something, anything, to say thank you, to tell Noa this was beautiful, to say that after all these years, I felt seen. Before I could say anything, Deacon's voice, laced with anger, exploded in my periphery.

"Absolutely not. Are you kidding me, Charlie?" He pushed between us, slamming the portrait of our mother down onto the table. "You've been home, all of what? Five minutes? And you're already bringing this shit up?"

I dropped Noa's hand, any semblance of comfort I was finding there chased away by Deacon's anger. I watched as her features crumpled and her eyes grew misty. Before she could open her mouth to speak, I rounded on Deacon. "She's your mother, Deacon. It's not weird to have photos of her at your engagement party. Some people might say it would be weird not to have them."

"She forfeited the title of mother easily enough," Deacon snarled, his green eyes murderous. A wisp of hair was still falling across his forehead, and instead of making him look playful like usual, he looked deranged. "I don't care how long you've been planning this, what staff you had to get to do your dirty work, get rid of it. I want it gone."

"No," I spit out, all too aware it wasn't just me Deacon was hurting. "You want the photos gone? Take them inside yourself. But that's probably more time alone with her than you're interested in, isn't it?"

"Quit being a fucking bitch!" Deacon's voice was still raised, and I noticed his knuckles were white where he was still pressing down the portrait, like he could force the photo down through the table, to the ground and into the earth where her memory could disappear along with her body.

"Deacon..." Noa began softly, placing a hand on his forearm.

"Don't defend her!" Deacon snapped, his eyes darting to his fiancée briefly before landing back on me. "She's always pulling this shit. At your engagement party, you're welcome to reserve an entire table for photos of her, but this isn't your engagement party, is it? You fucked up the relationship with the only man who could tolerate you for longer than five minutes."

A sound caught between a sob and all the air simultaneously being sucked from my lungs emitted from my throat. My eyes closed, and I tried to gasp for breath, but there was none. No matter how mad he got, how upset he got about our mother, or what he thought she did to him, he never, ever spoke to me like this. There was a line somewhere between us and he had crossed it, hitting me exactly where he knew it would hurt the most. Who knew that mere photos of our mother being brought into his relationship would be the breaking point after all these years, and that this new version of Deacon, whoever he was, just couldn't stand for that.

"Deacon!" Taylor's voice cut across the tent, fury dancing in her eyes.

Rage, guilt and humiliation swirled in a nauseating tornado in my stomach. And beneath all that, Deacon had just shattered the pieces of my heart I was only just beginning to sew back together. I looked at him, and it was like looking at someone I didn't even know. The Deacon I knew, the Deacon I loved with my whole heart, would never hurt me like that.

"Fuck. You," I bit out, each word punctuated with venom.

I felt Taylor grab my shoulder and attempt to pull me back. I jerked forward, half-tempted to reach out and pull his hair like when we were children. I couldn't remember the last time we fought like this—this viscerally. Deacon was on the precipice of speaking again, his mouth opening for what would surely be an angry retort when our father's voice sounded.

"Enough!" our father barked, eyes narrowed and mouth in a taut line. "I was under the assumption my children were fully grown adults, but clearly, I was wrong."

Deacon looked as if he was going to argue, rounding on our father, but he held up a hand in typical Steven Winchester fashion. "Enough!" he shouted again, eyes flashing. "Taylor, please take the photos back inside. Clearly, my children can't be trusted to act with any semblance of dignity."

A scoff escaped me, and I watched Taylor gingerly, reverently, begin to stack the photos before clutching them to her chest and leaving the tent. I knew she did so only for my benefit. Deacon would have preferred she threw them in the lake.

I whirled around, coming face-to-face with my father for the first time in months. Steven Winchester looked the same, perhaps a few more gray hairs than the last time. His blue eyes were dark, and as they stayed narrowed in on his children, there were maybe one or two additional lines of age wrinkling around them. It was a Friday, and he was still in part of a suit but had abandoned the jacket somewhere. As if this couldn't get any worse, David was standing just behind him, an expression that bordered on a grimace stretched across his face.

"That's it?" I asked incredulously, gesturing behind me to the display of photos. "He's disrespecting—"

He held his hand up again, interrupting me, "Yes, Charlie, that's it." No familial love or affection to be found in his voice or his features.

Deacon turned and stormed away, now gripping a glass of scotch he helped himself to at the bar at the other end of the tent. Holding my hands up in defeat, or maybe it was disbelief, I shouldered past my father, doing my best to avoid David's eyes. "Hi to you, too, *Steven*."

CHAPTER THREE

Sabine had procured a silk-covered pedestal from somewhere. It reminded me of the platforms that a bride-to-be would stand on when trying on wedding gowns. I had never seen it before in my life, but I was now standing atop it in nothing but a strapless nude bodysuit that bordered on lingerie to wear under whatever gown she decided on.

I rocked back and forth on the balls of my feet, careful not to tip the champagne flute I was clutching while I studied myself in the mirror. My eyes looked dull, but that was nothing new when I was forced to be here, suffocated by all my misdeeds that lived in these halls. My fight with Deacon was ringing in my ears, and his words burned against my skin as I replayed them against my father's expression of perpetual disappointment in me. I schooled my features into a bored expression, hoping I could will them away, and I brought the flute to my lips, clinking the crystal against my teeth.

"Sabine, don't you think your efforts would be better spent dressing Noa or Deacon?" I asked, watching her paw through the rack of designer gowns taking up residence in my bedroom.

It wasn't really my bedroom, not anymore, but for a man who didn't seem to give a shit about his family, my father had kept both

Deacon and my childhood rooms intact, exactly as they had been the day we left for college.

Her dark curls were pulled back into a tight bun that sat impossibly high on her head, and a look of concentration was etched on her features as she studied the gowns.

"Hmm?" she turned, her dark eyes sweeping over me, eyebrows narrowed. "Noa was gifted a gown by one of the designers she models for in exchange for the feature in Vanity Fair. Are you sure you haven't lost weight? You look thinner than the last time I dressed you. I'm a bit worried about how some of these might fit."

I shrugged, taking another sip of my champagne. It wouldn't be the worst thing in the world if none of the gowns she had chosen for me fit. There were far too many sequins and vibrant, screaming colors adorning that rack. I wasn't sure if I had lost weight.

Since moving to New York, I had really leaned into the cliché of the rich girl in her designer gear running through Central Park each day. It felt like I was accomplishing something each time I finished my circuit, but maybe it was just the same old me, trying to outrun the ghosts that nipped at my heels.

"Not to my knowledge. I have some other gowns here if nothing else fits."

She turned to me again, this time with an incredulous look on her face. "Charlie, you cannot wear a gown you've worn before to a party Vanity Fair is covering. We'll make it work, even if I have to pin you in."

I opened my mouth, about to suggest one of the options Taylor brought when a knock sounded on the door. It probably was Taylor, hopefully coming to rescue me with a simple, black gown. There was no way in hell Deacon, or my father, would be checking on me after that mishap.

"Come in," I called lazily, expecting Taylor to throw open the door and prance through my room like it was her own.

A head of messy blond hair appeared in the doorway as David ducked into the room. His mouth parted and whatever he was going to say died on his lips when our eyes met. He cocked his head, like an animal caught by headlights, surprised and unsure. I watched as his eyes swept over my body and heat spread across my cheeks, memories of his hands all over me, whispering across my skin. But it wasn't lust behind David's eyes—they were dark with concern.

"I'm sorry, I didn't realize. I was—" David began, immediately averting his gaze and ducking his head.

"Oh, come on David, don't be shy. It's nothing you haven't seen before," I chided, making light of the tsunami rolling through my stomach, boiling my blood and destroying my bones—all because my skin had been touched by David Kennedy's eyes.

I was speaking with a bravado that didn't belong to me. Every inch of my skin burned, the ghosts of his hands everywhere. The lace trim of the corset felt rough against my skin. Sabine hadn't even seemed to notice—I could see her out of the corner of my eye—examining the specifications and sizing of all the dresses, seemingly muttering to herself.

Something between a laugh and a choking sound came from David, and he leaned up against the doorframe, crossing his arms. "Be that as it may, I was just checking to see if you were alright."

"Oh, did you enjoy the show?" I asked, rolling my eyes before taking a sip of my champagne. "I'm fine, David. Thank you, but it's nothing I haven't dealt with before."

"Deacon didn't mean what he said," David said quietly, his eyes now roaming anywhere but me, not landing on one particular thing.

I scoffed, emptying my champagne before hopping off the pedestal and setting the flute down on the vanity pushed against the wall. "We both know that's not true. He meant every word."

David's eyes finally fell on me as I walked toward him, closer than we had been in almost a year, and certainly with one of us in significantly less clothing. I heard an irritated huff come from Sabine, but I ignored her in favor of moving closer to David.

"Deacon says you've been running. He says you do ten miles in the park every morning."

I narrowed my eyes, lips pursed. "So? Do you want to come running with me, Mr. Kennedy?"

I wasn't sure why I said it. Maybe the familiar nickname just slid from my lips by accident. But it was weighted, heavy. Being this close to David—my skin was crawling now, and I wanted nothing more than to drag him into this room and feel his callused, worn hands all over me, the real ones, not the faded memories that would forever pale in comparison. I wanted to go home.

"No, I don't want to run with you, billion dollar baby," he said, his voice remaining low. "For the record, Deacon was wrong. Five minutes never would have been enough. I could have tolerated you forever."

My mouth popped open, despite there being no words waiting there. All I could hear was my heart beating against my ribcage. It echoed in my ears as I stood there, gaping at him like some sort of demented fish. I was half-caught between wanting to throw myself at his feet, begging for his forgiveness again, and the other part of me wanting absolutely nothing to do with the Charlie

Winchester of the past. Billion dollar baby proved to be an untrustworthy, sad excuse for a human being. Before I could decide who I wanted to be, Sabine spoke, her voice interrupting and slicing through the possibility that felt palpable between us.

"Charlie, are you ready? I think we should try you in the Oscar de la Renta. This style runs small." She was pulling a dress off the rack, not bothering to look in my direction.

"Duty calls," I whispered, voice dry.

Planting my hand firmly on the door handle, David seemed to take that as his cue to leave and stepped back into the hallway. His eyes were still on me, gaze never wavering.

"Goodbye, David."

I turned, gently shutting the door before the burning tears could spill over my lash lines. Padding across the room, I stepped onto the pedestal with significantly more grace than I came off of it with. Rolling my shoulders back, I caught Sabine's eye in the mirror of the vanity as she held the gown, the swathes of metallic fabric, a mixture of gold and black falling between her fingers. It was a dress fit for a *rich girl* like me.

As I turned down the hall, I saw a faint light emanating from under the heavy oak door of one of the guest bedrooms—the one David was staying in. I exhaled slowly, bracing myself and trying to steady the gnawing sensation in my stomach. I adjusted my robe as it fell open on the walk across the house. The last thing I wanted was for him to think I was here on some pathetic mission to win him back. I would give anything, but I just wanted to be near him—the embarrassing fight with Deacon was still ringing in my ears, followed by the softer words David had said to me earlier when he came to my room during my fitting.

Like looking through the wrong end of a telescope, the image all small and distorted, I could picture Taylor grabbing the framed photo of my mother and following me back into the house, before breaking off and returning it to its rightful place in the study. She was sharing my room with me for the weekend and fell asleep on the chaise lounge at the end of my bed when she was checking her patients' overnight labs and doing research for some sort of upcoming surgery she had scheduled.

I braced myself, keeping hold of the bottle of scotch and two glasses I stole from the wet bar in my father's office as I padded across the house in the dark. I hadn't even looked at the bottle, no concept of what I took. I raised my hand and knocked softly on the door before pushing it open and peering my head around it. My breath caught as I took in David. He sat behind the giant desk that took up residence in the center of the room. The room was filled with dark wood and gold fixtures, incredibly ostentatious, and it was larger than most small apartments. All of the guest bedrooms were. If I hadn't known better, I would have thought my father designed them to be that way. Nothing but the best for a guest of the Winchesters.

His eyebrows were furrowed at whatever he was reading on his computer in front of him. His hair was pushed back off his face with that worn Tarheels hat on backward and a faded Princeton sweater that was pushed up to reveal his forearms. He looked up as I entered the room.

His lips turned down briefly, and he arched an eyebrow. "Charlie, what's wrong?"

I was wearing some ridiculous La Perla robe and pajama set Noa had left for me in my room. She left one for Taylor, too. Both were barely there slinky camisoles with some sort of lace embroidery Taylor told me was called *Frastaglio*. It was meant to make it look like a flower was framing your body and was apparently what La Perla was known for. The tiny shorts had the same on the side, and the embroidery flowed down the front of the robe. Taylor had claimed the pale blue set and thrust the black one at me, saying it matched my moody disposition. I shook the bottle of scotch in the air and forced a smile.

"I come in peace. Do you have time for a drink with me?"

David pushed back off the desk and surveyed me apprehensively. "That's quite the robe you have on there."

I shook my head, barely catching my eye roll as I said, "Noa gave them to me and Taylor. She said she modeled for La Perla and had tons of these just sitting around."

David removed his hat, running a hand through his hair, pushing it off his face again before setting it back down. He waved me in closer to where he stood up, gesturing toward the lounge identical to mine that was at the end of the king bed on the other side of the room. Chaise loungers in every room were a Steven Winchester staple apparently.

"You do know she is actually a model, right? You're saying that like you think she stole those off a truck in Dumbo."

"Oh, trust me, I know she's a model." I rolled my eyes before I could stop.

My cheeks flushed. I knew how that sounded. Like I looked down on her and what she did for a living, and I didn't. Not at all. I turned away and made my way to sit on the lounge, tugging my robe closed again as I did.

"Charlie..." there was a warning in David's voice, like he was chastising a child. He settled in beside me, narrowing his eyes. "Don't tell me you think she's not good enough for Deacon, because she's a model?"

My face warmed as I looked down, mouth popping open in dread when I saw the port-colored year on the worn label that read 1926, and the name above it. I grabbed a Macallan scotch. My father bought this scotch at an auction for almost two million dollars. There were only forty bottles ever filled. I was tempted to run away from David, from this room, scotch in hand and pretend it never happened. But then I remembered my father's face, how impassive and cold it looked when his gaze landed on the photos of my mother. How he let Deacon insult his wife like that. Insult our mother like that.

I started trying to work the cork out of the bottle with my thumbs. The truth had nothing to do with what Noa did for a living. I was so horrifically jealous Deacon was in love and getting married. So jealous the envy made my bones ache when I looked at them. I was in love like that, specifically with the man sitting across from me. It wasn't like I wanted the huge spectacle of the wedding, but I wanted what they had. I wanted my relationship back. And if I was being honest with myself, truly honest, I was terrified of the feeling that my relationship with my brother was fraying even more; that the invisible string between us was pulling and splitting.

"No. I mean, would I have rather they wait? Sure."

David arched an eyebrow, leaning back and observing me. "This seems kind of sexist somehow, and quite frankly, unlike you."

"They rushed into it, maybe she's using him!" I blurted quickly, the lie too easy and too convenient a deflection, even though I knew David would see right through it.

David grabbed the bottle from my hand, pushing the cork out easily with his thumb. "Again, sexist, and unlike you. So, she's using him because she's a model and a woman? Charlie, she was just on the cover of Vogue for Christ's sake. She probably has her own millions. You don't even know her. Deacon told me you don't spend any time with her. He said he thinks you've probably spent maybe a collective four hours alone with her..."

"They've only been together a year," I said, voice thick with fake justification, grabbing the scotch-filled glass David was handing me, careful to keep my fingers from brushing his.

David appraised me, taking a small sip of his drink before narrowing his eyes again. "I was going to propose to you after just a year. Do you think I was rushing into it?"

I knew this was a rhetorical question. I closed my eyes briefly, but the whole thing was there, ready to play on a loop, waiting to pounce and tear into my heart and rip it out. David standing on the steps of The Peninsula in Chicago, rain pouring down as he held out that vintage Harry Winston ring that had belonged to my mother in his bloodied hand.

I opened my eyes, staring determinedly down at my scotch, swirling the amber liquid in the crystal glass.

"No. I don't think you were rushing into it." My voice was small as I took a sip from my glass. "When you know, you know, I suppose."

"So, are you going to tell me what that was about today? With the photo of your mother? You had to know that would piss

Deacon off," David said, changing the subject. I couldn't tell if it was for his benefit or mine.

"I didn't do it. Noa set up the display as a surprise for him. I wouldn't have done that to him." I looked down again, tempted to pick at my cuticles. "He still won't talk about her. He still won't give her life, and I don't know, he's probably the one child she might have been proud of."

"And how did you feel about that? Noa setting that up, taking the time to do that for Deacon. For you," David asked softly.

I continued to look down, feigning interest in the way the amber liquid floated aimlessly around the glass.

Shrugging, I tossed back an overly large gulp of a scotch that was certainly meant to be savored. Or, at least, for two million dollars it should have been. "It was fine."

David was silent, and I watched the column of his throat from the corner of my eye when he swallowed a sip before setting the glass on the floor beside him. It was unfair that he made something as simple as swallowing look so fucking beautiful. There wasn't a movement, a twitch of muscle, anything his body did that didn't feel like it was made for me. He raised his eyebrows and a knowing expression stole across his face. He stayed silent for a few moments longer until he spoke, his voice quiet. "Why do you think she wouldn't be proud of you, Charlie?"

My eyes stung immediately at the question, and I blinked, bringing the glass to my mouth.

"Please," I snorted, shaking my head, wisps of my pin-straight hair falling in my face and obscuring my vision further. "I single-handedly decimated the entire leadership team at WH. I'm fucking teaching and doing a Ph.D. program, because I have no idea what I want to do. And I'm not...I'm not a good person."

David said nothing for a moment, waiting, and I could feel his gaze on me. Those honey eyes that were anything but boring. He placed his hand on my ankle where it sat exposed, resting across my opposite leg.

"Charlie, you're not—"

"I cheated on you. I'm a bad person, David," my voice, possibly as small as it had ever been, cracked horribly as I gulped between sobs that had somehow snuck up on me, wracking my body and stealing all the air from my lungs.

David remained silent, the sharp gasps I was making cutting through the night like a knife. Like I had cut right through the center of both our hearts. I felt his hand tighten on my ankle.

"David, I'm so sorry...I—" I gulped, losing my words and looking up at him. I loved him so much.

David sighed, and my infantile feelings increased. "Charlie, I know you cheated on me, and I know you're sorry."

He reached forward and grabbed my glass from my hand, setting it down gingerly on the floor alongside his previously discarded one. "I know all these things, and I still don't think you're a bad person."

I rubbed my hands furiously across my face, trying to scrub away the guilt and embarrassment that was so stuck to me it was probably the top layer of my skin at this point. "I love you so much, David. You're the perfect person, and my best friend....you were my best friend. You were the only person who ever understood me and—"

"Charlie. I know you love me. I know you loved me when you cheated on me. I know you love me, even though you hurt me. These facts don't negate that one," David interrupted me, and I glanced upward at him again.

His eyebrows were creased, and he looked torn between anguish and frustration. I reached out and grabbed David's other hand impulsively and cradled it between my two smaller ones, running my fingers along all his joints, veins and calluses, in an attempt to commit them to memory. The muscles in his arm jumped under my fingertips, but he didn't pull away.

"I would spend the rest of my life making things up to you. I would do anything—"

"Charlie," David said sternly, releasing my ankle and placing his hand under my chin, bringing my eyes to meet his. "I need to say this, and I am not saying this to be hurtful. But I've tried. Believe me when I say I've tried. I have both tried to forget what you did and forget you entirely. I can't seem to do either. I love you the same way I did when I first saw you. And I forgive you. But I can't forget what you did."

I closed my eyes and leaned into David's hand that was cupping my chin, grabbing it with both of my own. My skin warmed where it laid against his. Tears leaked out of my closed eyes. "David—"

I heard him sigh again and his fingers tightened, twitching against my chin. "Charlie, when I say I have tried, I mean I have *tried*. I tried therapy. More than once. I would give anything to forget, to move on. Anything. Do you think I love you any less? Do you think you're any less than the best dream I could have imagined for myself? I would give *anything*. Anything to be able to forget what you did. But I just can't. I can't forget it. And ignoring that fact wouldn't be fair to either of us."

I grabbed his hand tighter as I sobbed openly, leaning forward. I said nothing, continuing to cry, mouth open and gaping, and the noises coming out all gasping air. The skin of his hand grew sticky with my tears. I was close to literally dropping to the ground and begging at the altar of the person I loved most in the world for his forgiveness—begging for any piece of him, when he spoke again.

"Charlie, please stop crying," David whispered, pulling his hand away from my face and setting it firmly on my knee. "I can't. I wish I could, but I can't."

"When I first came back, you said maybe. I thought that if I waited, if we waited, that—"

"I'm sorry," David's voice was so loving, so tender, so fucking everything I didn't deserve. But somehow it stabbed right through my heart all the same.

"You never told people what happened. You said my dad didn't make you lie, but why haven't you told people the truth? You said I rejected you, but I would never—" I asked, my words punctuated with wet sobs.

"You did reject me, Charlie. In your own way," David's voice was harder than it had been, all the sharp edges of the heart that I broke. "But that's not why. I told people that, because I didn't want people to make assumptions about us. I didn't want to close the door on us, just in case I could forget."

My vision blurred, the hot tears continued to pour down my face, surely leaving stains on the silk pajamas. I nodded weakly, feeling somewhat like a child being told no. "This hurts so fucking much," my voice was a useless, wet gasp.

I looked up at David. His eyes were almost black and impossible to read, and at that moment I realized one of my worst fears—that they would never sparkle for me again.

"It hurts me, too," David's voice was low, the corners of his mouth pulling down slightly.

He ran a hand over his jaw before dropping it and grabbing mine in his. He interlaced our fingers, and I studied the way his hand engulfed mine. My eyelids fluttered briefly, and I traced his knuckles, the back of his hands, up his arms across the cords of muscle and the light dusting of hair with my fingertips. He felt like sunlight and love, and the way my fingers skated across his skin reminded me of the way it would feel to touch your favorite sweater, the one that was so worn and threadbare but fit you just right. The one you clung onto when you moved away from home. I was afraid to look up, afraid to stop tattooing his arms and his body on my finger tips, but when I finally did, I realized he had never looked away from me.

I wasn't sure how long we stayed there, hands joined, occasionally bringing the scotch to our lips, sometimes whispering to one another, like we were trying to hide from something—maybe we were. Our eyes never left one another, never looked away from the possibility, the promise—the home that could have been.

CHAPTER FOUR

The engagement party wouldn't have been out of place in a period piece set during the height of prohibition when bootleggers were making money hand over fist and throwing parties that had too many black and gold decorations. Or, at least, what Deacon thought those parties would have looked like. I really wasn't sure he got the point of The Great Gatsby, and the lavish display before me really drove that home. I wouldn't have been surprised if guests arrived draped with pearls or in feathered headdresses. I was also beginning to suspect that Sabine had ulterior motives in dressing me in this Oscar de la Renta gown beyond the sizing. I practically matched the decorations. The sweetheart neckline was tight to my skin, the twist bodice made of metallic gold lamé that stopped at my waist, the rest of the skirt flowing freely from my body, the crinkles of the material making it look effervescent in the light.

Pulling at the bodice absentmindedly, I shimmied my shoulders in an attempt to pull the neckline higher. Sabine wasn't wrong. I was down a size or two. I took this to mean I should probably try a different coping mechanism that didn't involve trying to outrun my ghosts ten miles at a time each day, while Sabine took that to mean the cuts of my gowns could be lower without being offensive.

Nails dug into my forearm, grabbing my hands away from my gown. I whirled around, finding Taylor standing there in a blood red, off-the-shoulder Alexander McQueen gown that I saw in Vogue just last week. It had gathered puff sleeves that would look ridiculous on anyone else. But not on Taylor. Her blonde hair was slicked back into a messy ponytail, eyes dusted with gold shimmer and lips painted the exact same shade of her dress.

"Stop pulling. It looks great." She wrapped her hand around my wrist, bringing it down to her side before she interlaced her fingers with mine.

"No, *you* look great." I tipped my head, surveying her pointedly. The tight chignon Sabine had my hair pulled back into was giving me a headache. "As usual, I'm not sure what I look like."

"You look beautiful. You always do." Taylor tightened her grip on my hand, offering me a faint squeeze of affection before dropping it and pointing toward the currently empty bar.

Guests had already begun to filter in, and somehow I avoided being a part of the welcome party. My father and Deacon stood on the left side of the tent entrance, both in classic black and white tuxedos that had been customized for them by God knows who, ready to greet guests as they were escorted down the sloping hill by a member of the family staff. Noa was on the right side, wearing some sort of white silk and feathered gown that was certainly custom made for her as well. I also knew the right side was her 'good side' for photographs, according to the recent Vanity Fair article profiling their engagement. That is, if a supermodel could only have one good side.

"Where'd you go last night?" Taylor asked, drumming her perpetually stubby fingernails against the bar countertop. "I woke up and you were gone."

"Oh, I'm sorry. Were you waiting up for me?" I asked, slapping a hand to my chest. "When I left, you were snoring away on the chaise, your ass hanging out of the silk La Perla's Noa oh so graciously donated to us."

Taylor's brown eyes narrowed instantly. "What's the matter with you?"

"Nothing," I shrugged, turning away from her and smiling politely at the bartender who was serving another guest. I was a liar.

There was something wrong with me, and maybe there always had been.

Noa was nothing but nice to me, and I couldn't seem to get over my own baggage to publicly recognize it.

"Charlie, don't let whatever's going on in your head ruin this for you, or for them," Taylor spoke softly, but there was a harsh tone to her words that she usually reserved for others and was rarely directed toward me. "Noa has been through a lot, and she's a good person."

The words fell from my lips before I could stop them. "Oh, I know. I read all about it in the Vanity Fair article. Parents killed in a car crash in Malta, she moved stateside to live with her aunt, she's discovered while she's waiting tables in high school, and then her aunt tragically dies, too. It has all the makings of a Lifetime movie."

I still wasn't looking at Taylor, staring resolutely at the champagne tower directly in front of me. But I knew she was glaring at me; I could practically feel the disgust radiating off her. In the corner of my eye, I could see her upper lip peeling back while she stared at me.

"Cut the shit, Charlie. What is your issue with her?" Taylor's voice was low but sharp.

"Please. You just like her because you introduced them and because you dated one of her best friends!" I scoffed. I didn't even believe what I was saying.

I accepted the coupe of champagne from the outstretched hand of the bartender. The words felt heavy in my mouth, accompanied by a sour taste that followed them. I didn't like how I was acting, but I couldn't stop myself, and nothing seemed to be worse than my own disgust with myself. It was like digging my own grave, because I knew I deserved to lie there.

"Okay, what is the matter with you?!" Taylor hissed, grabbing my forearm and dragging me to the corner of the bar, bubbles of champagne slopping over the side of the delicate crystal coupe.

I looked at her, my lips parting to lie or to deflect, but her brown eyes were now clouded, not with anger but concern. I could see it in the way a frown pulled at her expertly painted lips, making her sharp, pointed features appear less angular. The harsh bite of her fingers against my arm turned into a soft brush. If I couldn't be honest with her, my best friend, my only friend really—one of the only people I felt really knew me—then, *who* could I be honest with?

"I'm fucking jealous, Taylor! I am so envious, so jealous of my own brother, who deserves happiness, that I want to carve my own eyes out when I look at them! This should be me. This should be my fucking engagement party, which would be way less gauche, by the way. David should be greeting people over there with his stupid blond hair falling in front of his forehead. I should be wearing that dumb feather getup! I'm angry Deacon, DEACON, of all people, came out of all of this unscathed! I guess his powers of avoidance really worked wonders, because somehow he is the only functioning one of us all! Maybe I should have been pretending none of this was supremely fucked up my whole life, too!" I gestured widely with my arms, like the tent held all the secrets of the Winchester family, like the draped pearls and gold embossed crystal were whispering to us. "He has everything I want—all the things I don't deserve."

All the things that slipped through my grasp. I was furious with him, too, and angry that he somehow hadn't become a cheating, damaged person because our mom died. Angry at myself for falling so short. For failing her. Failing to notice her slipping away, and then failing to grieve her the way she deserved.

Taylor's features collapsed on themselves, all the sharp edges softening, and sadness stole across her face.

"Charlie..." her voice was a whisper, and she started forward like she was going to wrap her arms around me, but I shook my head and took a step back from her.

I blinked rapidly, tears having risen unbidden to my eyes. Taylor was a blur of red and gold.

I brought the back of my hand to my eyes, ready to wipe at them like a child, but I stopped myself at the last minute. My eyes were weighed down with false eyelashes and painted with varying shades of gold, and elegant, sweeping lines of black tipped off my eyelids. I couldn't be seen with smeared or smudged makeup. I could imagine the headline. Something along the lines of the bereft Winchester sister who couldn't control her emotions. And behind that headline was my father's face. Winchesters didn't cry in public. Taylor hastily grabbed a cocktail napkin, which was also gold, offering it to me. I dabbed my water line gently before tossing it unceremoniously over the bar and out of sight.

"Is it smudged?" I asked, my voice a whisper amongst the growing chatter of the crowd.

"No, no, it's not smudged," Taylor answered tenderly, her thumb resuming the comforting strokes across my forearm. "You look beautiful. You always, *always*, look beautiful, Charlie."

Blinking again, my vision cleared, and I took in Taylor standing there. Her head tipped to the side, messy ponytail falling down her collarbone to brush across her arms. A small smile pulled at her red lips, and she looked like she was about to speak again, but then my father's voice sounded from behind us.

"Charlie. Taylor. You're both looking beautiful this evening."

I turned, a smile stretching across my face, causing my cheeks to pull and burn. Between that and the slicked back chignon, my headache was getting worse. My father was dressed the same as he always was at these functions—standard tuxedo, with vintage Michael Kanners cufflinks his father gave him when he graduated from Harvard. They were kind of bizarre, and I always thought it was weird when he wore them. They had the face of some sort of rare nickel on them, and I was sure his father gave them to him with a lesson about the value of money. It seemed awkward to me for one of the richest men in the world to wear cufflinks with a nickel on them, but I was sure it was some sort of statement I didn't even want to start trying to wrap my head around.

I studied him for half a moment, ensuring my smile never faltered. He was aging, slowly, but I could see it more now since the distance between us edged ever larger. His hair was no longer peppered with gray but liberally streaked, and the lines across his forehead seemed more pronounced. We had barely spoken since my fight with Deacon yesterday. In an unusual move, I asked for my dinner to be delivered to my room between my fitting and my midnight escape to see David. Steven and I just exchanged vague pleasantries over a formal breakfast this morning.

"Father, you look handsome," I offered, the tight smile still pulling.

I rarely called him "Dad" anymore. He was always Steven, or father, when I had to address him directly.

"You really do, Mr. Winchester." Taylor stepped beside me, brushing her fingers along my arm again. "If you'll both excuse me, I see my parents. I'll be back in a moment."

I took the opportunity to widen my eyes at Taylor, pleading with her to stay. But she smiled in return before gripping my forearm briefly and turning on her heel, weaving her way through the crowd. I wanted her here, wishing there was someone, anyone here, to provide a buffer between us. My father and I couldn't seem to avoid brushing up against one another in a way that caused friction. But if I was Taylor or anyone else, I wouldn't want to be here when we were *forced* to be within each other's company.

I wanted to reach out for her, to call after her, to make her stay, but I knew she was trying to give me a moment with him. A moment where neither of us had yet spoken to ruin it, where there were endless possibilities of reconciliation stretching between us. My father turned briefly to the bartender, gesturing to a bottle of Scotch behind the counter.

"Your brother seems happy. How is your evening going?" He asked, his blue eyes swept over me, barely lingering on his only daughter before they settled on monitoring the crowd.

I watched for a moment as my father brought the generous glass of scotch to his lips and my lips pulled back—even the crystal was inlaid with gold.

"Why wouldn't he be? Deac has always loved being the center of attention, and now he gets to marry the most beautiful girl in most rooms. What's there not to be happy about?" I said, pointedly ignoring his question about how my own evening was going.

I brought the glass to my lips, the bubbles of champagne trickling down my throat as I surveyed the room, while guests filed in. My father and I stood beside one another in a less-than-companionable silence. In a different time, I might have opened my mouth to try and bridge the distance between us, to see if I could somehow reach him with words but standing here surrounded by the opulence and wealth he seemed to covet more than anything, the distance just felt larger than ever. But it wasn't just about my father, not really. Not when jealousy curdled in my stomach, and pangs of envy shot through me every time I looked at my brother. Deacon was my favorite person in the world, and I couldn't even see my way clear to be happy for him. I wasn't deserving of any built bridges, from anyone.

My father remained silent, occasionally sipping his scotch, or reaching out to shake the hand of a guest who approached the bar. I smiled politely and tipped my head the way I was taught, seemingly reverting to the "speak only when spoken to" mantra of my childhood.

"How is school?" He asked, breaking the taut tension that was growing and challenging both of our stubbornness as we each refused to move from where we stood.

I turned to answer, a truthful and hopeful one about how much I was enjoying my time at Columbia, how much I loved research and teaching was about to spill from my lips when camera flashes began going off in my periphery. I blinked, expecting to see one or two photographers. I thought Deacon mentioned hiring someone who was the photographer of the moment amongst celebrities and all Noa's friends for personal photos and the photographers from Vanity Fair, but there were dozens standing by the entrance of the tent. I narrowed my eyes, watching them clamor all over one another to get the attention of the happy couple.

Deacon's arm was around Noa's waist, and her hand placed demurely on his chest as they smiled and looked in a million different directions while the flashes continued to go off.

"Are there paparazzi here?" I uttered in disbelief, my eyes wide, swinging back and forth between my father, Deacon and Noa.

My father turned to look at me, bringing the scotch to his lips before arching an eyebrow, a wry expression taking up residence on his face. "It's part of Noa's job, Charlie."

My mouth gaped open in a surely unflattering expression, and I continued to stare at him incredulously. My father never allowed or approved of any type of unregulated press. So much so, it had been one of the breaking points for my future at Winchester Holdings.

"And why is this okay, Dad?" I whispered, disbelief coloring my words. I couldn't remember the last time I had even called him *Dad*. "You don't want this. You don't even want to be in Vanity Fair, let alone be photographed by random people! Why is this okay and my intimate moment with my boyfriend that was used against my permission not okay? You could have spun that...you could have—"

His next words sliced through the still tension-thick air and cut all the way down to my heart. "Enough, Charlie."

I opened my mouth, anger and rage clawing for first place against my sadness, wanting to explode from my mouth, but he continued to speak. "I promised your mother."

"You promised her what? She wasn't dying. She didn't have cancer. She didn't have—" I hissed, eyes still wide as I tried to understand what he was saying, what he was thinking, but his face was a blank mask like always.

"I said enough. Do not spoil your brother's evening." In an uncharacteristic move, I watched as my father knock back the remainder of his scotch, setting the glass behind him on the bar.

He turned to look at me, his expression still neutral and his eyes giving nothing away before he spoke, "I meant what I said. You look lovely this evening." Then, he walked off into the party.

I blinked—anger, confusion, guilt and the usual untethered sadness that came when my mother was brought up biting at my insides and sweeping through my veins. I was still so angry at my father for everything he did to keep me at arm's length, angry at myself for my inability to be happy for Deacon and for never being enough. I had no idea what he was talking about when he said he *promised* my mother. The only thing I could even remember about her that remotely alluded to her ultimate cause of death was vacant stares I never noticed until it was too late. I shook my head, puffing my cheeks before turning on my heel to deposit the empty champagne coupe on the bar.

"What was that about?"

I froze; my spine straightened, and my hand extended halfway to accept another coupe of champagne that the bartender had drawn from the bottom of the elaborate tower. I hadn't heard that voice in almost two years. Rolling my shoulders, I smiled tightly and grabbed the stem of the glass before turning around. Something akin to a grimace fell into place on my lips.

"Oh. It's you. I had a dream that you died," I said, words dripping with acid—but there was another feeling there, too. I could never pinpoint it, but it was always there when he was around. Maybe it was recognition of someone who was just as fucked up as me.

A lazy grin was stretched across Tripp's face. He stood, tilting his head to one side and his eyes, still chips of ice, roved over me. His hands were shoved into the pockets of his tux. Stubble dusted his jawline, and his dark hair was longer than the last time I saw him, pushed off his face just so and secured in place with what was probably a ridiculously expensive styling aid. He looked like a bizarrely unkempt version of himself, like he was trying out something new. It was jarringly at odds with the clean cut, movie villain look he usually sported.

"Were you crying at my funeral?"

"Dancing on your grave actually." Rolling my eyes, I turned around, tipping my head back and practically dumping all the champagne down my throat before grabbing another glass from the neat line the bartender was now setting up for the stream of arriving guests.

"I doubt that very much, Chuckles." Tripp's voice was low, and I felt his breath whisper past my ear when he came to stand beside me.

He laid his forearms on the bar, the elbows of his jacket buckling slightly, and he raised two fingers to one of the bartenders, nodding toward one of the many bottles of scotch. He turned his head toward me and brought the glass to his lips, eyes never leaving me. "Something's different about you."

I stared determinedly ahead, ignoring the swirling sensation in my stomach. I knew propriety would dictate that, as this event was being held in my family home, I should be mingling and greeting guests on Deacon and Noa's behalf. But here I was, somehow stuck with Tripp Banks—again.

"Oh, I don't know, Tripp, could it be the fact that I haven't seen you in almost two years? Haven't even spoken to you? Ignored all your calls and texts? Scrubbed you from my life effectively until this very moment?"

Tripp tipped his head to the side again, making an obvious show of studying me—eyes narrowing before an irritatingly pensive look stole over his face. His gaze seemed to land on my collarbone where it stayed. My skin felt hot where his eyes were on me, and a sharp exhale puffed from my nostrils. The silence stretched between us. I continued to take small, delicate sips from my glass the way I was taught, and Tripp continued to stare at me. I said nothing, sure he was about to come out with some sort of witty remark meant to disarm and discomfort me.

"Your boobs are gone. What happened to your rack, Chuck?" He asked, the annoying lilt he reserved just to bother me rising to the surface.

I turned, mouth open and ready with a response that would probably only further engage and encourage Tripp, but the words died a horrific death in my throat when my eyes caught on David just over his shoulder.

He was standing with my father, Ash, and his wife, Serena. His blond hair was pushed back off his face, and the low lights seemed to be catching his eyes more than usual. The cut of his tux indicated it had been tailored for him, and recently, too. Not a line was out of place. One hand was clutching the stem of a champagne flute, and the other was gently rubbing the exposed shoulder of a woman standing beside him. Soft blonde hair cascaded in maddeningly perfect waves down her back. She tipped her head back in laughter at whatever my father had just said, exposing the column of her long neck and the side of her face. David's thumb skated forward over her shoulder to trace her collarbone before he pressed a kiss to the side of her head. It was like watching a mirror image of him and me, but the person standing with him was all wrong. It wasn't me. It was Victoria.

CHAPTER FIVE

All the blood rushed from my head at once, and for the second time in recent memory, my mouth was gaping like a demented fish. But a fish who was caught on someone's hook, being dragged toward certain death. My skin was hot, and I wanted to vomit. This was wrong, all wrong. My eyes prickled with the telltale signs of impending tears that felt more like needles, and bile crept up my throat. This was all wrong, and it was all my fault.

"You didn't know?" Tripp's voice was uncharacteristically soft, forcing me to snap my eyes back to him. "They got back together a few months ago."

I shook my head, the sound of my heartbeat in my ears eclipsing the hum of conversation around me.

I knew that I had lost the right to be upset about what David did with his life a long time ago, who he dated, who he brought to parties, who he kissed, and I wanted nothing more than for him to be happy, but my heart broke all the same. My eyes flicked down to the champagne still bubbling in my glass, and embarrassment and shame sluiced through me. David hadn't mentioned it once. Not in the car, not on the jet, and certainly not in his room last night. I had no idea why I said it out loud, but the words fell from my lips in anguish anyway.

"I was with him all night. He didn't mention her once."

"Deacon didn't tell you?" He asked, his voice still maddeningly soft and laced with something like pity.

The thought of Tripp pitying me did nothing to stop my skin from growing hot, from the embarrassment threatening to choke me to death. But that was nothing compared to the broken fragments of my heart that shattered into tiny, irreparable pieces at those words.

"Deacon knew?" I looked up despite the hot, thick tears blurring my vision.

I felt one slip down my face, surely streaking my makeup. Tripp had set down his glass of scotch and took a hesitant step toward me like you would a wounded animal.

"Deacon knew, and he didn't tell me?" I reiterated, more for myself, because my brother breaking my heart like that seemed like an astronomical impossibility.

"Charlie—" Tripp started, shaking his head, and reaching out a hand to me.

I shook my head rapidly, depositing my drink on the bar unceremoniously before gathering the metallic skirt of my gown in my hands and turning toward the open side of the tent. It led out to one of the winding stone paths that would take me right back to the house.

"I need to get out of here."

In a bizarre way, history repeated itself, and I ran from the party like a twisted Cinderella yet again. But instead of running toward the mess I had made, desperate to fix, salvage and save it, I was running away from it—the mess made up of all my mistakes.

Throwing open the door to my childhood bedroom, I kicked my heels off and sent them flying in different directions. One crashed into the silk pedestal Sabine had clearly left behind, and another flew into the chaise lounge where Taylor's textbooks were still spread out. I slammed the door behind me, not caring how petulant and childlike I was being. I pressed my hand to my chest, like I could cradle my heart, and a gasping sob escaped me.

David was with Victoria—and Deacon knew, and he kept it from me. He knew it would destroy me, even though I had no right to let it, and he didn't even warn me. The one thing in our fucked-up family I had always been able to count on, that always, always had been irrefutable, was that Deacon and I protected one another, loved one another, at all costs, above everything, and he just let this hit me in the face. I couldn't tell what hurt more. The fact that the man I loved with my entire heart, the only person who ever saw me, was moving on right in front of me, and it was all my fault, or if my heart was breaking over the fact that maybe my brother didn't see me as a person worth protecting anymore. Maybe my mistakes had been too huge—too egregious. Maybe he hated me just as much as I hated myself.

I pressed my back against the wall, my hand still placed on my chest, and I allowed my eyes to close for a moment. I knew I needed to get back to the party, for my brother, for Noa, for Taylor, and to avoid the impending doom that would follow if my father noticed I was gone for an extended period of time. But I needed a moment, just one moment to remember to breathe, to remember David was no longer mine, to remember that—

"You okay Chuckles?" Tripp was leaning in the doorway of my room.

I hadn't even heard the door open. Seeing him standing there, where David had stood only yesterday, imposing and sucking all the air out of the room reminded me that my childhood bedroom was the scene of many crimes—where I failed to notice my mother slowly slipping away, where I failed my father and his expectations so spectacularly time and time again, but it was also where I failed to tell David that Tripp had kissed me for the first time. If I could have been honest, maybe I wouldn't be standing there alone at that very moment, and David wouldn't have been with someone who wasn't me.

"How many times do I have to remind you that when someone runs from a crowded party, it generally means they want to be alone?" I hissed, tempted to shove him out of the room and slam the door in his face, but he had already stepped across the threshold and closed it quietly behind him.

I stepped back, like a preyed animal trying to put distance between themselves and a predator, my feet sinking into the plush carpet that covered the room until I felt my shoulder blades hit the wall.

"You don't look like you want to be alone." Tripp cocked his head again, studying me.

He slid his hands into the pockets of his pants, and I noticed the platinum cufflinks, engraved with the letter *B* before they slipped out of sight. "You look like you need a friend," he pressed.

"You're not my *friend*. But if you were, I would tell you that wearing cufflinks with the initial of your last name on them is incredibly ostentatious."

I raised my eyes to meet his, irritated at his continued presence and constant ability to bait me. I watched, my stomach knotting as Tripp walked across the room and came to a halt in front of me. He tipped his head forward, his eyes like the bottom of the ocean, dark and impenetrable. I waited for him to box me in with both of his hands, but they stayed firmly in his pockets.

Tripp continued to watch me for another moment before he spoke, "If I'm not your friend, is there something else you need that I can provide for you?" My heart dropped, my eyes following suit, landing on his lips and the sharp planes of his jaw. "Maybe a...distraction."

Before I knew it, our mouths crashed together, my fingers wasting no time as they betrayed me and began ripping at the buttons of his shirt, desperate to shed everything between us, desperate to be distracted. Desperate to be devoured. *I am twenty again.*

David was with Victoria. David was with Victoria. It was a steady mantra in my head that I pushed against, worked to shut out as my hands roamed the muscles of Tripp's shoulders under his suit jacket and my teeth tugged his bottom lip. He shrugged out of the jacket without his lips ever leaving mine, and I undid the final buttons of his shirt, practically ripping it from his body. He grabbed the back of my neck, tilting my face upward, like he needed better access to my mouth. This was nothing like the last time we kissed, and nothing like the times before that. An involuntary shiver ran through me while we continued to bite at one another when I felt Tripp's fingers swiftly and deftly maneuvering around the clasp and zipper at the side of the gown. It fell from my body, becoming a metallic pool of fabric around my feet, leaving only the bodysuit between us.

I broke our kiss, pressing my forehead to his, breath ragged while my fingers began pulling at the buttons on his pants. I didn't care about anything else. The only thing I cared about was pretending nothing else was out there. That my heart wasn't shattered the same way it had been all those years ago. A soft moan escaped me as Tripp's lips moved from my ear to my jawline before landing on my neck. My fingers were on the zipper of his pants when I saw the door open from the corner of my eye. Like a startled deer, my head snapped back, and I looked to the door, another sick sense of déjà vu overwhelming me.

Taylor's eyes turned pitch black, and her mouth opened to form a perfectly round O, looking like she might erupt in a shriek at any moment. Instead, when she spoke, her voice was like ice sluicing through the room. She crossed her arms, the puff sleeves of her red gown somehow not looking ridiculous but imposing.

"What the *fuck* is this?" She enunciated every word with utter venom.

Her eyes narrowed in on Tripp and not in admiration of his shirtless form that had me pinned against the wall before they swung back to me.

I ducked under his raised forearm; his palm was flat against the wall. I wanted to run far, far away, but my feet were trapped in the fabric of my gown. I looked down, stepping out of it, unable to look Taylor in the eyes. My stomach tightened, and instead of whatever the hell I had been feeling, I could only feel vomit sneaking up my throat. "It's nothing."

"Well, it might have been something in a few minutes if you hadn't graced us with your presence, Taylor," Tripp drawled, pushing off the wall and beginning to shrug his button up back on, a lazy smile slowly creeping onto his face.

"Fuck off, Tripp," I hissed, grabbing his abandoned suit jacket and thrusting it into his still exposed abdomen.

He grinned at me, looking like a maniacal Cheshire Cat before shrugging his shirt back on.

"Yeah, fuck off, Tripp." Taylor's voice was still dripping with acid. She took a few steps into the room, raised a hand, and pointed behind her toward the still open door. "There's the door."

That maddening grin didn't so much as slip from his face while he looked at Taylor and began to walk past her toward the door, still taking his sweet time doing up the buttons of his shirt. "Always a pleasure, doctor."

The door clicked shut gently, and it might as well have been a clap of thunder right beside my ears. They were ringing endlessly. What the fuck was the matter with me? Taylor and I continued to stare at one another, and I opened my mouth to speak but any words I could think of died in my throat, so I swallowed the stale air instead, aware that I was still standing there in nothing but a bodysuit that was practically see-through. Taylor narrowed her gaze at me.

"Do you want to explain to me what's going on here, Charlie? Because it looks like I just walked in on you about to screw the person responsible for destroying your last relationship when you should be downstairs at your only brother's engagement party trying to win David back from that fucking Miss North Carolina wannabe. Unless I just hallucinated and I have an undiagnosed brain tumor? And to be honest with you, I'm hoping it's the latter."

She stalked toward me, brown eyes still swirling when she knelt at my feet, grabbing my gown, and forcefully shoving it back up my body.

"It's not what it looks like," I said uselessly, taking over the zippering of my gown from Taylor. "I just—"

Taylor's eyes widened, and she made a go-on gesture with her hands when my sentence dropped off. "You just what?"

I moved away from her, gathering up my heels before dropping on the chaise and shoving them back onto my feet.

"I wasn't expecting to see David with someone, especially her. It threw me. Deacon and I are fighting, and he didn't tell me about David being with Victoria. I don't know Taylor, I'm an imperfect person, sue me."

She dropped beside me, threading her fingers through mine. "Deacon knew, and he didn't tell you?"

I nodded, staring ahead, ignoring the tears that begged to be unleashed.

"I'm sorry," Taylor whispered, squeezing my hand with hers before dropping her head to my shoulder. "Fuck him."

"You have," I responded dryly, the attempt at humor felt foreign.

But a smile tugged at my lips when Taylor cackled loudly in response.

"Don't remind me. Why aren't you out there trying to win David back? We both know they're nothing compared to the two of you. Don't tell me you've given up."

"I tried, Taylor." I pulled my hand from hers, gently wiping my lash line to clear the rogue tears that had escaped. "Before I moved to New York, I went to his office and practically begged for him back. He said maybe. And I begged for him again last night, but it didn't matter. He says he forgives me, but he can't forget what I did. That he's tried."

"Well fuck him, too," Taylor whispered and wrapped her arms around my shoulders and brought her head to mine.

We sat there in silence for a few moments longer before we stood, holding hands like we did when we were kids, and walked back out into the world together.

CHAPTER SIX

The string quartet started a rendition of a song I vaguely recognized as belonging to a country artist-turned pop singer when Taylor and I slid back into the tent through one of the open panels at the back. The party was in full swing, with servers moving through the crowd, holding gold plates of drinks above their heads, or smaller ones of canapes and other hors d'oeuvres. Taylor pulled me by the hand to stand alongside the constructed dance floor. Elegant, swirling tiles took up a large portion of the floor that was laid out by whatever company Deacon and Noa hired.

I watched, feeling bizarrely detached as Deacon led Noa by the hand to the center of the dance floor. He looked at ease, the simple cut of his tux perfectly tailored as always, and one wisp of his chocolate hair styled to fall forward across his forehead. The feathers of Noa's dress twirled with her when Deacon spun her, perfectly in time with the music, his eyes never leaving her. I cocked my head to the side, studying them and trying to focus on the small, warm glow I felt at the way happiness radiated off of him. I breathed in and out, concentrating on that, watching my brother who deserved the normalcy and happiness of love, despite the fact that I was certain my heart was hemorrhaging inside my body.

Everything was uncomfortable, and everything hurt. I felt myself squeezing Taylor's hand, reminding me that she was here. My eyes bore into Deacon and Noa, watching their feet move in perfect timing with one another. I knew Victoria and David were somewhere in the crowd, and God only knew where Tripp had slithered off to. The last notes of the song came to an end, the sound reverberated through the tent before it was overtaken by the polite applause of the guests.

I arched an eyebrow as I watched Deacon drop to one knee and place his lips on Noa's hand. The ridiculous grand gesture was so like my brother that a laugh rose in my throat. Flashes from photographers strategically positioned across the room went off at once, like they were desperate to capture the moment that fit in perfectly with the opulence and grandeur of the event itself, to show the world all that they were missing.

Deacon stood, still holding Noa's hand to his lips before wrapping his arm around her practically non-existent waist and dipping her before kissing her in such an obvious display of tongue. I felt myself stifling another laugh. They didn't come up for air for what seemed like forever, and when they finally broke apart, a typical roguish grin was in place on Deacon's face as laughter and applause rang out from the crowd. Noa at least had the decency to blush. Her brown cheeks were pink, and she briefly rested her head against his shoulder before they each turned and began walking toward the watchful crowd.

Noa approached my father, the shy expression still on her face, and she honest to God curtsied in front of him. This earned a laugh from my father, and I couldn't tell if it was forced or not. I watched as he extended his arm and walked her to the center of the dance floor, placing one hand gently on her waist, much higher than his son's had been, and holding her other arm out. I was too busy watching their bizarre display to realize Deacon stopped in front of me and bowed with a flourish before holding his hand out. I blinked, narrowing my eyes at him before quickly replacing the look of disdain with one of good-natured humor. Flashes were going off around the periphery of the room again.

"Charles, may I have this dance?" Deacon asked, a smirk pulling at his lips. He knew this entire display would annoy me to no end.

I nodded, placing my hand in his and allowing him to lead me to the dance floor beside our father and Noa. I brought my hand to his shoulder, flicking my eyes up to him and purposely rolling them. "That was fucking ridiculous."

"I'm just giving the people what they want, Charlie." He smiled down at me, green eyes dancing and no sign of the anger he felt at me lingering there.

Another cover of a popular song started, and Deacon began leading me in sweeping movements around the dance floor, exactly in time and the perfect amount of space away from Noa and our father. Our etiquette teacher demanded Deacon and I both partake in Cotillion, forcing dancing lessons on us from a young age so I could be a perfect little debutante and Deacon an escort. We tried to make the lessons fun by ensuring we were always partnered together to make fun of everyone else as they struggled with the intricate steps.

"This isn't Game of Thrones," I hissed through my closed mouth. My painted lips were pulled up to the sides tightly.

"If it was, which Prince would I be?" Deacon asked playfully, our feet moving expertly together.

"A dumb one that gets eaten by a dragon."

A laugh escaped Deacon, and he tipped his head back before his eyes were on me. They flashed momentarily, and his mouth tugged down when he looked at me.

"You've been crying. Is this about yesterday?"

"Don't worry about it." I shook my head, cursing the fact that he knew me better than anyone in the world, and that any deviation in our identical eyes would stick out like a sore thumb to him. "I want you to enjoy your night."

This was true, I did want Deacon to enjoy his night. Contrary to what my father thought of me. No matter my jealousy, no matter my hurt—never in a million years would I dream of ruining anything for Deacon. More couples filtered onto the dance floor, and from the corner of my eye, I saw Taylor's red gown fanning out at her feet as her father spun her around.

"Why were you crying, Charlie?" He asked gingerly, his grip tightening on my hand.

Like a torturous magnet was at work, my gaze pulled from Deacon and landed on David and Victoria. They were dancing; his perfect hand caressing her waist through the material of her satin emerald gown. I watched, unable to look away, as David stroked his thumb ever-so gently along the seam of the dress. Their bodies were pressed close to one another, and my breath caught in my throat as yet again. Victoria threw her head back, emitting a throaty laugh while David gazed down at her, grinning.

Despite the pain in my chest, my feet never betrayed me, still moving me through all the motions alongside my brother mechanically until we had twirled around, and he was now facing David and Victoria. I blinked up at him, watching his eyes change when they landed on where they were dancing. Understanding crept across his features, and Deacon looked back at me, a clear ache in his eyes.

"I'm sorry this had to be the first time you saw them together," he said, pulling me in close for a moment and knocking our foreheads together, like we did when we were children, whispering about the world around us.

I shook my head, briefly removing my hand from his shoulder to wipe my fingers along my eyes as discreetly as possible. "It's not just that. I didn't know, Deacon."

He pulled back, his eyes narrowing. "He didn't tell you?"

"Neither did you," I whispered, hurt spilling from my lips and lacing my words.

My eyes were swimming when I looked at Deacon's, an exact mirror of my own. He was silent for a moment, seeming to struggle with the words he wanted to say. "I *am* sorry, Charlie. I thought it would be better if you heard it from David. I never would have dreamed that—"

I cut him off abruptly, sensing his voice spiraling closer to anger. "I know, Deac. I know. It just hurts me that you didn't tell me, but you aren't responsible for the actions of a grown man. No more secrets between us, okay? No matter what."

He looked like he wanted to object, throwing one more narrowed gaze toward David and Victoria before he nodded. "No more secrets. I'm sorry for yelling at you yesterday, Charles. I don't think David was the only man who could tolerate you for more than five minutes. It was just..." he trailed off, and I studied his face.

His eyes grew cloudy the way they always did when he was forced to speak about or remember our mother. I wished with all my heart that Deacon felt differently; I wished he would remember her, give her life, and I was tempted for a moment to tell him how no matter what, I was certain she would have wanted to share this with him. But my father's words rang in my ears, and I knew without a doubt bringing up our almost forgotten and dead mother would count as ruining his night. Instead, I swallowed my words and her memory down, practically stomping on it with my foot while her ghost tried to claw for a place in my life.

I smiled at him, shaking my head. "Don't worry about it. I'm sorry, too."

Deacon and I had continued dancing into another song, mindlessly changing our steps to suit the new style without even realizing it. When the last chords were struck, he folded me quickly into a hug and pressed a kiss to the crown of my forehead.

Before letting go, he ducked his head and whispered to me. "While we're about honesty and sharing, can you please make more of an effort with Noa? It hurts me that you barely know her."

Somehow, my already broken heart cleaved in half again. I tightened my grip on Deacon, nodding against his head.

"Of course. Of course I can," I whispered back, holding my brother for one more moment before I let him go, and my eyes landed on Noa.

She was waiting patiently at the side of the dance floor, holding a glass of champagne and her amber eyes wide and happy at the sight of us, like seeing her fiancé enjoying himself with his sister brought her so much joy. That might be beautiful, moving even, to someone else, someone whole—but all it did was make me feel like more of a failure.

———

I tapped my fingernails against the bar, smiling politely while I waited my turn to be served. I could vaguely hear the chords of a waltz starting, and I kept my back turned, having avoided both David and the dance floor all night.

"While no one's looking, want to sneak back up to your room and pick up where we left off?" Tripp smirked, appearing suddenly from nowhere—as was his custom. He stood so close to me I caught a whiff of his cologne.

I turned to look at him incredulously, taking a pointed step away.

"You're still here? I thought you might have found some poor unwitting girl to take back to your lair."

He shook his head, nodding to one of the bartenders who produced a stiff vodka soda for me, as per my instructions.

"The only one I have room for in my lair is you, Chuckles. You seemed like a willing guest a few hours ago."

"The moment's over, Tripp. I don't need a fuck buddy, be gone." I made an exaggerated shooing motion with my hand and widened my eyes at him before turning and leaning my back against the bar.

I brought the drink to my lips, taking a lengthy sip and allowing the liquor to burn against my throat. I shook my head as Tripp followed suit, resting against the bar and surveying the dance floor with me, a new drink in hand.

He gestured with his glass to the corner of the room where Deacon, Noa, and Taylor stood laughing with David and Victoria. They were only a few steps away, but it felt like I was watching them across an entire ocean, living out a life I no longer belonged in, no longer had a place in. Tripp tipped his head at me after knocking back his drink and holding out his hand.

"What about a friend?"

I looked at him over my glass, taking in his earnest expression. Once upon a time, Tripp had been my friend. One of my best friends. Until he became the villain. And I didn't know what version of him I was looking at now. His hand stayed lifted between us, like an olive branch meant for two outsiders who had no one else. Looking back, I watched with discomfort as Taylor and Noa flitted around one another, happily melding into one another's lives, and my brother laughed with David and Victoria, who were standing side-by-side with their arms wrapped around one another. I drained my glass and set it behind me, placing my hand in his before I could think better of it.

"How sad is it that you're my only option?"

Tripp didn't answer, but instead pulled me toward the still-crowded dance floor and positioned me directly in front of David's line of sight. He continued to say nothing but placed my arm on his shoulder, wrapping his other hand around my waist and pulling me flush to his body before seamlessly leading me into the steps. He waited until we were turned around, and I was facing David, who finally deigned to look at me. Our eyes met, whatever was left of my heart stopped beating, and an expression I couldn't place rose on his face, just as Tripp leaned down, pressing his lips to my ear. His warm breath skittered against my skin.

"I don't think it's sad at all."

I swung my bare feet back and forth, my heels brushing against the stone ledge. I was certain the rough stone was probably damaging my gown, but I couldn't really bring myself to care.

Noises from the party filtered down to where I was sitting, staring out at the endless expanse of the lake. Guests were slowly leaving, and Deacon and my father were currently stationed at the exit of the tent, shaking hands, and thanking everyone for their time.

It seemed as good a time as any to take a break. I spent most of the night dancing with Tripp, laughing and falling back into the secret world the two of us used to occupy back at Brown. It was surprisingly easy, partly because no one really paid us any attention. All eyes were on Deacon and Noa. But I felt David's eyes on me more than once, burning against my skin. I determinedly looked away from him at every opportunity, forcing my eyes to land anywhere but his. The anger, the hurt, the embarrassment that he didn't tell me about Victoria were ever present, wending their way through my body and infecting all my organs, trying to slowly kill me. Despite what happened between us, I had always thought of David as someone who would never hurt me, and I couldn't reconcile that with the person I knew.

"Charlie?"

My spine straightened, and my heart dropped. I turned, looking over my shoulder. Like I had conjured him, David was standing there on the gentle slope of the lawn looking down at me. His bowtie was undone, hanging around his neck, and both hands were shoved into his pants pockets. I said nothing but gently patted the spot on the rocks beside me before turning back and continuing my vigil of staring out onto the lake.

David settled in beside me, leaving enough distance between us so that our arms or our legs wouldn't accidentally brush. I eyed the distance between us and shifted farther away from him. He said nothing, joining me in staring out into the abyss.

"You didn't tell me," I said, breaking the silence.

My eyes blurred and forgetting all pretense, no longer caring about the integrity of my makeup, I rubbed them with the back of my hands.

"No," David answered quietly, still looking ahead at the lake. "I didn't tell you."

I wiped my hand across my eyes uselessly, the tears falling freely. "I feel so stupid."

David exhaled through his nose loudly before running a hand over his face and turning to me, grabbing my hands in his. "You're not stupid, Charlie. You're anything but."

I jerked my hands away from him. I didn't want to be touched or coddled by David.

"I'm not stupid? You let me sit there for hours last night, groveling for you! You never once said anything about Victoria. I thought that maybe...I don't know what I thought."

"I wanted to tell you, please believe that. No matter what's happened between us, I would never do anything to hurt you intentionally." David's hands were still hanging in the air, like he didn't know what to do with them. There had never been a time when I hadn't allowed him to touch me. "I didn't want to hurt you. I *knew* it would hurt you...but I didn't want you to look at me like you're looking at me right now."

"I'm not looking at you," I said bitterly, gesturing to the lake pointedly. "I don't want to look at you, because it hurts me, because I'm angry at you, because you embarrassed me. I know this is my penance for what I did to you, that I don't have a right to feel any of these things, but I always thought of you as someone who would never, ever hurt me."

I watched David drop his hands from the corner of my eye, where he wiped his palms up and down his suit pants before pulling on the ends of his styled hair, releasing it from the confines of the gel.

"Well, the same could have been said for you, once upon a time. Remind me who you were dancing with all night again? And don't think I didn't notice you two disappeared earlier."

I shook my head, scoffing. I pushed my palms against the rough stone, standing quickly and not bothering to brush any dirt or debris from my gown. I looked down at David through the blurred edges of my eyes. "Maybe you should spend your time looking at your girlfriend."

A strangled noise left David, and he turned to me; his eyes narrowed with a dubious look on his face.

"So, that's how it's going to be?"

"You tell me!" I bit out.

I knew I was being childish, but all of it—whatever I was made of now—was pouring out of me. All I could focus on was not being enough. Nothing I did was ever enough.

"You made it clear you didn't want me. I tried, I would have thrown myself at your feet for the rest of my life to show you how much I love you, how sorry I am. And then what? You lied to punish me? Wanted to hurt me tonight the way I hurt you? If you want to be mad at me, David, then be mad at me! Scream, shout at me! I deserve it. If you're so angry you want to punish me, then do it. Don't console me. Don't hold my hand all night only to embarrass me publicly the very next evening."

David stood suddenly and took a step toward me. His brown eyes were flat and hollow. His voice was a strangled whisper, "That's not love, Charlie. To spend the rest of your life trying to rectify a mistake you can't fix? You and I both know there's no future in that."

Those words—no future—echoed throughout my body, reverberating through my empty chest, because there was surely nothing left of my heart anymore, hurt me more than anything else David had ever said. It was childish, sure, but there was still a small part of me that didn't believe him last night—that had been holding onto a kernel of hope that one day, despite what he said, that maybe he promised me would be a yes, that just my love would be enough for David.

A strangled noise crept up my throat and that small bit of hope evaporated into nothing, and I felt stupid, so stupid because the future wasn't an endless expanse of possibility where I could prove myself. It simply didn't exist. "Goodbye, David."

Hiking up my dress in my hands, I turned and ran toward the stone path that would lead me around the side of the house. Against the blood pounding in my ears, I could vaguely hear David calling my name, but it fell flat. I couldn't bring myself to care. I wanted nothing more than to go home, go back to New York and the life I was trying to create, and forget the Charlie Winchester I used to be.

CHAPTER SEVEN

My townhouse in Manhattan was maybe the only grossly impractical purchase I had ever made—$3.9 million dollars to be exact. On the surface, it would have seemed like a property Deacon might have bought—too many bedrooms and too many bathrooms for one person—but it wasn't in one of the areas he would deem the most appropriate—it was on the Upper West Side, not the Upper *East* Side.

I bought my townhouse the second I stepped foot inside it. There was something about the smell, the crisp white walls and the winding rooms, and arguably poor layout—I could picture myself liking the version of me that might live there; this version of me was aspirational and didn't claw for her father's approval, and she didn't cheat on her boyfriends because she was sad. It was kind of unfortunate for that to be my bar.

The house itself was chunked off kind of bizarrely, and it was old, so there were dividing walls where modern architecture would dictate it should be an open concept. The narrow first floor gave way to two, easily accessible but hidden outdoor oases. If I wanted to be outside, feeling like I was still immersed in the city, I could go down the stairs and out onto the turfed garden terrace that was surrounded by wooden benches. Or, I could follow the creaky wooden stairs up to the rooftop. I usually only went there when I was feeling particularly mournful, or melodramatic and pathetic as Taylor called it.

I would sit up there, contemplating all the things I had done wrong, pointlessly ruminating on late wine-addled nights with David on my terrace back in Chicago. If I closed my eyes and tipped my head back, concentrating on blocking out the noises of Upper Manhattan, I sometimes felt like I was right back there; David's fingers tracing my shoulder, my collarbone, before being replaced by his lips. I could hear our laughter, rising above all the nighttime noises of Chicago. I could hear him saying "I love you."

But I stopped doing that when I realized Taylor was right. I had become quite pathetic, and there was no one to blame but myself. I didn't feel pathetic in the other parts of my home. In my kitchen, with the floor-to-ceiling white cabinets and the long, white waterfall island set off by black accent cabinets; or, in my bedroom where there was an exposed white brick wall and an old fireplace that led to a walk-in closet filled with creaky shelves. Or, in my office, which Taylor called mid-century modern.

After I bought this place, Taylor and I spent an entire weekend all over the city looking for exactly the right pieces that would go inside it. In those places, the ones we carefully built for this new Charlie—New York Charlie—I didn't feel pathetic. I felt like me. The familiar click of the door when I pushed it open sounded much more like home than the empty, echoing hallways of my family home in Lake Forest.

I pressed my back into the heavy wooden door of my house, closing my eyes and inhaling. This was where I belonged now. This was the home I was making for myself; just me, away from everything else. Dropping my bag, I kicked it to the side and padded down the hallway, relishing every creak of the floor as I made my way to my office on the second floor. I left my computer there, having promised Deacon I wouldn't answer any school-related emails during his festivities. The irony of one Winchester making that promise to another hadn't been lost on me.

My computer sat in the middle of my white desk, an almost-identical replica to the one that I left behind in my office in Chicago. I wondered briefly what became of my furniture there. Deacon had been responsible for clearing it out, but I never asked. Anything he thought I would have wanted went into boxes that were surely still collecting dust in a storage unit in Chicago somewhere.

But now, I thought of the leather couch I bought at a thrift store, where David and I spent so many nights laughing when we were new. I thought of the photo of my graduation from Brown that hung behind my desk, just me, my father and Deacon, alone in the world and missing my mother. I thought of the endless photos of me around the world, running constantly and never looking back at my home until I was forced to do so. I didn't want any of them crossing the threshold of this home. They were imbued with all the ghosts of my past—all my mistakes—and I didn't need the reminder.

I looked around the office I made in my townhouse, bookshelves lining either side of my desk not unlike my father's office back in Lake Forest. Various textbooks lined them, knocked over and in no particular order. Photos of Taylor and me throughout the years held up novels, and photos of Deacon were littered across the shelves. Not a single photo of my mother or father was there, and I think this version of me preferred that. I was trying to like who I was without my dead mother—and without my cold, distant father. A small laugh caught in my throat at the framed photo of Deacon and Noa on the cover of People magazine shoved into the corner of one of the shelves.

Taylor sent it to me after it was published, with a note in her lilting handwriting asking if I could get this autographed. Deacon came to visit me in the city, but mostly Noa, and saw it sitting on top of an unpacked box. He signed it immediately, as if that had been the signature she was looking for, and called Taylor demanding she give up her shifts for the weekend and come to New York to hang out with a celebrity.

She did it, which shocked me to no end. Taylor never skipped work. She even let him arrange the jet for her, and we had shown up in a limo Deacon procured with endless bottles of champagne. It was right after I moved to New York, back when I hoped every ring of my phone or notification of a text message would lead to David on the other end. David saying *maybe* really meant yes. David forgiving me. David loving me. Back when all I wanted was for New York Charlie to find absolution.

I blinked, my white desk and closed computer coming back into focus. Taylor was right. I was pathetic. That was before, and this was now. I was trying to be different. And I think I liked the person I was now, who I was in this house, in this city. I liked New York Charlie and fuck anyone else who didn't. Fuck David Kennedy. That's what Taylor would say. I settled into the chair behind my desk, dropping my phone on the desk. New York Charlie had Ph.D. candidate and teaching assistant things to do.

My email inbox was full of an alarming number of photos that were clearly cut and pasted from the Vanity Fair website. I hadn't looked at the article and had determinedly kept my head down when I passed a newsstand or bodega on the way back to my townhouse. I didn't want to see the professionally curated photos, let alone the random paparazzi shots. I scrolled aimlessly through them until I landed on one of Deacon and me during his bizarre medieval dance routine he subjected all his guests to. That one made me smile. It must have been right after we declared no more secrets between us—smiling at one another genially and moving through the steps of whatever waltz was playing. That one might deserve a frame on the bookshelf.

I narrowed my eyes when I spotted Damien's name, still my father's assistant, and the Winchester Holdings email domain. I never received any sort of company emails anymore. All the information I received came once a year, in a couriered package that I had to sign for. It was a printed tome of the companies' financials that I didn't give a shit about. I was still and would forever be a minority shareholder until my father died, and even then, I wasn't sure I would care. I was also certain Steven Winchester would outlive everyone, surviving in spite alone, so it didn't seem like a bridge I would ever have to cross.

A loud scoff escaped me as I opened the email. It was a fucking Outlook invitation to dinner with my father and Deacon the following week. He couldn't have sent me a text, or God forbid, called to let his only daughter know he was coming to town?

My father did come to New York occasionally, but it was almost always a fly-in, fly-out, no time for lunch affair. I rarely saw him when he was in the city, and the only time I could think of him being here for longer than a day in semi-recent memory was when he made a stopover on his way to see a WH board member in the Hamptons. I was half-tempted to decline the invitation out of pure spite—perhaps I was my father's daughter after all.

I begrudgingly accepted and watched as the event took up residence in my calendar. I quickly deleted the email from my inbox, hoping that would somehow push it from my mind until next week and began to filter through the emails from my supervisor and students. New York was just for New York Charlie. Winchester Holdings had no place here.

My heels clicked against the polished tile floor as I made my way through the halls of Columbia University's International Affairs building. Arms laden with various books, and my laptop stacked precariously on top of them, I wished I had a reasonable excuse for wearing sunglasses indoors. But, that would have likely drawn more attention to me. All week it felt like I couldn't go anywhere on campus without someone gaping openly at me or hitting someone beside them and pointing at me.

Deacon's face was splashed across every newsstand and bodega around the city, and unfortunately for me and my anonymous life in New York City, the news cycle hadn't changed. To make matters worse, photos of me from the party that weren't part of the Vanity Fair shoot ended up splashed right alongside Deacon's face and Noa's genetically perfect one on Page Six and every other tabloid magazine that existed. And they weren't just any photos. I had somehow earned my own little callout box with varying catchy titles like, "Has America's most eligible bachelorette found a new suitor?" Or, my personal favorite: "Move over, David Kennedy—Tripp Banks is in town."

Photos of Tripp and me standing at the bar together had been taken, and I didn't even know they had been. Our eyes seemingly only for one another and making it seem like a particularly heated or clandestine moment was caught on film. But I was certain I was probably seconds from yelling at him or had just told him to fuck off, and the shitty film quality of the paparazzi photos couldn't detect the difference.

At least I hadn't been entirely miserable when we were dancing together. Those weren't an entire farce. The real draw of the miniature spread about me was the detailed explanation of my relationship timeline with David, probably taken straight from the Society News article from two years ago, what was public knowledge about his family and his former role at WH before it moved right on into everything they could guess about Tripp Banks.

Every single magazine or outlet, no matter what medium, they all portrayed him as a dark, mysterious and shockingly handsome son of a banking executive from Boston who took WH by storm when he joined the executive team. That would then devolve into wild and depraved speculation about Tripp and me being a love story that spanned a decade, because someone who had nothing better to do with their time found an old photo of us hanging off one another during a mixer at Brown.

Some of the crueler tabloids would juxtapose that against a photo of David and Victoria, with clever captions indicating it looked like he had moved onto poorer pastures, quite literally, because Victoria's family net worth was estimated to be about a fraction of mine.

Chicago Charlie would have run to David begging for his forgiveness, apologizing at his feet forevermore, but I was still mad at him for lying to me about Victoria—again. Fuck David Kennedy. Tripp took the opportunity to text me whenever he felt like it, "as a friend," but would always end the conversation to let me know that if I was in need of any of his *varied services*, he could come to town at a moment's notice.

Rounding the corner, I was faced with an onslaught of what appeared to be undergraduate students lined up against the wall outside my supervisor's office. I narrowed my eyes at the line, peering over the stack I was still holding in my arms to see if I could make out the time on my watch. I started wearing an old one of Deacon's when I moved. It was some model of vintage Patek Phillipe that originally was our grandfather's, and then our father's, and then Deacon's—but he gave it to me before I left. And the pretentious clock face was currently telling me it was the middle of office hours for one of the undergraduate courses my Ph.D. supervisor taught.

I flicked my gaze back up, realizing every single one of the students standing there was either staring at me openly or pretending to look everywhere but me. I smiled tightly, resisting the urge to grimace at each and every single one of them before turning on my heel and propping myself up against the opposite wall to wait for office hours to be done, or for everyone to stop staring. Whichever came first.

The end of office hours came first, in a surprise to absolutely no one. I waited patiently, thumbing through one of the articles I had printed earlier, intently ignoring the students walking by and the audible whispers. I was doing my best to block them out, but I could occasionally hear someone say how beautiful Noa looked, how stunning her giant feathered dress had been, how hot Deacon is, and how they would give anything to have an engagement party like that. I had to resist the urge not to scoff at that one. I wasn't aware when having an engagement party befitting Daisy Buchanan became something to aspire to. The final students were filing out of the office when I finally heard something that made my neck snap up.

"Which one would you choose? David or Tripp? Do you think she's with either of them?"

Two young girls who looked like they could be around twenty, with the same nondescript and typical features that wouldn't have been out of place at any country club had their heads bent toward one another, causing their identical blonde waves to blend entirely together. Narrowing my eyes at them, I folded my pile of books and laptop to my chest again before pushing off the wall.

"I'm with neither. Have a good day, ladies," I offered, feeling mollified by the blush that crept over both of their cheeks and the way they quickened their pace down the hall.

Dr. Batra's office looked the same as any office in the department. Those grand offices with floor-to-ceiling bookcases and polished mahogany desks were for the movies, or for people like my father who couldn't get past their own self-importance. Her office was cramped, and it was full of books or various publications, but they were stacked precariously across the room, taking up the spare chairs and any available surface. But artifacts of her life were strewn across the room, too. Photos of her family and artwork adorned the walls. The standard issue desk was in the center of the room. Dr. Batra sat behind her monitor, glasses pushed up to hold her dark hair off her face as she stared eagerly at her monitor.

I leaned through the doorway, knocking quietly. "Are you still available to meet now?"

"Charlie! I'm so sorry, yes, please come on in." She pushed back from her desk and gestured for me to take the empty chair across from her. "How was your time back in Chicago?"

"Oh, you know, the usual. Paparazzi, Vanity Fair, and a famous bride-to-be. Nothing too interesting," I answered dryly, dropping into the seat. "Thank you very much for the time off, regardless. It meant the world to my brother."

"Your father, too, I'm sure. He must miss you living in Chicago."

I offered a polite smile—a Winchester smile—in response before changing the subject to my research. One of the things that drew me to Columbia's Sustainable Development program was the existing research on sustainable investing, and after the disaster that had been my charitable holdings portfolio at WH, it felt fitting. It was what I had been trying to do there, create something lasting and sustainable, and failed so spectacularly at, according to my father. But this, I could do. This I liked. I had legitimate opportunities to contribute and make a difference, something that might shape the way businesses functioned and invested in the future.

"I emailed you my updated proposal this morning. I'm not sure if you've had a chance to look at it, yet, but I primarily made the changes suggested."

She propped her chin up on her hand, smiling warmly at me. "I haven't yet. I intended to during office hours, but as I'm sure you saw, it was busier than usual. But I do have something I need to talk to you about."

My lips parted, and I felt my mouth dry out. I waited for the inevitable, that someone on the faculty, or in the department, had complained about the Vanity Fair article, the Page Six article, that I wouldn't be taken seriously as a researcher and my integrity had somehow been compromised. This was what I was afraid of from the moment I saw Deacon's face on a tabloid next to someone so famous, so known—that this little slice of my world I was trying so hard to protect would be taken from me by WH, too. No one in New York paid me much attention before that. There were far more interesting people running amok in Manhattan.

"It's not a bad thing, Charlie. You look terrified." She leaned forward, the corners of her dark eyes crinkling with laughter. "It's good news, I think. Depending on how you want to look at it."

"Okay," I nodded, waiting.

I forced another smile on my face, but her words did nothing to subdue the tide in my stomach.

She folded her hands across her desk in front of her, and an air of excitement settled around her. The smile she was wearing now radiated genuine happiness.

"I've been offered a new position. At the end of the summer semester, I'll be moving to the U.K. The position is at Oxford. I couldn't turn it down. It's one of the best development programs in the world."

A bitter tang coated my tongue, and the irony of it all pressed down on me. She was moving to practically the same place I had run away to—twice. My entire education here depended on her as my supervisor, as she was the only faculty doing research in this area and taking students. This thing I was trying to create for myself hinged on her—and she was leaving for the place I went when I couldn't face my life, and myself, any longer.

I schooled my features, another winning Winchester smile falling into place, that was all genetically perfect, whitened teeth and sore cheek muscles.

"Congratulations! What an opportunity and an accomplishment. You must be thrilled."

Her bright smile was still in place on her face, and she truly did look happy. This was her life's work, her career. Most people didn't just flit in and out of academia like me when they were lost.

"Thank you, Charlie. I am. I'll tell you all about the opportunity and the research another time. But I realize this puts you in a bit of a unique situation as my student."

I began to shake my head, a Winchester was always perfectly composed. I could cry and scream in frustration about my failed attempt at independence later, but for now, she continued.

"But you are also a unique student. I won't have secure funding for a doctoral student right away, but I know that's not a...how do I put it...concern or consideration of yours. Admission is highly competitive of course, but I would be willing to support your application. I know it's not ideal to switch schools or programs, but some of your coursework would be transferable, I would take you on again as a teaching assistant, and we could certainly repurpose your proposal and work on sustainable investing within the new program requirements."

I narrowed my eyes, my idiotic smile faltering in favor of a look of disbelief. "You want me to transfer to Oxford? Move to the U.K?" Again.

"I realize it's a lot to think about, but there's no rush, and I can certainly work to find someone who would take you on as a student." She continued to look at me, eyes starting to crinkle the longer she looked at me.

"It's not that, it's..." a choked laugh escaped my throat and suddenly I was shaking with laughter, waving her off as she sat up suddenly in alarm. "I'm sorry! I'm sorry...it's not you. It's not the offer. It's an unbelievable offer, a once in a lifetime one."

She looked at me, eyebrows raised and her mouth pulled back. "Are you alright?"

I waved my hand again before swallowing and fanning my face, tears having started to leak from my eyes. "I'm so sorry, I'm sorry. I used to live in the U.K. as you know. I've lived there twice now, and I've always gone there for reasons that...reasons that maybe weren't entirely my own."

"You're not interested? Charlie, this isn't only a good thing for me. It could be good, great even, for you as well." She leaned forward, a more maternal look of concern on her face now. "I think you have a very bright future."

A tiny breath escaped my nose. That's what I had been trying to find here in New York, a future without Winchester Holdings, and it had finally felt like I was doing it, on my own. Something no one could take from me. This was just like everything else—not something I had really earned. "I need to think about it. But thank you for the very thoughtful and very generous offer."

She gave me a small smile before sitting back in her chair and turning to her computer. "Alright then. Can you let me know by the end of June? For now, let's take a look at your latest edits."

I nodded, sinking down into my seat and grabbing the arms of my chair, hoping I could hold onto the semblance of this new life I had created here just a while longer.

CHAPTER EIGHT

Mercifully, the news cycle shifted the week the dinner with my father and Deacon was scheduled; Tripp and I fading away into obscurity and not even remotely interesting to the media any longer. I was not looking forward to sitting across the table from my father and feeling the judgment leaking off him. The photos of Tripp and me, and thank God the ones of David and Victoria staring into one another's eyes, slowly disappeared and were replaced by more current events. Taylor was very disappointed, claiming she loved hearing her patients talk about the engagement party, and the now clearly established Tripp versus David, Charlie versus Victoria vitriol the tabloids were spewing.

I tipped my head, eyeing my dress in the mirror. Dinner was at Harry's, which has been a Wall Street institution since the seventies. I had never been, and I'm sure Damien picked it based on price per seating. The Le Superbe Halter Dress was something I did pick myself, however. There was a small keyhole in the center of the chest, leading to a two-tone white and pale pink halter neck. It hugged my body and fell to just below my knees. An old pair of leather pointed-toe Prada pumps were strewn across the floor to my right. I pulled them out of the closet haphazardly and jumped around as I slid them onto my feet before deciding they were acceptable, and turned to study my face in the mirror.

I tucked my hair behind my ears, smiling at my reflection. My cheeks didn't feel like they were burning from forcing a smile, but that would surely change by the end of the night. I turned my head again, the straight sheet of my hair moving with me, and I watched the champagne tone of the shimmer on my eyes catch the light hanging from the top of my closet. I appreciated some shimmer when it wasn't the color of a fucking rainbow and forced on my eyes by Sabine.

My phone vibrated on the shelf beside me where it sat beside a large, black Saint Laurent Quilted Envelope Clutch. My father had awkwardly given it to me last Christmas as we sat around a ridiculous table setting that looked like it was out of a Hallmark movie. Deacon and Noa sat across from us, eyeing the interaction as he looked on with clearly no idea what the gift I was opening actually was. Damien bought every gift he had ever given me, and despite the fact that Taylor fell all over herself and quite literally let out a groan when she saw it, it was proof he didn't know me at all. I could guarantee he wouldn't even recognize it when I brought it to dinner tonight.

I padded across the carpet, eyes narrowing when I could make out the message on my phone.

Tripp Banks: It seems Page Six might possess a crystal ball. I have come to town. I'm in the city if you want to meet up.

I clenched my jaw as I aggressively pounded my thumbs against the screen to respond.

Charlie: Great news. When I was walking by the Hudson the other day, I thought it looked a little low on trash. Feel free to hop in.

Throwing the phone into the bottom of the clutch, it practically disappeared into the quilted fabric. The size of this thing really was fucking ridiculous.

The restaurant was dimly lit, and the low din of voices and laughter surrounded me. Two practically identical dark-haired women wearing the same slinky, silk black blouses tucked into figure-hugging black skirts, were positioned behind the hostess stand. Their overlarge and painted smiles greeted me. I suppressed a shudder, wondering if that's what I looked like to others when I was propped up beside my father at events.

"Winchester?" I asked, holding the stupid quilted clutch in front of me.

A flicker of recognition shone in both of their eyes, but they continued to smile politely as one of the two gestured to their left and grabbed a giant padded leather menu. I fell into step just behind her, both of our heels clicking in unison against the floor as we wove in between tables toward the back of the restaurant. Steven Winchester would hardly deign to sit out in the common area of an establishment. How embarrassing would it have been to sit with your son and daughter out in a public space.

The hostess came to a stop in front of a doorway, her tight ponytail swinging from the abruptness. The same overlarge smile slid back into place, and she folded her hands behind her back. "Right through there, Miss Winchester."

"Thank you." I offered her a smile before dipping my head and stepping through the doorway and down the short hallway to the room, careful of my heels on the polished hardwood floor.

The last thing I needed was to fall on my ass in front of my father. I'd done the proverbial version of that enough.

I could hear my father and Deacon before I saw them. I heard them laughing, but amongst that laughter there was another sound. Laughter that I heard all the way down to the marrow of my bones. Stopping suddenly, the toe of my heel caught against the floor, and I lurched forward before I steadied myself.

David was sitting directly across from where I was standing, lips parted ever so slightly at the sight of me. He was leaning in his chair, one arm slung over the back, and the jacket of his dove gray suit was unbuttoned, along with the white shirt underneath it. The other arm was propped up on the table, casually swirling a glass of scotch. The usual light or playfulness dancing in his eyes when he saw me was certainly dead and gone—there was nothing there. His gaze was flat and dull. I was sure mine looked the same as we stared at one another, our last words to one another ringing in my ears. Fuck David Kennedy.

"New heels?" Deacon asked, laughing, then standing to offer me a brief hug before dropping a kiss to the top of my forehead.

I cleared my throat, finally breaking my gaze from my staring match with David. "I didn't realize this dinner was open to the public. It was a surprise."

Deacon's mouth pulled down and something like guilt flashed behind his eyes. Our eyes. I looked at him pointedly, he clearly had already forgotten about our promise for no more secrets. Raising my heel, I brought it down onto the top of his brushed Prada derby loafer. They looked freshly polished. Deacon made a strangled noise, but I had already turned toward our father. The only thing that looked different about him from two weeks ago was that he was now in a suit instead of a tux. He was even wearing the same expression of perpetual disappointment at my and Deacon's behavior.

"Charlie, you look lovely," my father offered, kissing my cheek quickly before turning back to his seat.

I raised my eyebrows, shaking my head at the fleeting interaction and dropped into the chair Deacon pulled out for me.

"Thank you," I said, schooling my features before looking across the table at David.

He hadn't moved from his position, and his expression remained the same. David watched as I set my clutch on the table, swirling his glass of scotch and looking oddly reminiscent of my father. A server was standing behind a small bar in the corner of the room, and Deacon seemed eager to make amends for his forgetfulness by flagging them over to pour me a glass of wine. I smiled up at them in thanks, momentarily breaking my eye contact with David. Seeing David as someone who wasn't mine, someone who made abundantly clear that I could never fix things, was always odd, always jarring. But this version of David, the one from the engagement party who lied to me, who I left standing by the water in Lake Forest, made me feel like one of my ribs had broken off and stabbed a puncture in my lungs. Breathing around him hurt. It felt, for a moment, like I was looking at someone I didn't know, someone I didn't recognize.

Until he spoke. His eyes warmed, and his lips pulled up to the side in a sort of sad grin. His voice was low, and even though Deacon and my father were here, I knew the words were just for me.

"You look stunning, Charlie."

My lips parted, and suddenly the David I knew and loved with my entire being was sitting in front of me. It was no longer uncomfortable; it just simply hurt. My exposed skin prickled, and I could feel heat flush across my cheeks. It would be so easy to pretend none of that ever happened, and to fall back into my cycle of endless pining for him. But for the first time, I found that I didn't want to. New York Charlie didn't grovel. She was trying to learn her worth. Deacon cleared his throat, and I realized we had been silent, staring at one another for a few moments now.

"Thank you, David. It's nice to see you." I smiled softly in return, still unsure why he was even here, before taking a sip of my wine.

I turned to my father and offered the only question we ever seemed to ask one another. "How was work today?"

"I think I'll let your brother answer that question," he responded, somewhat ominously.

His blue eyes were blank as always, and I was beginning to wonder if any emotion that lurked behind them well and truly died with my mother.

Deacon cleared his throat, and an air of discomfort settled around him. I turned to him, sharpening my gaze. He rolled his shoulders and unbuttoned the top of his shirt before taking another sip of his scotch.

I raised my eyebrows at him expectantly and folded my arms across my chest. My heart started to beat faster the longer the silence stretched.

"I don't have all night, Deacon," I said sharply, irritation flaring alongside the anxiety about whatever he didn't want to say.

Clearly, he had been less than honest about more than one thing recently. I did indeed have all night; I had no plans other than a chilled bottle of wine, a promise from Taylor to call me when her shift ended at God knows when, and endless papers to mark.

"Do you keep a particularly busy social calendar, Charles?" Deacon asked playfully, trying to diffuse the tension that was growing ever thicker between us, but I continued to stare at him. "You know I'm getting married—"

I interrupted him with a feigned gasp of surprise.

"Are you really? That's not your face I see in every magazine in the western world? Your engagement isn't threatening the small semblance of privacy I try to retain?" I blew out a breath, a kernel of dread burrowing into my stomach. I could feel where this was going.

My eyes flitted back to David momentarily, while Deacon stayed silent. I could only think of one reason he was here now.

"No fucking shit, Deac. What does that have to do with WH? Spit it out."

"Noa works primarily out of New York. It's not feasible for her to move to Chicago. She would be gone more than she's home. WH did exceptionally well last quarter, which you would know if you ever bothered to read your shareholders' statements. It's the perfect time for expansion. I'm bringing a new office of the company to Manhattan. It's a great time to expand our portfolio even farther on the East Coast. That's what we were doing today. Seeing what office space was available in the few buildings WH owns and checking out some others on Wall Street," Deacon answered all at once.

It didn't even look like he had taken a single breath during that spiel, which was so clearly rehearsed I didn't know whether to laugh or cry.

"And that means..." I trailed off, disbelief coloring my words before my gaze swung back to David.

Another omission by my brother. I rolled my shoulders and pressed my eyes closed quickly, the dress felt too tight all of a sudden and everything was too hot. New York was mine. It was supposed to be just for me. Somewhere I could exist outside of WH, outside of my family, and outside of all my mistakes.

"I didn't realize you didn't know," David said, his voice strained.

My eyes flew open, and he was staring at me with something I couldn't place. I didn't know if it was sadness or pity. But I didn't want either from him.

"A lie by omission is still a lie, David," I whispered in return before turning back to my brother.

It felt like my face was collapsing on itself, just like this whole sanctuary I wanted. I cocked my head, sadness surely etching my features. Deacon looked torn—like he wasn't sure whether he should stand firm in his decision or reach out to offer me comfort.

"And that means you need to recruit new executives. That's what this is. You want David to come back to WH," I let out, solving some sort of riddle I wanted nothing to do with.

I knew better than to turn to my father. There would be nothing for me there. A derisive sort of snort escaped me as Deacon and I continued to stare at one another. I had never felt this far from my brother, not in all the miles and physical distance that separated us over the years, not when we were at odds with one another over our mother, not when we fought. All that time, and nothing felt as insurmountable as the distance that stretched between us now. It was like one piece of my soul, one that was never supposed to hurt me, always supposed to protect me no matter what, suddenly turned inward, hurtful and stabbing.

"That's why Tripp is also in town. He's moving here, too," I continued.

Deacon looked like he wanted to ask me how I knew Tripp was in town before closing his eyes momentarily. They were dim, seemingly stretching with endless regret and sadness. His hand twitched on the table, as if out of habit he wanted to reach for me, but he spoke instead, "Yes. It made more sense than asking Ash, or anyone else with a family or established roots in Chicago. Tripp and David were the obvious choices."

David grimaced across the table, raising his eyebrows while he stared into his glass. "I think there were probably some other factors you should have considered when making that decision and before springing this on me. Last I checked, no one else on staff had their hands, or their mouth, on my girlfriend."

"It's a business decision, Charlie," our father finally spoke, and I pulled my gaze away from my brother and David, expecting to see the same blank and monotone mask on my father that he always wore. But there were slight creases at the corner of his eyes, like what he saw unfolding before him troubled him somehow. But I knew better. Steven Winchester wasn't troubled by anything. "Nothing more, nothing less."

"Of course it was," I answered incredulously, shaking my head.

I took a measured sip of wine before I responded, not looking at any one of them in particular.

"Far be it from me to question a business decision. Please, go ahead. Proceed to woo David with an offer, the likes of which I am sure he has never heard."

Making a carry-on gesture with my hand, I looked away from my father, sure he would have something to say about my insolent behavior. I could feel David's eyes on me from across the table, but I didn't want to look at him, either. My gaze flitted over Deacon momentarily, and he looked on the precipice of saying something to me before I averted my gaze again. From the corner of my eye, I watched him swallow and shake his head slightly before taking another sip of scotch and turning to David.

I didn't want to look at any of them.

In typical Steven Winchester fashion, toward the end of the meal, my father excused himself to make a phone call that just couldn't wait. It had actually taken a bit more convincing than I think my father or Deacon would have thought to come back to the company, but I didn't find it surprising at all. Why would David want a daily reminder of the person who cheated on him from the person she cheated with? But the powers of Winchester persuasion won out in the end. I only politely engaged in the conversation throughout dinner, offering little in response to the prodding questions thrown my way by my brother and David. I could feel Deacon's eyes on me throughout the meal, but I refused to look back at him. I wasn't hurt like I had been at the engagement party when he kept the truth from me; I was fucking angry.

The two of them were talking about some colleague of David's they both knew that they thought might make a good addition to WH. I didn't care; I was taking the opportunity while my father was gone to scroll through my phone. David's phone began to buzz incessantly from its place beside his nearly empty scotch glass. My eyes lifted to watch as David leaned forward to see who was calling. A faint smile pulled at his lips at whatever he saw there. I fought a grimace, assuming it was Victoria, and that they were so blissfully in love that just her name brought a smile to his face.

"Excuse me," David said, standing and grabbing the phone before striding out of the room, off to wherever it was that people took calls at Michelin Star restaurants.

The second he was gone, Deacon turned to me. "Charlie, I'm sorry."

"You're beginning to sound like a broken record, Deacon," I snapped, draining the last of my wine.

The server was instantly there to refill it, and I couldn't even be bothered to look up in thanks. My eyes were boring into my brother.

"We said no more secrets! Less than two weeks ago! Did you snort so much cocaine in college that your memory short circuited?"

Deacon gave me a flat look and ran his hand through his hair, knocking it loose of its confines.

"It wasn't a secret. I approached Dad about it with the proposal last week after Noa and I talked through what was best. I assumed she would quit modeling."

"At the height of her career?" I asked, a choked laugh slipping from my lips at the unbelievable idiocy that was my brother at this moment. "Yeah, that sounds like something the soon-to-be most famous supermodel in the world would do."

"Don't worry, Noa and I already had it out about what an idiotic idea that was. I've served my time over that one." Deacon shook his head and knocked back what was left of his scotch. "Like I said, I wasn't keeping the secret from you. I thought you would be excited about me moving here. You hate coming home to Chicago."

"A little heads up would have been nice," I bit out.

This was such a Deacon thing to do that it was almost laughable. Little billionaire boy assumes that his soon-to-be wife would just drop her incredibly successful career to follow him to the Midwest, and when that doesn't work out, entirely disrupt his sister's life without telling her, and then not having the faintest fucking idea why she was upset about it. My corner of the world wasn't just mine anymore. Dr. Batra was leaving, and Winchester Holdings was descending.

"Like what the fuck, Deacon? This is my city, where I've been trying to make a life without the Winchester shadow, without all the dumb fucked up things I've done because of our stupid family. And now you're just re-creating the circumstances of what happened back in Chicago? Forcing David and Tripp to work together again?"

It was his turn to look incredulous.

"You don't have a monopoly on the city of New York, Charlie. And in case you were too busy during dinner being a goddamn martyr, David accepted the job willingly. Oh, and if I remember correctly, he was here first."

Anger flared in my stomach, and my cheeks burned. A retort rose on my lips, but Deacon cut me off.

"Charlie, I have sympathy for you. Empathy even. God knows I've made my fair share of mistakes, but you need to take some responsibility. Stop blaming Mom, Dad, me...whoever's on your villain-of-the-day calendar, for all the reasons you fucked up. You're the only one responsible for destroying what you and David had. Not Dad. Not Mom. Not me. Not Tripp. You."

Deacon looked one second away from pointing his finger at me, the way our father did when he was angry at us when we were poorly-behaved teenagers. I opened my mouth to respond, ready to tell Deacon exactly where I thought he should go—as if I didn't know any of that already, or that over the past year-and-a-half it hadn't occurred to me I was the one to blame—when I heard two sets of distinct footsteps entering the room again.

I shot a glare at Deacon before painting a perfect picture of contentment on my features. We could have it out later when our father wouldn't be breathing down my neck, waiting for my next mistake. I smiled balefully as my father and David re-entered the room, both taking their seats. David looked back and forth between us, his shoulders tight, like he could sense the tension settling between us; like he could see the thread connecting our two souls splintering. Deciding to go back to my plan of ignoring them all, I looked back at my phone and found another text from Tripp.

Tripp Banks: I assume Deac has made the big reveal by now? He's more suited for the Hudson than me. I'm wearing a custom Alan David suit.

Charlie: Already a Wall Street douchebag? I suppose Boston and Chicago weren't enough on the resume. A little heads up would have been nice.

Tripp Banks: I told Deac I wasn't getting involved.

Charlie: How friendly and chivalrous of you. I must have had an aneurysm, because I've decided to take you up on that drink. One night only. We're just about done if you want to meet me at the restaurant.

I dropped my phone face down on the table and folded my hands demurely in front of me. I hadn't been paying the slightest bit of attention to what they were talking about now, but it sounded like they were talking about meeting at whatever office space they decided on for David to sign his new contract in the coming weeks.

My father turned to look at me, and I noticed the lines of his face seemed sharper than they had two weeks ago. He was aging, and each time I saw him, it was like a countdown clock started in my head. My mother left with no notice. I had notice, and I was doing nothing with it.

"I'll be in the city until things are settled with the expansion. Perhaps we can have dinner again," he said.

Perhaps we can have dinner? I gaped at him before plastering another polite smile on my face. But here was another interloper in my life. I didn't need my father becoming Master of Manhattan the way he was in Chicago. I relished the small corner of Upper Manhattan I had cultivated for myself. The stoop of my townhome, free of security, free of paparazzi, people on the street freely ignoring me. I could feel that all slipping away now.

"That sounds great. I'll give Damien a call, and he can set something up. Where are you staying?" I asked in response, entirely aware the normal daughterly question would have been to ensure their father was staying with them.

I had extra bedrooms, bathrooms, and space. But I didn't want any part of this family there, any more than I thought my father wanted to be there. Deacon never stayed with me when he was in the city anymore. He didn't need a closet full of spare clothes at my house. He had one at Noa's.

"I'm staying at The Carlyle while things are getting settled."

I nodded, continuing to smile politely as I imagined my father taking up residence in his preferred suite—The Empire. I had always thought staying in hotels for extended periods of time grew too impersonal, too hostile. But not Steven Winchester. He thrived in a sterile environment.

"I think I'm going to head home now. Thank you for dinner," I said, the maniacal expression still plastered on my face.

My father nodded, making a vague noise while he signed the check a server had brought over. I stood and smoothed out the front of my dress before grabbing my clutch. I shot a cursory glance toward my brother and David.

"Goodnight, Deacon. And David, have a nice evening."

I turned on my heel quickly before either of them could respond and made my way out of the private room, weaving back through the tables of dining and smiling patrons. I wasn't sure what was becoming of my life when suddenly a drink with Tripp Banks was more appealing than sitting in a room any second longer with my father and brother, and David Kennedy. Hell must have really frozen over.

CHAPTER NINE

Inhaling deeply, I tipped my head upward to the night sky and closed my eyes briefly. That was saying something, if the smell of Manhattan provided relief compared to a private room in one of the best restaurants in the city. It might have said more that I would rather wait out on the sidewalk for Tripp than sit in there a moment longer. I felt like I could breathe out here. So, I stood, chin still tipped toward the stars, to savor it for just a little longer, before Winchester Holdings surely invaded every corner of the city.

"Charlie! Wait!" David called from behind me.

I opened my eyes suddenly, peering over my shoulder, and watched him smile at the doorman before stepping out onto the sidewalk. He ran a hand through his hair, tugging on the ends like he was nervous. I stayed silent as his long legs closed the distance between us.

"I hate the way we left things after the engagement party," David said, a rueful expression on his face.

He looked like he was in pain, the creases around his eyes more prominent from the frown he was wearing. "That's not who we are. That's not...that's not who I want us to be. I don't want to be those people, the ones who can never be in the same room again, always at each other's throats like that. I want to coexist, at the very least."

"It's not who I want us to be, either, David. But you lied to me. What was I supposed to do? Say thank you?" I answered, offering him a nonchalant shrug.

I was attempting to channel Taylor. I could practically hear what she would say. Fuck David Kennedy and fuck Victoria, too.

David's eyes widened before a noise of disbelief sounded in his throat. "You want to talk about lying? You fucking cheated on me, Charlie."

My mouth popped open, surprise decorating my features. I had only ever heard David say those words once before. I wrapped my arms around myself despite the warm breeze, tipping my head and looking at David, really seeing him. Discomfort radiated off of him, and his lips were twisted into some sort of grimace. He looked like saying those words, saying that out loud, had caused him real, physical pain. I closed my eyes, trying to pretend the reality, the consequences of what I had done in my carelessness, weren't staring me in the face. Those words hurt me; they sunk their claws in, ripped and tore at all my skin and my heart.

"I know. I know. I cheated on you."

I opened my eyes, the edges burning and blurred as I took in David. His posture was tight, and I could see his hands fisted in his pockets. I watched as his jaw popped before he started rubbing a hand across his face.

"What are we going to do?" I whispered uselessly. I would rather cut off my own arm than stay away from David.

Clearing his throat, David rubbed his jaw again. "I don't know. I don't know what to do. We're in each other's lives now regardless of what we do."

I wondered if those words meant to David what they did to me. We were in each other's lives, sure, but that was a gross oversimplification. His name was stamped on the inside of my heart, he was tattooed on my veins, and his smile inflated my lungs with air.

I tipped my head again, trying to catch the way the streetlights were reflecting off David's eyes, searching for one more glimpse of sparkling honey; one last time I could pretend his eyes were the stars put in the sky just for me. I considered his words for a moment and weighed them against everything else I knew. There was no fixing what I had broken. I knew David's eyes, his hands, his heart—that I could no longer claim them as my home. But they still were despite my best efforts, and I would probably always want them to be. If I had to choose between some form of life with David Kennedy, or one without, I would pick *with* every time. I would exist on any scraps he wanted to throw my way for the rest of my life.

"Maybe that's all it is. An acknowledgment that we're in each other's lives now. Just a fact," I offered, repeating David's earlier words back to him. They felt heavy and foreign against my lips.

"Should we try to start over? Do you think we could try to be friends?" David asked, the words seeming to catch on his own lips, like he couldn't believe he was saying them.

"Friends?" a choked laugh escaped me, and my mouth stayed open in shock.

I wasn't sure if I was capable of being friends with David. How do you become just friends with the only person who ever saw you, really, truly saw you? But if it was that, or the alternative, a bleak life without the stars and sunlight that made up David Kennedy, I would take any piece of David he was willing to give.

"Okay. Friends," I answered, choking back another laugh when David extended his hand. "I'm sorry, are you trying to shake my hand, Mr. Kennedy?"

"I have it on good authority that Winchesters know the importance of a good, firm first impression handshake, billion dollar baby," he said, stepping closer to me and starting the usual somersaulting of my heart.

I took a deep breath, willing it to quiet down. That was not what friends did.

I took a tentative step toward David, extending my own hand. "See for yourself."

David's hand brushed against mine, and my heart dropped. After all this time, I still had no idea why they were so rough and worn. I just knew I loved it. I loved everything about him.

David laughed, rubbing his jaw with his other hand while our hands remained awkwardly suspended between us. "I'm not sure I know how to be just your friend, Charlie."

"Well, I don't think friends constantly acknowledge their shared romantic history, or the continued sexual tension between them. I also don't think they shake hands all that often," I said, withdrawing my hand from his.

This was more for my benefit than David's. I was trying to temper the urge to throw myself at his feet and beg for forgiveness again, and I could practically hear Taylor in my ear, telling me how pathetic I was. It was time to move on. *We were in each other's lives now. It was just a fact.*

"You're probably right." David smiled again, shoving his hand back into the pocket of his suit pants. "We can figure it out as we go."

Nodding, I wasn't sure what else to say; my heart was still torn, shredded entirely, tatters of the muscle tissue beating uselessly in my chest. But I was spared, because as if right on fucking cue, Tripp stepped out of a black town car that had pulled up to the curb. A grin spread across his face, his eyes glinting mischievously as they darted back and forth between David and me.

"Well, well, well...if this isn't quite the reunion."

"Tripp," David nodded, his voice tight and a forced smile fell into place.

"Shut up, Tripp." My words were punctuated and irritated, his constant need to bait everyone around him never failed to get under my skin.

"What are you doing here?" David asked, an edge to his voice. "Steven and Deac said you signed your new contract last week in Chicago."

"I did. I'm not here for the big reveal, or to try and convince you to come back. Chuck and I are going for a drink. She's welcoming me to the city." Tripp stepped closer to me, casually throwing an arm around my exposed shoulders.

A noise of disgust came from my throat, and I ducked out from under his hold, exaggerating a shiver, which only made the cat-like grin on Tripp's face grow.

"You're going for a drink?" David asked, his voice and his eyes sharpening. "Just the two of you?"

I angled my head at him. "Friends, remember? *Friends* are okay when *friends* have drinks with other *friends*, David."

David dipped his head, and I watched the muscles in his neck tighten before he looked back up and spoke. His words were clipped, harsh even, "I guess in this new world you have lots of *friends*. I'll have to get used to that."

"You wanna join us, DK?" Tripp asked, his words casual.

My lips parted, and I looked at him in disbelief, and in disgust, immediately second-guessing my choice of "friends."

David huffed, brown eyes skating over me with an emotion I couldn't place before he schooled his features.

"No, I need to head home. Victoria is visiting this weekend."

"Well, say hi for us." Tripp smiled, looking more like he was baring his teeth.

"Do you ever shut up?" My lower lip jutted out as I hissed at Tripp. "Seriously, do you come with an off switch?"

I turned to David, about to politely rephrase, that he *should* pass on our greetings to Victoria, exactly as a Winchester would do, as etiquette would state, but he was looking back at me, eyes soft now.

"Goodnight, Charlie."

My breath caught, and it felt like one of those moments in the movies where everything around you stops, and you feel like you're on the precipice of something and your life is hanging on tenterhooks. Like your choice at that moment might change your entire trajectory. But there was a line in the sand between us that David had drawn, and our life together was behind it. We were *just friends* now.

"Goodnight, David."

———

Manhattan at night was so different from Chicago. Deacon and I always referred to Chicago as our corner of the world, and in so many ways, it really did feel like it was just for us. It was quiet, almost quaint in comparison. But in Chicago, there was nothing quaint or quiet about being a Winchester. Here, I felt like I was anonymous for the first time in my life. Despite Noa's fame—and how mine and Deacon's escalated by association—no one really noticed me here amongst the other almost nine million people. At least, it had been my own. Now, Winchester Holdings was all around me...again.

Tripp fell silent the second David went back into the restaurant, only gesturing in a general direction for us to walk before falling into step beside me. Our shoulders brushed occasionally, and neither of us said anything while we navigated through the throngs of people. I was annoyed at him for baiting David, annoyed at myself for putting myself in this situation, and annoyed at myself for caring so much that David seemed upset I was with Tripp when he had made it abundantly clear it was over between us.

But I didn't stop walking. I didn't turn around and tell Tripp to fuck off like I probably should have. Tripp was another see-saw in my life. One second I was teetering away from him, hating him with every irritated breath I took in his presence, and the next I was tipping toward him, brought in by whatever magnets seemed to exist in our two bodies. It was like that with us and always had been from the day we met.

When I was young and stupid, my sorority sisters would always laugh and say that we were two halves of one whole, two people who must be destined for one another, because we couldn't seem to stay apart. Now, it was like we were two drowning people in the way that the first person to go down often ends up drowning their rescuer out of sheer panic, just a tangle of limbs, fear and hysteria; and I had no idea who was who.

"Where do you want to get a drink, Charlie?" His voice was uncharacteristically gentle, but it was the use of my real name that caught me off guard.

I stopped in the middle of the sidewalk, turning to him and crossing my arms. "Charlie? Since when do you call me *Charlie*?"

"That's your name, isn't it?" Tripp stopped alongside me, his hands in the pockets of his worn khakis, and he gazed down at me.

I noticed his eyes, that maddening blue that seemed fake, glinted in the light, sort of like David's. But where David's were all warm, Tripp's eyes sparkled like tiny, frozen snowflakes caught in the sunlight.

"I wasn't sure you knew my real name," I muttered, rolling my eyes, and beginning to walk along the sidewalk again.

"Where do you want to stop for a drink?" He asked again, ignoring me.

I shrugged, my arms still crossed as we walked. I wasn't entirely sure this was a good idea anymore, but I knew I didn't want to be alone. The thought of David going home to Victoria, despite our decision to be friends and my commitment to have him in my life no matter what it cost me, made me nauseous.

"Somewhere no one would expect us to go."

Tripp came to a sudden halt, tipping his stubble-lined chin toward a doorway in front of us. It looked like a typical Manhattan hole in the wall: the dark windows were papered with advertisements for events and bands, and it looked dimly lit on the inside. The worn, scratched door was set back from the sidewalk with a heavy-looking, tarnished door handle. He looked at me, arching an eyebrow.

"I highly doubt this bar has ever seen the likes of a Winchester."

"Pfft. I don't even want to know half the places that have seen the likes of Deacon." I shook my head, stepping forward to open the door, but Tripp beat me to it, pulling the handle and gesturing for me to go first with his other hand.

"How gentlemanly of you."

"I'm nothing if not chivalrous," he spoke from behind me, and I realized how close he was standing to me.

His breath was warm against my ear, and my spine straightened out of habit when I felt Tripp place his hand against my lower back.

A rough laugh rose in his throat. "I thought we were friends now?"

"Just because we're friends doesn't mean I want you pawing at me," I said, stepping away and weaving through the assorted tables and mismatched chairs before dropping down on a chair and table shoved into the corner of the bar.

Light from a candlestick shoved in a wine bottle illuminated the graffiti on the tabletop, and the wax dripped freely leaving tracks down the side of the bottle and drying on the surface. I dropped my clutch, kicking it unceremoniously under the table, practically able to hear Taylor shrieking in my ear about the YSL clutch and the sticky, dirty floor. Tripp bent over the bar, and I watched his jawline pop while he spoke to the bartender, who was leaning an ear toward him, cleaning a glass with a questionable rag, before he made his way back to me.

Tripp dropped into the seat across from me, holding two bottles of beer by the neck. He held one out to me, and I grabbed it from him, noticing the ripped and torn Stella label. It had seen better days. Tripp's eyes were on me while I brought it to my lips.

"Since when do you drink anything but top shelf?" I tipped my head, raising an eyebrow at him.

My hair shifted with the movement, and I noticed Tripp's eyes tracking it.

"Did you want to drink from one of those glasses?" He asked, voice dry.

"I've had worse." My eyes wandered around the bar, and I tapped the bottle to my teeth.

I was unsettled, untethered and unmoored, sitting there with him. It wasn't as easy to be Tripp's friend, to pretend that the past wasn't all around us whispering in our ears when we were outside the confines of the engagement party. Tripp sat in silence with me, occasionally pulling out his phone and tapping away, or taking a sip of his drink. When he set it down, his large hand wrapping around the bottle, I noticed with a pang how neat, how clean, his hands were. There wasn't a callus to be found.

"Do you get manicures?" I blurted suddenly, enjoying the disdain that rose on his face, making him look even more like a movie villain.

"No, I don't get manicures." Tripp took another sip. "Why are you looking at my hands, Chuck? Would you like to hold one?"

His voice dripped with the usual arrogance that annoyed me to no end, but I watched him extend a hand, leaving it palm up for me.

I remembered being eighteen, pulling Tripp by that same hand through parties and bars, holding it when we danced together at various formals, all the while he whispered in my ear.

Impulsively, I reached out and laid my palm flat against his. Tripp curled his fingers around mine, dwarfing my hand. His skin was too soft, too cared for. There was no way he wasn't secretly getting a manicure—or two—on the side.

"David's hands are all rough and full of calluses. But yours aren't." I felt his hand tense around mine but only momentarily.

"What happened between you two earlier?"

Shrugging, I took another sip of my drink with my free hand, leaving my other one where it was cupped in his. "He wants to be friends."

"What do you want, Charlie?" His voice was low.

Tripp's thumb skated over my knuckles briefly before coming to rest back on top of my hand.

"To turn back time," I whispered in return, looking up and meeting his eyes.

I wasn't exactly sure what I meant—where I wanted the hands of the clock to reverse to, where I wanted them to stop. The possibilities were endless.

Tripp paused and seemed to weigh my answer before he extracted his hand from mine, his face showing nothing.

"So, Kennedy's the one then?" He looked up at me, thumbs rolling over the label on his beer bottle.

The light hanging above us glinted off his eyes, and he arched a dark eyebrow as he waited for me to answer.

"David is David." I shrugged again, a smile playing on my face, because instead of the harsh, biting and heartbreaking parts of our love, I was thinking of the good ones. He would always be Mr. Kennedy to me. "He has something no one else has."

"And what's that?"

"He notices my laugh is louder in private. He knows who I am when no one is looking. He sees me. He's always seen me."

It might have seemed like a cop out, like maybe to the average person that wasn't much. But it was everything. It was all I could say to explain the intangible hold David Kennedy would always, *always* have over me. "Did you know humans and animals sleep when they feel safe? It's evolution. We evolved to sleep when we were safe and protected, away from threats. I could bore you and tell you how neglected children don't sleep well or explain the effects of attachment theory. But it's that simple. He's the first person who has ever made me sleepy. I'm sleepy around him."

Tripp narrowed his eyes. "And I don't make you *sleepy*? I don't see you?"

I placed my palms flat against the table, leaning forward. "What's the first thing you noticed about me, Tripp?"

His trademark grin fell into place, lips quirked up to one side. "That you had a great rack for a freshman."

I slapped my hand against the table, my palm sticking to the tacky wood and raised my eyebrows at him.

"I knew who you were. Everyone did. But that's not why I stayed," he said, staring at me, eyes never leaving mine.

Smiling sadly, I took a sip of my beer. "But it's why you came. It's why everyone has shown interest in me over my whole life. But that's never why David came to talk to me. David loved me."

Tripp leaned forward, too, placing his hands flat so our fingers were touching again. "You didn't invite me for drinks to talk about David Kennedy. We're supposed to be friends now, Chuck. And as your friend, I'm going to do you a favor. Don't take the bait and talk so much about David. The constant stream of consciousness about your lost love is very fucking boring."

A loud laugh, almost a cackle, erupted from my lips, and I slapped my palm to my mouth to cover it. It wasn't really all that funny, but Tripp was right. When did I become such a broken record? I tilted my head, reaching forward and grabbing his hand. He tensed under my fingers again, but I felt him relax when I didn't let go.

"You're right, I'm sorry. Tell me a story."

Tripp's head pulled back and his eyes widened. Those were the words I said to him when we fell asleep together before I kicked him out of my house and left for North Carolina with David, but he nodded and his lips parted to a grin.

"Okay, Chuckles. I'll tell you a story."

CHAPTER TEN

When I finished class for the afternoon, my own and a tutorial I was supervising for a first-year economics course, I emerged from the lecture hall and promptly flagged down a cab, ending up on Fifth Avenue. I hadn't really been thinking; I just listed off the first destination that came to my mind.

I was never in awe of Manhattan, not the way you were supposed to be as a young, listless soul. But I was today, for some reason. Everything about it captivated me—the people milling around, rushing somewhere, the sounds of the traffic and the thick, oppressive heat of the looming summer. Everything this place was before Winchester Holdings would descend on it.

My ancient Louis Vuitton from Taylor was heavy on my shoulder, and I found myself looking up at the doors of Saks Fifth Avenue. I meandered through the store, occasionally stopping to sift through a rack of shirts before being confronted with a wall of floor-to-ceiling bags. I ran my fingers over the leather, wondering if something more practical, with two straps and evenly distributed weight would be nice. I stopped in front of a black leather Rebecca Minkoff backpack. It was folded in on itself, and I knew there was a specific name for it that Taylor would know for sure. There was one of those large, signature clips in the middle that were on all their designs. My fingers had just brushed the cold metal when I heard a voice behind me.

"Charlie?" Noa asked, a smile on her face and sounding genuinely pleased to see me.

I turned, taking in Deacon's fiancée, the one love of his life as he put it. Her face was bare, exposing her angular features that lent so well to photos and the bright lights of a runway. Her dark brown hair was pulled off her face, the slick bun looking effortless and chic. I knew my hair would be sticking out at awkward angles if I tried anything like that. An oversized, seemingly unassuming black hooded sweatshirt, save for the fact that it was certainly designer, dwarfed her and the small pair of bike shorts hugging her legs.

"Noa." I smiled.

She was truly beautiful, and it was easy to see how Deacon fell in love with her. She was kind and unassuming, and somehow always whispering things to him that had him bent over in hysterics. She indulged him, played with him like the child he was—he told me the moment he fell in love with her was when she suggested they play hide and seek, one wine-addled afternoon. But she was the temper to his storm, too. His own gravity to keep him from drifting out into the stratosphere.

"What are you doing here?" Noa asked, her eyes bright.

I watched as a man in a nondescript outfit lingered a few steps behind her. I arched an eyebrow at the way his eyes roved over me, assessing for any threat. This had been part of my fear about Deacon and Noa from the beginning, any tiny bit of anonymity we had would evaporate. He would become the kind of person who was photographed and stalked by press and paparazzi, and now that he was moving here—I would, too.

"I don't actually know," I offered with a shrug. "I was at school, and then I ended up here. What are you doing?"

A blush rose on her cheeks, and I noticed her suddenly hiding one of her hands behind her back. "Deacon's coming back to town tonight to see the new office space, and he uh, I thought that maybe—"

My mouth popped open as the scrap of lace she was holding fluttered while she hurried to hide it. I didn't even have any space in my brain to be angry, to be sad, that he hadn't told me he was visiting, to remember that I was no longer his first priority. I was distracted by the lingerie I was certain she was holding. It was just an endless rolling tide of disgust. This was absolutely the type of thing my brother would love. I could picture him sending her on an errand for something that he could "enjoy," salivating over his fiancée picking something out just for him.

"Please don't tell me that you're here picking out some gross lacy contraption for my brother to peel off you later. You know what? I'm temporarily without hearing, without vision. Let's pretend we never saw one another today."

Noa cringed before a loud laugh escaped her, holding up what looked like a lace bodysuit in defeat before dropping it on the closest table. "I'm glad I ran into you. I wanted to see how you were doing after Deacon's...announcement about the company expansion. I told him he shouldn't spring it on you like that. It always seemed like you wanted to be alone here, like New York was something you wanted to experience by yourself."

I chewed my lip, awkwardness overwhelming me. She wasn't wrong. She had lived here this whole time, and I let my desire for having something of my own—escaping and outrunning who I used to be—overshadow all of that. I never took her up on any of her offers to do things together in the city, faking excuses or feigning illnesses and going to see the plays she suggested we take in together with Taylor when she came to visit, pretending I was too busy with school when she asked me to join her for dinner or drinks with Deacon, because I was scared I would see David and remember that his maybe was still a nothing, only to have my hope and heart crushed again.

"I'm sorry that my brother is such an idiot that he thought it was reasonable to simply expect you would just uproot your entire career. But don't worry about me, I'm just a massive bitch it turns out."

Surprise dotted her features, eyebrows popping up her forehead, and she looked at me in confusion. "Charlie, you're hardly—"

"Do you want to have lunch?" I blurted before I could stop myself.

I thought I was furious with Deacon for so much more than him bringing WH here, for interloping on my life. I had been so mad at him—for forgetting to call me when he came to the city, for coming for one night and not stopping in. But at the end of the day, I looked at Noa, really looked at her. Standing there, the perfect match to Deacon's chaos, and I realized I was sad. Sad it wasn't just me and him against the world anymore. There was someone else he loved with his whole heart, too, and he was right. I needed to try harder with her. I barely knew her when it came down to it.

A look of quiet happiness overtook the surprise on Noa's face. A smile that I could tell was so genuine slid into place, and it made my heart ache for all the ways I had tried to shut her out before now, for things that weren't her fault. I was starting to wonder if she was too good, too pure, for any Winchester. We had a tendency to stomp all over the people we loved in designer footwear, and I wished with all my heart she was kept safe through it all.

"I would love that. I can come back here later, if you want to just go now?" Noa's eyes lit up as she spoke.

"Please, I definitely do not need to see whatever it is you were going to pick out for Deacon. And I would actually love nothing more than to disrupt his plans for what was sure to be a depraved evening. Come with me, I'll protect you." I laughed, and it wasn't forced.

Maybe it would be nice to have someone to mock Deacon's antics with other than Taylor. Maybe there was room for one more. I was also alarmingly short on friends. My only real friend lived in Chicago, and as we fell into step beside one another, and Noa's bodyguard lingered behind us, it occurred to me she might understand what it felt like to be me sometimes, what it was like to carry a weight that sometimes felt like it was just too much. Maybe Noa could be my friend.

––––––––––

I knew Noa lived in Tribeca, but as I sat on her couch, which was one of those insane white cloud couches that took up practically the entire living room, a pang of guilt shot through me. I had not once set foot in her apartment. Now my feet were tucked under me, and she was pouring me a glass of wine in her kitchen.

I looked around, the lights from the city streaming in through the floor-to-ceiling glass windows and what could only be described as her tasteful but minimal decorations. Abstract art hung on the white walls, mostly black and white, the occasional pop of color coming from coffee table books spread across the apartment that featured Chanel, Prada and the like. The kitchen was all white marble, and it looked exactly like the place you would expect a supermodel to live in. There was even a bowl of what looked to be decorative fruits in the middle of the waterfall island.

She gave me a tour when we arrived back here, after she hugged her security guard goodbye once she was safely in the building. It wasn't as big as my townhome, without as many useless and empty rooms, but three bedrooms and two bathrooms were sprawled out across the one floor. The entire apartment was crisp and clean, but somehow it wasn't devoid of life. There were framed photos of Noa walking on different runways, or on the cover of various magazines scattered throughout. In her bedroom, a framed photo of two people I knew to be her parents sat in the center of a large dresser, flanked by a photo of Noa and her aunt on the beach in California. I noticed photos of her and my brother, and even some that featured Taylor on her nightstand.

Laughing, she showed me what she said was the most typical model feature of her apartment—her walk-in closet. It put mine to shame and was significantly more organized. Her shoes were neatly placed on lit up shelves, and each bag had its own spot on the opposite wall. All of her clothes were hung perfectly, and I made a mental note not to show her the disaster that was my closet.

It was the type of apartment I could picture my brother living in. I could imagine him walking through the door, suit unbuttoned and hair falling onto his face. Him loosening the neck of his tie and dropping his briefcase on the mysteriously empty end table by the door. Maybe it was waiting for Deacon. Maybe this entire apartment and everything in it was waiting for him. Maybe Noa had always been waiting for my brother. I could see him walking to the sideboard in the corner of the living room and pouring a drink before collapsing on that ridiculous couch, with his arms spread out over the back, and the lights of the city where he was a master of the universe would shine in and cast a glow across his features.

The idea of Deacon seamlessly blending in here, and finding a new life and happiness, made me want to kill him slightly less. I might have had an epiphany, but he was still a moron.

"I hope white is okay. I don't usually drink red when I'm going on casting calls." Noa smiled at me, her feet padding gently against the polished hardwood floor and interrupting the picture I was painting of Deacon's life here in my mind.

"Oh? How come?" I asked, accepting the stemmed wine glass from her.

It was a beautiful, elegant and rigid crystal. Again, it seemed like something my brother would love. It screamed of understated opulence. Though nothing Deacon ended up doing was particularly understated.

"I'm afraid of staining my teeth," Noa offered in honesty before sitting across from me on the section end of the couch and folding her feet under her like mine.

"Does that ever get challenging? The...pressure? The expectation to look a certain way?" I tipped my head, studying her.

Her curls were still pulled back in a messy bun, and her face was bare, save for what I assumed was a tiny bit of blush, but I was beginning to wonder if she just naturally looked like someone had done a "no-makeup" makeup look on her at all times.

Noa nodded thoughtfully, taking a small sip of her wine. "When I was a teenager it was harder. It's really easy to get caught up in the...toxicity of the world. I never wanted to be a model. It wasn't something I aspired to be."

"What did you want to be?" I was curious, because it had never really occurred to me that maybe this wasn't her dream, and that maybe Noa and I had more in common than I ever thought.

"A veterinarian or a marine biologist." She laughed before continuing, "I love animals, and I mean I grew up in California. I was always on the water surfing or swimming."

"You surf? David surfs. He used to compete, actually." I cringed, the words having slipped from my lips before I could stop them.

I didn't want to bring up David at every opportunity. It *was* really fucking annoying, but he always seemed to be lurking in the periphery of my mind, ready to spill out into my real life.

Noa smiled, bobbing her head in agreement and seemingly skating over my too-casual mention of my ex.

"He told me that, yeah. I mean, I'm not great. I'm sure David would surf circles around me, but everyone did it when I was younger."

I cleared my throat, hoping to drown the mention of David's name with the mouthful of wine that followed. "So, from marine biologist to model? You know you could go back to school if you wanted now. God knows you don't have to worry about money. Deacon wouldn't care."

"I actually like modeling now. Maybe it sounds...shallow, or I don't know. But I look at it as art, honestly. I think fashion can be art, and runway and print modeling both allow me to do that, to contribute to society in that way, provide inspiration to a photographer or a designer, whatever it is. I know it's a problematic industry, to say the least, but I like my career. I don't feel the need to change who I am now because it might be considered less than to some." Noa shrugged, her words bare and honest.

"What's that like?" I burst out laughing. "I feel like no matter what I do, I am constantly disappointing my father. I'm caught in this vicious cycle of not wanting to care and caring more than anything."

"I don't think you disappoint your father, Charlie. I just don't think he understands you," Noa said softly, her dark eyes focused on me.

Her words reverberated against the wall I had constructed to keep out anything that might give my father humanity after he fired me. I'm sure there was a business case for it, when I thought about it logically. But all I wanted at that moment, in the entire world, was a parent. Someone to hold me and tell me it would all be okay, wipe my tears away and tell me they loved me, that I was more than the sum of my mistakes. But all I got was Steven Winchester, president and CEO, set on keeping up appearances.

"Well that makes two of us, because I don't understand him, either," I said flatly, taking another large sip of wine, much larger than the tiny sips my etiquette instructor told me were appropriate. "Do you know why you don't have our mother's ring, Noa?"

She shook her head, puckering her lips and holding out her left hand to look at her ring. It was almost an exact replica of the ring that would be on my finger right now had I not been so stupid. The three-carat emerald center stone had two tapered baguette diamonds on either side, giving way to a platinum band that wrapped around her dainty finger. It was Harry Winston, too. But the diamond that belonged to our mother was a vintage cushion cut, and God only knew where it was. The last time I saw it was back in my father's possession.

"The reason you don't have the ring is also sort of the reason I don't work at WH anymore. My father gave it to David to give to me, and well, as you can see I am no longer with David. I don't know what Steven did with the ring, but I highly doubt Deacon would have given you something I tainted." I had meant for my voice to sound deadpanned, funny even, but it cracked and got smaller the longer I talked.

Noa looked away from her ring to me, her eyes and features soft. Something that looked like sympathy or understanding was written there.

"What happened with you and David? Deacon always said it wasn't his story to tell, and that it just didn't work out. But it seems so obvious you two still care about one another. Just things I've observed from you, from him. Things I've heard Deacon say."

"Deacon never told you?" I asked quietly, almost in disbelief.

As she shook her head, what was left of my anger at my brother lessened. Dissipated into nothing. Maybe he did still think I was worth defending, protecting. I contemplated what to say next, how to explain to Noa that my decisions were never about David, but about me, my mother, my father, Tripp, who I wanted to be versus who I was. But there was only the truth at the end of the day.

"I cheated on David with Tripp," I blurted out.

I swallowed the bile that rose in my throat at the admission. No matter how long I had to sit with what I had done, my actions didn't disgust me any less. I waited for the outward signs of repulsion or disappointment, even anger, to appear on Noa's delicate features, but they never came. She continued to look at me with the same expression, looking maybe like she wanted to hug me or offer me comfort, like I deserved those things, but she stayed silent; an offering of permission for me to continue.

"I loved David with my whole heart. He was perfect...he is perfect...and I would have kept him forever. I don't really know how to explain it other than to say it wasn't about him. He wasn't even a factor. It was about me and who Tripp used to be to me, the time in my life he represented. We went to Brown together and being around him again was like being the person I was before my mom died. I don't know, it's really fucking stupid actually. But it felt like maybe there was absolution for the mistakes I made when she died, like if I was worthy enough now for Tripp, it would make up for the fracture in my family." I sucked in a breath before draining the rest of my wine.

My eyes began to burn, and as I looked at Noa, I realized they were burning with unsaid apologies. Because my lack of interest in her hadn't been about her, either. "And now Victoria has him, Tripp is still Tripp, my relationship with my father is practically non-existent, Winchester Holdings is about to be everywhere around me again, and you and Deacon are living out my dream."

Noa was quiet, and the tears were fully blurring my vision now, so I couldn't tell if her expression of love had given way to irritation or anger. But I watched as her blurred figure stood from the opposite end of the couch and padded across the cream high-pile rug and felt the couch sink as she sat down beside me. I felt her hand on my shoulder, and I quickly rubbed my eyes with the back of my hands before turning to her.

"Is that why you've been distant?" Noa asked, her voice low, and I choked back a sob at the gentle, unwavering understanding in her words.

"I've been a bitch. I'm sorry, Noa. I am. And I am so, so happy for you and Deacon. But I am also so, so jealous. Sometimes it feels like a reminder of what I could have had," I offered, shrugging.

It felt foreign and odd at first to receive physical affection from someone who wasn't Deacon or Taylor, but I placed my hand on top of hers anyway. It was like an offering, signaling we could try again.

"I would love to be friends, if you wanted," I continued. "But I have to warn you, according to the only other two friends I have, I talk about David too much, and it's fucking annoying. And according to Deacon, I don't take responsibility for my actions."

A loud laugh, followed by a snort, escaped Noa and seemed so at odds with the tiny, composed person in front of me. "Deacon said YOU don't take responsibility for your actions? Has he looked in a fucking mirror?"

I laughed again, wiping away tears at the corner of my eyes without a care in the world as to whether I was smearing my mascara, and I watched as Noa did the same, draining the rest of her wine with an undignified swig that would have made my father shudder. She grabbed my empty glass from me and made her way to the kitchen to pour more. Maybe there was something salvageable about my little corner of New York City after all.

CHAPTER ELEVEN

Takeout containers littered the previously spotless marble island in Noa's kitchen, along with an empty bottle of wine. We had devolved into sharing the most ridiculous stories about Deacon we each had, continuing to laugh so hard we were crying. We only paused when Noa's stomach emitted the loudest noise I think I had ever heard, and she demanded we order from her favorite Maltese restaurant.

I listened with interest while she spoke animatedly in Maltese over the phone, and when the food had arrived she introduced me to each dish and explained whether it had cultural significance or significance to her and her family. I swirled my wine, rolling my shoulders back and relaxing into the cushion of the couch. Closing my eyes briefly, I understood why these couches were so popular. It really was like sitting on a fucking cloud.

Noa had stepped away to answer a call from her agent, something about a luxury watch deal they were back and forth on. I stayed, waiting on her couch, and straining my ears to hear the sounds of the city around us. Her apartment was much more soundproof than my townhouse.

Spending the day with Noa had been easy, enjoyable even. I wasn't sure the last time I had thoroughly enjoyed the company of someone who wasn't Deacon or Taylor. It felt like she had always been in my life. She was like a gentler version of Taylor. Where Taylor was all sharp edges, iridescence, and severe honesty, Noa was soft and reminded me of a gentle shimmer that guided you toward a difficult truth. I could see clearly why they were such good friends, and why Deacon was drawn to both. Maybe there was something in the Winchester genes that required us to be guided and herded like sheep, to not run ourselves toward destruction.

My head was still tipped back, resting on the back of the couch, chocolate hair spilling around me when I heard the distinct sound of a key turning in the lock of the front door. I snapped my neck up, my spine straightened automatically.

"I have been fantasizing about this all day. I am going to absolutely wreck you," Deacon's voice was low and gravelly, and nausea rolled in my stomach at the realization that this must be how he sounded when he was turned on.

His head was bowed as he stepped through the door, dropping The Row Gio leather duffel bag I had gifted him last Christmas beside him before kicking off his loafers and his hands already moving to his belt.

He looked up at the same time my mouth popped open in horror. A wisp of chocolate hair had come undone and had fallen onto his forehead, completing the wild, and what was to me, incredibly disturbing look across his features.

"EW!" I shrieked, standing and covering my eyes.

I jumped back and forth on the balls of my feet like a child, but the thought of this version of Deacon living here was not one I had wanted to entertain.

"Jesus!" Deacon yelled, slamming the door behind him, and I heard the telltale sounds of his belt being done back up.

A shudder ran through me while I waited for him to speak again. "What the fuck are you doing here? I did not expect my sister to be the first thing I saw in this apartment."

Disgust rang through his words, and I finally peaked an eye through my fingers to ensure Deacon was indeed fully clothed. He strode across the room to the bar in the corner, pouring a drink immediately and knocking it back.

"I'm sorry, am I interrupting whatever disgusting fantasy you concocted for yourself when you sent Noa on her little 'errand' for lingerie?" I drained my wine and grabbed the nearest throw pillow, whipping it across the room toward Deacon. "You're fucking gross, Deac."

"Oh, I'm sorry Charles, does a man enjoying his fiancée offend your morals? Where were those all the times your tongue was down Tripp's throat?" Deacon scoffed at me over his glass.

He had topped it off with another measure of scotch.

"You know, here I was, enjoying a day with my future sister-in-law, and in comes my depraved brother to ruin it." I spread my arms wide, waving my wine glass around before turning and making my way to the kitchen to pour myself another much needed drink. "Also, by the way, telling someone you're going to 'absolutely wreck them' isn't hot. It's alarming."

I made exaggerated air quotes as I spoke while Deacon continued to glare at me from his spot by the bar. "What are you doing here anyway? I didn't think you'd be interested in seeing me after dinner last week."

"You're right, I'm not interested in seeing you." I raised my eyebrows at him while I tipped the bottle of wine practically upside down to fill my glass as quickly as possible.

Deacon and I hadn't spoken since the dinner. It might have been the longest time we went without speaking, and neither of us seemed particularly inclined to bridge the gap or apologize first. "But I ran into Noa today at Saks. She was shopping for her little *errand* and decided that it would be much more enjoyable to come have lunch with me. We ended up spending the day together and came back here for a drink and ordered dinner...and now you're here."

"You spent the whole day together?" He asked, his features softening as he spoke. The corners of his lips twitched, and the ghost of a small smile was there.

"Yes, and she didn't mention you coming here tonight once, so clearly the prospect of getting 'wrecked' by you was not all that appealing." Pursing my lips, I took another sip of my wine.

A grin spread across Deacon's face, and he bounded across the room exuding such a childlike energy my perpetual grimace almost split into a smile but suddenly he wrapped his arms around me in a hug, lifting me off my feet and, honest to God, spinning me around. A gag snuck up my throat, and I immediately pushed off him, brushing my clothes off.

"Deacon, do not hug me right now. Barely ten minutes ago you were storming in here ready to do whatever disgusting things it is you like to do. Don't touch me for a while, or ever again, preferably." I shuddered and took a measured step back, holding out a hand to stop any of his other unsolicited acts of brotherly affection.

Deacon raised both his hands in surrender, but the grin remained in place on his face. The rogue wisp of hair was still brushing his forehead, and his green eyes were sparkling.

"I know you're still mad at me, but it means a lot to me that you spent the day with Noa, that you're here with her right now."

"Well, I'm not mad at Noa," I muttered over my wine glass, eyeing Deacon skeptically.

He was still grinning at me, and the boyish look on his face was endearing. This is what he always did when I was angry—he would apologize and grin at me endlessly until I forgave him. "But I am mad at you. You aren't going to talk your way out of this one."

"I know, I know. You're mad at me, because I've taken your little slice of exile on American soil and infiltrated it with the evils of Winchester Holdings. We can talk it out. You can scream at me, you can hit me. But tonight, I'd like to take you and Noa out. My two favorite girls," Deacon said, finally lowering his hands and looking at me with an uncharacteristically nervous expression.

I continued to stare at him, irritated to find my anger slowly ebbing away. "Don't tell Taylor you said that."

Another grin slid back into place on Deacon's face, and he slung his arm around my shoulders and steered me toward the hallway, assuring me Noa would have something suitable for me to wear for what he said would be, *a night to remember.*

In true Deacon fashion, it was shaping up to be a night to remember, though that wasn't always a good thing. He changed his suit into one he deemed more "appropriate" for the venue, and I practically spit up my wine when he emerged from the bedroom in a white suit jacket and white pants. The whole thing was offset by a light brown leather belt, and a pale blue dress shirt with the top buttons undone. I refrained from telling him how ridiculous he looked, certain the suit was custom, because I couldn't think of a single designer that thought the Miami Vice look was back in. Somehow, his preposterous suit chipped away at it all further—I was annoyed with him now at best. It was so undeniably Deacon that I took comfort in it.

What I didn't take comfort in was the Alice + Olivia silver Chicago sequined Fringe Mini Dress Noa shoved me into. I also wasn't taking any comfort in the back of the honest-to-God limo that Deacon somehow procured while Noa and I were getting dressed.

I knitted my eyebrows as I watched him expertly unroll the foil on the top of a bottle of '95 Dom that had been sitting chilled in the back of the limo when it arrived.

"How did you arrange all this so quickly?"

Deacon flashed me a cat-like smile, hair still falling across his forehead. He debated pushing it back with styling gel but told Noa and I he felt it really "completed" his look. I had no fucking idea what look he thought he was going for, but that never stopped Deacon. He palmed the cork in his hand, barely making a sound as he popped it off. That was one other weird thing our etiquette teacher had taught us during Cotillion season—it was considered improper to allow a champagne cork to eject from the bottle and make a loud noise. "Charles, you know as well as I do, money talks."

"You seem to enjoy speaking with yours quite frequently," I said, raising my eyebrows at him before accepting the champagne he was holding out.

Noa snorted beside me, taking her champagne from Deacon. She was wearing a honey-colored Herve Leger draped cut-out minidress she had been gifted that I was certain would look ridiculous on anyone else. But she looked flawless. Somehow, she had simply swept her hair back into a messy ponytail and looked red-carpet ready. This was never a problem or real possibility for me, because my hair always hung around me like a sheet, just like it was right now.

Deacon leaned back in his seat, green eyes sweeping between Noa and I shrewdly. "I'm having second thoughts about this. Just because you two are friends now, it's not a license to gang up on me."

"It's nice to have someone who understands the...complexity and uniqueness that come together to make you, babe." Noa smiled slyly, amber eyes glittering at him.

I turned to her, a smile I usually only reserved for Taylor when we were making fun of him on my face. "He really is one-of-a-kind, isn't he? Did you know the first words he managed to say between the silver spoon in his mouth were, *Dolce and Gabbana*?"

Noa tipped her head back, emitting another loud laugh that seemed so at odds with her tiny, waif-like figure, but it suited her. It made her more magnetic.

"Is that why you were so excited when I walked for them last year? Don't you have a print from that show hanging in your office?"

Deacon rolled his eyes, making a chatting motion with his hand before draining his champagne.

"Ha ha. Compared to yours, Charlie? I'm pretty sure your first words were, 'I'm going to grow up to be the poster child for daddy issues!'"

"Okay!" I said indignantly, raising my middle finger to him. "Point taken but don't forget you're on thin ice with me already."

The limo rolled to a slow stop, and Deacon made a motion for me to finish my drink. I started doing a mental calculation of how far we had driven. There were only a few places that my brother would deign to visit that were this close by. Despite the tinted windows, I could see masses of moving shadows on the sidewalk and what looked to be camera flashes. I whipped around to look at Deacon, irritation pulling my lips downward.

"I'm guessing I'm about to be on thinner ice." Deacon shrugged, running a hand through his hair, devil may care attitude not disturbed in the slightest. "Before you start yelling, I didn't call them. It's Manhattan, and it's the Soho House. Paparazzi are always waiting around outside."

"WHY are we at Soho House?" My voice was practically a screech, and I leaned forward, shaking my hands in exasperation at my brother.

Deacon leaned forward, grabbing my hands and speaking in a maddeningly calm voice. "Because they don't allow photographs inside, and given your recent foray into the press, I thought you might appreciate that."

I snatched my hands back from him, not quite past the fact of the incident back at Noa's apartment. I continued to stare at him shrewdly, unsure if this was some attempt at staying in the spotlight by ensuring he would be photographed in that ridiculous suit, or if this was the Deacon version of a peace offering—ensuring you could only be photographed for part of your evening.

"Fine," I conceded, gesturing for Deacon to open the limo door.

Of course, he was beaten there by a doorman who stepped aside and held the door for us, and the flashes of photographs being taken began.

Sitting back, I watched Deacon step out and hold up a hand for the press, his billionaire boy smile falling into place, and with his other hand, Noa expertly laid hers delicately on top of it and swung her legs out of the limo without her dress so much as shifting an inch. I noticed she led with her left hand, giving them a glimpse of the flawless Harry Winston on her hand. The corners of my lips twitched. They really were perfect for each other. I would gladly take second place in my brother's life if it meant she was first.

I slid forward and hooked my feet at the ankles, grabbing Deacon's hand that was now waiting for me. I raised my eyes to him, arching an eyebrow before turning to smile politely at the waiting photographers. Deacon stepped between Noa and me, who was engaging in what appeared to be courteous conversation with the nearest photographer and slung his arms around both our shoulders.

I caught myself rolling my eyes and quickly schooled my features. It was such a typical Deacon gesture, ever the carefree quintessential billionaire. The press clearly loved that, and shouts began for us to look in every direction, the flashes near blinding me. I watched from the corner of my eye as Deacon melded into the role seamlessly, his eyes that usually mirrored mine were alive with what looked to be laughter. He really was meant for this. He had always thrived on attention. My lips pulled at the corners. Just because I didn't want this, doesn't mean he didn't. And it didn't mean he didn't deserve to have everything he wanted, despite my inability to understand it.

Deacon paused when we reached the door and turned, raising his hand in a wave. Widening my eyes in exasperation, I tugged on his arm sharply.

"This isn't a fucking red carpet, get inside. Steven will love that photo, by the way."

"You're the only one that gives a shit what Dad thinks, Charles," Deacon said through his smile.

He looked down at me for a moment, eyes gentle, like the idea that I didn't even realize how preoccupied I was with what Steven Winchester thought was sad to him.

His grin never faltered until he turned away and gestured for Noa and me to walk through the door that was being held for us. Maybe he had a point. My entire life did feel like a perpetual see-saw. One minute, I didn't care at all, and the next I was swinging in the opposite direction, clawing for any semblance of his affection or attention. I felt him squeeze my exposed shoulder before dropping his hand and interlacing his fingers with Noa.

The noise and shouts of the photographers outside were cut off suddenly when the doorman closed the door behind us. The rounded reception desk was padded with a dark, worn leather buttoned in the middle. The top of the desk was a sparkling, lacquered wood. It looked like it might be oak, and I was certain if I ran a finger over the top of it, not a single speck of dust would come off. I had never actually been here, and I wasn't even sure if our family had a membership, but I watched Deacon walk up to the desk, his shoulder brushing with Noa's ever so slightly, and I remembered that it didn't really matter. Being a Winchester was like an all-access pass to anywhere in the world. It just didn't often occur to me to treat it as such. The woman behind the desk smiled in greeting, and it looked like the hostess version of a Winchester smile—too fake, too bright, too forced, and entirely empty inside.

Looking around, I surveyed the various heavy wooden doors that were painted a dark gray, clearly leading off to different areas of the lounge, and the distressed wood paneling that lined the walls. The lighting was dim, with lamps scattered throughout to cast what I assumed was meant to be a mysterious glow or ambience.

Unease settled in the pit of my stomach. I didn't particularly enjoy frequenting places like this: exclusive or semi-exclusive. I hated them. I had appreciation for Deacon trying to spirit me away to somewhere where my photograph wouldn't be taken at will.

But it was another bizarre juxtaposition of my life. I loved my father; I hated my father. I hated Tripp; I couldn't seem to stay away from him. I wanted nothing more than anonymity and privacy, but I never felt comfortable exercising that Winchester all-access card to get it. Maybe I was just a giant fucking hypocrite.

"This way," the woman stepped out from behind the desk, revealing her cream-colored bandage dress.

I eyed it, recognition flaring in me. It was the same Herve Leger bandage dress Taylor had made me buy but in a different color. That David wanted to devour me in, that Tripp first pressed his body against mine in a leather-padded hallway not unlike the distressed leather present here. I watched her for a moment as she made her way to a door across the room, opening it to reveal another carefully curated distressed wooden staircase, wondering if she had ever committed as many atrocities as I had. If she had ever destroyed the very fabric of her own soul, and someone else's in the process.

"Charlie?" Noa spoke, her voice soft.

Her head was tilted, wayward curls escaping her messy bun but not looking out of place. She held out a hand, turning it palm upward. "Everything okay?"

I shook my head, reaching out to grab her hand. I could tell my fingers were stiff in hers, and she squeezed them before tugging along behind Deacon and the hostess, who was laughing uproariously at something my brother had said, something that surely wasn't that funny. Our heels clicked almost simultaneously while we followed them up the stairs. The walls were lined with the same wooden panels and brass torches with a cylindrical globe surrounding the bulb screwed into them.

The hallway was suddenly cast in the reddish glow of the dimming sunlight, and I jerked my head away from the sconces on the walls and realized that the door at the top of the staircase was opened, revealing the rooftop. Noa continued to tug me along, and as I followed her, heels moving from the smooth wood to the cement tiles of the rooftop, scattered cushion chairs surrounding various marble-top tables came into view, all offset by the glass railing.

I arched an eyebrow at the view of the Brooklyn Bridge. I would give them that—exclusivity could buy one hell of a view. We wove through the tables, and I felt Noa squeezing my fingers sporadically. I noticed some minor celebrities, some of Deacon's future Wall Street master of the universe colleagues, and some people I recognized solely for being in the same stratosphere of wealth all scattered throughout the chairs. Shadows from the tabletop lanterns were stretching across the concrete as the sun sunk lower against the Hudson River.

"Is this suitable, Mr. Winchester?" The hostess stopped, gesturing to a rectangle marble table surrounded by chairs, just off the glass railing of the rooftop.

"This is perfect, thank you." Deacon smiled.

It was so different from the flirtatious smile he usually threw every which way, but I guess those days were behind him now. She nodded before stepping away, and Deacon pulled out two of the cushioned chairs for Noa and me before dropping down across from us. He leaned back in the seat, instantly taking up more space than necessary, like Deacon Winchester couldn't possibly be contained by one of these chairs on the Soho House rooftop.

"So," Deacon leaned forward, a smirk forming on his face, "has Tripp Banks 'come to town?'"

"Do you exist solely to piss me off?" I asked, plucking a leatherbound drink menu from the table and began to flip the pages aggressively until I got to the list of Vodka.

He leaned forward and snatched the menu from me before closing it with a snap. "David told me you two had drinks after dinner with Dad last week. Back to your old habits?"

"David has a big mouth," I said through gritted teeth. "I've known Tripp for a decade, and despite my best efforts he continues to be present in my life. I might as well make the best of it."

"You seem to be gaining friends at an alarming rate, for someone who is so selective. First Tripp, then David, now Noa. And you're just friends with them all?" Deacon questioned, delight rippling in his eyes.

Thirty-one years old, and he could never resist baiting me.

"Leave her alone, Deacon. It might surprise you to know that people can just be friends without falling into bed with one another. Though I know that hasn't been your usual style." Noa rolled her eyes.

Deacon looked aghast for a moment before holding up his palms and shaking his head. "And it hasn't always been hers, either. I'm just asking. I don't need Tripp and David at each other's throats over my sister. Again."

"Thank you for that, Deacon. Might I remind you that David has well and moved on? And in fact, I'm ready to move on from this topic of conversation." I grabbed the menu from him again to signal this conversation was over.

"That might be hard," Deacon's voice sounded strained, and I looked up from the list of Vodka to see a contorted expression on his face. "David and Victoria just walked in."

CHAPTER TWELVE

My stomach turned over and my heart started to beat erratically, and when I opened my mouth to say something, anything that might get my brother to somehow get them to go away or convince him we needed to leave—his phone started ringing. Deacon held up one finger at me and a gleeful look settled on his face when he looked at his phone.

"Hey man," Deacon said into the phone, leaning back in his seat again with that perpetual air of ease around him. "Yeah, at Soho House. Just got here. Are you coming down?"

I narrowed my eyes at him, snapping my fingers loudly in his face to get his attention. He continued to hold up his finger at me as he nodded at whatever was being said. I widened my eyes at him and was tempted to grab the phone and throw it off the building when he finally hung up.

"Who was that?" I hissed, tempted to shrink down in my seat to avoid David and Victoria seeing us.

I was trying to be on board with trying to be his friend; I was still very confident life with David Kennedy was better than any life without him, but I wasn't interested in making Victoria a regular part of my social repertoire.

"Tripp. He's going to come down. He just got the keys to his place today," Deacon responded, nonchalance lacing his voice, like this wasn't my worst nightmare playing out.

"Why are you only friends with your employees?" I bit out, wishing there was a drink in front of me to drown in, but no server had been by yet, because apparently that's just how my life was.

No drink when I needed it desperately, even at a private club that was supposed to have five-star service.

"Why are you only friends with the men you cheat on and cheat with?" He deadpanned, looking over my shoulder.

I watched as the fake look of recognition slid into place, and he raised his hand in greeting.

I opened my mouth to say something, anything in response, when I read the telltale sound of heels clicking behind me; so I reached out and grabbed the exposed skin of Deacon's wrist between my fingers, twisting and pinching it like a child. He hissed a breath and immediately retracted his arm, glaring at me and looking like he was about to respond before Noa cleared her throat and turned in her seat.

The breeze from the river picked up, blowing the loose curls that had escaped her bun around her face. Like Deacon, she raised an albeit, much more delicate, hand to wave at David and Victoria. I pressed my lips together tightly, before pivoting in my own seat and steeling my features.

Dusk had started to set, and somehow this time of day suited David Kennedy more than any other. Those last rays of sun were catching every piece of gold in the waves of his hair, and they looked like threads woven in to emphasize how unearthly David was, how beautiful. I wouldn't have been surprised to find his likeness in a painting from the Roman empire—bronzed skin on display just so beneath white cotton and hair wreathed in a golden circlet. Every inch of him looked sharper, harder, somehow more defined under the softer light. He must have changed from the office before coming here. He was wearing what looked to be a black wool Theory crewneck sweater with the sleeves pushed up, revealing the tanned, corded muscles of his forearms.

Against my will, my eyes roved across his shoulders, down to those forearms and muscles in the back of his hands that seemed to be flexing on their own accord. I wanted to reach out and grab one of his hands, slowly interlace his fingers with my own. But they weren't mine to touch anymore. My gaze tracked down the rest of him, muscled thighs in what I was pretty certain were a pair of Rag & Bone Twill pants I bought him.

I knitted my eyebrows together, jealousy and irritation rising in me that it was Victoria, not me, who would have sat there while David was fresh from the shower selecting his clothes for the evening. Victoria, not me, who would get to be there when he shucked them off for the night. In another life, that could have been us every single day, just me and him. But that wasn't this life. I was sitting on the rooftop of the fucking Soho House with my brother and his famous fiancée, and it looked like the love of my life and his new girlfriend were going to come and sit with us, all the while Tripp Banks was set to arrive.

Victoria looked as effortlessly beautiful and distinctly southern as she did the first time I laid eyes on her. Her blonde hair, all ashy and perfectly toned, cascaded in waves around her exposed shoulders. The dress she was wearing was probably something I would have picked for myself, and I was pretty sure it was circled in the regular portfolio Sabine sent me of options for upcoming events. It was a black Galvan dress that was offset with a crystal chain that came down from her neck to sweep around and accentuate her chest, leaving a tiny keyhole of exposed skin.

I felt myself shift in my seat, cognizant of the ridiculous fringes of sequins that surrounded me in this mini dress of Noa's, feeling somehow entirely less composed and infantile in comparison. The sheath of the dress went just past her knees, and I watched as her muscular calves flexed with each step in her classic patent Louboutins.

Narrowing my eyes in concentration, I pushed my toes into the bottom of my Jimmy Choos, wondering if my calves could flex like that. Casually lowering my arm, I dragged my fingers across the back of my calf. It felt the same as always. I suppose we couldn't all have southern beach volleyball legs.

"What are you two doing here?" Deacon asked genially, standing when they reached us.

He grabbed two spare chairs without a care in the world from the neighboring tables and clearly without a care as to whether any of us wanted to sit together.

Victoria paused, her fingers tracing David's arm before running down to slide into his palm seamlessly, like they were at home, like her fingers knew exactly what patterns to trace to find their way to fit in between his.

"I'm in town for the night, and we wanted to grab a drink before our dinner reservation later," Victoria offered, smiling in a way that seemed fake and entirely unlike a polite Winchester smile, which was its own special kind of artificial. This smile seemed vaguely threatening, and like she was ready to rip into anyone who challenged her with her teeth.

Unbidden, my eyes swung to David. A dinner reservation? In Manhattan? That seemed decidedly un-David Kennedy. David

Kennedy would be more likely to grab food from a random cart on the street and eat it on a late night walk. I would know. I had lost count of the number of food trucks we ate at together in Chicago.

His eyes swept over me with something like a cool indifference, lingering only for a moment. I recoiled into myself and found my hand snaking out for Noa's. With a pang, I realized her hand was sitting palm up right beside her thigh, as if waiting for the moment I needed it. David gestured for Victoria to take one of the empty seats Deacon had dragged over to the end of the table, waiting for her to settle in before he tucked it into the table and dropped into the chair next to Deacon.

"Victoria's away for work next week, so she's only in the city tonight," he offered, like it was in way of explanation, eyes flitting back to me but still giving nothing away.

Noa turned to Victoria, her fingers tightening on mine and her thumb sweeping smooth, soothing strokes against the back of my hand. I watched as she tipped her head toward Victoria, and there was something predatory in her features. It was so like Taylor I wanted to laugh.

"I'm not sure I know what you do for a living Victoria?" Noa asked her.

"I'm a lawyer," she answered, taking the drink menu David offered to her.

Before Noa could respond, a server materialized by our table, and Deacon spoke before he could ask if we had any questions, "I think a round of shots for the table. Whatever you think is best. And then what do you think, two bottles of champagne? Whatever's driest." He grinned at the server before turning to Noa, brushing his hand along her free one that was placed on the table.

"I actually wanted a double vodka soda. Extra ice." I smiled tightly at the server, hand still clutching Noa's.

Noa turned back to Victoria, her full lips parting to ask another question when a set of hands snaked around my head. I felt my stomach plummeting, but then the smell of them enveloped me. They were small but worn hands that smelt like alcohol and disinfectant. The back of my eyes burned and not from the chemicals surely pressing against them. My second favorite person in the world, next to my brother, smelt like that.

I brought my hands up, grabbing the ones pressing on me with them, sure as soon as I touched them. Something like a choked sob escaped me and I turned. Taylor was standing there, blonde hair pulled into what might look like an artfully messy bun to some, but I knew that was two twists of her wrist with an old elastic. It looked like she had just thrown on her dress—another Herve Leger here to remind me that bandage dresses were forever. But that one had a half-moon opening around her chest, and semi-sheer sleeves running down to her wrists.

"What are you doing here?" I whispered, standing and wrapping my arms around her.

Taylor hugged me tightly in return before pulling back and gripping my shoulders. She looked pointedly over my shoulder. "A fashionable little birdie called me today and told me big brother over there steamrolled your life with a sudden announcement. I thought you could use your best friend."

I turned, looking at Noa, words drying in my throat. She shrugged and winked at me before turning back to Deacon, who was looking at Noa in a way that made my lips part and tears continue to well. He was looking at her like the world started and ended with her, like she hung the moon.

I couldn't help but look at David, thinking of when he used to look at me like that. How his own mother had pointed it out and warned me to keep him safe. Instead, I ripped out both our hearts and stomped all over them with designer heels. I half-expected Deacon to be irritated or annoyed by Taylor's choice of words, but he didn't take the bait like usual.

I cleared my throat, realizing I was still just standing there staring and grabbed a spare chair from an empty table for Taylor.

"Didn't you have a big date this weekend, Taylor? With a radiologist? The poor girl must be devastated." Deacon grinned, finally breaking away from the look he was giving Noa.

Taylor placed her chin on her hand, the smile she reserved solely for ribbing Deacon falling into place. "Mhm. I did, and she was. But we rescheduled for our next free weekend. I'll be just as good of a conversationalist then."

I shifted, turning to Taylor before Deacon could respond but before I could speak, my gaze snagged on Noa. Her features were stretched into an almost normal smile, and I would have thought nothing of it had I not noticed the way she rolled her shoulders, like she was brushing off their bizarre banter. Deacon and Taylor had always just existed in that way, it had never occurred to me what it might be like to be on the outside looking in, no matter how clear it was to anyone with a pulse how obsessed Deacon was with Noa.

I dropped my hand and opened it up toward her, just in case. I finally looked at Taylor, my gaze softening immediately. I could give her shit for the weird flirtation vortex she and my brother got sucked into later.

"You canceled your date for me? You didn't have to do that."

Her smile shifted into something kind and familiar. "Anything for you," she said, grabbing my hand quickly before an entirely different Taylor look stole across her face. "David, Veronica. So lovely to see you again."

David closed his eyes briefly, exhaling through his nose before fixing a smile on his face. "It's Victoria, Taylor."

"What did I say?" Taylor asked, absentmindedly flipping through the menu, not bothering to look in their direction.

Reaching down under the table, I pinched her exposed thigh, barely able to get purchase on anything, because all that was there was muscle. Without reacting, she dropped her hand and plucked mine off her thigh. Before David could answer, or God forbid Deacon jumped into the conversation, a lilting voice came from behind us.

"Doesn't this look cozy," Tripp drawled, and I felt him drop his hands to my shoulders.

I tensed under his fingertips, my spine ramrod straight. His fingers were smooth against my exposed skin, the warmth of his hands suddenly making me feel sweaty. There were too many things skittering across my skin, little lightning bolts from his touch that caused involuntary drops in my stomach followed by flares of irritation.

Taylor pursed her lips and narrowed her eyes at him. "Tripp, to what do we owe the...pleasure of your company?"

Tripp gave her a lazy grin, helping himself to an empty chair before swinging it around and placing it right beside Victoria. Instead of answering Taylor, he turned to Victoria and held out his hand. "Nice to see you again after all these years. I think the last time I saw you DK and I were in business school together."

Victoria nodded, extending a stupidly toned arm to grip his hand. "Life really does come full circle, doesn't it?"

Tripp nodded in agreement before looking back at me, ice blue eyes glinting mischievously. "I certainly hope so."

My stomach rolled uncomfortably at his loaded words, and I thought of our bodies moving together all those years ago; and I found myself wondering what it would be like now with this Tripp, *adult* Tripp with his never-changing eyes, his filled-out chest and shoulders, and the sharper edges of his face.

I grimaced at the betrayal from my own thoughts, thankful that the vodka soda appeared in front of me in an intricate crystal glass. I brought it to my lips, taking an undignified swig. I would need more where this came from. I watched as the server sliced the foil on the bottle of champagne expertly and prepared a tasting glass.

"Are we celebrating anything?" She asked politely, a seemingly forced smile on her face.

I waited for Deacon to open his mouth, offering some dumb comment about how every day of his life was worth celebrating when Victoria spoke.

"Actually, yes. The champagne was an astute idea, Deacon. Did David tell you?" Victoria smiled, her pillowy lips artfully glossed, and her stupid tan somehow sparkling despite the fading sunlight.

My grip tightened on my glass, the ridges of the crystal digging into my palm, and I bit my tongue to keep from asking myself. But Victoria didn't wait for anyone before continuing, her face now a picture of smugness. "I accepted a new job today. I'm moving to New York."

My glass was halfway to my mouth when it slipped through my fingers, shattering on the table, and before I could stop myself, my internal monologue spilled from my lips. "Oh, you've got to be fucking kidding me!"

Deacon barked a laugh that was immediately silenced by a sharp glare from Noa. He schooled his features but was clearly having a hard time, because he started coughing loudly and thumping his chest with his fist.

Tripp arched an eyebrow at me, grabbing the champagne flute that was just sitting there while the server seemed frozen in time, eyes swiveling back and forth between all of us as she made no move to clean up the drink that was now dripping onto my legs.

"New York has become quite popular, at least amongst the members of this table. You're right." Tripp winked at me before turning his gaze to Victoria. He continued, breezing past my outburst like it had never happened. "Where's the new job?"

Victoria cleared her throat, briefly flashing me a look of disdain before launching into an explanation of her new position at Merrill Lynch. Taylor's hand found mine under the table, and I looked determinedly downward, concentrating on a crack in the cement floor beneath me that I hoped would open up and swallow me whole.

CHAPTER THIRTEEN

One of the benefits of Deacon's obnoxious nature was that he never failed to fill silence. He was an easy crutch to lean on when I had nothing to say, and tonight, I really did not. I spent the night sipping a steady stream of strong drinks, ignoring the bottles of champagne that kept appearing at the table. My hand was clamped in Taylor's, and I listened intently as everyone else spoke and drove the conversation, my eyes swiveling back and forth between David and Tripp.

It seemed like they had reached some sort of tolerable understanding of one another's presence in their lives. I wondered briefly if they ever had it out over me. One punch at a charity gala two years ago really didn't seem like it would be enough to emerge from the rubble of that disaster and be this cordial. But my alcohol-laden brain might have been making me to be a figure of greater importance than I really was.

David and Tripp had a *before* me. They were friends, once upon a time. Now, they would be a large part of making up the three-person executive team of the WH office, so they were going to have to learn to live with one another. I had no fucking clue what my brother, or father, thought they were doing, but our father's words echoed in my head: *It was business. Nothing more, nothing less.*

I spoke when I was spoken to, answering bland questions from Victoria that seemed like she had to force herself to utter, that were mostly about school. What I taught, what I was researching, and what I thought I might "do" when I was done with my Ph.D. Deacon responded that I didn't have to do anything—I was a Winchester.

It was supposed to be a joke, but it had never really dawned on me before, the truth in that. It was an irrefutable fact that I didn't *have* to do anything, and I was sure there were people who didn't expect me to do anything. It didn't matter if I left Columbia, if I stayed. I could run away. I could go with Dr. Batra to Oxford. People like me were always getting things they hadn't earned, didn't deserve, and most people wouldn't even bat an eyelash. They might whisper about it behind my back but nothing really, truly mattered—and that made my entire heart so fucking heavy I thought it might fall out of my chest.

As I listened, I learned about Victoria and a sort of agitation filled my veins. I didn't know who she was when she was younger, when she and David first got together—but the person she was now, was so decidedly un-David.

I always felt like one of the things David and I had in common, at our very core, was the fact that we sort of just existed in this world. Not out of a desire to be here, but like we were placed here. It wasn't a terribly sympathetic quality, and neither of us were looking for sympathy, but there was an acknowledgment, a recognition of a soul that also longed for something else, to be anywhere else. It had always felt like the one secret our souls shared, like we were two children, holding our pinkies in a promise of what could have been. I imagined somewhere in the multiverse, David was surfing his days away, and maybe I was teaching. High school English or something my father wouldn't approve of. In that universe, we lived in a bungalow on the beach and watched the sunset from our front porch over sweating beer bottles each night.

But that was not who Victoria was. She talked about her career as a corporate lawyer, which sounded so goddamn boring I fought to keep my eyes from glazing over, about her family real estate business and subsequent personal real estate portfolio, and her passion for tennis.

I could picture her in a stupidly stylish tennis outfit, playing at whichever private club her family belonged to in North Carolina, sun-kissed skin glowing, and the perfect waves of her hair falling just so.

Feelings of guilt started to eat at me. I knew it would be giving myself too much credit to think that I had forced David here, and that he truly had no feelings for Victoria, but it just didn't seem like the choice he would have made for himself; the one that was true to who he was. He was saltwater, he was tousled hair, he was the taste of beer on my lips, he was staying up too late because we just couldn't stop laughing. He was everything. But he certainly wasn't this.

"Shit, we should get going, Vic. Our dinner reservation is in about thirty minutes, and it'll take a bit to get there. I'll sign the tab and call a car," David interjected, interrupting whatever Deacon was saying that I was paying no attention to.

I watched as he looked down at his watch, the vintage Rolex that once belonged to his grandfather, his favorite person ever. He never took it off, so at least that remained the same. I remembered what it was like for that watch to be right beside my face, David's hand gripped against my headboard or fisted into my pillow while we moved together. Nausea rose in me when I realized it wasn't my body he was moving against now, and it never would be again.

Taylor looked at me, having taken her hair out of the messy bun. It was now a wild mane around her head, and it provided a shield as she mouthed to me in distaste, "Vic?"

Etiquette would dictate that I should have asked where they were going, but I really didn't want to know, and I really didn't fucking care. I'm sure it was somewhere overpriced and exclusive. That seemed like the type of place *Vic* would like.

"Oh, you're right. We don't want to miss our reservation. I'll just use the restroom." Victoria smiled at everyone, taking the last sip of her champagne before standing. "It was really nice to see you all. Thank you for letting us be interlopers on your evening. I hope you have a great rest of your night."

I watched her grab her quilted black Chanel clutch, taking a moment to run her hand over David's shoulders, and had I been a character in a fantasy novel, I might have growled. Because that's how I felt—possessive and angry, but David wasn't mine anymore; and in my new reality of Winchester Holdings invading Manhattan, I was going to have to get used to seeing them together.

David gripped Deacon's shoulders, and even managed to shake Tripp's hand before he hugged Noa. All that was left in his customary goodbyes was Taylor and me. His eyes found mine, and he smiled. "It was great to see you two."

"Was it?" Taylor inquired with a cat-like grin before taking a slow sip of her champagne.

I shot her a sideways glance, but she didn't look back, staring firmly ahead at David. She had taken to doing this ever since we broke up, needling at him in an unnecessary and undeserved defense of me.

"Always," David answered, his eyes never leaving my face, before he turned and made his way toward the stairs.

I pushed myself out of my chair, ignoring the heaviness of Tripp's stare that was now glued to me.

"I'll be right back." I trailed after David, keeping back far enough that we didn't run into one another at the bottom of the staircase.

I might have been insane, but I wanted to talk to Victoria. To apologize for all the headlines pitting us against one another. No one deserved to be treated that way so publicly. I waited at the bottom of the stairs, peering around the corner, and watching David turn and disappear down the hallway that led toward the bathrooms. After a moment, I quietly stepped off the stairs, afraid he might have suddenly gained supersonic hearing and would be able to recognize the telltale click of my Jimmy Choos from a mile away. I ducked down the hallway after him, the lights significantly dimmer than the reception area.

The length of the hallway was illuminated by those same dumb lamps as the other rooms, shadows cast along the polished hardwood floor I was practically tiptoeing along and trying to locate the women's bathrooms. This place was an unnecessary labyrinth, the hallway turning into another. I looked up as I walked around, and I wanted to look away; I really fucking did. But I couldn't. I was frozen, a deer in the headlights watching as the hunter loaded and subsequently cocked their rifle, index finger feathering briefly on the trigger before they fired.

But instead of a hunter, it was David Kennedy. And instead of a bullet, there was Victoria. And we weren't in a forest. We were in

Manhattan. Instead of the headlights of some random pick-up truck, the lowlights of a random hallway in Soho House were shining on them, providing the most heartbreaking, ill-timed spotlight of all time.

I was frozen, one foot suspended in mid-stride. They could have seen me if they broke apart. But David had Victoria pushed against the wall, hands gripping her waist, moving to her hips, to her ass, and then down to her thighs to hike up her dress. Her stupid golden, toned arms were snaked around his neck, hands tangling in the hair curling at the nape. I watched, no air in my lungs and certainly no blood flowing to my extremities, because my heart must have quit, utterly died, as her hand came down and brushed across the broad muscles of his chest, down the ridges of his abdomen where they stopped at his waist, toying with the button on his pants that I bought him. Her hands, maybe I could have gotten past; I could have cradled my disintegrating heart and provided shelter from.

But not David's hands. As long as I lived, and I was certain it wouldn't be much longer, because there was no fucking way my heart was beating, I would never forget what it looked like to watch David's hands tense and grip someone else's thighs, to skate inward and move up the front of their dress. I wouldn't forget the noise I heard coming from the back of his throat, or the way I saw his tongue test the seam of someone else's lips.

I wanted to die. This was what wishing for death felt like. I walked backward out of the hallway, into the one that led me here to my certain death, and I kept moving until my shoulders hit the wall, and the bones of my shoulder blades dragged against the wall until I hit the ground.

I wanted to scrub the visual of their limbs and tongues, and the sounds they were making from my brain entirely. I wanted to pluck my eyeballs from their sockets and skewer them with the heel of my designer shoe so I would never have to see it again. Maybe Taylor had some sort of medical device that would remove an eyeball from its socket; she always had weird shit in her bags. But in the meantime, I pressed the heels of my palms into my eyes. I knew I should get up, run away as fast as I could and send the sequin fringes of this dress flying, because some sort of giggle that could only belong to Victoria was followed by the telltale creak of a door being pushed open.

"What are you doing?"

I knew who that voice belonged to without having to remove my palms from where they were digging into my eyes. "Hiding," I whispered, my voice strangled.

Before he could respond, a low moan that I recognized all too well sounded from around the corner. Something between a gasp and a sob caught in my throat. Victoria hadn't been the bullet. That was the sound of David moaning, voice all rough and harsh and guttural. That was the bullet, and it ripped through my heart and my spine for good measure, leaving my body floating immobile, aimless in space.

The door finally slammed shut, effectively cutting me off from my torture, and I opened my eyes. Tripp was crouched down in front of me. My vision was blurred at the edges, but I could tell his posture was tense, his shoulder bumping mine as he settled in beside me on the floor, saying nothing.

"I guess that's one thing that hasn't changed. David and I...I mean, David always kind of had a thing for hooking up in public places," I said, the fake bravado of my voice falling as it cracked horribly.

The memories of us poked at my brain. My desk at WH. The coat closet in Deacon's office. The yacht club. Wrightsville beach. Naively, I had summed that particular proclivity was exclusive to me. David Kennedy wasn't a voyeur, but I drove him insane, and he just couldn't resist *me*.

"Spare me. Fucking guy can't do you the decency of waiting until they've left? Didn't they have a dinner reservation?" Tripp scoffed, his voice harsh and cutting.

"He probably didn't expect me to see them..." I answered, with a small voice.

Was this what I had done to David? No, he never had to see it. But I wasn't sure what was worse. Because I had been imagining them together, pretty much on a loop since the engagement party, and nothing, *nothing*, came close to the real thing.

Tripp looked at me, lips pulling up in disdain. "You can't tell me he's not doing it on purpose. Parading her around. Acting like he's so into her. Some twisted form of revenge. It's cruel, Chuck."

"Well, you'd know a thing or two about that." I rolled my neck, voice thick with tears, so I was finally looking at him sitting against the wall beside me. "Why'd you do it? The stupid board. Writing all our names down with points like that. Why'd you do it?"

Tripp looked at me, lips pulling to the side before his eyes stopped on the tears tracking down my face. He reached out, brushing his thumbs under my eyes quickly before answering, "I wish I knew. I was young and stupid, and I don't know what I thought. I guess I thought a lot of things that did matter, didn't. It started as a stupid joke, and it wasn't meant to be some cruel game we were playing, and then as with most things, it went too far."

"That's such a cop out, Tripp." I rolled my eyes, staring determinedly ahead at the emerald paint on the walls.

He leveled me with a look before rubbing absentmindedly at his jaw. "I didn't have great familial role models growing up, shocking as that may be. I didn't really learn much about respect, or anything, really. It's not an excuse, but I went from one microcosm of toxicity to the next, and afterward, I realized there was a whole wide world out there that was entirely different than where I came from."

I pursed my lips, nodding through the tears that continued to fall. It wasn't a fully formed answer, and it wasn't an excuse. But it made sense. A person like Tripp with all his sharp edges had to have been forged somehow.

"I'm not proud of that, Chuck. If I could take it back, I would," he continued, eyes now staring ahead at the wall, too.

"I never said you were." I shrugged, angling my head to look at him. His eyes, sharp and frozen, suddenly landed on my lips. I jerked my chin, widening my eyes at him. "I'm not proud of *that*, either."

"I know." Tripp's words were low. He extended his palm to me, almost childlike in his expectant display. "I'll take you back upstairs?"

I arched an eyebrow, still looking at his hand warily. "My legs didn't stop working."

Tripp stood with one fluid movement, and now he was towering over me. But his palm was still extended. "Come on, forget them."

I looked up at him through my wet eyelashes. He looked earnest, somehow. That type of facial expression wasn't in Tripp's usual repertoire, and I decided to take that as a sign. I raised my hand to slap my palm against his, his fingers immediately circling my wrist to haul me upward. Anything beat sitting there waiting for Victoria and David to finish up. My palm, sweaty in his, twitched, even as we made our way back upstairs.

Taylor was standing at the top of the stairs, my purse in her hand, tapping her heeled foot. Her eyes narrowed in on my hand in Tripp's, and she made an exaggerated shooing motion, continuing to tap her foot until Tripp looked down at me one last time, worrying at his bottom lip with his teeth before making his way back to the table.

"Let's get out of here, we can go back to your place...drink some expensive wine and watch tv in bed. You can tell me what that was about, holding hands with that demon and running after David like that," Taylor said.

"I wasn't running after David. I went to apologize to Victoria about all the press headlines," I muttered, continuing when Taylor gave me a dubious look. "I'm serious. But then I had the ah...misfortune of catching them doing something rather untoward."

A small noise like a wounded animal escaped from her throat, and Taylor instinctively wrapped her arm around my shoulder, steering me back toward the table. "I'm sorry. What are they? Wild animals who can't wait until they get home? Disgusting."

I knew for a fact Taylor did not find public sex to be disgusting, quite the opposite in fact. She always said she found it sweet, endearing somehow that two people couldn't keep their hands off one another. I forced a small smile and leaned into her arm as our heels clicked in sync against the floor. It was going to take a while to forget that, if I ever managed to.

Tripp was still standing when we got back to the table, one hand clapped against Deacon's shoulder.

I raised my eyebrows at him. "I was just coming over to say goodnight to everyone. Taylor and I are leaving."

"What a coincidence, I'm heading out, too. I'll walk you both out." Tripp smirked, dusting off the front of his sweater before crossing his arms and pointing his chin toward Deacon and Noa. "Go ahead, say goodnight to them. You can say goodbye to me outside."

"And let the press run away with new photos of us? No, thank you. Your escort services aren't needed any longer. The hallway to the rooftop was enough." I rolled my eyes, trying to turn away from him to Deacon and Noa, but as always, he needed the last word.

"How about you say goodbye to me up here then? Don't want to risk anyone overhearing, so maybe something entirely non-verbal?" Tripp raised his eyebrows at me, taunting me.

Before I could even dignify that with a response, Taylor raised her middle finger and arched an eyebrow. "That should do it." I smiled tightly at him before finally turning to Deacon and Noa. "Noa, I had a really great day. I'm so glad I ran into you. I'm sorry I interrupted your plans, but Deacon, I'm not sorry I saved her from an evening of whatever depraved things you were up to."

Taylor slapped her hand over Deacon's mouth, who looked primed to offer up some disgusting remark, green eyes glinting mischievously. "Goodnight, Deac. Goodnight, Noa. I'm sorry you're stuck with him."

Noa smiled, eyes solely focused on Deacon, like she didn't mind that at all. She stood holding her arms out to me, and I stepped into them. Her arms wrapped around me, and for such a small person, there was something comforting about the way she hugged me. Like she really, truly, cared. Maybe she did. She pressed her cheek to mine and whispered to me, "Night Charlie, thank you so much for today."

Deacon's arms enveloped the two of us, and he pressed a kiss to my forehead. "Aren't we just a big happy family?"

"Probably the first time anyone has said that about a Winchester and have it be true," Taylor remarked. "Let go of your sister, she and I have things to discuss and expensive, billionaire quality wine to drink."

I pulled away, extending my hand to her, wiggling my fingers. Taylor laced hers through mine, but not before turning to Tripp, lips pulled back to display her perfectly white teeth. "Tripp. Another night where you foisted your company upon us. Have a good evening."

She pulled my arm sharply, dragging me through the tables and chairs before I could tell her off for being rude. Her brown eyes narrowed at me, and she whispered from the corner of her mouth, "What is this whole friends thing you two have going on? It's fucking ridiculous. Do you know what you're doing?"

Craning my neck over my shoulder, I looked back at Tripp. I could see his lips moving, his face bearing the dry expression it always did as he spoke to Deacon. I couldn't tell what he was saying, but Deacon's head was tipped back in laughter, even Noa looked vaguely amused. Like he could feel me looking at him, Tripp flicked his eyes up. A smirk pulled at the corner of his lips, and my heart constricted.

There was a time when Tripp Banks looking at me like that would have made it skip a beat, and that was followed by a time when his gaze would have caused nausea to roll in my stomach. Now, I wasn't sure what it made me feel.

I rolled my shoulders before looking away and muttering, "I have no clue."

CHAPTER FOURTEEN

Having Taylor in my house all weekend was like living in a bubble where the best parts of New York Charlie and Chicago Charlie could coexist. We did exactly as she said, changing into sweat suits and piling into my bed with the most expensive wine in my house. Taylor insisted on berating David for having sex in public before showing me hours of recorded surgery footage, pointing out particularly interesting techniques, or letting me know when the surgeon was, in her opinion, "a fucking idiot who probably went to med school in a barn."

I watched her from where I was sitting, propped up on the island in my kitchen, my first morning cup of coffee between my hands. She was moving around the house, grabbing her belongings that in typical Taylor fashion had been scattered throughout the whole house in her brief time here.

"Are you sure you have to leave?" I asked.

"Yes, I can't trade another shift, or I'll be working every fucking weekend until Thanksgiving," she answered, followed by a triumphant noise when she pulled her wallet from where it was lying on my couch.

She turned, walking across the room to stop in front of me. Gathering her hair, she expertly wound her hand around it and snapped an elastic into place to create a low messy bun.

"Remember what I said, don't let anyone take this from you. Who you are, what you're doing here. It doesn't fucking matter that Deacon wants to be the Master of New York, that WH is coming here. You love teaching. Even if your supervisor leaves, you're still there. You can find another one. You're still at Columbia. Don't let David and Tripp ruin that."

I hadn't told anyone about Dr. Batra leaving, the irony of it all. The easy escape it posed, the way the muscles in my legs were taught and poised, ready to run as fast as I could and never look back at this place. But I told Taylor that weekend as we laid side-by-side, city lights filtering in through the open window of my bedroom, that I didn't want to leave, didn't want to be the person who ran no matter how good the opportunity may have been.

I nodded, saying nothing when she brought her forehead to mine. "You're my best friend, Taylor."

"Yeah, yeah. Just don't replace me with Noa now that you're all buddy-buddy. I must love you, too, you know, if I was willing to take a last minute commercial flight to get here." She smiled offering an exaggerated shudder at the word 'commercial' before winding her hand around the back of my neck and squeezing briefly. "Seriously, don't get tangled up with those two again. We don't need another gala disaster like at The Peninsula."

"Thank you for that." I pushed her away and took a sip of my coffee.

My phone began to vibrate beside me, and I picked it up, groaning when I looked at the text on the screen. It wasn't even a text really; it was a meeting invitation from Damien to meet my father at the new office and sign some paperwork.

"Well this day just took a turn. I've been summoned."

I pushed off the island, tossing Taylor my phone. A snort came from her while she read the message. "Daddy Winchester too busy to send a text?"

"Apparently." I waved a hand over my shoulder, gripping my coffee and heading up the stairs to prepare to face my father and Winchester Holdings. "Love you."

"I'm off again in two weekends, so I'll come back, and we can do something fun. Fuck David, fuck Deacon, fuck Tripp, and fuck your father. Fuck everyone but you and me," Taylor called, and I turned, raising a hand and offering her a smile that she returned before leaving; I listened to the recognizable click of the old door lock, and then I was all alone.

I headed back up the stairs to my closet to find an outfit that my father would deem appropriate for a majority shareholder signing paperwork. I'm sure he would want a pretty photo, or two, with me, smiling blandly over a piece of paper and holding an ostentatious pen. It would be staged, pretend even. There was no way he would let press in the room when we were signing anything of importance. But most things Winchester were pretend now, anyway. Pretend I could do.

The town car pulled up to the curb of a towering skyscraper in the financial district. I craned my neck, peering through the tinted window at the endless mirrored panels. I didn't think my father owned this building, so they must have had to buy or rent space in another tower. I never really read my quarterly updates that I received. I skimmed them and committed random facts about how the company was doing to memory in case my father ever asked me about them, and I was fairly certain I read that all of the New York properties were at maximum profitability, which meant they were entirely occupied.

"Thank you," I offered to the driver, who gave me a bland smile in the rearview mirror in return.

Pulling a pair of oversized Versace Pilot sunglasses from my purse, I jammed them onto my face quickly before stepping out of the car. It wasn't particularly bright out, but I didn't feel much like putting my face on display for the world to see. I stepped out onto the curb, finding the door unattended and the sidewalk mercifully empty.

The wide legs of my black wool Versace pants billowed out around my heels while I crossed the lobby. A matching blazer was slung over my shoulders, and I had tucked a white t-shirt into my pants. I almost left the blazer but imagined a look of distaste on my father's face if I wasn't wearing a suit for any photos.

The office was on the thirtieth floor of the building, and I was alone the entire way up, forced to stare at myself in the spotless mirrored elevator. From what I understood, the entire floor was currently empty and would soon be home to the WH New York office. I imagined it looked the same as they all did and would likely be a mirror of the Chicago office down to the standard issued black ballpoint pens my father favored.

I remembered my mother used to tease him in the evenings, switching out his pens for ones of different colored ink. Deacon and I ran around their office playing whatever childish game we had invented that day, and I could hear her voice now, or what I imagined she sounded like after all these years. She would wrap her arms around my father's neck, and her chocolate hair that was straight like mine would fall over his shoulder. She would whisper to him that the world wouldn't end if he used a different pen.

I frowned, thinking of how pedestrian and mundane it seemed, it was a weird memory to stick with me after all these years. But it was more than just a pen, after all. She had that effect on him. She could make him step outside the rigid lines he drew for himself. She made him a bit more human, and whatever shreds of that humanity were left seemed to have died with her.

The doors to the elevator suddenly slid open, and I shook my head quickly, banishing thoughts of my mother and the person my father might have been if she hadn't left us. I stepped out onto the floor, taking in the floor-to-ceiling windows that offered an unparalleled view of Wall Street and the shining marble tile floor. There was an empty reception desk rising from the floor right across from me. It was white with padded ivory leather covering the top. I walked through the floor, moving past glass-walled conference rooms and offices until I came to a sudden stop when I heard my father's voice.

"Charlie will have nothing to do with Winchester Holdings again, so you don't need to worry about her...interference. She represents the company in name only, and her controlling shares remain of course. However odd, I think that's the way she prefers it, and that's for the best," my father's voice sounded out, cutting across the empty office.

"Thank God for that." Deacon laughed.

My stomach dropped, a sick feeling beginning to churn there. I wasn't sure why Deacon and I couldn't seem to keep things straight, or when I had become something to joke about, to laugh at. My heart hurt; there was something about hearing my brother toss around my mistakes so casually, like they were funny, made them seem infinitely worse to me at that moment. I waited, breath caught in my throat, pushing myself against the closest wall. They could only be talking to one person.

"Careful," David finally spoke, his voice low and cutting. "She may be your daughter, your sister. But you're still talking about the woman I planned to marry."

"I'm just joking around, David." Deacon's voice remained playful.

"I'm not laughing." David's voice was hard, and I pressed myself into the wall, wanting to shrink down and die there. "Charlie's involvement or lack thereof is not a condition of my return to Winchester Holdings. As her family, I suppose that entitles you to think what you will without my interference. But as far as I'm concerned, she is, and always will be, the love of my life. Regardless of how it played out. So, one more word about her like that, and I will rip that contract out of your hands and shred it without hesitation. My loyalty is always to her."

I closed my eyes, dropping my head back to the wall. I desperately wanted not to care at all about what I just heard. To not be confused by his words, to not feel a tiny spark of hope despite everything else he said to the contrary. To not think that maybe, just maybe, when he was with Victoria, he was pretending it was me. To not care that despite everything I did to ruin us, David still saw something good in me. That was and had always been David. He was always seeing things I couldn't. I wanted nothing more than to still be mad at him, to hate him if I could, for lying to me. But I just couldn't. Those words made my heart stretch and swell, and I didn't think any part of me would ever be able to hate David Kennedy.

"What are you doing?" My eyes flew open at the low whisper of Tripp's voice. He was standing in front of me, icy eyes looking at me shrewdly. His dark hair was pushed off his face and stubble lined his jaw. Tripp's hands were in the pockets of dark navy pants and a gray three-quarter zip sweater was pushed up his forearms. "Are you eavesdropping, Chuck?"

"No," I said, flustered and pushing off the wall. "It's not my fault that Deacon's voice is so loud. What are you doing here?"

Tripp arched an eyebrow like he didn't believe a word I was saying before answering, "I was bringing some things to my office. I'm off until next week. What are *you* doing here?"

"Signing paperwork. A Winchester's duties are never done."

"No school today?" Tripp asked, stepping toward me.

I felt myself pushing back against the wall again, half-wondering and half-hoping he would raise his muscular arms and box me in.

I shook my head. "I don't teach or have class on Mondays."

"Lucky girl." His voice was still low, and he was staring at me intently. "You might be waiting awhile for your dad. I think he and Deac had a lot to go over with David. I can show you around if you want."

I didn't want to spend any more time here than necessary, but I fell into step beside him, moving down the opposite hallway and away from where I had been listening to them speak. Tripp pointed out various things, like a large conference room Deacon was planning on using for executive meetings, another for all staff meetings. We stopped at one of the offices toward the end of the hall, which had glass surrounding it as well, and I spotted the standard mahogany desk taking up residence in the center of the room.

"Is this where the magic happens?" I asked wryly.

Tripp grinned at me, holding the glass door open and gesturing for me to walk in.

I was right. Most of the standard furnishings from the offices in Chicago had already materialized here. The same desk, the same desktop, the same chairs, and the same bookcases. There was even the same patterned box of Kleenex sitting on one of the side tables that I threw at Tripp in a fit of irritation back in Chicago.

"Do you have much left to bring in?" I eyed the sparse settings before turning back to Tripp. He was lounging against the door, one foot kicked up against the glass.

"No," he answered plainly, and I knitted my eyebrows. Did he not realize how barren and sterile the room still was?

"Have you felt compelled to feed a stray kitten to an ATM machine recently?" I asked dryly, sweeping my eyes over the office once more before looking back at him.

Tripp tipped his head, bringing his mouth to the side in a smirk. "You should reference more topical films, Chuck."

I narrowed my eyes at him before propping myself up on his desk and crossing my legs at the ankles, heels swinging back and forth. I watched as Tripp's eyes ran down the length of me before landing on my Louboutins.

"I didn't realize you were a film critic, or an expert in anything artistic for that matter."

His lips curled up to the side and he pushed off the door, walking forward with an effortless confidence I would never be able to master before stopping short right in front of me. His thighs were pressed against my knees, and I could feel the hard muscle beneath the thin layer of his pants. Tripp cocked his head, studying me. His eyes roved over my face, seemingly categorizing every inch before he spoke again. I hadn't heard this voice, this Tripp, since I was twenty.

"I'm an expert at a lot of things, if you're interested. Can I show you?"

My breath hitched, and an altogether new feeling settled in my stomach. It wasn't anger, irritation, or anxiety. It was none of the usual feelings I had with Tripp; it was nervousness, rather. This close, I could see all the different striations in his irises; how much they really did look like seeing a snowflake close up, or a frozen lake. I could lift my hand and run my fingers across the dark stubble peppering his sharp jaw.

I didn't know what I was doing, or why I was doing it, but I was confused, and I could hear David with Victoria, and then I was nodding softly. Tripp brought his face ever closer to mine; his nose brushed mine and his breath was warm on my lips. I tensed as he brought one of his hands to my jaw, grabbing it lightly between his thumb and forefinger, and tipping my head upward. His other hand found my waist, and he gripped it, thumb stroking upward across my ribcage.

We continued to stare at one another, neither of us moving. It felt like there was some sort of finality hanging in the air, like if one of us moved even a millimeter, things would change and doors would close. We weren't two young, dumb kids with nothing better to do than chase one another around; we weren't two adults forced back together and trying to find salvation for our previous choices. We were here, and maybe it really was just him and me. I wondered—

"Ahem," my father cleared his throat, and I snapped my head up, jerking my body backward on the desk, like I could somehow manufacture distance between us.

I pushed Tripp away from me, his hands dropping from my chin and from my waist. He grinned at me before turning around, the picture of casual elegance and holding out a hand to help me hop off the desk.

I swatted it away and jumped down onto my heels, brushing off my shirt and the waist of my pants before finally looking up. My father stood, a bored and perpetually disappointed expression on his face, arms folded across his chest. Deacon was leaning against the doorframe, hands tucked into the pockets of his tan suit pants, looking like he was choking back laughter. He raised an eyebrow at me. But my eyes skipped over my brother to the other person standing in the doorway, to David.

Guilt swirled in my stomach, and I heard his words echoing in my head. His loyalty was always to me, and here I was about to...I didn't know what. I was afraid to look directly at him, afraid of what I would find there. I wasn't sure what would be worse—if I looked up and found nothing in his eyes, if he didn't care, or if he did.

Finally, our eyes met. And my heart started to hurt all over again. There was sadness, there was something that looked like ire there, too, but there was a sort of resignation about his features, his posture that hurt the most. His shoulders, usually all hard lines and edges of muscle, seemed like they collapsed in on themselves. His lips downturned. Like he was finally accepting this, or maybe the new reality that I was no longer solely his. I'm sure my eyes looked similar when I first saw him with Victoria and had looked the same ever since I saw them grabbing at one another. I offered him a little shrug, unsure of what else to say. He was with Victoria, and there was no us anymore.

"Charlie was kind enough to help me test out the capabilities of the new furniture," Tripp offered, voice dry.

He propped himself up against the desk beside me, hands both shoved casually in his pockets, like my father, my brother, and my ex hadn't just walked in on whatever that was.

My father raised his eyebrows, continuing to stare at me. "How charitable of her. But I'm sure you have better things to be doing with your time. I know for a fact that Charlie does. She's needed for some signatures."

I nodded, saying nothing, high heels clicking loudly, as I allowed my father to summon me from the room like a dog. Anything to get me away from how David was looking at me and leave behind whatever feeling Tripp's hands on me—and his body that close to me—had done to me.

CHAPTER FIFTEEN

Exactly as I predicted, Rebecca was in New York with my father and Deacon while they had set things up for the expansion and to deal with any press-related inquiries. After moving through and signing all the required paperwork on my end, none of which I read myself but was explained in horribly boring detail by Helen, still the head of legal at WH, Rebecca rolled in a rack of Sabine-approved suits for me. Just a few photos needed to be taken that they could use for the formal announcement.

I wasn't sure why it mattered if I was in them at all. My father and Deacon could get a full spread in the Wall Street Journal for all I cared. I wasn't really in the picture any longer, anyway. Most publications were no longer curious, nor did they really care what I was doing now, but Rebecca had of course spun the dissolution of my portfolio by making it look like academia had been my lifelong dream, and my father had graciously allowed me leave the company.

I personally thought letting everyone know he fired me might have been a better headline and really cemented his status as a ruthless businessman. In typical fashion, he disappeared shortly after the obligatory family photoshoot, shutting himself in one of the empty offices to take a phone call. Deacon was walking me through his vision for the office, all the way down to the specific art he wanted on the walls.

We stopped at the end of the floor, where the two largest offices sat side-by-side. One already had various boxes strewn throughout, and from the personal effects, I could tell would be Deacon's. He opened the door, gesturing for me to enter, and I saw a massive, blown-up print of Noa's most recent cover on Vogue.

"Do you want everyone who comes in here to know your wife is more beautiful than theirs?" I raised my eyebrows at him before shaking my head.

Deacon grinned, dropping into the leather seat on the other side of the desk and kicking his feet up to the table, revealing another pair of Prada loafers. "It's a business tactic, Charles."

I sat in the seat across from him, hooking my feet at the ankles. "Ah, far be it from me to question the reach a Master of the Universe will go to intimidate the competition."

"Speaking of business tactics," Deacon began, taking a moment to peer over my shoulder to make sure no one was lingering around, "what the hell was that?"

I schooled my face and plucked my bottom lip with my teeth. "What was what?"

He slapped his hand down on the desk playfully. "Was that some sort of lame ass attempt to make David jealous? I'm not sure taunting him with the guy you cheated on him with is the best move. Maybe try someone a few towers over. I'm sure all you'd have to do is walk through the trading floor at Goldman and shout your name."

Continuing to pull at my lip, I finally puffed out my cheeks and exhaled before leveling my brother with a look. "I heard Steven when I came here."

Deacon opened his mouth to say something but paused and scrubbed his face with his hands before laying a hand flat on the desk. He flipped his palm up, and I resisted for a moment before dropping mine down onto his. His voice was a whisper when he finally spoke, "He's still your dad, Charlie."

My eyes burned and I raised them to the ceiling, taking a measured breath. I quickly wiped along my lash line before looking at Deacon. He hadn't felt like my father in years, but I wasn't about to open that door today. "I heard you, too...and David."

"I'm sorry," he whispered again, squeezing my hand. His forest green eyes were soft as he continued to stare at me. "I am sorry. It wasn't about you. It was just a stupid joke. I thought it might make David feel more comfortable, or God forbid, laugh about the situation. But I'm sure you heard it had the opposite effect."

"What am I supposed to do with that, Deacon?" I shook my head, whispering back. My eyes were still blurry, and I could just see the outline of his quaffed, chocolate hair. "He says things like that, but he won't...he can't forgive me. He's with Victoria, and he lied to me. We spent the entire night together before the engagement party, and he's a fucking liar. Just like me."

I dipped my head, tears beginning to track down my face. I felt Deacon place his other hand on top of mine and squeeze it between both of his.

"Let yourself off the mat, Charlie. Do me a favor, do Taylor a favor, do yourself a favor. You don't deserve to suffer for the rest of your life because of your mistakes. I know that doesn't change anything. That doesn't turn back the clock. But you need to move on. At least for now. David is going to do what he's going to do, and you don't deserve to sit here while you wait for him to figure out if you're worthy of forgiveness or not. I forgive you. I say you're worthy. So, if you want to go have fun and fuck Tripp, fuck Tripp. Sleep your way through Wall Street for all I care. I just don't want to see you like this anymore."

Something between a sob and a laugh escaped me, and I dropped my head to our joined hands for a moment. It was such a Deacon proclamation, like he was the authority on when it was appropriate to dole out forgiveness. His speeches were always in the same vein, but since Noa, one of his mantra's was absent. I couldn't remember the last time he told me I was his favorite person, and I knew I wasn't anymore. That had hurt me, angered me, set me adrift more than I ever would have thought. But my gaze flicked up to the print of Noa, taking up all the space in this office the way she did his heart. Second place was okay.

I laughed, shoulders shaking. "How many older brothers' advice would include sleeping their way through Wall Street?" I took my hands back, wiping the sides of my fingers at my eyes.

Deacon smiled, leaning forward and painting a fake, demure look across his face. "I've thought about starting a blog, you know. I think a lot of people could use advice from someone like me."

"That has the makings of something that belongs on the dark web. Stick to finances and whatever it is you do." I smiled at him, pushing myself to stand. "It's weird, right? This world where we both...where it's not just us against the world anymore? I didn't think it would be hard, but it feels like we're constantly grating on each other or something, I don't know."

My brother studied me, lips twitching and glancing sideways at the portrait of Noa. "It uh, it never occurred to me because you were gone for so long that I should have tried harder, too. Showed you how important you were no matter what. My priorities might look different, but you'll always be the other half of me, Charlie."

I smiled, nodding at him before reaching forward and ruffling his hair, freeing it from the confines of all his styling gel, partly because this is how I thought he looked best—most like the person I knew with my whole soul and loved, but also because I knew it would drive him nuts.

Deacon jerked backward, immediately running a hand through his hair to try and salvage it. Our moment of sibling tenderness passed, and he jerked his finger toward the door and narrowed his eyes at me, but he was smiling. "Get out of my office. I fucking hate it when you do that."

"Consider me gone. Might pop on down to Goldman and see what they have to offer me," I offered dryly, shouldering my bag that I had discarded by the door, along with my Versace blazer.

Deacon pointed at the door again but not before he flashed me a smile. At that moment, he looked like a little boy again—all messy chocolate hair, eyes too bright, and smile too wide. My heart constricted, and I found myself wishing again, this time for altogether different reasons, that we could go back in time. Not away from who I was becoming now—not even away from Tripp Banks and whatever the erratic beating of my heart meant at the thought of his thighs pressed between mine—but to a time where we could exist with our mother and father, just the four of us, just for a moment longer.

CHAPTER SIXTEEN

The elevator doors opened, revealing a much busier lobby than when I arrived at the building. I hadn't bothered to try and track down my father to say goodbye, as he was probably still on the phone, and I had served my purpose to him today. I diligently played my part as a good little rich girl and smiled for the photos like he asked, and I was happy to step out into the lobby and move closer to leaving this building behind, to getting back to my life—my life that doesn't involve Winchester Holdings.

I fished my hand around blindly in my tote until I felt my phone and started thumbing through my emails as I crossed the lobby exit, happy to be blending in with everyone else going about their day. The sunlight was brighter through the revolving door than it had been earlier, and I stopped to grab my sunglasses, pushing them onto my face before stepping out into the world. It was still my world. My world without my father, without Winchester Holdings.

"Where are you headed in such a hurry?" Tripp drawled, and I whipped around, spotting him propped up against the side of the building, a pair of Ray Ban Clubmaster sunglasses shielding his eyes.

"Jesus Christ!" I slapped my hand to my chest, mouth popping open in irritation. "You should come with a bell."

Tripp pushed off the wall, shoving his hands into his pockets and walking toward me, the ever permanent catlike grin on his face. "And here I was, thinking you might want me to wait for you after our little tryst earlier."

"Well you thought wrong. In fact, I'm actually on my way to the hospital right now, because I clearly had a stroke earlier," I said, turning on the point of my heel and heading down the street away from him.

I had actually intended to call a car, and I was going to head to my office on campus and do some reading, but I needed to put distance between us. I didn't want to end up at his mercy again, and by the way my heart was beating at the sight of him and my palms were growing slick with sweat, it seemed like a distinct possibility.

"Are you asking me to play doctor, Chuckles?" Tripp asked, falling into step beside me.

I stopped suddenly, crossing my arms and practically sneering at him in disbelief. "What is wrong with you? Can you be normal for even a second?" I gestured widely at his dumb grin and cocky stance as I said, "Not whatever this is. You must have other thoughts that don't involve riling me up and sexual innuendo."

Tripp arched an eyebrow and slowly pushed his sunglasses down his nose to peer at me. His mouth parted, and he looked on the precipice of another dumb remark, but I continued.

"I'm serious. Cut the shit. I'm sick of having to defend why I choose to spend time with you, because this is all people see. We both know there's more to you than that."

He paused, considering me and a wistful smile, the likes of which I wasn't sure I had ever seen on Tripp Banks's face, tugged at his lips. Pulling off his sunglasses and folding them, his eyes skated over me, and there was a softness there, too, that wasn't usually found in the frozen expanse of his stare.

"You know how you say David is the only person who ever really saw you for who you are?"

"Yes?" I asked, lips pulling down in confusion.

Tripp continued to stare at me, and for a moment it reminded me of the way David used to look at me. Like I was something special, something worthy.

"Sometimes I think you're the only person who sees me," he offered quietly before gesturing for me to continue walking down the sidewalk with him, like he hadn't just reached right down into soul, plucked my heart out with his hands, and whispered language that I knew all too well.

———

Tripp sat opposite me in my office at school, his legs kicked up on my desk and shoes sitting on top of a pile of printed economics articles I hadn't leafed through, yet. Leaning back in the chair, he crossed his arms behind his head, shirt lifting ever so slightly to reveal a strip of taut abdominal muscle and a line of dark hair that disappeared into his khakis. He was still wearing his fucking sunglasses, which somehow just completed whatever look he was going for.

I sighed loudly, leaning forward to push his feet off my desk. They fell to the ground suddenly, causing Tripp to lurch forward in the chair, grabbing the arms at the last second and sending all of my papers crashing to the ground.

"If you insist on sitting here while I read, please don't put your feet on my desk. And make yourself useful and clean that up."

"You invited me here, Chuck," Tripp said dryly, pulling off his sunglasses and setting them on my desk before bending down out of my view to gather the papers.

"No, I didn't," I shook my head incredulously, "I said, and I quote, 'I'm going to head to my office on campus to get some work done.' And you said, 'I'd like to see where you work now,' and then you followed me here like a lost little puppy dog."

He lifted his head back up, a wry grin on his face. "What kind of puppy dog would you say I am?"

I narrowed my eyebrows at him and made an exaggerated motion for him to continue cleaning up the stack of papers. "An unfriendly one who gets passed by in the pound."

"I think I'd be a purebred Australian Shepherd. I mean, have you seen these eyes? People would pay big money for eyes this blue," Tripp continued to talk, voice dry.

A laugh escaped me, and I clapped my hand to my mouth, like I could silence the sound that was now ringing through the small office. A low whistle escaped Tripp's mouth, and he tilted his head to the side, grinning at me. "Did I just make you laugh, Chuckles?"

"There's a first time for everything." I rolled my eyes, looking back down at the article I was annotating.

Silence fell between us, but it wasn't uncomfortable. It was companionable, and the thought of that unnerved me more than anything. My gaze was unfocused as I breathed in and out, trying to concentrate on the words in front of me while the sound of papers shuffling came from the floor. I raised my fingers to my lips absentmindedly, thinking about how close we had been to kissing earlier, how warm his hands felt on me, and how it did feel like I was twenty again, but not in the way it used to. Sitting here in this room, it felt like we were the same two people again from all those years ago. Not the ones trying to rectify colossal, unforgivable mistakes, just two people who saw each other.

But then I pictured David's face. The resignation in his eyes, the sadness. Like maybe there had been some small, miniscule hope still in him that Tripp and I managed to shatter all over again.

"What's this?"

I blinked, vision clearing, and I dropped my fingers from where they were still brushing my lips. Tripp was seemingly on his knees on the other side of the desk, somehow still taller than me where I was sitting in the chair. His knuckles were white, and he appeared to be clenching a thick, white envelope. I looked at it in confusion for a moment longer before I realized what it was: the Oxford application package that Dr. Batra dropped on my desk last week when I still hadn't said anything about her offer.

My eyes flicked over to Tripp's, and it was the second time that day there was something in them I had never seen before. Confusion, sadness, and something that looked sort of like betrayal lingered in the frosty striations of his irises.

"Running away again, Chuck?" he whispered.

I tensed, registering the harsh undertone that wasn't there earlier. The playful, albeit annoying drawl was nowhere to be found.

"No, I, uh—" I shook my head, stumbling over my words before I rubbed my palms across my face.

I never meant for anyone to see that. I knew how it would look, how it would seem: Deacon lands himself in New York with David—and Tripp in tow—and instead of facing any of my problems, I leave the continent—again. I didn't want to be the person who ran anymore, who backed themselves into such unforgiveable, fucked up corners they had no choice but to flee.

"Give me that. It's nothing." I leaned forward to grab the envelope from Tripp, but he snatched his hand backward and tipped his head at me, eyes filled with darkness.

"Don't be a child," I hissed, standing, and reaching forward again, but Tripp stood in one, fluid motion and pulled the package even farther out of reach.

"Most people would say running away would make you the child," Tripp said, anger lacing his words. "Am I that big of a mistake to you? So colossally vile, unforgivable, that you can't even exist in the same city as me?"

"Tripp, please just give it to me," I murmured, falling back into the chair and scrubbing my face again.

It had never occurred to me until this very moment that Tripp might have been a casualty of Charlie Winchester, too. In my quest to find absolution for my regrets and mistakes at twenty, to try to change my wish that I mourned and grieved my own mother properly instead of looking for salvation in someone else—I took advantage of him, used him, and played on his feelings the exact way I thought he had done me.

"I'm not going. I'm not planning on leaving New York, Tripp."

He stood, apprehension etched in his dark features. I cocked my head, studying him for a moment. Somehow, he and David were both all sharp edges and jawlines, although Tripp's was more triangular while David's was broad, square almost. But that was where the similarities ended. Where David was light and honey, and home, Tripp was dark and shimmering icicles, and an uncertain frozen lake you didn't know if you would make it across. I wanted to laugh, looking at the two of them was like looking at a literary foil in the flesh.

"You aren't vile. I mean, you are," I chided, a poor attempt at lightening the mood, "but I don't think you are a colossally vile mistake. I think I made a colossally vile mistake. More than one actually, and you just happen to be tied up in both."

Tripp tossed the envelope onto my desk, and it skidded toward the corner where it stopped, balancing on the edge. He finally dropped into the chair, one arm slung over the back, and he continued to stare at me. The anger seemed to be ebbing away, and I wondered for the second time, if underneath all of his sharp, pointy edges, there was someone who was deeply hurt, and been made to feel deeply uncertain. In all of these years, even across the distance, it had never occurred to me to even think about, let alone ask, when we were in one another's lives.

"You're not going?" He finally asked, his voice now even and impassive.

"No, I'm not going. I like it here. I like New York Charlie. I'm not going to let Deacon steamroll that. He can't have my little corner of the world. And between you and me, Winchester Holdings can get fucked." I raised my eyebrows at him.

It was a lie. But a white lie. The envelope *had* tempted me. The promise of the work I could do, what I could contribute, was tempting me. It was tempting, the idea to place myself thousands of miles away from all of it again. Away from my father and Winchester Holdings, as far away as I could really get when I lived primarily off my trust fund that I only had access to because of both. I didn't need the company or the expansion.

The trust fund felt like a bottomless pit, at least to me. Deacon would probably manage to blow through his during his lifetime. It would be easy to pick up and go, but it felt like a bit of a cop out, childish and cowardly. I didn't want to go anywhere again just because everything I wished I could avoid was all around me. I was trying to learn, to grow, to change.

An aloof, almost offside grin slid into place on Tripp's face. "Well, thank God, because I simply wouldn't get the same reaction from your father if I had some other girl pinned against my desk." Tripp slid his sunglasses back down his face and resumed his position, head tipped back and his Ralph Lauren shoes finding their way to the top of my desk again.

Maybe he was my friend after all. Maybe he could really be my friend. This Charlie, this Tripp. Maybe we were each more than our mistakes.

CHAPTER SEVENTEEN

I had meant what I said to Tripp, to Taylor. I chose New York, and I didn't want to run again. Just because they were all here now, didn't mean Winchester Holdings would have such a chokehold on my life anymore. That ship had long sailed. I would be lying if sometimes I didn't daydream about my father apologizing and begging for me to come back, realizing that all the work I was doing on sustainable investing here at Columbia showed him how much value-add I would really bring to the company, telling me he loved me, that he always had, always would.

I had asked Taylor before what she made of that from any of her psychiatry rotations. She always answered the same way, saying even fucked up people with more fucked up parents still craved their love. And I guess that was true, because just like I would never willingly choose to live in a world without David Kennedy, Steven Winchester could come back begging for my forgiveness at any time, and I would happily grant it to him. I was beginning to suspect that deep down, the see-saw, the endless back and forth with my father was just a defense mechanism. At the end of the day, I think I just wanted my father to love me for who I am.

But all of that was hard to remember, hard to recall why I was so vehemently against going to Oxford with Dr. Batra as I stood in the staff lounge in the international affairs building. It was decorated in the same Oxford blue—from the balloons to the streamers, to the tablecloth covering a table laid with cutlery, plates and plastic champagne flutes all in the same color. There was a giant white cake, the Oxford crest printed on it. All of this to celebrate Dr. Batra and her once-in-a-lifetime opportunity; the same opportunity that had been given to me freely, that you could argue, like many other opportunities I was given, that I didn't have to work for at all.

I teetered back on my heels, one hand holding the stem of a plastic champagne flute, the other tucked into the pocket of my wool wide leg Michael Kors trousers that were practically identical to the Versace ones I wore for my father's dumb impromptu photoshoot last week. A camel-colored, cropped Saint Laurent t-shirt was tucked into them. Usually, I never would have spent that much on a t-shirt alone, but Taylor had no such reservations and had dropped it into my bag. The ultimate irony came when I checked my statement later. I never looked at the total when I bought anything. I was beginning to wonder if my entire life was a juxtaposition that bordered on hypocrisy.

I had just finished one of my required courses, a lecture on International Political Economy, and made my way to the staff lounge with some of my classmates who were all pursuing either PhDs in Political Science, or Sustainable Development. These were people I had seen almost every day for the better part of a year, presented with, researched with, shared shitty food at graduate mixers with, and had traded teaching sections with; but I wasn't sure I would consider them my friends. We were collegial, and we shared inside jokes about graduate life and certain professors or faculty, but that's where it ended. It was the same sense of otherness I had possessed all my life. I wasn't the same as everyone in my social circle, all those girls I was friends with by proximity, all the people Deacon knew, our family. And here, I wasn't the same as anyone, either.

I didn't accept any funding packages, I donated my TAship money because I was required to take it, and I didn't run to the grad student lounge when there was free food, I didn't go out for the happy hours at the local bars because it seemed disingenuous. But I could see the bond they all had with one another, the shared experience I would never truly understand.

So I stood there, smiling politely over the plastic glass of champagne wearing fifteen-hundred-dollar pants. God knows how much the shoes I was wearing cost. I hadn't even looked at them when I put them on that morning, just pulled them down from the shelf in my walk-in closet. Scott and Tenzin, the two people I probably saw the most here, because we taught seminars for the same class, left the table across the room, each not so conspicuously holding a second glass under their blazers and came to stand with me.

"So," Scott cleared his throat and peered at me from behind his thick, black acetate glasses, "is it true?"

I furrowed my brow, swallowing the sip of champagne before answering. "There are many things that are true, Scott. You're going to have to give me more to go on than that."

"Dr. Batra. She asked you to go with her, that she would keep supervising your work if you went to Oxford." Scott gestured with one of his champagne flutes to where Dr. Batra was standing across the room.

She was laughing, one arm crossed over her stomach, the other bringing champagne to her lips.

Tenzin eyed me, curiosity piqued. She tipped her head, waiting for me to respond and her thick, black hair fell from her shoulder. Somehow, it always looked like it had been freshly blown out, gently curing at the ends.

"Well?" she asked, clearly not interested in waiting for me any longer.

"She said if I wanted to apply, she would be happy to continue to supervise me there. If I wanted to apply, not that she was taking me with her," I answered, an edge to my voice.

This was one of the many things that I had worried about, that it was just another opportunity laid at my feet in front of my golden shoes.

Both of their eyes went wide, and Scott quite literally shoved my shoulder like what I said was so unbelievable. "Who in their right mind would turn down Oxford? It's one of the oldest academic institutions in the world. They have one of the top development programs in the world. This place is fine, but it's not Oxford."

"This place, as in this Ivy League institution?" I asked wryly, raising my eyebrows and draining the rest of my champagne.

"OXFORD!" Tenzin hissed, her eyes practically bugging out of her head now.

"To apply. The invitation to apply to Oxford," I began, and they both opened their mouths to protest. I held up my hand to stop them. "I know, I know. She said she would supervise me. It's as sure as you can get when it comes to an acceptance. But it's an opportunity I didn't earn. I didn't apply and get selected for admittance based on my own merit, against how many other applicants. It's piggybacking on her hard work, no?"

Scott tipped his head back, black curls falling with the column of his neck, and let out a loud cackle of laughter. "Says the Winchester. Isn't every opportunity you've had in your life one you didn't earn?"

My cheeks grew flushed, and my mouth opened a fraction, my mind scrambling for some retort that would make what he said somehow untrue, or justify it, but he kept talking, "I'm not saying that to be harsh. I'm saying as far as I know, you didn't buy your way in here. You didn't pay Dr. Batra off to invite you to continue to study with her. This might be one thing you could say you earned all on your own, Charlie."

He looked at me pointedly for a moment longer before launching into some story about one of the students in his TA section. I nodded along politely, holding the plastic blue flute in front of my lips, occasionally tapping it against them. My gaze kept finding Dr. Batra, watching how she was being lauded by her colleagues, our colleagues, how happy she seemed, and how genuinely excited. She had earned it, and despite all of my vehement promises, I wondered what it would be like. As I stood there on the periphery, one foot in this life and the possibility of it, and one foot in my old one, I wondered. I wondered what it would be like if I let myself earn it.

————

Rolling the pen I was holding between my fingers, I continued to stare down at the envelope with the Oxford crest embossed into the corner. I mapped the lines and ridges with the tip of my finger before moving across the surface of the envelope to the top where I skated around the edge that the glue was lifting up on. One simple movement, and I could open the whole thing and look through the package, through the course catalog and begin to imagine even more what *earning it* would look like.

A knock sounded from the doorway, and I lifted my head, breaking eye contact with the envelope that was only serving to taunt me. Dr. Batra was leaning against the frame, arms crossed over her chest and her dark eyes crinkling at the corners from the smile she was wearing. She tipped her chin to the envelope and visible Oxford crest.

"I'm heading out for the weekend, and I saw your door was open. I don't mean to intrude, but after having the Oxford colors and crest assault my senses for the last few hours, it's hard not to notice. Are you having second thoughts at all about the offer?"

I considered her words, crossing my own arms and tipping back in my chair to look up at the ceiling, like it might hold some answers for me there. But all I found was ceiling tile that looked like it needed to be replaced. I pinched the bridge of my nose and exhaled, looking back at her where she waited patiently for my answer. "No. I mean, I don't think so."

She arched an eyebrow. "That doesn't sound very certain, Charlie. I said it before, and I'll say it again. I think it would be a great opportunity for you."

"Columbia is a good opportunity for me, too. One I earned," I said, words harsher than I intended. "I just mean that I've made a commitment to this program, to this city and to the life I'm trying to build here."

"It strikes me as interesting that you think this program is the only opportunity you've earned. It's not my place to judge when I only know what the public knows about your personal life, what all of America knows about families like yours. Your positionality, your wealth—yes, they are a privilege. An unearned one foisted upon you at birth." She paused, seeming to weigh her next words while they swept over me. "In my opinion, that unearned privilege might just make you uniquely suited to make a difference, though. A real, tangible one. I can see it in your eyes, in your work. How passionate you are about your research. The topic of sustainable investing might be boring to the average person, but you are uniquely in-tune with the reality. Your name, your family, have social capital in that world. You keep doing this work, keep going down this path...maybe you stand a much higher chance than most at making a difference. You have the connections and the avenues to have your work seen by the people who control most of the wealth in the world. It seems to be like an advantage you shouldn't want to waste."

A childlike petulance rose in me as I rebuked her words. "Be that as it may, that doesn't mean I've earned the opportunity to have a place secured for me at one of the best institutions in the world because of my talents alone."

Dr. Batra shrugged, her arms still crossed over her chest. I watched her large computer bag move up and down with her shoulders. It was fraying at the seams, and the material looked like it would scratch you and snag at your fingertips. I instinctively kicked my Saint Laurent computer bag farther under the desk, an uncomfortable sensation swooping in my stomach.

"I can't tell you what to do, Charlie. But I didn't ask you to consider joining me just because you're wealthy and just because you're a Winchester. I asked you because you're smart, you're dedicated, and I think our work together is only just beginning.

You earned the opportunity to be my student here without those pieces of you. Why not there, too?" She offered me an encouraging smile, and it reminded me of one a preschool teacher might give. "You should head out for the weekend. Go do something fun. It's Friday night in Manhattan. You're young, and you can do whatever you want. Tell me you aren't just going to sit here into the wee hours of the morning staring at that envelope and begrudging things about your life you can't change?"

I snorted, offering her a smile. "I was actually going to call my brother's fiancée to see if she was free to grab dinner or something."

"Ah." Dr. Batra laughed, a funny sort of irony hanging between us. "The supermodel. Enjoy dinner, Charlie. I'll see you Tuesday."

"Goodnight," I said, beginning to gather some of the papers and other things I wanted to bring home with me for the weekend, purposely avoiding the envelope that was still sitting there when she spoke again.

"You know you're allowed to enjoy it sometimes, right? Enjoying the privileges that you have and being honest about that doesn't make you bad, Charlie. It doesn't make your work worth any less. It just makes you human." Smiling one more time, she pushed off the door and turned away leaving me alone in my office.

I sat there for a while longer, the casted shadows from the setting sun growing ever larger. When I finally decided to leave my office, I pushed the envelope into the ridiculous designer bag along with everything else.

CHAPTER EIGHTEEN

I twirled the stem of the cherry from my vodka soda in between my fingers, eyes wandering around the restaurant, Cathédrale. The lights were intentionally dim, casting what I assumed were meant to be mysterious shadows across everything, furthered by the twinkling candles on each table. I looked down at the cherry, wondering why they insisted on putting it in the drink in the first place, before bringing it between my teeth and ripping it off the stem.

Noa picked the restaurant. I guess it was more of a gastropub, but it was close to a shoot she was wrapping up. I had texted her when I left school, and she seemed genuinely thrilled to say yes, following up by saying she was absolutely starving and miserable at what she called "the shoot from hell."

I wasn't sure what would qualify as *the shoot from hell*, but I was sure she would let me know. I picked up my phone, taking an absent-minded sip of my drink. My email inbox typically remained empty on weekends, a far cry from what it looked like when I was at WH.

There was a text from Taylor, saying she wouldn't be back like expected, because she had a "can't miss" surgery she was assisting on. I smiled, imagining the morbid delight and curiosity that would grow and grow over the coming days as she imagined herself making precise incisions and sectioning away diseased tissue. Her father had been the chief of surgery at Northwestern Memorial for her entire life, and in the way Deacon grew up wanting to be our father, she wanted to be just like hers, too. Maybe that was a normal thing for children, wanting to be like a parent.

I twirled the cherry stem again and couldn't imagine a single thing that would make me want to be like either of my parents. I could aspire to be like my mom, all empty stares and forced smiles, and you know, dead. Or, I could aspire to be like my father, void and vacant but surrounded by piles and piles of money I would never spend. I already had piles and piles of money I would never spend; I had never aspired to that, and I certainly didn't want to aspire to the rest.

"Charlie!" Noa called across the restaurant, standing on her tiptoes to peer across the tables.

Her hair was pulled back in a tight bun, a cropped white t-shirt rising above oversized light wash boyfriend jeans and an oversized black monogrammed Givenchy tote hanging off her shoulder. Her face split into a smile, and she waved at me again before turning to the bodyguard lingering behind her and saying something to him. He smiled at her and nodded before walking purposefully through the tables and finding an open seat at a bar that took up half the space.

Noa wove through the tables, blatantly ignoring the heads that lifted, or the obvious shoulder smacks people made as she walked by. She dropped into the seat beside me, letting her tote fall with a dull thud before kicking it to the side swiftly. I could see Taylor, shrieking in shock at the both of us in unison, unable to believe someone treated designer items with the same disregard as me. Noa's whole body sunk into itself, and she let out something between a sigh and a moan, rolling her head back before leaning forward and dropping her elbow onto the table, chin in palm and continued smiling at me.

"I'm so happy you called."

"Shoot that bad?" I raised my eyebrows, pushing the menu across the table to her.

She flipped through the menu, running a lithe finger down the paper, stopping and tapping the last line. Noa looked up, her face bare and glowing.

"Do you want to split a bottle of Louis Roederer with me?" She asked, temporarily ignoring my comment. "It has the lowest sugar content on the menu, and I don't really want a cocktail or mixed drink. I'm worried anything else will make me break out."

"Sure," I nodded, draining the last of my vodka.

I watched as Noa raised her hand, a bright and kind smile on her face. She was still smiling as she waved over the server. On anyone else, it would have looked like a horrifically entitled, douchebag move, like they were demanding attention. I imagined my brother doing it, and I had to resist the urge to grimace. But on Noa, it didn't look off-putting.

The server didn't seem to mind, either. He came to stand in front of us, arms crossed behind his back. His blond hair was shorn close to his head, and his eyes were a blue that could have rivaled Tripp Banks.

"Ladies." He smiled, revealing a row of teeth that were almost as white as mine. "What can I do for you this evening?"

"You know, I have had the absolute worst day," Noa stated, laying her hands out flat against the table.

Her engagement ring seemingly caught every single flicker of light in the restaurant, somehow looking brighter than it did in the daytime. I was beginning to realize she was one of those people, in much the same way Deacon was, that the sun just shined on. No matter what happened to them, no matter how life tried to keep them small, they were simply too big, too bright, too special to be contained.

"And because of that, my future sister-in-law and I really, really need to share a bottle of champagne." Noa pointed at the menu with her perfectly rounded fingernail.

"Coming right up," he grinned, before his eyes roved over Noa.

They moved to me, dragging over my arms, across my chest before landing on my face. I felt my lips pulling back when he turned away.

Noa opened her mouth in horror, a silent gag shuddering up her throat. "Ew," she whispered, rolling her eyes.

"Are you going to tell me what made the shoot so awful?" I pressed, genuinely curious. I had no idea what would make a model's day so horrible.

"Where do I fucking start?" Noa rolled her eyes again, pushing her palms farther into the table. "The art director for this designer is...difficult to say the least. Most print shoots are longer, but this was exceptionally lengthy. I got there at five this morning and sat in hair and makeup for I don't even know how long. But my face wasn't right, so we started again. And then it was just okay, but nothing I did in front of the camera was right. My arm looked weird, my legs looked too loose. I could go on and on and on. But it's fine. It's just a different sort of bad day. You know, Deacon's idea of a bad day is when he loses a few million. Mine is that I get told I look weird. Yours...I don't know what a bad day is for you. What are those like?"

"I don't think it's quite as simple as being told you look weird," I said gently, noticing that her eyes were rimmed red and underneath her eyes looked swollen. "Deacon can stand to lose a few million, and to take a few hits to his ego. A bad day for him is no worse than it would be for you."

She smiled softly at me, waving her hand like it didn't matter.

Before she could say anything, the server materialized with our bottle of champagne. I waited patiently and smiled politely as he showed us the bottle and offered us each a taste before depositing it in an ornate and very impractical crystal ice bucket. Noa took a small sip and her eyelids fluttered, a brief hum of enjoyment coming from her.

"So, what does a bad day look like for you?" She asked again, curiosity radiating off her.

"I don't have many bad days anymore, at least not at work." I shrugged.

It was the truth. Walking into Winchester Holdings had often felt like dodging landmines. Some were shaped like Steven Winchester, some like Tripp Banks, and some were of my own making. "Usually they're good. Sometimes they're just average. Today was, uhm, weird. I guess."

"How so?"

I weighed my words, taking a sip of champagne and letting the bubbles fizz against my lips before swallowing. I hadn't told Deacon about Oxford, and I hadn't intended to tell anyone other than Taylor. There was something about it—between the sheer irony of it all and another opportunity I hadn't earned placed at my feet that would allow me to run away from all of my problems.

Again. I debated sloughing her off, sharing a half-truth as I usually would, but a lot of my problems came down to my inability to be honest, so I thought I would try telling her the whole truth.

"My supervisor accepted a job at Oxford, and she essentially asked me to go with her. This was before I found out about Deacon bringing WH here. And you know, I've been trying to...I don't know. Trying to do something here, existing outside of the company. But leaving, running back to the UK again seemed so...ironic and uninspiring. It would feel a bit like classic Charlie, running away again. I was mostly hoping I could avoid it, but then Tripp found the application package in my office from my supervisor."

"What was Tripp doing in your office?" Noa asked, the crystal champagne flute poised at her lips, like she was about to take a sip, but my words stopped her. "What's the deal with you two? I can't figure it out. You told me what happened, but anyone can see how much you and David love one another, even now. But you and Tripp...it's like magnetic or something. You always seem like you're on the precipice of fury with him."

"That's probably because at all times, I am on the precipice of taking whatever sharp object is nearest and ramming it into his jugular," I answered, again debating the truth that sat right behind my teeth, ready to spill from my lips. "Tripp and I have a much longer history than I led anyone at WH to believe, including David, until it was too late. We went to Brown together, and we were...friends. Best friends in a constant will they/won't they tug of war. There's a lot of history there that would take forever to get into. But the day I found out my mom was dead, we slept together. And then...he disrespected me more than anyone ever had, and more than anyone has since. Or, at least I thought he did. Long story short, years went by, and then there he was again."

"Why didn't you tell anyone? I mean, why keep that a secret?" Her voice was gentle, and she leaned over the table, like she wanted to get closer to me.

A deride sort of snort came from me. But not at Noa. At me. At twenty-year-old Charlie, unmoored, unanchored, desperately thrashing around to find the closest and only comfort.

"I tried to fuck away my mother before her body was cold. She deserved better. She deserved better when she was alive, and when she was dead."

Noa's eyes glimmered, like there were tears she was waiting to shed for me. "Wouldn't you say that's called being human, Charlie? You're allowed to make mistakes. Some would say that's *what* makes us human."

My eyes started to burn, and I began to chew on the inside of my lips with my teeth. "I seem to make a disproportionate amount of those."

"Deacon never talks about her," Noa murmured, voice barely discernible above the noises of the restaurant.

"No, I can't imagine he does. Some of the only fights Deac and I have had are about her. I mean, you were at the engagement party," I said, wiping my lash line discreetly.

The last thing I needed was a photo of me crying at dinner all over the tabloids.

Noa brought her flute to her lips but pressed the crystal there before setting it down. "He's never even told me how she died. I mean, I'm not an idiot. I can guess what happened. But he's never so much as brought her up. You know, when Taylor introduced us the first thing she said was, 'You both have dead parents, so that's something you have in common.'"

I rolled my eyes and shook my head. "Of course she did. I really wonder about her social skills sometimes. But, I'm not surprised. She's been dead almost nine years, and I don't even remember the last time my father or Deacon so much as said her name. I'm sorry about that, for you, too. I'm sure it would be...nice? I guess, to have someone to talk about it with who gets it."

"I won't ask you to share anything about her that you feel would infringe upon Deacon's privacy, but if you ever want to talk about her—give her life again, I'm always here. You look like her, you know, from the photos," Noa offered, ignoring propriety and grabbing the bottle of champagne, topping up both of our flutes.

I nodded, David's words from the first time we ever discussed my mother echoed in my head. It was the day after we decided to be together, for real. The day we drank three bottles of wine and stayed on my terrace until morning, the day we couldn't keep our hands off each other and had sex on my living room rug. He told me I looked like her, and it was the first day he provided me a safe refuge for her, a place I could maybe open some of those doors and allow her back in the way Deacon and my father never did.

That was also the day Tripp showed back up in my life. There was a bitter sort of irony there, the way he had been in my life the day she left it, and then he showed back up just as I started to dig her out of the grave in my head.

I looked at Noa, and her smile was so wide, so genuine and offered her what I could. "You could tell me about your parents, too, if you wanted. I don't know anything about them, and I would like to."

Tears were still glimmering in her eyes, but they looked happy. I surveyed her as she spoke, her hands waving every which way, telling me stories about her parents and her childhood, what it was like to move from Malta to California after their death. I could feel the distinct differences between grief like hers, and grief like mine. Hers was open and raw, but there was something stunning about it. She seemed so happy to be talking about them, even though the back of her hands were wiping her eyes more often than not. Mine, Deacon's, and our father's grief, if he had a soul, was hidden, volatile, and angry.

It seemed so obvious to me at that moment I almost laughed. The solution had never been Tripp's body against mine, banishing any thoughts of my mother from my mind to give it solace. The solution had never been to somehow cosmically make it up to her by making that mean something. It was by seeing her, all of her, the way none of us seemed to in her life. She was very, very dead to Deacon and my father. But as I watched Noa tip her head back and laugh as she recounted the way her father was a terrible cook, the way she gave her parents life with every word she spoke, I realized she didn't have to be dead to me. I could breathe life back into her.

CHAPTER NINETEEN

Turning the key in my door, I shouldered into my foyer. My headphones were still shoved firmly into my ears, blasting punk music that was way too loud, but I liked it because I couldn't even hear my own thoughts. I was probably going to damage my eardrums, but I couldn't bring myself to care about that and changing my running music to something quieter wasn't on the table. I kicked the door behind me and pushed off my shoes before walking into my living room. I tossed the plastic bracelet for my keys that I kept around my wrist when I was running onto the sideboard pushed against the wall.

I pulled out my headphones, finally looking up and into the living room, clutching my hand to my heart. David was sitting on my couch, the picture of casual elegance, as if he fucking lived here. He was leaning back, foot resting on the opposite knee, and one arm swung wide across the back of the couch. His eyes flicked to me in acknowledgment before casually raising a beer to his lips and looking back to whatever ESPN replay he had on my TV.

As always, my heart dropped into my stomach, and I studied him for a moment longer before asking what the hell he was doing in my house. His hair was pushed back off his face and looked windswept, somehow. The sleeves of his charcoal quarter zip

Patagonia sweater were pushed up on either side, revealing his muscular forearms. I would die for those arms.

"You scared the shit out of me. What are you doing here? How did you get into my house?" My hand was still on my chest, and I could feel my heart hammering rapidly. David Kennedy was in my home. I would be a liar if I said I didn't often dream about us sharing this perfect, poorly laid out, creaky-floored old townhouse together. "And is that my beer? Did you just make yourself at home here, like some kind of predator?"

David smiled lazily at me, and he brought the bottle to his lips again. "Deacon gave me his key."

"That's still trespassing," I hissed, stomping by him and into the kitchen to grab water. Fucking Deacon. "Deacon needs to learn that just because he was given a golden key to life upon birth, it doesn't mean other people's keys are his to give out at will."

David stood and trailed behind me into the kitchen. "Well, I'm actually here about your brother."

"Shouldn't you be at work?" I tapped an invisible watch on my wrist. "Tick tock, David. I'm losing dollars here."

I felt David's warmth behind me, and I could almost picture his throat as I heard him swallow another sip of beer. "Last I heard you weren't even living on the Winchester dime, Charlie. So, it's not your money I'm wasting here in this kitchen."

I stopped in front of my fridge, my arm extended and ready to pull open the door. My mouth opened and closed, but David spoke again.

"Deacon told me you haven't taken a dime from your father or from your Winchester trust since you got back. All that money just sitting there. It took me a second to realize. I knew you had sold your townhouse in Chicago, but that wouldn't have been that much money. Not enough to pay for this place. And then I—"

Cutting him off, I opened the fridge at last and pulled out a bottle of water. I closed the door and turned, pushing my back against it. I took a small sip of water before I spoke, "It's my mother's money. What she left to me. My inheritance. And the ten million dollar trust her father left me that I got when I turned twenty-five."

David studied me for a moment, eyes creased before placing his hands on either side of my head, "Go shower and get dressed. Let's get out of here for the day, Charlie."

I pushed back into the fridge, afraid to inhale, afraid to breathe. David was so close to me—and I knew exactly what he would smell like. If I inhaled, I would smell the ocean, I would smell warmth, the way his skin always felt hot against mine. My shoulders brushed his palms as he caged me in, and I raised my eyes, meeting his. The amber flecks in his eyes were more pronounced, and before I could swear they were sparkling for me, I picked a point just over the edge of his broad shoulder and stared at it resolutely.

"How do you know I'm not teaching this afternoon?" I breathed, still looking at the wall beyond him.

"You don't teach on Mondays," David answered, and I closed my eyes briefly.

His breath whispered past my cheek. His lips were right there. He was right there. "I need your help this afternoon. Deacon asked me to plan his bachelor party sooner rather than later."

A laugh slipped from my lips, and I pushed my head back against the fridge even farther. "They don't even have a date set yet.

Doesn't he know the bachelor party typically happens right before the wedding?"

David laughed, bringing his head forward, so close our foreheads almost touched. A wave of his hair would have touched me had it not been for the hat on his head. "I think he wants two. One to celebrate his engagement now, and one to send him off into marriage later."

"Of course he does." I rolled my eyes, finally landing on David again.

There he was, as perfect as ever. I wanted to ask him why he was so close to me, why he was all around me. But I didn't. I just stared at him, tracing the lines around his eyes and the line of stubble on his jaw. My hand twitched at my side, and my fingers must have been desperate to touch him. "Anything for Deacon. If you'll uncage me, I'll go shower."

David pushed back suddenly, clearing his throat. He snatched his hat off his head, running his hands through his hair before trapping all the waves underneath it again. "I'll be waiting down here."

The air felt thicker than it had before, when it was just us existing without the rest of the world. It was like he had temporarily forgotten there was a Victoria, that there had been a Tripp. It was just me and him for a brief moment in my kitchen. I smoothed out my ponytail, sweat having slicked it back against my head. "I would say help yourself to a drink, but you've already done that."

David arched an eyebrow, grinning at me, the awkwardness seemingly forgotten. He turned and bent down to open the bar fridge that was built into the waterfall island that took up most of the kitchen. I wanted to study him, the taper of his body, for a moment longer, but I cleared my throat and forced myself to turn around and walk up the stairs. I heard the telltale crack of the bottlecap and tried not to think about the column of his throat, the way David's full lips would look pressed to the lip of the bottle. I tried not to think about David Kennedy, casually sitting on my couch, taking up all the space in my home in the best way possible.

I tried not to imagine what it would be like if this was our home; photos of our lives, photos of David, dripping saltwater and wavy hair plastered to his face dotting the walls. I tried not to imagine those things, but he was David Kennedy, and I was me.

As I wiped the steam from my bathroom mirror after my shower, face bare, straight hair soaking wet and tucked behind my ears, I looked at my green eyes and took note of the fact that at the thought of him, they were sparkling. They were light and alive, sort of like my brother's always were. Any life with David Kennedy in it was better than one without.

The branches of the trees were heavy, boughed with the green leaves and buds that were just opening in the early summer sunshine. Just like they had been this morning when I was at the park for my run.

I hesitated when the town car pulled up, to the same entrance I ran through every morning. My lips pulled back, about to suggest we just go back to my house, unsure if he really wanted to be in public with me. But David stood, hand extended on the sidewalk to help me out of the car. He didn't have a care in the world, smiling politely at everyone as we fell into step beside one another.

There were people scattered across the park, running by us, walking, sitting on wooden benches worn with age, or lying on the grass, limbs stretched out and loose in the sunshine. We walked in silence, and I studied him from behind my sunglasses. As easy as breathing, I could picture him back in Chicago, exactly like this. Less lines around the eyes, but the same carefree, easygoing David Kennedy.

"Haven't spent enough time in Central Park since moving?" I asked, tipping my head to try to catch the way the sunlight fell through the treetops just so to illuminate his features.

"I wanted to see where you run every day. What you might be running from." David's voice was uncharacteristically quiet, and his eyes were hidden behind his sunglasses.

My lips parted, and I was going to tell him the truth. That I was running from all sorts of things. From myself, from my father, from my mother, from him. But he tipped his chin toward a coffee cart that doubled as a boat rental for the lake. Those overpriced, overworn, row boats tourists could take.

"You ever been on one of those?" David cocked his head, grinning at me now. It was probably the sunshine, warm against my skin and all the natural serotonin that gave a person, but it felt like that entire ball of fire that hung in the sky was sitting inside my chest when he looked at me like that.

"Do you think I've ever been on a tourist trap rowboat?" I asked, arching an eyebrow and trying to pretend there wasn't a supernova exploding inside me.

"Not a chance, billion dollar baby." David laughed and tipped his chin again in invitation.

I wrapped my arms around myself and nodded.

This is what my life could have been like with him. Doing ordinary things every day. But they would have all been heart-stoppingly beautiful. Because that's what it looked like, watching David smile politely while he ordered us coffee, bought us an hour on one of those stupid boats, him holding his hand out for mine while I stepped into it, careful to make sure I didn't tip it over, clutching the already sweating plastic cup of iced coffee and him dropping effortlessly into the boat beside me, shoulder muscles flexing as he pushed us off the shore. In theory, they were all simple, mundane acts. Boring even. But they were perfect, because they were his.

We floated aimlessly for a moment in the lake, saying nothing and taking small sips of coffee. I don't think either of us knew what to do now that we were both metaphorically, and literally, adrift.

He looked up at me, his hands wrapped around his now perspiring coffee and cleared his throat. David shook his head, gripping his jaw before breathing out again. "I didn't think this through. I don't know how to do this," he said, letting out a small laugh, pulling on the ends of his hair before running a hand through the waves and pushing them down with his hat.

The oars of the boat were bowed in front of him, secured in the rusting iron holders on either side of the tiny boat. Our knees were almost touching.

"Me neither," I confessed, looking around at the other boats floating around us; people with their heads tipped back, chins pointed toward the sunshine, or mouths open in laughter. I turned back to David, and if I couldn't have him, I wished with all my heart for a life where we could exist around one another like that. "What did we do before we had sex?"

"Before we fell in love?" David's voice cut across my skin.

My breath caught, and I wanted to tip over this stupid boat. To just disappear under the water. I meant it as a joke. Even when it was just sex, it had never been just sex. Not with him. I let myself look at him, sunglasses folded on the front of his sweater, green eyes meeting his beautiful honey ones, and I could feel the ghost of his hands on my waist; his warm breath on my neck, David's lips against my ear whispering how beautiful I was, how good I felt while we stole moments in the WH offices.

But it wasn't just our bodies moving together, how perfectly they fit. I could hear the peals of our laughter when we played tag around my house in Chicago; it was the way he hooked his feet with mine under the conference table, the way we would lay together and fall into easy, comfortable conversation. It was the way David became my home, more than Chicago, more than being a Winchester was.

"We could try making fun of Deacon?" David continued, his easy grin breaking whatever was stretching taut between us. I watched him empty the rest of his coffee, nestling the plastic cup at his feet before he grabbed the oars of the boat and started rowing again. "That always works."

"Why are you nice to me?" I asked, the straw pressed against my parted lips.

His muscles flexed and strained under his sweater as he rowed, steering us toward the Bow Bridge. I didn't care where we were going. I would stay out on this little lake with him forever.

David looked at me for a moment, pausing his rowing, but his hands never let go of the oars. His mouth pulled down in a frown. "Because someone needs to be. I don't think you're very nice to yourself. You're not—you're not the villain in my story, Charlie."

I wanted to tell him that I should be, that I was the villain. In his story, in Tripp's story, in my own story. Instead, I asked him a question I didn't really want the answer to. "What's it like with Victoria?"

"Easy. Simple. Familiar," David said, shrugging like there was nothing more to it as he rolled his shoulders back to start rowing again. And maybe there wasn't, and that was okay for some people. But to me, David deserved an indescribable kind of love.

"Is that a good thing?" I asked quietly.

I focused on the steady slice of the oar through the water, ears straining to drown out the bubbles of the lake, the sound of laughter from couples in their boats around us. I had no right to ask, but I did anyway.

"What's it like with Tripp?" David deadpanned.

I raised my eyebrows, choking on the sip of coffee I had taken. "I guess I had that one coming. I'm not with Tripp."

"That's not how it looked the other day at the office," he said coolly, one pullback of his shoulders, his honey eyes sweeping over me and landing on a tangle of reeds to the left of us.

I could hear what he said in the office echoing endlessly in my head, the image of him and Victoria together stamped itself on the back of my eyelids, and even though we were in a cramped boat on a tiny lake in Central Park, we were so far from one another. From the people we used to be. The people who would have conceivably been together forever.

David exhaled, pausing to rub his jaw before looking at me, features all falling in on themselves. "I'm sorry. I'm not trying to start anything. I just mean that it's obvious you two have...something. I don't really know how I didn't notice the chemistry between you two before. It's palpable."

"You and I have chemistry," I whispered lamely.

I wasn't even sure why I said it, because it didn't fucking matter. But I never wanted David to devalue what we were, what we had, and he was looking at me at that moment like he was suddenly in on a terrible secret. "I meant what I said back then David. It had nothing to do with you. It was about me."

David looked away again, and I savored the view of his jawline, the column of his neck leading down to the breadth of his shoulders. He stared out at the lake a moment longer before turning back and schooling his features, suddenly looking like those words and what I did weren't hanging between us. Wouldn't always be hanging between us. "Tell me about school, your research."

Part of me wanted to press more, to let a thousand reassurances spill from my lips, to get on my knees before him in this fucking boat, but the moment had passed, and it wouldn't change anything at this point. Instead, I eyed him shrewdly, skepticism lacing my words. "You really want to know? No one ever wants to know about my work."

He nodded, laughter slipping from his lips.

"You're laughing at me," I narrowed my eyes, pulling my lips into an overexaggerated pout.

"I'm not laughing at you, billion dollar baby." David paused before dropping his voice so low I couldn't be sure I heard him right. "I think you're wonderful."

If I was a stronger person, I would have told him not to say things like that. Not to tell me I'm wonderful and tell my father about his unyielding, unending loyalty to me. How I would always be the love of his life. But I wasn't a strong person, and I felt myself smiling at him, my heart beating against my ribcage in happiness and desperation; I tucked those words away with all the other words of love and admiration David had ever given me, and I let my entire being curl up around them and hold them close.

I cleared my throat, setting my almost empty coffee down beside his. "So, my Ph.D. is kind of unique. The Sustainable Development program is small, but it's based in the International Relations program, so there's quite a bit of crossover with those students. Part of the reason I chose Columbia was because there is an entire field of research and work that's already been established in sustainable investing. That's what my work will focus on. And you know, I think it's what I was trying to go for with the Charitable Givings portfolio at WH, but looking back, that wasn't a sustainable model for so many reasons...I was reading this fascinating paper the other day about..." I trailed off, noticing the way David had stopped rowing, the way he was leaning forward, forearms propped up on either oar, tanned skin glowing.

The faint dusting of golden hair was even more evident in the sunlight. His fingers gripped the oars loosely, but he didn't look bored. He was looking at me like I was the most fascinating thing he had ever seen. His eyes were dancing, the honey flecks glinting at me, and his lips pulled to the side in a grin.

I imagined this was what Taylor looked like when someone's diseased body was open on her table. My heart continued to hammer against my ribcage as it always did, begging to be let loose and go back home. I closed my eyes briefly, trying to remember the bad things about David, the way Taylor instructed me to. To remember he was becoming "quite a little liar" in her words, and that I could say fuck them all. My eyelids popped open, and he was still looking at me.

"I'm sorry, am I boring you?"

David shook his head, eyes never leaving mine. "Not at all," he said earnestly.

"But my supervisor accepted this amazing opportunity at Oxford, so...I'm not really sure what's next for me at school now," I said, jumping to the next train of thought. I couldn't remember where I left off.

"So, she's leaving? Who's going to supervise you now?"

I laughed loudly, the irony of it all pressing around me again. I looked at my knees, knocking them together and watching the frays of my denim shorts swish back and forth against my thighs. "I don't know, and I guess that's the thing right? It doesn't really matter. She asked me if I would be interested in going with her, but it seems...too convenient. Little rich girl can just go wherever she wants whenever she wants, even after she's made a five-year-plus commitment to one institution. Silver spoon and all that. I want my time, my work to matter, and I want it to matter here."

"Why wouldn't you go to Oxford, Charlie?" David asked quietly, enough strain in his voice that I raised my gaze to see the sadness that was scrawled across his features. "The things you do, the things you like, they matter. Silver spoon or not. It's not nothing—it's important to you."

"Don't you think that would constitute running again?" I breathed.

His opinion mattered more to me than almost anyone's. I wondered if there would ever be a time when I didn't care what David Kennedy thought.

"It's not running if it's your choice, Charlie," he answered, words bare and honest. "You think you don't deserve any opportunities that come your way. And I understand that, maybe not quite at the same level, but I get it—and I promise you it's not true."

My eyes prickled, and my heart reached out to grab that sentiment, those words, and placed them in the special spot I had for all of David's love inside me. I shook my head, straight hair fanning around me. Placing my hands flat against my legs, I forced a smile and a change of subject, lest my heart finally escape from my chest and ruin David's clothing with the blood splatter. "Let's talk about bachelor party number one. What does he want?"

David tipped his head back, the waves of his hair gently falling backward against his ears. His lips pulled into that flawless grin, and I resisted the urge to lean across the boat and trace them with the pad of my thumb.

"So, for event number one, he's asked for the entire floor of a hotel in Monaco during the Grand Prix. Originally, it was the entire hotel, but I let him know that probably wouldn't be feasible on such short notice. Now, we haven't gotten to event number two, yet, but knowing Deacon, I can only imagine we will be expected to top it."

I rolled my eyes, and my shoulders started to shake with laughter. Fucking Deacon. Soon, David was laughing, too, and it was easy to pretend that we were just two people laughing at the absurd behavior of someone we both knew and cherished. It turned out Deacon was as good a neutral ground as any, and that maybe there was really a way forward for an okay life with David Kennedy in it.

CHAPTER TWENTY

I wrapped my arms around myself as I walked side-by-side with David. The evening air was a bit crisper than usual for this time of year, and it made goosebumps rise on my exposed shoulders. I watched David from the corner of my eye, noting the way his hands were shoved firmly in his pockets, and he never strayed too close to me on the sidewalk. In his defense, there was probably nothing worse than our skin touching. Maybe it set him alight the same way it did me. But he was the one who suggested we take the subway, his tone had almost been goading.

"Billion dollar baby could never take the subway," he whispered when I pulled my phone out to call a town car.

And now we were walking in silence toward my townhouse. He hadn't really said anything when he hopped on the subway line and walked out onto the street with me, seemingly content to walk me home. The streets were surprisingly quiet for a Manhattan evening. The stoop of my townhouse loomed ahead, and I stopped short of it. David came to a halt beside me, his hands still firmly in his pockets. I shrugged my shoulders toward the steps.

"Do you want to come in? Have a drink? I'll show you the house. I'm assuming you've only seen the living room after your little break and enter." I leaned forward playfully, my arms still wrapped around myself. "I own it. Really expanding my real estate portfolio out here."

David flipped his hat off expertly, running a hand through his hair. His mouth pulled back, and it looked like he was chewing on the inside of his cheek, debating. "As tempting as it is to pass judgment on your real estate portfolio, I don't think it's a good idea."

"Oh, come on David." I laughed, leaning forward and smacking the back of his forearm. "What am I going to do? Seduce you? I've tried that, and it hasn't worked."

"Charlie..." he started, looking at me ruefully before shaking his head again.

I held up both my hands in surrender, disappointment curdling in my chest. I wasn't inviting him in for any ulterior motive. I just didn't want the night to end. Time with David felt like a precious commodity.

"Your choice. But, I do have some of Steven Winchester's best wine here. That I may or may not have stolen from his cellar when I was home for the engagement party."

My favorite smile fell into place, and David jerked his head toward the stairs. "Who am I to turn down Winchester wine? Let's go, show me your investment, billion dollar baby."

I smiled at him once more, turning and starting up the steps. I could feel David behind me, and as the lock clicked on the front door, I looked over my shoulder at him, extending a palm. "I'd like my key back, please. I'm restricting Deacon's privileges, because he apparently thinks it's his to give out at will."

David grinned at me, fishing in his pocket and producing the key. He dropped it in my palm but not before I felt the brush of his fingertips against my sensitive skin. A small shudder ran through me, and I wanted to close my eyes at the contact. I rolled my neck, trying to banish the feelings and made my way into the kitchen.

"You've already made yourself acquainted with my living room and apparently my kitchen, seeing as you helped yourself to beer when you were here earlier. But feel free to start opening my drawers in case you missed anything." I dropped my bag onto the floor and called over my shoulder, "White or red?"

"Either's fine, but I know you prefer white," David answered, and I dropped down, pulling open the wine fridge and peering in at the contents.

He was right. I did prefer white, much to my father's chagrin. He thought red was more dignified and indicated a more refined palate. That was probably why he never noticed when I pilfered the expensive bottles from his cellar whenever I was in Chicago.

"You remembered," I murmured more for myself, selecting a bottle at random.

It turned out to be a bottle of sauvignon blanc from Screaming Eagle in Napa Valley. I had no idea why my father would have had this. He didn't like American wine, let alone an almost seven thousand dollar bottle of white.

David was leaning against the island, his hands still planted in his pockets. He tipped his head and raised his eyebrows, and I resisted the urge to lunge forward and run my fingers through the waves curling against the nape of his neck under his hat. "White wine and vodka soda. I remember."

"How are your parents? Your brothers and sister?" I questioned as I began maneuvering the corkscrew into the bottle.

I knew David had told a different story about what happened between us to most people, but there was a part of me that wondered if he had kept the truth from them, too. His mother had practically warned him to stay away from me at his father's sixtieth birthday party. It was like she looked at me and could see everything I had done laid bare, all the ways I didn't deserve her son even then.

David pushed off the island, unhooking two wine glasses from where they hung under the black shelves.

"Parents are good. My dad's looking to retire soon and have Jackson officially take over the practice. Ryan's there now, too, and Sophie's at Yale Law now. She'll probably end up there, too."

"Have you been home much?" I looked up, filling both our glasses above the acceptable level.

"A few times. Victoria works mainly out of Wilmington, but she traveled so much for work, she came here most of the time. It made sense for her to move." David took the wine glass from me, swirling it out of habit before taking a sip. "Thank you for the wine."

Before I could stop myself, the questions that were burning a hole in my throat, pounding away at my brain at all hours of the day since I saw them together, slipped out.

"It must be pretty serious. She's moving to New York. Are you planning on sharing all that extra closet space in your big fancy Manhattan apartment?" I blinked rapidly, stupidly, at him, hanging on tenterhooks waiting for the answer at the same time as wanting to cover my ears so I wouldn't be able to hear it.

"We talked about it. But she wants to buy an investment property in—" the rest of David's words were cut off by a loud ring from his pocket.

I watched him fish his phone from his back pocket, a crease forming between his eyebrows when he saw whatever was on the screen. "Just a moment, I have to take this."

Nodding, I leaned against the doorway, waiting for him. I pulled out my own phone and began mindlessly flipping through emails. I had texts from Taylor to return and another dinner invitation from my father, via Damien. Sent to Deacon and me via Outlook. Fucking Microsoft. He wanted us to have dinner with him at The Carlyle later that week. No doubt there was some ulterior motive or business discussion to be had. Why would Steven Winchester deign to spend voluntary time with his two children?

David had walked into the hallway, but his voice carried. A sour taste settled in my mouth that even seven-thousand-dollar wine couldn't fix.

"Hey, babe. Sorry I missed your text earlier. Yeah, I was out." I narrowed my eyes, knowing if I listened any longer to David's terms of endearment for Victoria, I was going to end up feeling significantly worse and have a David Kennedy-esque relapse up on my terrace, but I didn't move. "Oh, I'm just at the new offices with Deacon."

The lie seemingly fell from his lips easily, and I wasn't sure what disturbed me more. The fact that I was now something he needed to lie about, or that David was suddenly turning into a person who lied. Maybe there was only one person to blame for that; he didn't lie before I railroaded his life. Blood pounded in my ears, and I couldn't concentrate enough on the rest of the conversation to hear what other truths he conveniently left out.

David rounded the corner and gestured with his wine glass to the staircase behind me. I noticed his eyes were dark. "You going to continue my tour, Charles?"

"You're turning into quite the little liar, aren't you?" I said, my voice low. I gazed at him sharply. "Why would you lie to her?"

He exhaled loudly through his nose before taking an overlarge sip of his wine. David walked toward me, setting his glass on the island. I stayed silent, arching a brow as he rubbed the back of his neck.

"Charlie, come on...I'm in your house, drinking wine with you. We spent the day together."

"I thought we were friends?" I offered with a casual shrug.

I took another sip of my wine, eyes never leaving his.

"We are," David said earnestly, taking another step toward me.

I felt myself lean back farther against the doorway. He stopped, brown eyes surveying me, like he noted the change in my posture. "I don't think Victoria would be comfortable with the amount of time I spent with you today. I thought it was easier to keep it to myself. I'm trying to figure out how to have you in my life, Charlie. How this can work."

"Oh!" I threw up my hands. My voice dripped with sarcasm as I continued, "Of course. It'll be our little secret, because you want to have your cake and eat it, too. Instead of wondering why you're suddenly spinning this elaborate web of lies to spare both Victoria and me from whatever the fuck it is you're feeling, this is the solution? I'll be your secret friend. No. No thank you."

"That's not—" David started but fell silent when I held up my palm.

I drained my wine and pushed off the doorway, slamming the glass down with a little too much force. "You know what I like about Tripp, David? He doesn't ever pretend to be anything else than who he is. Friends don't need to lie about being friends. I know I hurt you. I know what I did was unspeakable, unforgivable. You've made that clear, and I'm trying to move on. And I am sorry, I will be sorry forever. But you need to make up your mind. I heard you in the office the other day, you know. I'm the love of your life, and your loyalty is always to me, you say you forgive me, but you just can't forget what I did? This feels like an awful lot more than simply forgetting. Admit it. You're *choosing* not to forgive me now. And I *saw* you with her at Soho House. And somehow, I was still stupid enough to think that maybe that didn't change anything. So thank you for this moment of clarity, because I don't want to be friends with someone who thinks I'm something to lie about. Who's ashamed of me and the way I make them feel. I might not be a good person, but I deserve more than that at the very least. Victoria deserves more than this. I think it's time for you to go."

David looked at me, his eyes trailing my face and tracking the tension in my posture. He shook his head, and I noticed his hands twitch, like he was going to reach for me but changed his mind. "You weren't supposed to hear that, and you definitely weren't supposed to see *that*. I'm not ashamed of you, Charlie. I couldn't be ashamed of you, even if I tried. You confuse me. The way I still feel about you confuses me—one minute I have forgiven you and the next it's like it just fucking happened! Things would be so different if you had just told me what happened when he first kissed you!"

"Well I didn't! That fuck up? That person that did abominable things? That's not who you wanted, who you were in love with. I didn't want to give you a reason to leave me, too. To show you the ugliest parts of me. You deserved better. And now things are the way they are."

I could see David's heart crack in his eyes. Those sparkles—those stars that lived in those eyes—I wondered if that's what it looked like when one died. Exploded into dust and never to be together with the atoms that once made it up ever again.

His lips parted, and he started to shake his head. "I would have understood—"

"Would you have?" I asked pointedly, words dripping with bitterness. "You can bill me for whatever it is you decide to book for Deacon's bachelor party. Just let me know the dates as soon as you can. I'll need to rearrange my schedule. Most Ph.D. candidates don't jet off to Monaco on a moment's fucking notice."

The corners of my eyes started to edge in, burning and blurring with unshed tears, but I stood there resolute in my anger at David. I knew, not even particularly deep down, that there was more to this, and my anger was most likely misplaced. It belonged only with myself and the hole I had dug, but through my tears I raised my hand and pointed toward the door again. "Out."

I could see David run his hand down his face through my blurred eyes, but instead of turning around like I had ordered him to, his long legs closed the space between us quickly, and he grabbed my outstretched hand between his. My spine stiffened as David's arms wound around me, and I felt his chin press into the crown of my head. His chest was warm, and my tears threatened to spill over. I wanted to stay here, to close my eyes and inhale him, to forget everything. All the reasons I didn't deserve him back then, and all the reasons I didn't deserve him now.

"I'm sorry," David murmured, his voice cracked and laced with hurt.

"Me too," I pushed back from his chest, wiping my eyes with the back of my hand.

"Please go, David. I don't think we can be this kind of friends. Everyone involved deserves better."

I watched David walk away after a whispered goodbye, and I tossed the rest of his wine down the sink in some sort of childlike act before pouring myself another glass and making for the garden-level terrace. All my memories of what a shitty person I had been, that I was still proving to be, could stay up on the rooftop terrace along with David's lies.

Tonight, I wanted to sit outside with my father's expensive wine and listen to the sounds of the city. For some reason, I grabbed a worn leather photo album that was sitting sideways on my office bookshelf. There were photos of my mother there. Maybe tonight, I would drink my father's expensive wine, listen to the sounds of Manhattan, and look at photos of the family I used to have.

CHAPTER TWENTY-ONE

Deacon was sitting beside me in the back of the town car, his foot propped up on his knee to reveal a charcoal pair of Falke Merino Silk socks underneath the leg of his navy suit pants. The rest of the ridiculous socks were hidden in a pair of cognac-colored burnished leather Tom Ford Oxfords. He was jiggling his foot non-stop, one arm slung over the back of the headrest, flipping through emails.

"Why can't Noa come to dinner? She's always a good buffer with Steven," I asked, my voice bordering on a whine.

"She left for Japan this afternoon. She's shooting there for the next week. I'm sorry my fiancée will be unable to provide her *buffer* services for you this evening." Deacon rolled his eyes before looking over at me. "Can you and Dad just bury the hatchet over whatever this is?"

Indignation flared across my cheeks and my lips pulled back. "Whatever this is? Deacon, he fired me and tried to pretend he didn't!"

Deacon scoffed and tossed his phone in the seat beside him. His green eyes were narrowed at me. "Charlie, you decimated his entire leadership team at a very public event in the span of ten fucking minutes. You're lucky all he did was fake fire you."

"Be that as it may, all that it did was serve to remind me of the fact that he doesn't love me. He doesn't love anyone," I muttered, bitterly aware I sounded like a very annoying broken record.

"Has it ever occurred to you that you're the one who doesn't love yourself?" Deacon asked, voice suddenly tender.

I jerked back at his words, anything I wanted to say in response lost when the driver announced we had arrived. Deacon was still staring at me, his eyes darker than usual. He reached out and squeezed my hand before leaning across me and opening the door. Fortunately, with the absence of Noa, there were no photographers waiting outside the golden doors of The Carlyle. There was just a doorman wearing an impeccably pressed suit, who tipped his head at us in a sort of deferential bow that disturbed me and stepped aside for us to enter.

"Thank you." I looked back at him with a smile as Deacon and I stepped through the door.

I smoothed down the front of my black Badgley Mischka Pinwheel Dress. Deacon was quite literally sauntering to the concierge, hands in the pockets of his custom suit pants. He looked a second away from whistling a tune about how wonderful his life was.

He knocked once on the desk in greeting, leaning forward on his elbows and smiling at the woman behind the concierge. A wisp of hair fell forward onto his face, and with a casual sweep of his hand, it was back in place; the roguish grin never faltering.

"Winchester. We're meeting our father for dinner. He's staying in the Empire Suite," Deacon offered in a smooth voice that had me pointedly rolling my eyes behind him.

"Ah, yes. Mr. Winchester decided to dine..." she smiled, simpering at Deacon and quickly flipping her eyes to the monitor in front of her, "at the Champagne Bar at Dowling's. If you'll follow me."

She gestured with a perfectly manicured hand to her right. Folding her hands behind her back, her heels clicked across the polished floor.

The Carlyle was my father's preferred hotel in Manhattan and had been for as long as I could remember. It was meant to be emblematic of a New York City gone by. It was built in 1930 and reminded me of most of the buildings in Chicago, leaking wealth around every corner with loud, mid-century finishings. It was designed by some famous architectural firm I could never remember. Steven Winchester preferred the Empire Suite, one step down from the Presidential Suite. I think that had more to do with the person who designed it, whose name I also could never remember, and the panoramic views of Central Park. He loved being near nature. It was one of the reasons he never moved into the city and stayed in that giant, empty house in Lake Forest. He probably felt like the true Master of the Universe up there, lording his wealth over all the plebians of Manhattan who didn't occupy the 28th and 29th floor of a New York City landmark hotel.

Dowling's was a newly imagined fine dining option at The Carlyle, boasting a new menu that was a luxurious take on traditional American fare. It was decorated in the same way as the rest of the hotel—understated and somehow unique, while remaining the pinnacle of opulence. Our father was seated at a winged back, green velvet chair. His suit jacket was unbuttoned, as was the neck of his crisp, white shirt. He wasn't looking at us, and in true Steven fashion, didn't really look like a man eager to see his children. His eyebrows were creased, and he was staring resolutely at his phone.

The concierge attendant stopped in front of the table where our father was holding court in the center of the room. I arched an eyebrow as he swirled an extravagantly detailed crystal champagne coupe before bringing it to his lips. He never even looked up from his phone, typing a response to an email with his left thumb.

"Mr. Winchester, your guests have arrived."

I pinched the back of Deacon's elbow, biting down on my own lips to avoid responding. The way she presented us, as his guests, as opposed to I don't know, his own flesh and blood, caused my stomach to curdle. Was the great Steven Winchester so high up above us into the stratosphere that something like family, or his children, would make him seem normal?

"Ah, thank you." He offered her an obligatory smile, standing and brushing off the front of his shirt in a smooth motion.

He held out his hand for Deacon, blue eyes giving nothing away. I watched while they shook hands before Deacon clapped him on the shoulder. My father stepped to the side of the table, placing one of his hands on my bare shoulder and briefly kissing my cheek.

"You look wonderful as always, Charlie."

"Thank you. It's nice to see you," I offered in return, quickly pecking his cheek before folding myself into the velvet chair my brother had pulled out for me.

Deacon kicked me under the table, and when I whipped my head in his direction, he widened his eyes at me and jerked his head toward our father. My delivery probably left something to be desired; I started reverting to robotic-like conversation with our father after I left WH. I knew Deacon wanted me to try harder, to understand that our father was a complicated man like I used to, and to take the offerings he provided. I cleared my throat and turned back to our father, who was looking at his phone again, before he placed it face down on the table.

"How is everything going?" I asked, hoping I was appropriately feigning enough interest to satisfy Deacon.

He didn't kick me again, so it must have been passable. Or, he didn't want to risk scuffing his Tom Fords.

Steven raised his hand, gesturing above our heads at someone behind us before looking back at me. "That's why I've asked you to have dinner. We have some things to discuss."

"God forbid we just have a normal family dinner," I muttered under my breath, snatching the bright yellow napkin off the table and making a show of folding it properly across my lap.

But apparently, I wasn't quiet enough when I spoke.

Steven's gaze narrowed in on me, his eyes bordering on unfriendly. "And would you be interested in attending a family dinner if I invited you to one, Charlie?"

Deacon coughed loudly as I tried to muster up an intelligible response.

Steven raised a singular eyebrow that I noticed was peppered with gray now before answering his own rhetorical question, "I thought not."

I was saved from responding when a server materialized at the table, holding up a golden tray with two identical glasses to the one my father was drinking from. I listened and nodded along as he explained they had a rotating menu in the champagne bar, that included specific pairings with various appetizers and hor d'oeuvres. He placed the glasses in front of Deacon and me, with a promise to be back momentarily with our first food pairing.

Deacon raised his glass in an offer of cheers, his usual smile in place. I felt my lips curling up but pulled them back into a tight smile and raised my glass to meet my father's and brother's. I took a small sip before setting the glass down. I kept my fingers loosely around the stem, imagining I would need another drink very soon. If Steven Winchester said he had things to discuss, it usually didn't mean anything good for me.

"What's so important you can't send us an email?" Deacon asked, his voice chiding our father in a way I would never dream of doing anymore.

I glanced over at Deacon, and he reached his hand down and gently squeezed my wrist. I knew the comment was for me. Deacon never seemed to care that he rarely communicated with us like a normal parent. All of those innate senses humans were supposed to have, that desire for a family, to be loved unconditionally, seemed to shut off in him with regard to Steven the moment our mother died.

Either the art of subtlety was lost on him, or he didn't care enough to reprimand Deacon for what I assumed he would perceive as a slight. Steven launched into what sounded oddly reminiscent of a business pitch.

"As we are currently seeking to solidify a foothold in the market here, I think it's well worth our time as a family, and as an organization, to establish ourselves as patrons of the city, as well. I've consulted with Rebecca, and we've decided it's best to officially launch Winchester Holdings New York with a charity gala. As a family, we will each select a charity or organization to donate to. The organization can be one of your choosing, but I would prefer they have deep roots in Manhattan. The money will come individually from each of your trusts and mine from my personal holdings to demonstrate our commitment together and individually to the city."

"Why does it have to come from my trust?" Deacon blurted, a sour expression pulling at his features. "The company covers these things."

My mouth gaped open in disbelief and disgust, as I turned my head slowly toward Deacon. "Your trust has more than 100 million dollars in it, Deacon. Surely you can spare a few million to help the people of New York."

"You know, you must be lonely all by yourself in that big townhouse and all the way up on that high horse, Charles. Maybe you should get a cat," Deacon said contemptuously, flashing me a smile that was mostly teeth.

"I'm not getting a fucking cat." I rolled my eyes, bringing the glass to my lips and taking a more generous mouthful this time. "But maybe I will donate to a cat shelter. There must be hundreds and thousands of disenfranchised cats in Manhattan. Or, you know what, a rat sanctuary! The rats could use some of our money, because God knows we could never use it all."

Deacon's eyes glinted at me, and a smirk formed on his face. But before he could answer, two loud finger snaps sounded from across the table. We both turned, Steven was sitting there with a look of poorly veiled irritation on his face. He raised his glass, punctuating his next words by pointing at Deacon.

"Enough. Both of you. You will take the money from your trust. End of story. And you," he moved on to pointing at me with the glass, "will not be donating to a cat shelter. Pick something else. That's final."

Laughter rose in my throat, and I clapped my hand to my mouth to stifle it. This was so stupid. So endlessly stupid and seemingly normal for two siblings to be fighting like this. I looked over at Deacon again, and his features had softened to reveal the lines that formed around his eyes and his mouth when he laughed.

"I really hope someone overheard that," I said dryly, taking another sip of champagne. "Imagine the headline? Winchester Family feud over too much money and rat sanctuaries."

Deacon choked out a laugh and knocked my shoulder with his hand. He shook his head and ran a hand through his hair, and I noticed he straightened his shoulders, like he was composing himself.

Steven did not look amused. I studied him, scouring his face for any trace or hint of a laugh line or smile. But there was nothing, just impassive features that bordered on displeasure.

My chest felt warm and heavy as disappointment settled against my skin. It was stupid, so stupid, but it was a bizarre human moment amongst our family who rarely had any at all. Preposterous to someone else, but it was so fucking ridiculous that our fights were about who took money from their trust when and who donated to what charity. But Steven's humanity was seemingly good and dead.

"Rebecca is working to coordinate everything for the gala in a few weeks' time. Please let me know the charity or organization of your choosing before then as I would like to extend an invitation to a representative. Speaking of invitations..." he cleared his throat, and my eyes widened when he adjusted his collar. Steven Winchester looked uncomfortable. I could feel Deacon's eyes on me, and the expression he seemed to be wearing matched mine. "I have decided to invite a guest."

"Do you mean a date?" Deacon questioned, his mouth parted.

We both continued to watch our father shift in his seat. He rolled his shoulders back and raised his hand again to whoever he had waiting at his beck and call in the restaurant.

"Yes, a date." He drained the rest of his champagne. "As such, I would also ask that you each bring a date to make it seem less official. Deacon, I'm assuming you will bring Noa if she's in town. If not, I would kindly ask you to escort Taylor. It's well-known she's a family friend and it will appear casual. Charlie, I thought perhaps—"

"She can bring her cat," Deacon deadpanned.

I narrowed my eyebrows, ignoring Deacon, save for an annoyed glance in his direction, and really looked at my father. This felt impossible to reconcile in my head. I wasn't even sure that man had mourned our mother, and if I didn't have memories that suggested otherwise, I would probably suspect now their marriage was a business arrangement. And now he was sitting here and had the audacity to look uncomfortable in front of us. I had tried for years to give life to her, to keep her with us, and he shut me out at every turn. Rarely mentioned her again, and now he wanted to bring a date to a company function? It had been almost a decade, whatever was left of my mother, his wife, was dust and bones. But he didn't even have the decency to lead with something about her? To say anything to acknowledge her existence?

"Who is she?" I asked quietly.

I wasn't sure I wanted to give life to this person. Not when my mother had been robbed of hers by everyone around this table.

"You'll be able to see for yourself in a moment. She's joining us for dinner."

It turned out the woman to wake Steven Winchester's cold, dead heart was an editor he met when Vogue was covering Deacon's engagement party. Her name was Marta something. I was pretty certain I was having a sort of emotional rage blackout during dinner and missed her last name, because I couldn't hear anything but the pounding of my own heart in my ears. I sat there, leaning back in my chair, abandoning propriety with one arm crossed over my chest and my legs crossed at the knees, eyeing her shrewdly.

She couldn't have been more than six or seven years older than Deacon, and if she was forty, she was certainly taking advantage of the wealth of extensive facial treatments available in Manhattan. As my eyes roamed her face, taking in the taut skin and lack of lines or sunspots, I was trying to categorize the work she had done—but then I ran my tongue over my teeth and remembered the sheer cost of having them professionally whitened my entire life. I sunk back in my seat a bit at that point, trying to keep my lip from twitching upward.

Her blonde hair was slicked back, parted in the middle and gathered in a low ponytail, and she looked like she was freshly back from some sort of luxury beach destination. Her blue eyes sparkled, and she kept flashing Steven tiny, coquettish smiles with lips I was certain weren't naturally that pillowy. High cheekbones gave way to an angular face that looked like it belonged somewhere in Europe.

Our mother had looked like us: chocolate hair that couldn't be anything but straight if it tried, the exact same green eyes, and I couldn't recall a single time she had ever been seen with a tan. She always looked like she had a secret, and as it turned out, she ended up having several. Marta looked like an open book, like someone who wore exactly who they were on the outside. I could have probably guessed her zip code correctly, where she summered, where she spent her winters, without even trying.

Deacon had no such reservations about her. He was leaning forward on the table, arms folded and seemingly enraptured by everything Marta had to say. His irritating, billionaire golden boy charm oozed from him all night, and at times, he was even bordering on flirting with her, despite how many times I stomped on his foot under the table with my braided golden Jimmy Choo mule. The playful smile never moved from his face. He was really bringing out his best material, his most charming stories. And soon, he was playing the part of the ever-loving fiancé, busting out his phone and showing her all his favorite pieces of Noa's work.

At one point, she had tried to engage me in conversation and asked me if I was seeing anyone. It was one of the few times I appreciated what being a Winchester and what my father had taught me. I could always come up with a saccharine and socially acceptable answer to any question. Laughing and tipping my head to the side, my hair mirroring the movements of Deacon's, which was flopping around all night, fell over my shoulder like a curtain. I responded by saying we simply didn't have enough time for that conversation, and that she and I would have to have drinks on our own so I could give her the sordid details. I smiled tightly at her as she tipped her head back in what I could only assume was fake laughter before dropping a manicured hand to my father's shoulder.

My father eyed me sharply all evening, like he couldn't quite believe I would just sit there without some sort of outburst or comment. That only further spiraled my rage, because it was like he knew—he knew this would bother me but not Deacon. I had tried to keep our family together when I was too young to be shouldered with that responsibility, and he shut the door on her, on me, each and every time. And now it felt like he poured cement over her coffin, filling her grave all the way to the top so she could never, ever escape.

I said nothing other than polite formalities as the evening drew to a close. I even laughed at the end of the dinner when Marta and Steven decided to excuse themselves for a "nightcap" in his suite. I gave my father the perfunctory Winchester smile when he rose to kiss my cheek goodnight. It might have been my best one yet, because he had the decency to look unnerved.

When Deacon closed the door to the town car, the silence was overwhelming as it was just us, I finally came unglued. The entire walk to the doors of The Carlyle, through the golden revolving entrance, I thought of nothing but the first words I would screech at my brother when we got into the car—that she was clearly a gold digger, and that Steven Winchester was an unfeeling piece of shit. It didn't occur to me until much later that it was probably the longest stretch of time I went without a wistful thought about David Kennedy passing through my mind.

But when the door closed, I didn't scream; I didn't even so much as raise my voice. Something akin to a gasp or a sob rose in my throat, my eyes watered, and then I was crying. I swatted at my face furiously, not caring about my mascara or my lash line or anything our dumb etiquette teacher taught me, until Deacon grabbed my hand.

"Charles, come on. At least try to see the humor in it." His voice was a bizarre mix between soothing, and playful, like he could encourage me to laugh at our father and his much younger girlfriend he was no doubt taking to bed at this moment. "I'm surprised it's taken him this long. It's what men like him do. He's practically a robot. I'm surprised he hasn't cycled through any of Noa's friends. It's what people expect from a widowed billionaire."

I yanked my hand back, scrubbing at my eyes again as an undignified hiccup came from me. I wasn't even sure why I was crying this much. I had learned long ago many ways to compartmentalize my father and his cutting behavior, and how to keep my mother in her box. "Don't you think mom deserved just a bit more than that?" *Maybe we deserved more than that.*

Deacon exhaled, his lips sputtering as he did. Out of the corner of my eye, I watched him lean forward and yank open the mini bar in the back of the car. He expertly uncapped some tiny bottle of scotch and drained it in one tip upward to his lips. "Let's not get into what she does and doesn't deserve."

"You can't be serious! They were married for how long? She was our fucking mother—she is our mother, despite the fact that we all like to pretend otherwise. He could have at least led with a, 'Hey kids, your mother has been gone a long time now, and I think it's time I move on.' But did he? No. He didn't even acknowledge her existence!" I hissed, sitting up straight and grabbing his forearm when he reached for another bottle in the mini fridge.

He shook me off, grabbing two bottles this time—another scotch and one miniature bottle of Grey Goose he lobbed toward me.

"People who do what she did don't deserve to have their existences acknowledged. She left us, Charlie. She willingly left us, left this earth. Left us alone." His voice was sour, bitter and laced with agony I don't think he even realized was there, like it had taken root so deep in him, planting itself in his very fibers that it was just a part of him now, so he thought it had always been this way. But I remembered his grief, his pain. I remembered crying with him, and I remembered drinking it all away. At least we did it together. This—whatever this was—wasn't something we could do together.

"Can you honestly say that's what you believe, Deacon? That she was a willing participant in what happened?" I lowered my voice and extended my hand, hoping he would grab it. He didn't. He flicked open the second mini bottle of scotch and drained that, too. "I think she must have been in immeasurable, inexplicable pain to have done that. I think she was suffering, and none of us noticed. I don't think we have anyone to blame but ourselves."

"Look around!" Deacon raised his voice, bringing his arms wide, one hand still holding the empty bottle. "What is there to be sad about? The world was her oyster. An oyster that had the biggest fucking pearl ever seen, by the way."

"Deacon," I started, lurching forward.

I had entirely forgotten that I was mad at Steven, furious and hurt. All I cared about was my brother, and his inability to grieve that I was certain would come back to bite him in the ass. But he cut me off, a sharp gesture with his hand to stop.

"I don't want to fight about her. I hate fighting with you, period. But I can't fight with you about this. Not about her." Deacon breathed, looking at me, green eyes earnest and pleading.

His cheeks were flushed, one tendril of chocolate hair brushing his forehead. He was looking at me straight on, and I debated pushing, fighting with him. Not for my sake but for his own. But when I looked at him, I saw myself. We have the same nose. The straight, Greek nose. The same eyes. Forest green. One of the rarest eye colors in the world. The same, pin straight hair. Chocolate brown. He is me, and I am him. Deacon is, and always will be, the other half of my soul. It was like looking at myself in many ways, and it made me uncomfortable.

I didn't like to look at myself much, not if I could help it. Every horrible, misguided thing I had ever done would come screeching in my ears when I looked in the mirror. But the longer I considered it, David's words whispered, too; that maybe I wasn't very nice to myself. And Deacon's face from the car ride over, a sad set to his smile when he said that maybe I was the only one who didn't love myself. There might have been some truth to that statement.

I nodded softly, fingers working around the cap of the vodka before tipping it back down my throat. "Do you want to go get a drink? I promise I'll laugh about Steven and Marta."

He pulled his phone out of his suit jacket, eyes widening and an unbridled excitement rose on his face. Turning to me with wild eyes, he shook his head. "Sorry, no. Noa finished her shoot, and she wants to FaceTime."

My mouth parted, words about how disgusted I was ready to spew out of my mouth, but the happiness radiating off him made my cheeks twitch instead, the ghost of a smile somewhere. It was a childlike excitement, except not in a perverted way. Though, I was certain Deacon's perversions knew no bounds. Instead, I asked what it was like for him.

"What's it like? Being in love?"

Deacon looked at me, unabashed. "It's the best goddamn feeling in the world. I have no idea why I waited so long."

"You were waiting for the right person." I smiled through tears that had resurfaced.

"What was it like for you? To be in love?"

My breath caught in my throat, a million memories swimming behind my eyes. What was it like? What had being in love with David Kennedy been like? Scratch that. What was it like? Because who was I fucking kidding? There was no other love for me.

"It's like coming home. Opening the door and realizing your entire being, your whole heart lives inside another person. Where they go, you go. And you're home. It's anywhere with him. It's the smell of the ocean. It's unruly blond waves. It's callused hands that are always warm. It's inappropriate laughter. It's him chasing me around my house. It's my terrace back in Lincoln Park. It's Chinese food. It's looks across the conference table that suddenly go on too long—"

"It's David," Deacon finished for me, some sort of sad and wistful look in his eyes, like he knew what it was like to be me. To have fucked it up so spectacularly you'd be missing all that for the rest of your life.

"It's David," I answered, my own voice small.

Because it would always be David, no matter the fact that he was now a fucking liar like me, that he picked Victoria, that Tripp Banks was also there and probably always would be.

The town car came to a slow halt, and I peered past Deacon out the tinted window, recognizing the blurred outline of Noa's building. My eyebrows collapsed onto one another, and I didn't want my night with my brother to end. I felt seen, and despite our differences that we could address another day, there was only one other person who understood me; and he wasn't an option right now. I opened my mouth to protest, to beg that he forget whatever weird fucking thing he was going upstairs to do over FaceTime with Noa, but Deacon leaned forward. There was a crisp, hundred-dollar bill folded between his fingers. I don't even know where it came from, but it was something Steven used to do. Produce money out of nowhere. Maybe it was something only Winchester men learned. I never carried cash.

"Rector and Washington," Deacon supplied, the driver swiping the bill from his fingers with a nod.

"No," I interrupted in confusion, leaning forward to correct him. "I live—"

"I know where you live, Charles. And I wouldn't dream of making this poor man drive to Upper Manhattan. It's not only far, but you should really consider a more desirable zip code." Deacon gave me a grin, slapping my shoulder, like I was his buddy, before throwing open the door and ducking out onto the sidewalk.

My eyebrows were furrowed, mouth pulling down in confusion, but he leaned back through the door. Gripping either side of the car, his suit jacket now unbuttoned, and that annoying wisp of hair blowing across his forehead in the breeze, he spoke, "Tripp's renting down there right now until he finds a place. I'll text you the address. You don't only get one singular love, Charles."

With that, he slammed the door in my face, and I lurched forward across the leather seats, but the driver was already pulling away from the curb—far be it for him to deny Deacon Winchester and one of his whims. I thought about protesting, my mouth parted, and my hand grabbed the back of the passenger seat. I was ready to insert myself through the opening and demand I be taken home. But Deacon's words were ringing endlessly in my ears and behind my eyes was my father's hand sitting on top of stupid Marta's. Maybe you didn't just get one.

CHAPTER TWENTY-TWO

The lobby of the building Tripp apparently lived in was littered with abstract sculptures and modern art hung from the walls. It was also home to an endless parade of drunk, fresh out of their Harvard or Wharton MBAs, Wall Street boys. They were all dressed in different versions of the same outfit: Hugo Boss or Armani shirts, giving way to Tom Ford chinos and Oxford shoes.

A group of them poured from the elevator opposite the revolving door just as I stepped through it. Their loud, cantankerous laughter stopped the moment they saw me. I arched an eyebrow as they all basically ran into one another. A tall, blond one, who looked like a cheap version of David, smacked his hand against the abdomen of the one standing beside him.

"Fuck, I think that's Charlie Winchester," one with dark brown hair whispered. I could tell they were drunk because they definitely thought they were speaking quieter than they were. "What's she doing here?"

I raised both eyebrows at them this time, striding across the lobby. The click of my Jimmy Choo mules resounded across the entire floor. Stopping in front of the concierge, I opened my mouth to speak but could hear them clear as day. They were still waiting by the elevator bay, staring.

"Her dad and brother had a meeting on the investing floor the other day. I saw them with that guy from the papers. Tall, black hair? The one from Boston. Banks, something. I think he's renting the penthouse right now."

Rolling my eyes, I placed my palms on the marble counter. "I'm here to see Tripp Banks."

The security guard looked up at me, a bored expression on his plain face. "Name?"

"Charlie Winchester," I leaned forward farther, practically mouthing my name with a cringe on my face.

"Who?" he narrowed his eyes, making a gesture toward his ear. "Can you speak up?"

I gritted my teeth, leaning forward even farther in this ridiculous Badgley Mischka dress. The crepe pinwheel embellishment that took up my entire chest crumpled as I pushed into the marble countertop. This felt like a pointless endeavor. I highly doubted Tripp had put me on a sort of pre-approved list. Or, maybe he had. It did seem like a thing he would do.

"Chuckles?"

I whipped around, grateful for what was possibly the first time, for one of his ill-timed interruptions. Tripp was standing there, head cocked to the side and a wry grin stretching his lips. He had as much stubble coating his jaw as I had ever seen him with. His dark hair was pushed back, and the arms of a black hooded sweatshirt were pushed up. I didn't think I had ever seen him in something so casual. I'm sure it cost hundreds, if not thousands of dollars, though. But it gave the illusion of casual nonetheless. Those were still Tom Ford chinos, after all.

"Tripp. The man of the hour. Just who I was hoping to see."

"To what do I owe this pleasure?" He asked, the shit-eating grin still marring his handsome features. "Do you need me to 'come to town'?"

"Don't quote Page Six. It doesn't become of you," I said, finally pushing off the countertop. "In a shocking twist, I'm here to see you. Deacon was feeling...particularly meddlesome this evening and re-directed our car to drop me off here. And here I am, but I don't think your concierge was going to let me in. I'm not sure I'm on the list."

Tripp's eyes swept over me, and the ice warmed for a moment. The grin softened into a familiar smile before it was just the sharp set of his jaw. "I think Deac might have been doing me a favor. You look particularly striking this evening."

He stepped forward, another cat-like grin falling into place. Tripp reached out, grabbing the fabric of the pinwheel on my chest between his thumbs and tugging on it lightly. "And what do you mean you aren't on the list? The name Charlie Winchester has been inked on every list imaginable since you were born."

"See!" a loud shout came from down the lobby where my audience was apparently still standing, watching me. "I told you, that's Charlie fucking Winchester. She's hotter in person."

Irritation flared behind Tripp's eyes, and they froze over as he looked over my shoulder. His jaw tensed in a predatory sort of way, and he tilted his head. "What's with the audience?"

"Oh, they realized they spotted a Winchester in the wild." I waggled my eyebrows at him.

Never taking his eyes off them, Tripp spoke out of the corner of his mouth to the concierge. "For the record, she's always welcome."

He strode forward, wrapping an arm around my shoulders. He dropped his mouth to my ear. "Do you want to come upstairs? Away from the prying eyes?"

I nodded, too aware of where I was and what I was doing now. I could have left, insisted the driver take me home after my brother left. But I didn't. And I had willingly walked into this lobby, willingly asked for Tripp Banks. And I did want to go upstairs. He was my friend if nothing else. I don't know why, but I brought my hand up to rest on his, the one that was draped around my bare shoulder. "Do you have pretentious East Coast wine?"

"Always," he breathed against my ear, his lips lingering on my earlobe.

"Why are you wearing a hooded sweatshirt? You look decidedly...undouchey," I asked, my hand still resting on his as we made our way across the lobby to the elevator bay where the little group was still standing.

"I was at some sports bar, meeting a friend from Harvard. He's a sports agent now. He only ever wants to meet in places like that."

Tripp's lips were against my temple now. But the way his head was cocked, I could tell he was still looking at them. They were all still standing there, wide-eyed and punching one another in the shoulder or the stomach. They couldn't have been more than twenty-two, and I imagined they were exactly what my brother, David and Tripp probably were at that age. Fresh off their business degree, an analyst at Goldman or Merrill Lynch, ready to master the world. The universe.

We drew ever closer, and their eyes never left us. Me in the dumb cocktail dress I needed to wear for a dinner with my father, because anything else would be unacceptable, and Tripp in his bizarrely casual sweater.

They all stopped jumping around, pausing the swipes they did through their hair to stop and stare at us. I raised my eyebrows, half-caught between laughter and self-consciousness, annoyance maybe. I don't know if I was channeling Taylor and what she would do from hundreds of miles away. Maybe it was Tripp and the way we always antagonized one another. Or, maybe it was simply the fact that I knew he would get a kick out of it. That it would make his smile pull from that bizarre, angry and predacious set of his lips right now.

"Hi boys." I smiled, my face the epitome of a Winchester—polite smile but not too polite, welcoming enough but not so much you thought you could be one of us.

"She is beautiful, isn't she?" Tripp finally spoke, but there was a distinct edge to his voice. "But if I hear another word, she'll have to send her brother and father after you. I promise, they aren't as nice as me."

I tipped my head back, leaning into the crook of his shoulder. This felt comfortable, real, at least for right now. "You make them sound like gang lords."

Tripp finally extricated his arm from me, only to push the button for the elevator. He leaned back against the wall, arms crossed, accentuating the breadth of his shoulders. It was muscle tone I hadn't really noticed before. He had always been fit, but I think a part of me had categorized him in my brain as the boy I knew. Skinny, no fat but muscular all the same. Now, he wasn't the same. His shoulders, his chest, his arms had filled out. He wasn't a boy anymore.

"Well, I'm sure two of the richest men in the world can pose as gang lords just fine. Or, they might know some," Tripp supplied, with an arched eyebrow.

He was still watching the group, who seemed suspended in time, staring at us with gaping jaws. Tripp jerked his chin toward them, and then pointed toward the door at the end of the lobby. "You boys don't have somewhere to be?"

"Don't mind him, gentlemen. He has terrible social skills. Enjoy your evening." I held my hand out for Tripp for some reason, and there was a hesitation or apprehension in his eyes, but it passed and he grabbed my hand, lacing his fingers through mine.

The elevator door slid open, and he tugged on my arm. Tripp spun me around, wrapping one arm around my stomach and dropping his chin to the crown of my head. I didn't know why he was doing this. We didn't really casually touch like this, not anymore.

Right as the door was about to close and finally separate us from the bizarre little audience of baby Wall Street boys, one of them shouted to ask if WH was hiring and a flash went off. Tripp leaned forward, about to grab hold of the door, but I swatted his hand away.

"Just leave it," I muttered, nausea settling in my stomach.

"No, fuck them. They don't get to just take your photo without your permission," Tripp said, the anger in his throat reverberating against the back of my head.

"It happens all the time now," I said, shrugging like I didn't care. But I did.

It was one of the things I hated most about Deacon catapulting our family into the spotlight by dating an internationally known supermodel.

"Since Noa?" Tripp leaned forward and pushed the button that read PH, his arm never moving its hold from my stomach, so I was forced to lean forward with him.

I nodded, not really wanting to open up that particular can of worms. I was working on accepting the fact that this was just a part of them being together, and it was the price I had to pay to support them. We stood in silence, his chin still pressed firmly into the crown of my head, and his arm still wrapped around me. I could only imagine what the tabloids would make of that one. I wasn't sure why I didn't just push him off, but he was warm, and I felt comfortable there.

The loud bell of the elevator announced our arrival at the Penthouse, and the doors pulled open to reveal a modern foyer that looked like a replica of the building lobby. Tripp gestured toward the hallway with his hand, and I finally stepped out from his hold. There were two heavy wooden doors on either side of me, and one at the very end. Tripp had already crossed the short hallway and was shouldering into the door facing us. He stopped, leaning back against the door to hold it open for me.

I raised my eyebrows at him, ducking through the door. "So chivalrous. Leaning impassively in the doorway waiting for me to cross the threshold."

"You know me. Chivalry will never be dead in the lair, as you like to call any places of residence I occupy." Tripp closed the door, and I peered into the apartment.

It also looked like a replica of the lobby. There was an odd modern sort of statue in the center of the room, separating a sterile-looking kitchen and dining area for a sunken living room. A giant black leather sectional couch spanned the floor, edging against a Moroccan style rug. Atop that was a coffee table that looked like a giant chunk of smooth rock, but I knew it probably cost tens of thousands of dollars. A gas fireplace was built into the wall, where the flames were low but still flickering, and above that was a television I couldn't even guess the size of.

"You aren't much for personal touches, are you?" I crossed my arms, feeling cold and exposed standing there in the middle of his home.

The only home I ever pictured for Tripp were the ones I knew—the shitty couch in his frat house, and the room he occupied on the top floor with the dumb king-sized bed, impeccable black Millesimo by Sferra sheets that were always made and perfectly tucked in and the massive oak desk that was piled high with economics textbooks.

Tripp was standing in the kitchen in front of a giant wine fridge, eyeing the endless shelves of bottles. "It was a furnished rental, Chuck. My real estate agent hasn't found anything I like, yet. You okay with..." he reached forward, plucking out a bottle from the top rack of the fridge, eyeing the label, "a Sauvignon Blanc by Screaming Eagle?"

A derisive snort escaped my nose, and I shook my head. "Is that a joke? Did Deacon or David say something to you?"

Turning, Tripp's eyebrows rose. "Deacon or David? Your brother said nothing, but I do see I have a text from him saying, *you're welcome*, which I take it means I'm welcome for him sending you here. Which, if I'm going to be straight with you, Chuck, is a weird thing for your brother to say. And as for DK, we have an unspoken agreement. We speak about the years before you, and the years after you. Never the ones with you in them."

The years before me and the years after me. I paused, feeling the weight of his words on me—on my heart. There was a before me, and there was an after me for both of them. And I guess, there was a before each one of them, and an after each one of them for me, too.

The text from my brother was weird, but that was Deacon. He never met a boundary he didn't cross. But I didn't really care about that and the weighty implications of him sending me here. I cared about this black hole, this vortex of torment and pain I had created in all of our lives. I cleared my throat, looking at Tripp with the same eyes I had in my office—that he was a casualty of my general fucked-upness, too.

"I'm sorry for that," I whispered, my eyes clouding over quickly, before I blinked away the impending tears.

"I'm not," Tripp said, his words firm. "I have a lot of regrets in my life, and I'm sure there are many more to come. You have never been one of them, and you never will be. The fallout or what's happened after we've...collided, sure. I regret how things turned out. But not you. Never you, Chuck."

I flicked my gaze up, eyes blurring at the edges again, but I could make out Tripp, leaning against the wine fridge now, the bottle gripped loosely in his hand. Part of me wanted to be spiteful, to tell him that I couldn't say the same. But when I combed through my memories, it wasn't exactly true. Tripp, as he was to me in all those moments past, wasn't the regret. He wasn't the pinch of guilt I felt when I looked at David, when I looked at the life I used to have. It was all just for me. I debated telling him that, telling him the truth; that just like I wasn't the villain in David's story, Tripp wasn't the villain in mine. I was the villain in my own. But he spoke again, breaking the thick tension that hung between us.

"What does the wine have to do with it? You don't want this one? I can pick another."

I shook my head, the words about to tumble from my lips banished to the back of my mind. "The wine is fine. It's wonderful, actually. I made the mistake of trying to share a bottle of this exact wine with David Kennedy, my alleged friend the other night. Didn't go so well."

"Is that what you're so fucked off about?" Tripp asked me, turning to grab two stemmed glasses that were hanging beside the fridge.

"Fucked off about? That's very British of you." I stepped out of my mules, almost letting out a moan when the arches of my feet touched the cool floor.

I grabbed them and padded to the front door, setting them down neatly in case I felt the need to make a quick getaway.

The telltale pop of the cork echoed around the practically empty apartment. It might have been a furnished rental, but it was one of those sad "less is more" furnished rentals that made Wall Street boys think they were something, because it had random art in it. I walked back into the living room, dropping down onto the unfriendly looking leather couch. The leather was freezing against the bare skin of my thighs.

"Yeah, I've been watching a lot of Geordie Shore with my mom," Tripp offered, his socked feet quiet against the floor.

He handed me a glass of wine that I began to swirl out of a pretentious habit. I really didn't give a shit what the legs on my wine were like.

"Pardon me?" I asked through a laugh.

Tripp fell back onto the couch about one cushion away from me, tossing an arm over the back. His sweatshirt was still rolled up, and I tracked the muscles on his forearms. There was a light dusting of dark hair over his olive skin, and I almost laughed again, picturing him as a scrawny frat boy, but somehow still the epitome of every girl's desire. "You watch Geordie Shore with your mom?"

"She likes it. We used to watch it when I was younger and since I left Boston, we sort of just started FaceTiming whenever there was a rerun on." Tripp shrugged, indifferent. Like he didn't realize how at odds that was with who he was in his life, how he carried himself.

It was sort of hard to picture Tripp Banks as someone with parents, someone with a family, someone who had been a child. I had never actually laid eyes on his parents, only glimpsed the outline of his father behind a tinted driver's window once before Thanksgiving break, and he rarely spoke about him. He always seemed so like a ready-made version, a mold, of what someone like him was supposed to be. He was rude, entitled, and dry most of the time. I couldn't imagine him as a child with unkempt hair, dirty hands and messy clothes—as someone who once needed love and guidance.

There was a dull ache in my chest, and I tipped my head to look at him. This person who quite literally looked like a Bond villain brought to life, who sometimes *was* a Bond villain brought to life, FaceTiming while he watched a shitty UK reality show with his mother. I asked before I could stop myself. "What's that like?"

"The show?" Tripp asked dryly, but the way he looked at me, I knew he was fully aware I wasn't talking about the show. He swallowed his wine, and I watched the column of his throat as it went down. He swirled his wine once, not bothering to look at the glass before answering, "It's nice, comforting maybe. My mom is complicated, and so is my whole family really. But it feels normal, and that's why I do it. Not just for me but for her."

His words felt heavy, weighted. Like he was saying so much more without saying anything at all. I wanted to ask him why she was complicated, why *he* was complicated, and I was going to, but I got the distinct impression he didn't want to say anything else.

Tripp took another swig of his wine and hastily grabbed the remote, beginning to flick through music channels until he landed on something. I wasn't looking, as I watched him the whole time. Without him saying anything at all, I sort of felt like I understood who he was now a bit more. His jaw was clenched, and I could tell by the way the muscles popped in his neck. His eyes were frozen, and instead of looking like ice they suddenly looked like the Atlantic Ocean, and he was pushing the buttons of the remote harder than necessary. A sudden urge to make whatever this was better for him overcame me, and I shifted self-consciously in my cocktail dress. I leaned forward conspiratorially, grabbing his forearm and shocking him out of whatever contemplation he was lost in.

"So anyway, don't alert the press. But David and I did have quite the fight over a bottle of Screaming Eagle, and then tonight, at dinner—Steven brought a date. Marta something. She's an editor at Vogue." I breathed, a lightness lacing my voice that I didn't really feel. But I just wanted him to feel better.

"Marta from Vogue?" Tripp's voice was laced with mockery, an exact reflection of my own earlier. "Do you want to change out of that dress, Chuck? I'll get you some sweats, and then you can tell me all about Marta from Vogue, and how she's a gold-digging bitch, because I'm assuming that's where this is going."

I took an overexaggerated sip of wine, nodding at Tripp primly. "You might be right. But I won't say no to getting changed."

Tripp surveyed me, his eyes still icy and an aloof air about him. "You going to stay awhile, then?"

"Yeah, I think I'll stay awhile."

CHAPTER TWENTY-THREE

And I did stay awhile. Tripp left out a heather gray, matching Hugo Boss sweat suit that made me laugh hysterically, because it was so stupid-looking but also the exact type of thing I imagined he would wear when he was lounging alone at home.

We were sitting, propped up on his bed, an array of Thai food between us. His room was as sterile as the rest of the apartment, which wasn't surprising. When he was showing me around the apartment, making dry comments about the benign nature of it all, he had thrown open the closet without thinking, and then quickly tried to close it when my eyes went wide, in a sort of feral delight that mirrored the one he always wore. His suits were pressed and hung according to color in his closet, and everything that needed to be dry-cleaned was hung on the opposite wall of the walk-in closet. It was all still color-coordinated. Jackets were paired with pants, and shirts were hung on the inside of the jackets. Socks, ties and pocket squares were tucked into the pants pockets.

Tripp was holding a carton of noodles, expertly rounding them around his fork with one hand. He pointed to the television with his elbow. "My mom loves that guy."

We were watching Geordie Shore. I wasn't sure how I got here, but I found I didn't really mind. I was propped up by one of his many giant, no-doubt expensive, feather pillows, my body dwarfed by his Hugo Boss sweat suit. The bottle of wine was perspiring in a stainless steel ice bucket Tripp produced from a cupboard in the kitchen. It was almost empty, and he still hadn't asked why I was there. I wasn't sure why I was still there, either. But I didn't want to go home to my big empty house and think about my father and Marta, David and Victoria, or God forbid, my mother's ghost would come knocking. I wasn't ready for that.

"This is the dumbest fucking show I have ever seen, Tripp. I am terribly sorry for Mrs. Banks, but I don't even know what this is about." I gestured to the screen, one hand clutching my wine glass and the other absentmindedly picking a snap pea from a rice dish.

"Well, it's obviously not going to win an Emmy, Chuck. But that's not the point. The point is it's a bunch of fame-thirsty reality stars that work all day and party all night, with all the intricacies and dramas that come from living in the UK."

Tripp dropped the box of noodles on his bedside table, grabbing his wine glass. He tossed back the rest and held out his hand for mine before standing to fill the glasses.

"I've lived in the UK, Tripp. There are no *intricacies*. I can promise you, it's nothing like this." I watched as he topped up both of our wine glasses.

He ditched the Tom Ford Chinos shortly after I changed and was still wearing his sweatshirt and a pair of black Armani Exchange jogging pants.

Tripp looked at me, a wry expression on his face when he passed me my now full wine glass. "Remind me your area code in London, Chuckles?"

I rolled my eyes, grabbing an egg roll and whipping it at his chest. "My flat was in Chelsea."

"Oh, your 'flat' was in Chelsea, one of the most undesirable areas in London." He made air quotes around the word 'flat' with a stupid lilt to his voice. Tilting his body, he easily side-stepped my egg roll and let it fall to the floor. "I think my point has been made, and you can clean that up."

"I'm sorry, Mr. Bateman. I know how much a mess upsets you." I narrowed my eyes, bringing my wine glass to my mouth.

Tripp fell back down onto the bed, rolling his neck to look at me with his eyes that seemed to soften, melt almost, over the course of the evening. "We talked about this. You need more current references. We can find you a more topical movie, if you would like."

"Is it my fault the men in my life bizarrely resemble a fictional serial killer? Or not, I suppose, depending on how you interpret the movie."

"Are you going to tell me what happened with David?" Tripp asked, his voice quieter.

I couldn't help but look over at him. He was staring at me intently, and my heart dropped because the usual hard edges of his face seemed softer, more boyish.

I chewed on the inside of my mouth before tossing back a mouthful of wine. I knew wine was meant to be savored, especially bottles of wine that cost thousands of dollars, but my last interaction with David was sitting heavy in my chest.

"He came over the other day, wanting to talk about Deacon's bachelor party. We spent the day together, and it was all nice and normal, but then later when I invited him in for a drink, he was weird about it but came in anyway. And then Victoria called. And then he lied about where he was and what he was doing."

"Chuck," Tripp said, exasperated. "You aren't telling me you're shocked he lied? Of course, he lied."

My mouth popped open into an indignant circle, but my voice was small when I spoke. "He made it seem like he was, I don't know, ashamed of me. I don't want to be someone people are ashamed of being with."

Tripp reached forward and grabbed my wine glass, setting both down on the bedside table in a smooth motion. He leaned back toward me, his head tipped down and his dark hair falling around his forehead. But for some reason, I was focused on the way his sweater sat against him. If I reached out, I could grab the hood.

"Charlie. Are you kidding me? Of course he's not ashamed. Victoria might be—"

"I believe you told me she was 'hot in an obvious way,' but I was worth a fuck lot more." I made my own exaggerated air quotes, trying to put on a deep voice like his.

He reached forward, grabbing my fingers. "She might be hot in an obvious way, Chuck," his voice was measured, and I could hear him in my ear the way I did two years ago, "but you're the most beautiful woman I've ever seen in real life."

"You've seen Noa Dahan in real life," I breathed, not taking my eyes off Tripp.

I waited for the wry expression to steal across his face, and for him to say some off-putting or antagonistic joke. But it never came.

"Statement still stands," he whispered back. I started, pulling my head back slightly, surprised. "Why did Deacon send you here, Chuck?"

"He was just being an asshole," I could barely discern my own words.

His eyes were boring into mine, and I couldn't look away; and I realized I didn't want to look away. I wasn't sure what we were doing here, but it felt like another one of those moments there was no coming back from. My heart was doing something weird. Usually, my stomach soured or dropped from anxiety when he was around, and it was still fluttering, but it felt more like a nervous tap against my ribcage.

"Is that the story you want to stick with?" Tripp asked. There was a taunting edge to his voice, but the low, gravelly tone remained.

I shook my head almost imperceptibly. Part of me was holding back, because there was an invisible line between us that our hands were still clasped over. I knew that if I leaned over, if I crossed it, I was firmly planting myself in the years after David Kennedy. There really, truly, was no going back. But I felt myself leaning forward ever so slowly, eyes shifting from Tripp's blue ones to the hood of his sweatshirt that I wanted to grab in my hands and down to his full bottom lip, the lines of dark stubble across his jaw.

Exhaling, I tipped my head, my hair fluttering around my face. I leaned closer, over the top of our hands. Tripp raised his other hand, placing his fingers against my mouth stopping me just before my lips brushed his. I jerked backward, embarrassment flushing across my cheeks, but Tripp wrapped his hand around the back of my neck, laying his forehead against mine.

"I want you to do that again when you're not mad at your father or David Kennedy. And if you find that you don't want to, that's okay. But I'm not doing this with you again when I don't know if you're doing it because you really want to, or you feel pissed off and you're looking for some twisted form of revenge. I want you to want to. Wait a while and see if the urge is still kicking around."

"Tripp Banks turning down a sure thing? A ready and willing girl in his bed?" I said reproachfully. Our eyes were so close, but I could still see the way his pupils expanded in that sort of wild delight he expressed only when we were at one another's throats. "That's not the boy I knew."

I watched Tripp's lips pull up into a grin as our foreheads continued to rest against each other. "I'm not a boy anymore, Chuckles. I look forward to the day I can show you just how much I've changed and how much I've learned over the years." His voice dropped several octaves, and I felt myself swallow.

"Are you going to kick me out now?" I finally pulled back, taking him in fully. His eyes were dark as they continued to focus solely on me. "Seeing as you're not going to put out? Is that my cue to leave?"

Tripp laughed, finally leaning back against the pillows on his side of the bed. He brought our still joined hands to rest on his abdomen, and I could feel the ridges of his muscles through the sweater.

"No, you can stay if you want. We have plenty of episodes of Geordie Shore left to watch, and there's a fridge full of wine here. We can steer clear of the Screaming Eagle, or anything else that brings up untoward memories for you. But that might be hard, you have more fucking baggage than anyone I know."

"Oh, fuck you," I bit out through laughter, laying back down against the pillows, aware that Tripp had started playing with my fingers as my hand laid on his stomach.

"It seemed like you were just about to try to fuck me, Charlie," he deadpanned, eyes shifting over to me for a moment, glinting like a frozen lake. "Now, shut up, this is one of my favorite episodes."

I fell silent but found I kept glancing over at Tripp, watching as he watched the television, the way his throat looked when he swallowed his wine, finally reaching up and grazing my fingertips across his jaw, the muscles in it feathering and twitching against my skin. He did look different. All the boy-like softness gone, replaced with the sharp edges that much better reflected his personality. But I wondered how different we really were from the people we used to be, and whether people like us could really, truly change.

———

I was sitting cross-legged on Tripp's bed, still wearing the same gray sweat suit from the night before. He was standing across from me in the middle of his walk-in closet, doing up the buttons of his white Burberry cotton stretch shirt. I could tell it was tailored to fit him by the way it tapered down his sides, highlighting his oblique muscles. He left the top few buttons open, and I continued to watch him as he shrugged on the jacket of his matching black, slim fit Burberry suit.

"See something you like, Chuck?" Tripp asked, arching an eyebrow wryly.

"I'm actually wondering how I'm going to get out of here without being seen in either your sweat suit or last night's cocktail attire. The dress might be better. I only have gold Jimmy Choo mules with me. I don't think they go with this outfit." I raised my eyebrows in response.

I was kidding, but the closer morning crept, anxiety settled in my stomach about the very real possibility I would be photographed leaving here. I hadn't really intended to stay the night, but we were lying there in the same position as the shadows in the room grew longer, stretching toward us and wrapping the night around us. And at some point, the spaces between our conversation grew, stretched like those shadows surrounding us. I felt myself shifting closer to Tripp, body beginning to fall sideways against the pillows until my head was pressed against his chest, and the movements of his hands as he toyed with my fingers grew gentler. My eyelids fluttered and grew heavy, despite the loud noises from the television. At one point, when my cheek was pressed into his chest growing ever warmer from his body heat, my own limbs growing leaden, I could have sworn I felt him press his lips to the top of my head and rest them there for a while.

We woke up in the exact same position, with Tripp gently prodding my shoulder. He swore that if I freaked out like the last time we fell asleep together and tried to kick him out of his own apartment, he was going to send the catalog of embarrassing sorority-era Charlie Winchester photos he claimed he still had to every tabloid in the entire United States. It hadn't freaked me out, not really. I laid there for a moment, eyes swiveling around and taking in my surroundings, remembering how barren and devoid of life his apartment was.

I registered the presence of arms around me that didn't belong to David Kennedy, the fact he was no longer the last person I shared a bed with like this—no sex, just sleeping and the entirely new level of intimacy being vulnerable and exposed with someone else like that brought on. It occurred to me as I smoothed out my hair and rubbed my cheek where the impressions of Tripp's sweater were indented on my skin, that each time I did something like this, regardless of who it was with, I was living in the years after David, and that slowly but surely, he would no longer be the last person I did all sorts of things with.

"Do you want me to leave first, and you can call a car after an appropriate amount of time has passed?" Tripp said over his shoulder, now assessing himself in the full-length mirror in his closet.

I watched him tug on the sleeves of his shirt, so each arm peeked out the same amount under his suit jacket. It was like looking at Deacon in the morning. He preened until everything was just right, down to ensuring his socks were pulled up to the exact same height under his pants. David had always just thrown his suits on, somehow looking effortless, and like he had stepped off the pages of a menswear magazine.

"I think the damage was probably already done by the photo taken of us last night in the elevator. I'm sure it has no doubt made its rounds through trading floors across the city, and some tabloid is next." I shrugged, pushing off the bed and coming to stand in front of Tripp with my hand out. "But I wouldn't say no to some socks or slippers, so I don't need to pair my mules with this sweat suit."

Tripp grinned, eyes never leaving mine when he reached out toward one of the drawers beside him built into the closet. He pulled out a pair of thick, wool socks that he probably wouldn't be caught dead in. "You can wear these. Just throw them out when you get home. I don't need socks that have touched the streets of Manhattan."

I snatched them from his hand, my breath catching in my throat when Tripp grabbed my wrist with his hand, stroking his thumb across the inside of my wrist.

"You're welcome," he murmured, jerking his chin toward the open closet door. "I'll walk you out."

Tripp tightened his hold on my wrist, raising it and spinning me around, so I was facing the bedroom again. His other hand came to rest on my waist, and I felt his breath against my ear. It was cool and skittered across my cheek. His stubble scratched at the side of my face where his face was dangerously close to mine. My heart was doing that weird thing again. I couldn't quite recognize it, because it wasn't the feeling I equated with attraction, like or love now. To me, that permanently felt like my heart beating itself bloody against my ribcage in a desperate bid to get to David. But it was fluttering, dropping, and beating erratically the longer Tripp had his mouth hovering by my ear. It felt familiar, and as I breathed in, catching the scent of his cologne, it clicked. It was the exact same thing my heart used to do around him when I was twenty, before everything between us changed. In the before David years.

"How chivalrous," I managed quietly, finally leaving the closet.

Tripp dropped his hand from my waist but kept his hand around my wrist, trailing behind me as we left the apartment.

I stopped in the foyer to grab my things and shove his ridiculous, apparently disposable, wool socks on my bare feet. Tripp momentarily helped me balance, and then kept his hand wrapped around my wrist the entire ride down in the elevator. I kept looking over, glancing down at our sort-of joined hands and studying the sides of Tripp's face. His expression looked normal, bored even. Like holding my wrist, with his thumb ever-so casually stroking the sensitive skin on the underside, was something we did every single day. It left me with a weird, sort of infantile feeling. It seemed like something you would do to usher a child around.

I looked over at him, aware of the different skittering sensation in my chest, and realized doing this with him every day was within reach. A muscle jumped in his neck and his thumb tapped against my palm, and I wondered if he wanted to hold my hand. Tripp rolled his neck, finally turning to look at me, eyes glinting.

"What's going on in there, Chuck? You're looking particularly pensive this morning." His voice was bored, but there was an undercurrent of hesitation, of nervousness there, like he was afraid what my answer might be.

I extracted my wrist from his hand, rubbing it in my other hand and noticing how warm it was from Tripp's fingers. I could see his eyes darken and his face fall momentarily before the same, indifferent mask slid back into place.

"I'm still angry at you, you know. Not for David or any of that. That was just as much my fault, if not more." I held up my hand when I noticed his lip's part, like he was going to say something in protest. "I know you say you didn't do it...you didn't write my name down...you didn't delete the message...you didn't know about it until later. But you were still a participant in all that. You're culpable, whether you want to be or not, Tripp. You say it was something you wanted, that you were so happy thinking something was starting between us. But you never called me, either. Never checked in when I was grieving. It was radio silence, regardless of whether your stupid brother deleted my message."

Tripp ran a hand through his hair, puffing out his cheeks and seeming to consider something before reaching out and smacking the emergency stop button with the back of his hand. I jolted forward, grabbing his forearms to steady myself.

"What the fuck, Tripp!" I hissed, pushing myself upright and brushing myself off like I had hit the floor when I lurched at the sudden stop. "The emergency button is for emergencies. I have things to do today that don't include being trapped in here with you."

"I'm going to talk, and you're going to listen to me, Chuck. You can't seem to help yourself, and I'm sure you'll be primed to interrupt me and bite my head off at any moment. But I'm going to say this, and you're going to listen, got it?" Tripp said evenly, looking at me sharply before continuing. "I can't change what happened. You're right, I wasn't there for you. I can use the excuse that we were kids all day and all night, but it doesn't justify it. You left without saying goodbye, my pride was wounded, and I assumed you didn't want anything to do with me. I did not write your name on that board, but that doesn't change the fact that there was a board. That I should have ripped it up. Post deleted the message, and it just felt like...so far gone. Years had passed by the time he brought it up. But I never forgot about you. I thought about you. I grabbed any copy of Business Insider or Forbes to see if your name popped up. I ended up in Chicago, and I heard you were coming home. And then there you were. The most beautiful girl I had ever seen."

Tripp paused, still looking down at me, and I pressed my fingers to my forehead, trying to formulate some sort of response, but he continued, "It was wrong, but I don't regret it. I'm sorry for what I did to you and David. I'm sorry for what it cost you, that it ended up hurting you. I never said I was a good man, Charlie."

He was right, my mouth had popped open more than once during his little speech, ready to jump on anything he said like always. But I considered his words and realized maybe it wasn't just shared history that always shoved us together, not the mistakes I made. Maybe we were both the same kind of bad. Maybe we understood one another. Those were the things that made whatever magnets we each had constantly pull toward one another. Maybe I could forgive him, and maybe I could forgive myself in the process. "For what it's worth, I don't think I'm that great of a person, either."

"Thank God, because that would be really fucking boring," Tripp said, eyes darkening. "Like I said, think about it. Try kissing me again if you find that you want to. This is who I am. That's all I can offer you, Chuck."

"I'm sure you heard about the charity benefit Steven is so generously hosting to establish WH in Manhattan," I said slowly, unsure if I really wanted to commit to the idea that was half-formed in my head, but it seemed too late to go back now. "Steven has asked that Deacon and I each bring a date to make a grand entrance with to take some of the heat off him, because he's bringing his new *friend* Marta. It's probably going to be awful. I'm already dreading it. I don't think I trust you, Tripp. To be honest, I don't really trust myself. I make terrible decisions. This, along with last night, but why don't you come with me? You can be my date."

Tripp's teeth scraped his full bottom lip and held onto it for a moment. "You hate Winchester Holdings' events. You're really going to go through with this one?"

Something between a laugh and a scoff sounded from me. "Do you think Steven Winchester gave me a choice? Trust me, if I didn't have to be at any of these events, I wouldn't be. So, what do you say? You're not going to make me beg you, are you?"

"The idea of you begging me for anything is very appealing." Tripp's voice was laced with insinuation that made me narrow my eyes. "I'm not going to make you beg. I would be honored to accompany you to an official Winchester Holdings' event."

He reached out and hit the emergency button, and the elevator sprang back to life. Tripp looked me over again, the annoying look of smug superiority sliding back into place.

I turned forward, crossing my arms across my chest, trying to look anywhere but Tripp. "Don't make me regret this. You're still on thin ice with me."

"Yeah, that ice seemed real thin this morning when I woke up with you in my bed," Tripp whispered, voice laden with sarcasm, brushing past me to hold the elevator for me as it opened. "Let's go get the front desk to call you a car, and you can carry on with your day and pretend you didn't wake up with me this morning."

Tripp was wrong. The ice I was standing on *was* thin, and I had no idea what I was doing.

CHAPTER TWENTY-FOUR

The Oxford application was peeking out of the corner of my Saint Laurent tote. Sitting behind my desk in my office, it was like it was taunting me. Every time I put my head down, even when I arranged my pin straight hair in front of my face, I could see the envelope in my periphery. The words blurred on the page in front of me, things like international economy, disaster relief, and gross domestic product blending together and meaning absolutely nothing. The semester was technically over. I had no classes left to teach, no tutorials to supervise. Just my own research and the looming deadline for Dr. Batra.

David and I had maintained a stony silence since I kicked him out of my townhouse, and to my knowledge he had nothing to say about the photos of Tripp and me in the elevator appearing online. It took less than twenty-four hours, in which I had to endure a very unpleasant forty-five-minute group FaceTime call with Deacon and Taylor. They each took opposite sides of the Tripp versus David argument stirred up again by the media; Deacon firmly in camp "second-chance romance," and Taylor saying in no uncertain terms that I needed to be doing anything I could to pry David from Victoria's manicured fingers.

I was hounded by Rebecca and the new publicist for the New York office, Cal, who shockingly reminded me of Damien. They had the same wire-rimmed glasses, the exact same preppy fashion sense—wearing too many paisley shirts and ridiculous brogued footwear. The calls had been so persistent they finally had to release a bland statement saying that I was no longer an active executive staff member, as I had cordial relationships with all of the executive team. Steven was determined to stay out of it, saying that anything New York was Deacon's problem.

Deacon wore a shit-eating grin anytime I saw him afterward, saying that I would have him to thank when "all was righted in my love life," because he directed the town car to Tripp's apartment building. But thankfully, I quickly became the least interesting thing to the press again when Deacon and our father announced the invite list for the upcoming Winchester Holdings' charity gala.

I wasn't really sure you could call it that, because it was the equivalent of my father pissing all over the other major holdings' companies in Manhattan. I was pretty certain it was a personal vendetta against J.P. Morgan and Goldman Sachs. Steven Winchester made an incredibly generous donation to Memorial Sloan Kettering Cancer Center, which felt so obvious and boring to me. Deacon donated to the International Rescue Committee. I was fairly certain he had someone Google "New York charities for refugees" and see where it landed. Which, I supposed, was fine because I was pretty sure it was for Noa.

It also confirmed for me that neither Steven nor my brother ever listened to a word I said when I established a charitable giving's portfolio based on community engagement. I chose a small organization in the Bronx that supported vulnerable individuals with mental health and public health programming.

I exhaled, cheeks puffing out as the words on the page in front of me continued to blur. I had to read this article, and another three, before next week. My gaze flicked up to look at the clock. I had been sitting here trying for about two hours and not retaining anything, mostly because my eyes kept wandering toward that envelope.

And then my mind would start to wander, and I would begin to wonder what it would be like. To go back to London, to choose to go there and study at one of the best institutions in the world. But then I would remember my personal life was such a fucking disaster again that it wasn't entirely likely I was making that choice on my own. It was too convenient of a getaway car. Again.

My phone started to vibrate against the stack of papers on my desk, and I peered over it, seeing an incoming FaceTime alert from Taylor. I knitted my eyebrows, having her rotation pretty much memorized, I was sure she was supposed to work this weekend.

"Taylor, to what do I owe the pleasure? Are you on break or something? A world-altering surgery you need to tell me about?" I hit the answer button without picking up the phone, starting to gather the stacks of paper around me.

"Wow, could you at least do me the decency of picking up your phone so I'm not staring at the fugly Columbia ceiling?" Taylor shrieked, fake outrage lacing her voice.

"You know what I look like, I thought you might be interested in seeing the tiles I stare at in existential dread around this time every afternoon." Leaning forward, I grabbed the phone and brought it up to my face. I was about to offer an overly fake, all teeth, Winchester smile, because it was her favorite thing about me to tease, but I narrowed my eyes when I saw the cupboards behind her. "Is that my kitchen?"

Taylor grinned, fingers tapping the phone and switching the view. The camera panned to my kitchen, and I could see Taylor's feet swinging into the screen, which must have meant she was sitting on my island. "Surprise!"

"First, get off my island. Second, I really need to stop giving out copies of my house key. Third, you told me like not even two weeks ago that you couldn't trade any more shifts. What are you doing here?" I asked, but the fake smile on my face stretched into a genuine one. I always felt better, more myself, when Taylor was around.

"Oh my God, that's the best part. What's his face, that new surgical oncology resident who transferred? He asked me to swap. And then I thought, wouldn't my service be put to better use at that Glow fashion show thing Noa invited us all to tonight instead of walking around the oncology floor at Northwestern Memorial?" Taylor switched the camera back toward her face.

Her brown eyes were sparkling somewhat impishly, and I could see that the sharp edges of her face had been contoured, and her eyes dusted with a shimmer that would make Sabine proud.

"I would hope to God, Taylor, that your services would be better put to use as you know, a doctor. That thing you went to school for over eight years to be?" I squinted at her before continuing. "And his name is Dr. Taber. You've told me how annoying he is pretty consistently since he arrived."

Comprehension lit her eyes, and she pointed her index finger at the screen. "That is his name. You're right. When are you coming home? I'll order us dinner, and we can get ready for that bizarre little Guerilla fashion show Noa is so excited about."

Noa was doing some sort of photoshoot for a small, up-and-coming designer that was mysteriously taking place at a club before an exclusive, invite-only party. There was some sort of dress code described on the invitation, but I was so behind on my own readings I wasn't planning on going.

"Yeah, I'm not going to that."

"Oh? Do you have other plans? Busy with Tripp Banks?" Taylor asked snidely, her gaze narrowing on me through the camera.

"No, I don't have plans with Tripp. I told you...my moment of weakness has passed. I tried to kiss him, but he gave me some impassioned speech about waiting for a new moment. We fell asleep watching fucking Geordie Shore, because he watches it with his mom. It was nothing. End of story," I said in a poor attempt to brush it off, but it was much more complicated than that.

Taylor made a vague noise of disbelief before continuing. "Come home! It'll be more fun to pretend your little dalliance with Tripp was nothing when I'm crimping your hair."

I agreed, only to shut her up. As I was stuffing everything in my tote, careful to avoid touching the Oxford envelope, my hair swung in front of me. I tugged on the straight strands momentarily. Taylor could try, but there was no way in hell I was going anywhere with crimped hair.

I bounced my legs, running my palms across my bare thighs. The white t-shirt I was wearing was strategically torn to reveal my black lace La Perla bra and the shiny black Lycra shorts left little to the imagination. Taylor was wearing something similar, but her shorts were a neon green. I had no idea where she even found clothes like that, but I was sure if I checked the tags I would have seen a designer's name. I couldn't believe I let Taylor talk me into this.

I took a sip from my drink, one of the many glasses scattered across the table in front of me. I could feel the splatters of neon paint across my face pulling tightly as I took a sip. There were two attendants at the door whose job it was to splatter anyone who came into the club with strategic specks of said paint.

Taylor ran off to talk to the designer. Noa and two of her friends were standing on a platform not far from our room. I studied them, watching keenly while they posed for various photos. I think the one on the left, Mika, was the one Taylor used to date before ending on amicable terms—which also somewhat explained her overenthusiastic interest in this event. They were wearing outfits almost identical to ours. I watched Noa lean forward, biting the earlobe of her friend with a playful grin. If it was possible, the camera flashes went off even quicker. I couldn't wrap my head around what kind of campaign this was.

The bar had been transformed into some sort of eighties or nineties rave house. Bright colors, shooters in test tubes and bizarre grungy-style decorations were littered everywhere. I was unsure what I was looking at, but I was certain Taylor was over there complimenting the designer on their vision brought to life. Having Taylor here always righted everything in my world. But not for the first time, I wondered what it was like for her back in Chicago now. I was gone, Deacon would soon be gone from Chicago. But Taylor probably didn't care. She was, and always had been, her own person with her own distinct life separate from us. She didn't need Deacon or me there for it to be her home.

Noa suddenly flopped down on the leather couch across from me, a sigh that seemed much too large and much too deep for her tiny body escaping her. Her brown hair was straightened to become almost a replica of mine and was teased beyond belief, pushed back with some sort of black, athletic headband. There were two streaks of neon paint across her cheeks, and the rest of her exposed skin was peppered with paint flecks in varying colors.

"Long night?" I asked, pressing the rim of my glass to my lips.

"Print and editorial stress me out." Noa leaned forward, her fingers deftly turning all the bottles of liquor toward her, amber eyes narrowed in concentration as she studied them. "Runway is my happy place."

I was about to tell her I wasn't sure I understood the difference when Taylor sat down beside me, swinging her long legs around to quickly cross them at the ankle. She leaned forward, grabbing Noa's wrist. "This set is incredible. I love the juxtaposition—"

"Nope, no." I held up my palms before slapping a hand down to grab Taylor's shockingly muscular leg. I could never figure out how she developed quad muscles like that. It must have been all the hours she spent sprinting around the hospital Grey's Anatomy-style. "If she gets going about this, the artistic vision and the art direction and whatever the fuck else, it's all she's going to talk about tonight."

Taylor turned her head to look at me, lips pulling back like she was irritated before she flashed Noa a cat-like smile. "She's right. In another life, I think I was a high-powered editorial art director."

"But in this life, she was made for slicing open living human beings," I laughed, reaching forward, grabbing the tequila bottle, and waving it at Taylor. "Open up."

Taylor cackled before resting the back of her head against the top of the cushioned leather seat. Her overly crimped hair splayed out around her. She nestled her body down into the couch before snapping both of her fingers. This was a dumb game we used to play with Deacon when we were kids who had no business drinking tequila.

The rules were pretty simple. One person got to pour until the other person said stop. I raised my eyebrows at her tauntingly before tipping the bottle forward. I watched the tequila splash into her mouth before she reached out and grabbed my wrist to signal me to stop. Taylor sat up, delicately wiping the corners of her mouth before a tiny shudder rolled through her. She turned to me, eyes sparkling dangerously, and she tipped her angular chin toward the bottle still hanging loosely from my hand.

"Your turn," Taylor stated pointedly, hand open and beckoning for me to hand it to her.

"No!" I laughed, pulling it backward. "The last time you didn't stop when I said so."

Taylor narrowed her eyes. "That was like three years ago. Time to move on."

Noa cleared her throat, holding up her phone with a defeated sort of collapse to her features. "Deac just told me he's on his way with Tripp, David...and Victoria. So, you might want to take her up on that."

"Oh, the Tripp she's not sleeping with?" Taylor looked at me sharply, grabbing the tequila bottle from me. "Open up."

Rolling my eyes, I leaned backward. Right on cue, the mention of David and Victoria caused the typical sour waves of nausea in my stomach. "I'm not sleeping with him. We slept in the same bed. There is a distinction between the two you seem to forget."

"Deacon told me you tried to kiss Tripp, and he said no because he wanted you to do it when you weren't under mental duress," Noa prodded, one eyebrow rising up her unmoving forehead.

On anyone else I would have assumed they were at the two-week mark of a fresh Botox appointment, but I was pretty sure Noa just produced more collagen than the average person.

"Wow!" I sat up straight, widening my eyes at Noa. "Is nothing sacred?!"

Taylor scoffed loudly, pushing against my shoulder to shove me back down against the leather couch. "Have you met your brother? Open up. You're going to need it to deal with *Vic*." She made overexaggerated air quotes and pulled her mouth in a weird direction as she shook the tequila bottle.

"Behave. I don't need to give David any more fucking ammo against me." I rolled my eyes, settling against the leather and wrapping my arms around my bizarrely ripped shirt.

I suddenly felt self-conscious with bits of my skin on display.

"Mmm. I'm sure kicking him out of your house earned you a lot of brownie points." Taylor smiled tightly at me, finally tipping the bottle against my mouth.

I felt the plastic spout that was shoved into the bottle press into my bottom lip, a shudder rippling through my shoulders at that lingering taste of tequila there before it started to splash against my tongue. I closed my eyes, and all I could see were David's honey ones, dark and staring into mine in my kitchen.

CHAPTER TWENTY-FIVE

The first thing I noticed when my brother crashed into our private booth, pouncing on Noa immediately and showing an indecent amount of tongue as he kissed her, wasn't even my disgust at their public display. It wasn't Taylor who was sitting there, mouth pulled back and eyes wide. It was the way David's fingers were interlaced with Victoria's, how his hand dwarfed hers. My mouth dried and I tilted my head, eyes blurring at the edges as they walked toward us.

The thought of his worn hands touching someone else's skin so casually like that felt like someone had taken the heel of their Louboutin and repeatedly hacked at my heart with it. Before seeing them together at Soho House, it had never really occurred to me until that moment that he touched her with his hands. *My* hands. The hands that brought me home. The hands that used to belong to me. I felt Taylor brush her fingers along the side of my arm subtly, like maybe she could hear blood spurting out of the heel-shaped holes in my heart.

The next thing I noticed was the strapless, iridescent Bottega Veneta sheath dress Victoria was wearing. The silhouette was similar to the Galvan dress I last saw her in, with a deep cut-out sweetheart neckline. I didn't want to be looking at her, but I knew

Taylor's eyes would be popping out of her head. It was exactly the kind of dress she would salivate over. It wouldn't surprise me if she dragged me around Manhattan in search of it first thing in the morning.

I blinked, forcing a smile to stretch across my face, despite how dry my mouth was and how loud my heart was pounding in my ears. A glass appeared in front of me, perspiring and ice clinking against the sides. I looked quickly at Taylor who was holding it out to me, everything about her casual save for the slight pinch to her eyebrows and the way her eyes softened as she looked at me.

Smiling, I took it from her like I had been expecting it. The burn of the vodka only seemed to exacerbate the feelings in my throat and chest. I allowed myself to stare down at the ice cubes in my empty glass for a moment, blinking rapidly to subdue the tears that threatened to spill over at the thought and memory of David's hands on someone else.

Queasiness rolled through my stomach, and I swallowed, wanting to wash away the images of David and Victoria's bodies moving together that threatened the borders of my mind. I wondered if he looked at her the same way he used to look at me: eyes dark and sweat slicked blond hair falling across his forehead as he moved over top of me, whether her back arched into his body, perfectly fitting the way mine did. Or, if he followed every kiss on her body with a nip from his teeth and—

Deacon snapped loudly in front of me. He was leaning forward, green eyes narrowed in concern and chocolate hair falling all over his forehead in a mess. He had abandoned his suit jacket somewhere, a crisp white shirt was unbuttoned at his throat, sleeves rolled up and belted into slim fit gray Armani pants.

"You in there? Where are those Winchester manners? You know as well as I do that's not how you greet new arrivals to an event, let alone your own flesh and blood."

Blinking rapidly, I swatted his hands away and stood, pulling at my shirt, like I could somehow cover myself up more or pretend I didn't look like a dollar store version of Victoria in her stupid eight-thousand dollar dress. Her new job must have come with a nice signing bonus. Taylor pushed up beside me, sliding her hand down my arm until our fingers were interlaced. She squeezed my hand three times in quick succession, and my eyes fluttered closed. It was another thing we used to do as kids to let the other know we were there.

"So sorry to have disappointed you, Deacon. But you seemed a little preoccupied trying to eat Noa's face off, so I didn't think you would mind."

"What can I say?" Deacon grinned at me, tossing an arm carelessly over Noa's shoulder.

I turned immediately to plaster a fake smile for David and Victoria before Deacon could devolve any further. Victoria was smiling tightly, two perfectly styled waves of blonde hair framing her face, the rest of those annoying "fresh from the ocean" curls pulled into an artfully messy low bun at the back of her head. Her pillowy cheeks were dusted with some sort of highlighter that perfectly matched her gown and refracted the light just so.

I was purposely staring at her, trying not to notice the way that David's slim fit light blue Hugo Boss shirt stretched against his broad shoulders. But just beyond Victoria, Tripp was leaning against the wall that enclosed our booth.

He cocked his head at me, impossibly dark hair pushed off his face and thick stubble dusting his jaw. His hands were tucked into the pants of his tailored black suit. I couldn't recognize the designer from here in the low light. But it was probably Tom Ford, or maybe Ralph Lauren. Slim fit black wool pants, tailored stark white shirt with the top buttons undone, open black jacket that skimmed the sides of his stomach so closely you knew it was tailored, and an impossibly shiny black leather belt to complete the look. He arched an eyebrow at me before pushing off the wall, long legs closing the distance between us quickly.

Tripp snaked his arm around my shoulders, his hand warm through the thin fabric of my t-shirt. I opened my mouth to say something in greeting to him, to Victoria, to David—who I was still looking determinedly away from—when I felt him press his lips to the side of my head; his stubble rubbed against my skin. I pulled back on instinct, but Tripp kept me firmly pressed into him, his lips moving against my skin in a whisper. "Play along," his voice was practically indiscernible.

Victoria seemed to perk up, her eyebrows rising before something like a haughty smile settled across her lips. "When did you two get together?" She asked, her smile never wavering, like it was polite, but I noticed the way she pulled David tighter against her.

"We aren't together. Tripp just doesn't understand boundaries when it comes to me." I ducked out from under his arm, pushing closer to Taylor who was still squeezing my hand.

"Could have fooled me," David muttered almost imperceptibly, his eyes flashing dark.

I finally looked at him and recoiled at the way his eyes passed over me with something like indifference. My mouth popped open, an indignant response rising in me. I was firmly back in the Fuck David Kennedy camp.

"I introduced Chuck to the wonders of Geordie Shore the other night when she stayed over at my place," Tripp said, his stupid Cheshire Cat grin making him look maniacal. I gave him a flat look, wanting him to shut up, but of course, he did no such thing. "She gets handsy when she's drinking, just like she did when we were younger."

"Shut up, Tripp," I hissed, tempted to lean forward and smack the dumb look off his face. He was trying to get a rise out of David, and judging by the set of his jaw, it was working. "Pretty sure I wasn't even allowed to touch anything in your bland, serial killer apartment, because you were worried about smudges."

Deacon was looking back and forth between David, Tripp and me, his green eyes wide and seemingly unsure which side of whatever was developing here he wanted to fall on. I felt Taylor tug on my hand like you would to redirect a child. David pulled Victoria toward the sofa at the same time, her dress catching every light hanging above us, making her shine like the stupid sun as she gently folded herself down beside David. Her hand placed on his knee and her body angled toward him, she was still leaning over him like some sort of predator ready to stake her claim on a particularly interesting carcass. I settled against the leather seat again, Taylor intermittently squeezing my hand, and I smiled blandly at her and David. That was fine, she could have him, and I didn't care. Judging by the way my heart felt like it was still bleeding out, I knew that wasn't entirely true, but I could pretend.

"Well this is fucking awkward. Did not think that through when I sent Charlie over to your place the other night. Kind of slipped my mind what an antagonistic bastard you can be," Deacon finally said dryly, extracting himself from Noa and leaning forward to grab a random bottle.

He palmed it, rolling it over to see the Grey Goose label before pointing it at Tripp.

Tripp dropped down beside me, casually placing one of his perfectly polished Gucci loafers on top of his knee. His suit pants pulled up just so to reveal charcoal dress socks. I knew without looking that the other sock would be pulled up to the exact same place on his other leg. He draped his arm over the top of the seat just behind me. Taylor eyed his hand with disgust and shimmied farther down the couch away from it.

"Not one of your finer moments." Taylor flashed Deacon a look, and then her eyes moved over Victoria quickly, a sour expression arose on her face before she glowered at Deacon again, like it was somehow his fault she was here. "But I suppose Daddy Winchester holds the blame for that one. You probably felt obligated to try and do something nice for Charlie after he sprung his little girlfriend on you. Who knew after all these years he would decide to date a card-carrying member of the Manhattan social scene."

"Your dad's dating?" David asked, somewhat incredulously.

He looked from Deacon to me, where the sharp set of his jaw softened, and his eyes warmed ever so slightly, like he knew just how much I was hurting.

Deacon nodded, hurriedly swallowing the measure of vodka he poured himself, making a hurry up gesture, swinging his hands wildly before slamming the glass down. "Yeah, Marta something. She's an editor at..." Deacon trailed off, brows crinkled in confusion, and he began snapping his fingers trying to recall where she worked.

"Vogue," I supplied quietly. "Marta Berg. Senior fashion news editor at Vogue Runway."

David's nostrils flared, and I noticed the way his shoulders tensed under his shirt. Deacon jumped right back in, regaling everyone with tales from our unexpected dinner, but I wasn't listening. I was watching the way David was watching me. A pained expression pulled at his face, but his eyes were soft, like the honey I loved, almost but not quite. He was looking at me like the fact that this happened to me, hurt me, was hurting him, too.

"Anyway, she's pretty hot," Deacon finished with a shrug, eyeing Noa playfully. "He's bringing her to the Charity Gala, and he asked that Charles and I bring dates to 'take the pressure off.' Charlie says she's going to adopt a cat to be her date."

I rolled my eyes, preparing to tell my brother to fuck off when I felt Tripp's fingers brush against the bottom of my shirt sleeve.

"That won't be necessary," Tripp said coolly. "Chuck practically begged me to be her date the other night."

Every inch of warmth, longing, grounding I felt had instantly evaporated from David's face. His eyes sharpened, and the crease between his eyebrows that might have been concern for me straightened immediately. I could see the pop of his jaw grinding again. Worst of all, might have been the way his fingers started sweeping and brushing across Victoria's exposed skin—up her arms, to her shoulders and across her collarbone—slowly, lovingly, the exact way he used to move his fingers across me.

My heart began to hemorrhage again, and I felt myself squeezing Taylor's hand in rapid succession. She turned her gaze to me before looking over at David and Victoria.

"Shots!" she announced, much to Deacon's delight.

She squeezed my hand in return—one, two, three times. She was here. I could turn away, turn toward Taylor, turn toward Tripp, look anywhere but David and Victoria, who were now whispering to one another. David's other hand had made it to her thigh, fingers tucked just under the hem of her dress. I could look away. I probably should have, but I couldn't. It felt oddly like watching a car wreck in slow motion—wheels and machinery and steel exploding all at once, leaving only carnage. And in this particular wreck, the carnage was me.

CHAPTER TWENTY-SIX

I was sandwiched between Taylor and Noa, my legs pressing into either of their thighs. Taylor was still clutching my hand, squeezing it tighter every time I tried to pry mine away, telling her my hand was getting sweaty. I don't know what she thought I was going to do if she let me go. Throw down with Victoria? Who was actually no longer engaging with any of us but just sitting there on her phone, with one hand firmly planted on David's thigh.

David, Tripp and Deacon were all deep in conversation, any awkwardness between them seemingly forgotten. David did seem to be in a decidedly better mood, but any time he looked around, his gaze just skipped over me like I wasn't there. That might have been why he seemed happier; I was just a stain of blood on the highway from the wreckage that was us now, nothing worth resting your eyes on.

Taylor and Noa were leaning across me, heads together discussing some recent spread in Vogue or Vanity Fair for some designer that I didn't know. The entire club had now given way to some sort of 90s rave vibe that fit perfectly with whatever vision the designer had been trying to achieve earlier. I noticed there were still photographers weaving in and out of the gyrating crowd, snapping candids.

I leaned back, bouncing my legs. I was restless and didn't want to sit here any longer, with nothing to say and David pretending I didn't exist, and Tripp looking at me with one of his dumb smug smiles or occasionally tossing me a wink. "Do you guys want to dance?" I asked, looking hopefully between Noa and Taylor.

Taylor's eyes widened, placing a hand to her chest. "Charlie, these shorts cost a thousand dollars. I'm not going down there to sweat."

"I can't dance," Noa held up her hands.

Her hair was starting to curl around her face, despite the hours probably spent straightening it for the shoot.

"You can't dance?" I asked, a single eyebrow rising. "I refuse to believe that you, *you*, the supermodel of the world, can't dance?"

Noa shook her head, shrugging before leaning forward and pouring herself another drink.

"I'll dance with you, Chuck," Tripp said, interrupting whatever it was Deacon and David were talking about.

I looked up at him, his mouth pulled to the side in a smirk and frozen eyes seeming to taunt me.

Deacon was in the midst of waving his hands around widely, and he dropped them, shifting to look at me. We looked at one another for a moment, and a small smile stretched on Deacon's face. He raised his eyebrows in encouragement before jerking his head toward the dance floor. Our conversation from the other night rang in my ears. I could hear my brother telling me to let myself off the mat, to live my life and to stop punishing myself. Looking determinedly away from David, I nodded at Tripp, standing and extending my hand to him.

His hand engulfed my own, and I tried to focus on anything but how different his hands felt from David's. No calluses, no worn skin. Just a warm hand much bigger than my own. I trailed behind him, his taller figure navigating the crowd leading us God knew where. I focused on the way our fingers fit together. It was different but different didn't necessarily mean bad. Everyone would feel different than David. And I found that I didn't entirely mind that this hand, Tripp's hands, were different. He stopped abruptly, at the very edge of the seemingly makeshift dance floor by the corner of the bar. He didn't drop my hand but simply brought our joined fingers to rest at the side of his leg, his thumb brushing over my knuckles.

"Kennedy's a fucking idiot," he said plainly, eyes directed over my shoulder staring in the direction we came.

"Oh, I think David is perfectly happy with Miss North Carolina." I glared back at them and up to him. Even in the dim light of the bar, Tripp's eyes remained impossibly blue.

His gaze dropped back to me, and he pulled his lips back incredulously. "You're kidding me, right Chuck?" He tipped his chin toward the booth. "This is driving him fucking nuts."

In spite of myself, I craned my neck to look over my shoulder and found he wasn't exactly wrong. David was still beside Deacon, who was continuing to talk animatedly. Victoria was sitting beside Noa, seemingly fine to engage in conversation now that I was gone. She also looked significantly happier, leaning forward and nodding her head, smiling widely at whatever Taylor and Noa were saying. She wasn't clinging to David like a second skin; she wasn't even looking at him.

But he was looking at us. I could see the tight cords of muscle in his neck, how his jaw was grinding back and forth. He looked anything but happy to be sitting there. I turned back to Tripp, waving it off. "He's over me. I'm sure we're just offending his sensibilities in some other way."

"Oh, come on, of course he's not over you. Look how mad this is making him. It's written all over his pretty face." Tripp gestured behind me with our joined hands, not a care in the world for how obvious he was being.

I ripped our hands from the air, wrapping my other one around them to keep him from making any other sort of antagonizing gesture. "Why are you like this?"

"Like what?" Tripp asked blandly, his eyes sweeping over our still joined hands before landing on me.

"Why do you have to antagonize everyone around you?" I asked softly, really studying him.

His jaw tensed uncomfortably in the low light, and there was something, some sort of emotion, passing behind his eyes that I couldn't get a read on.

Tripp shrugged, bringing our joined hands up to his lips, brushing the back of mine lightly. "Eventually you just become what everyone expects of you. But I'm not doing anything. Like I said, it's all over that pretty face of his."

"It is quite pretty, isn't it?" I said, even though I wanted to stop, to peel back just one of the layers he wore around him at all times. To pause the grating music pressing in on us, to stop everyone moving past us, the people dancing around us and ask him why. What he meant, what expectations he felt shouldered with.

But the day someone managed to crack open Tripp Banks and start to understand his inner workings would be the day the world fell off its axis.

"He might be annoyed with us, but he's here with his girlfriend, Tripp. A girlfriend that once upon a time he failed to tell me about. Scratch that. He has conveniently omitted Victoria twice, and I'm starting to believe it was to hurt me. I promise you, David Kennedy is not pining for me."

Tripp scoffed, ire in his eyes before he leveled a look at me. It was incredulous and beneath that there was something unsure. Like the idea of David still wanting me was hurting him, slowly eating away at his insides. "You can be really dense, Chuck. That man will pine for you for the rest of his life. You've got no idea, do you? You just run circles around all of us."

I shook my head, cheeks flushing and my skin prickling uncomfortably at the idea. It hit too close to home. Maybe I really was a fucking wrecking ball. I looked away, finding myself chewing on the inside of my cheeks and finally extracting my hands from his.

"You think he doesn't care? Want to test that theory?" Tripp asked, tipping his head down and bringing his face so close to mine I could see all the frozen striations of his eyes. They glinted under the faint lights and his mouth twitched into a smirk. "We can do something about it."

"What are you talking about?" I crossed my arms and rolled my shoulders uncomfortably.

He was too close. If I tipped my chin up to meet him, I could grab his full bottom lip between my teeth as easily as breathing. I hated how quickly that thought sprung to life, and how it didn't feel foreign or sour.

He shrugged, bringing his hand up to tuck my hair behind my ear. I stilled at the touch, the way his fingers skated across my skin.

"Nothing we haven't done before. What's a kiss between friends?"

"I thought you said you didn't want me to kiss you until—"

Tripp brought his lips down to mine, but it was nothing like the other times we collided. His mouth wasn't crashing against mine, biting and stealing and eager to take as much as he could. I wasn't clawing desperately for a distraction, for absolution or healing. His lips were soft against mine, tentative, nervous, even. This kiss was our first kiss in a corn maze when we were nothing but teenagers. This kiss was two people who made one another laugh more than anything. This kiss was the two of us falling asleep crushed together in my tiny sorority bed, this kiss was the tiny bubble that existed around us on that dilapidated couch in his frat house. I could feel the cracked leather against all my exposed skin. This kiss was all the good parts of us.

He pulled away, hair coming undone and flopping against his forehead. His frozen eyes looked like they might have been melting. Tripp jerked his chin over my shoulder and whispered to me, "Take a look."

But I didn't care what David looked like. I cared that Tripp looked like he was thawing. Instinctively, I reached up and wrapped my hand around the back of his neck, bringing his forehead down to press against mine. "Do that again."

Tripp grinned, his lips pulled into a taunting smile and his eyes glinting playfully. "Where are your manners? Aren't you going to say please?"

His voice was low, wrapping around me and something about the way it skated across my lips had them parting to utter the word, "please," when a loud, throat-clearing noise sounded from behind me. I whipped around, dropping my hand from Tripp's neck. He grabbed it in midair, pressing it into his chest quickly, eyes sweeping over me fondly before pulling me into it. I felt him drop his chin to the crown of my head, and it was oddly reminiscent of the elevator at his apartment.

"Your sense of timing is impeccable, doctor," Tripp said loudly over the noise of the bar, the incessant beat of the rave music was starting to pound against my eardrums uncomfortably.

I felt the rumble of his voice in the column of his throat as it pressed against the back of my head, and I was at odds with how comfortable, how familiar it felt.

Taylor was smiling at us both blandly, her eyes narrowed shrewdly. "Some might say it's intentional. I just came over to see if it was okay that I headed out...Mika and I were going to grab a drink somewhere quieter and catch up. But you seem otherwise occupied."

"Charlie was just about to beg me for something. I'm not sure what she was going to ask for, but I'm sure I'll find out before the night is through," Tripp said with that dumb lilt to his voice he reserved just for me.

A sour expression rose on my face as I cringed and slowly dropped his hand from mine in an exaggerated movement. "And in a surprise to no one, you've ruined the moment."

Taylor opened her arms expectantly and smiled at me before an expression that could only be described as suspicious fell back into place as she gazed at Tripp. Her lips were pursed, and she continued to appraise him as I wrapped myself around her.

"You have your key?" I asked, closing my eyes briefly when she hugged me in return.

"Do you know what you're doing?" Taylor whispered, propping her pointed chin up on my shoulder, likely so she could continue to stare at Tripp. "It doesn't look like I should wait up."

I inhaled, pushing my nose into her wild, crimped hair. I could smell the lingering Tom Ford Rose Prick perfume she wore. She claimed it was the only thing that covered up the smell of antiseptic and masked whatever lingering scents left the hospital with her. That was her justification for why she kept the largest bottle possible in her locker at work, her car and in the various bathrooms in her apartment. I wasn't really much for perfume, but I loved it on Taylor. It immediately wrapped around me, lulling the erratic beating of my heart and reminding me of all the ways we had always been there for one another. If Deacon was one half of my heart, my soul, then Taylor was the other.

I closed my eyes, pressing into her hair. I could see us—Taylor holding my hand in the yard of our prep school when I was too nervous to join a game our classmates were playing, crying into one another's shoulders when it was time to leave for opposite coasts for boarding school, taking a red-eye out to her when her first girlfriend broke up with her, and drowning our sorrows in tequila and poor choices.

I shook my head; I really didn't have a fucking clue what I was doing.

"Not really," I whispered into her hair, pulling back. "But the other night, that night there...things all felt different than before. It's time to move on, isn't it?"

Taylor gripped my shoulders, and she stared at me appraisingly. "If that's what you think is right. I'm with you no matter what happens."

Her words felt ominous somehow, like she was predicting another great downfall of mine. She squeezed my shoulders one last time before peering over at Tripp and pointing her index finger at him.

"Watch it," she said flatly, eyes boring into him.

Tripp grinned at her, all feral delight before he raised his eyebrows. "Wouldn't dream of looking away from her now."

Taylor's lip curled momentarily before she looked at me and turned away to weave her way back through the crowd to wherever her drink date was waiting.

"Want to get out of here?" Tripp pressed his lips to the corner of my ear suddenly, and I felt my back straighten automatically, but he placed his hands on my shoulders where Taylor's had just been. I rolled them back, relaxation melting down my spine.

His hands were soft and warm, and I didn't find myself missing the brush of someone else's rough hands. I nodded, feeling myself leaning back into him. My brain immediately began to mark the different ways my body fit into his, all the ways he wasn't David. But no one would ever be David. I had thought we were one another's puzzle piece, that I would never find another that fit any of my edges the way he did.

Deacon's words rang in my ears—that maybe you didn't get just one singular love. I could feel Tripp's chest against my shoulder blades. He wasn't David. But no one would ever be Tripp, either. They were different, they made me feel different, and maybe that was okay. That maybe was allowed.

Blinking, I focused on the way his hands were warm against my shoulder. It was a different, foreign, and a softer warmth, but it was nice all the same. I leaned over my shoulder, looking back at Tripp. His eyes bore into me, and they really were a thawing ice.

"Yeah, let's get out of here. I'll just run to the restroom. Can you go tell Deacon we're leaving? I don't feel like dealing with whatever he has to say."

Tripp nodded, fingers pressing into my shoulders one more time before he shoved his hands in his pants pockets and brushed past me before threading through the crowd toward our table. I felt suddenly, shockingly alone. More alone than I should have felt surrounded by throngs of sweaty, jumping people covered with bright splashes of paint. Pushing up onto my toes, I craned my neck to look over the ever-moving crowd for some sort of restroom sign. I spotted it, flashing, and alternating between various neon colors. I wasn't sure if it usually looked like that or if the art designer had it changed for the evening. Pushing through the crowd, I finally stepped out of the sea of people and into the dim, secluded hallway.

"Have you fucked him?"

I whirled around, startled, and brought my hand to my chest. My palm was sticky against my already sweaty skin. David was now leaning against the wall that led back toward the club. His arms were folded across his chest, and his forearms were splattered with the various colors of neon paint across them, only accentuating the cords of muscles and veins. His face was giving nothing away, but his lips were downturned.

"What?" I asked, disbelief coloring my words. "Have I fucked who?"

David pushed off the wall suddenly, coming to stand right in front of me. His eyes never left mine, and I stepped backward, my own back bumping into the hallway wall. "Tripp. Have you fucked him?"

"Excuse me?" I scoffed, hardly able to believe what I was hearing. "Since when do *friends* care about things like that?"

I watched as David's jaw popped, shifting back and forth. The lights from the club flashed just beyond the hallway, illuminating his eyes, making me realize they looked exactly like pits. The stars in them were well and truly dead. No sparkling honey to be found. He leaned forward, his palm coming to rest beside my face and a tendril of blond hair falling onto his forehead. He shook his head before speaking.

"He doesn't deserve you."

I felt myself pushing harder against the wall, trying to escape whatever version of David had me caged in right now. A bitter laugh pushed past my lips. It wasn't that long ago I was in this exact same position, but with Tripp leaning over me, baiting me in a bathroom hallway. I shook my head, sadness lacing my words.

"Don't. You don't get to do that. You don't get to say things like that. You don't want me, David. So, what's it to you if I let Tripp in my bed? Or, anyone else for that matter? Am I supposed to believe that you and Victoria have turned over a leaf of celibacy? You're born again? I know for a fact that can't be true, because I heard the two of you in the bathroom of Soho House." My voice cracked with anger, but the constant hurt, the bleeding out of my heart, was leaking into my words. Because David didn't want me anymore. He made that clear. "You don't want me so yes. Eventually I was going to find someone else who did."

"That's not true," David ground out.

"What's not true?" I bit back, folding my arms across my chest to try and create distance between us.

My entire body prickled, and my skin felt sticky.

"That I don't want you. You're all I want. I want you every second of every minute of every goddamn day. When I close my eyes, you're the one tattooed on the back of my eyelids. Those fucking perfect, green eyes. This hair, this nose, this chin." David punctuated each word with the brush of his thumb against my face.

First, he pressed it into the side of my face right by my eyes, cupping my cheek momentarily before twisting my hair between his fingers, his thumb swiping the end of my nose before coming to rest in the center of my chin. I felt his fingers brush alongside my jaw.

"You. I only ever see you. Don't you think I wish it was my own girlfriend? But no. It's only ever you. I have to be so careful, so fucking ever-present when I'm kissing her—when I'm in bed with her—that my thoughts don't stray to you. But you're always there, banging away incessantly on the door in my mind begging to be let in. You're all I ever want but the one person I can't have, because you ruined it."

I squeezed my eyes shut, praying to whoever might be listening that when I opened them David would be gone. That he wouldn't be right here, a breath away. That I had imagined it all. He wasn't standing in front of me, simultaneously saying everything I wanted to hear but ripping whatever was left out of my heart with his teeth. I shook my head, trying to shake his thumb off, hoping it would just disappear. I opened my eyes, and he was still here, head tipped down and his hand formed into a clenched fist beside my face.

"That's not fair. This isn't fair, David. I deserve—" I swallowed, my eyes watering around the edges. "I know what I did was wrong, and I'll be sorry for the rest of my life. But if you really can't forgive me, you need to let me go. Please let me go. I can't do this with you forever. I won't survive it."

David dropped his hand from my chin and took a measured step back from me, offering me a small jerk of his head that resembled a nod. He exhaled, his cheeks puffing out in something like resignation before opening his mouth to speak.

"Everything okay here?" Tripp's voice came from the hallway entrance, and I looked away from both of them, wiping at my eyes before turning back and plastering a smile on my face.

"Everything's fine. I was just telling David that we were leaving," I said tightly, immediately making my way toward where Tripp was standing.

Tripp nodded with raised eyebrows, and I watched as he poked his tongue into his cheek, looking like he didn't believe a word I was saying. "That okay with you DK?"

David shrugged noncommittally, like he didn't have a care in the world before speaking. "Can I have a word, Tripp?"

"This is a new one," Tripp said, meandering every so fucking slowly down the short hallway until he was face-to-face with David.

I watched, unable to look away as Tripp raised his eyebrows again, waiting for David to talk. David leaned forward, seemingly whispering something to Tripp that I couldn't make out over the pounding noise of the club music. Whatever he said was brief, and my eyes widened as David stuck his hand out for Tripp.

I wasn't sure if I was horrified or devastated when Tripp reached back out, gripping David's hand in his. David clapped his hand on his shoulder when they broke apart, and Tripp walked back toward me, hand outstretched for me. I didn't know where to look, what to focus on, so I slipped my fingers into his and let him tug me toward the club again.

I thought the other doors that closed on us, on me and David, had been it. The final one locking me out of the best home I had ever known. But I was wrong each time. Because nothing was as final as this. Nothing felt the way this one did, I could feel it—an impenetrable, solid steel door whose edges would soon be sealed with cement, nothing in or out. Tripp's hand was warm in mine, and I stumbled along behind him, still looking over my shoulder at David. I raised my hand, offering a small wave in goodbye. Because it was goodbye; the real one this time.

David smiled at me, sadness etched in his features. He tipped his head, nodding one more time before scrubbing his hand across his jaw and over his eyes, shoving his hands into his pockets. The space stretching endlessly between us disappeared, overtaken by the throngs of people who had no idea the finality that hung in the air, that this very club was the sound of two hearts severing.

I couldn't make out David anymore, and I wanted to crane my neck, to stand on my tiptoes to get one last look, but the door to the club opened and the night air blew past me, washing over my skin and welcoming me into a new world. I finally looked up at Tripp, and he was assessing me carefully, eyes somewhat frozen over again, and as we waited in silence for a town car, I hoped this was a new world I would survive.

CHAPTER TWENTY-SEVEN

Tripp was silent the entire car ride from the club, his eyes looking like ice creeping over a bottomless lake. But he never let go of my hand, his thumb occasionally brushing the back of it. The car pulled up to his apartment building, and he finally spoke, thanking the driver for his time, and extracting his hand from mine to pull a crisp bill from his wallet.

I felt oddly bare, exposed with my hand just sitting empty and open, fingers still outstretched for his. I shifted uncomfortably, too aware I was in this strange outfit that was entirely out of place anywhere but the one-time art installation we had been at.

Tripp opened the car door, still saying nothing to me. I pushed myself along the leather, offering up my own thanks to the driver. Tripp leaned over the door, inky black hair spilling over his forehead, eyes impassive and an extended hand reaching toward me. Instinctively, I reached up, interlacing our fingers once again. I ducked out of the car, falling in step beside a silent Tripp.

I wanted to say something, anything, but I really wasn't sure what. I was confident in only one thing—I had absolutely no idea what I was doing. But the jerk of David's head, the confirmation that he would finally do what I asked, what I needed; that he would let me go, played over and over behind my eyes. But it wasn't grief or despair spreading across me. It might have been relief with sadness staining the edges but relief nonetheless. Maybe I could finally move on, and maybe I could work on forgiving myself.

We crossed the lobby in silence, and I found myself studying the planes of Tripp's face, lingering on his bottom lip, the way it had felt against mine. The way that kiss felt as a whole. Tripp tipped his gaze toward me when he held the elevator open, and I passed him, never letting go of his hand but continuing whatever vow of silence had taken over us since leaving the club. He raised his eyebrows at me before leaning his head back against the mirrored elevator wall and kicking a foot up against it.

"Just ask, Chuck. I know you're dying to." Tripp rolled the back of his head to look at me while the elevator started to rise up to his apartment.

I *was* dying to ask. I wanted to know what David said to him, but I narrowed my eyes and carefully peeled my fingers from his, crossing my arms stubbornly. "I'm not sure what you're talking about."

Tripp pushed off the wall, coming to stand in front of me, both palms flat on either side of the wall behind my head. He looked down at me, lips pulling up smugly. "You want to know what Kennedy said to me."

"No, I don't." I shrugged, pressing my head back and acting like I didn't have a care in the world.

Tripp leaned forward, placing his lips at the top of my ear. "He told me I didn't deserve you, and that he didn't, either. That no one deserves you, and to be careful with you."

My heart dropped, and I pressed my eyes closed. He was letting me go, pushing me to Tripp of all people. This really was the final door closing. That home had been boarded up and left vacant. I lifted my head, Tripp moving to place his forehead against mine.

"Well, I could have told you...that no one deserves me," I deadpanned, deflecting and watching the corners of his eyes begin to defrost.

"Happy to see you're finally recognizing your worth, Chuck." Tripp grinned, pushing off the wall as the elevator dinged to announce our arrival at the penthouse floor.

He shoved his hands in his tailored suit pockets, strolling leisurely out of the elevator and down the small hall.

"I was kidding. The only person conceited enough to believe something like that about themselves would be you," I offered, trailing behind him, arms still firmly crossed over my chest.

Tripp glanced at me sideways from where he stopped and leaned against the doorframe, lazily punching in the security code. "You're right, I wouldn't be thinking highly of myself if I was wearing...whatever it is you're wearing. Did you get dressed in the dark? Don't worry, you can wear one of my sweat suits."

The door swung open, and he backed out through the doorway, making an exaggerated gesture into the apartment. I frowned, walking pointedly past him. "I'll have you know, Taylor dressed me. This was exactly in line with whatever the fuck was going on at that...fashion show tonight."

"Taylor would know best," Tripp called, his voice a drawl from behind me as I walked down the hallway through the still barren apartment. "Help yourself to some clothes. Top drawer in the dresser."

I snorted, looking over my shoulder at him. Tripp shrugged out of his suit jacket, folding it expertly before setting it down on the marble island that spanned the length of the kitchen. "Of course you have an entire drawer for sweat suits specifically."

"They're coming in handy now to save you from your little *fashion statement*," Tripp said, moving to the wine fridge and drumming his fingers against the glass. "Any preference?"

"Screaming Eagle?" I asked, my voice wry, turning from him and making my way toward his bedroom.

I really didn't want to be in these stupid shorts a second longer.

Tripp's bedroom looked exactly the same as I had last seen it: sheets pulled tight and tucked into the corners of the bed. The walk-in closet was open, and I rolled my eyes, noticing the way his dry cleaning was hanging entirely in order. The dresser was immaculate, spotless and annoyingly shiny. I pulled open the top drawer as instructed, cringing at the fact that I was standing in Tripp Banks' sterile, serial killer closet, pulling open one of his dresser drawers. This was the epitome of being in the lair.

I rose up on my toes, peering into the drawer. A laugh escaped me. It was four rows of evenly folded, color-coordinated sweat suits. The gray Hugo Boss I wore the last time I was here, a black Versace set, a navy set I didn't recognize but felt like a cashmere blend, and a soft cotton, chocolate brown set. I grabbed the brown sweat suit, dropping it unceremoniously to the ground before eyeing the perfectly folded clothes still in the drawer.

I reached out, unfolding them all and mixing the matched up coordinated colors before closing it. I knew Tripp would lose his mind whenever he opened the drawer and saw it. I could vaguely hear the pop of a cork from the kitchen as I shut the door to the ensuite bathroom. It was the same as the rest of the apartment—sterile with no personal touches save for the bottle of

Tom Ford Oud Wood cologne that sat to the left of the sink. Even the fluffy, black hand towel was perfectly folded, looking like it was fresh from the dryer. More likely freshly pressed by the cleaning service.

I was happy to change into the sweat suit, finally discarding the black shorts and bizarrely ripped shirt. Catching my reflection in the mirror, I paused. The hooded sweatshirt engulfed my body, the arms falling past my fingertips. I could still see tiny flecks of neon paint peeking out from the neck of the sweater, dotting my skin. I moved my head back and forth, watching as my eyes caught the light above the mirror. My hair flopped back and forth, straight as always, and I choked back a laugh. This was not what I predicted for New York Charlie.

"Chuck?" Tripp called from behind the closed door, followed by a faint knock. "You all good?"

I blinked, turning away from my own reflection, because no good ever came from me studying and dissecting my own soul. I pulled the door open to reveal Tripp leaning against the wall, a flute of champagne extended. He had ditched the remnants of his suit, now wearing the black Versace sweat suit I had left in a disorganized mess in his dresser.

"Champagne?" I cocked my head, reaching out and snatching it from him, padding away into his room. I wasn't sure I trusted myself if he kept looking at me the way he was. "What are we celebrating?"

I felt Tripp behind me as I walked through the room, entirely unsure of where I was headed until I impulsively dropped down on the side of the bed I fell asleep on the other night. I settled against the outrageous amount of pillows he had, bringing the champagne to my lips.

"We're celebrating your clever little desecration of my formerly organized clothes," Tripp replied before propping himself up on the other side of the bed.

He had pushed his hair back, and he really did look like a Bond villain. He was all dark edges—stubble peppering his jaw, impossibly dark hair and a matching black Versace sweat suit.

"Very funny." I arched an eyebrow at him, taking another small sip just for something to do with my hands, with my lips.

My eyes couldn't be trusted, because all they were doing was roving Tripp's face, tracing his jawline to his lips, and falling on his bottom lip for longer than was appropriate. I could feel his eyes on me, and I looked up and there they were. Not frozen but thawing. It was like looking at the person he used to be to me, once upon a time. It was going back in time, in the best ways. It was unsettling, unnerving, jarring. I wasn't a child trying relentlessly to shove the broken pieces of a favorite toy back together. We were just us, and maybe that was okay. Mistakes and all.

"Why did you do that? Why did you kiss me?" I asked hesitantly.

Tripp slowly brought his flute to his mouth, like he was considering my question.

"I wanted to see what would happen. I thought you'd either run screaming for the hills, or Kennedy would come to his fucking senses and quit the holier than thou act, and that it was something I could do to help you be happy. When he didn't, I thought maybe it was time I made it clear that I'm all in with you. Messiness and all."

I shook my head slowly, chewing the inside of my cheek. "I've tried with David. I've thrown myself at his feet. I've begged. I've pleaded. But he can't get over what I did. He can't forgive me, but he can't seem to let me go. I asked him tonight to let me go."

"Where does that leave us? You asked me to kiss you again," Tripp asked quietly, seeming to weigh his next words before continuing. "But you still love him."

"I'll always love David. I told you before, the best way I can describe it is that he was my home. The first home I felt comfortable in, sleepy in—safe in. But we don't get to keep our first homes forever," I offered truthfully, shrugging my shoulders in the giant sweater overtaking me.

"Are you in the market for a new one?"

I paused, considering his words over my champagne. Tripp simultaneously existed in my before and after years. The years before my family fell apart, before my mom left me, before I became whoever I was to have hurt Tripp and David both so badly. But unlike David, he was still here in the after years.

"I could be, but I'm not sure I trust you to be there for me. I know you say you didn't do it, but I spent a long time thinking you abandoned me during the worst time of my life."

Tripp's eyes flashed, freezing over for a moment before they gave way to softness again. "I understand that. I can't change the past, Chuck. What would it take for you to trust me again?"

What did trust mean to me? My eyes began to burn, unbidden, and the answer rose up, in and amongst all the painful memories. My mom leaving me—this earth—my father shutting all his doors for years; my brother abandoning me in my quest to breathe life into our mother, continuing to conveniently shut me out whenever he deemed it necessary to protect himself. But I was looking at Tripp now. Looking at who he was to me. He was many things—some bad, some good. But they all clicked together to form the endlessly confusing, endlessly frustrating, and endlessly appealing puzzle that he was. What did trusting Tripp look like? It was the combination of all those things that seemed to exist for just us. Two fucked up people who saw things in one another no one else could.

"Make me laugh like you do. Make me furious like only you do. Antagonize me. Call me Chuck. Be a pretentious matching sweat suit-wearing douchebag. Understand me. Be there for me this time."

"Okay," he nodded solemnly, tipping back the glass of champagne and draining it in one swallow.

I watched with fascination how he swallowed, the sharp jawline giving way to the taut muscles of his neck that disappeared beneath the hood of his sweatshirt.

"Can I kiss you now, Chuck?"

I continued to stare at Tripp, a small smile tugging on the corners of my lips before I slowly finished the rest of my champagne. Tripp continued to watch me, grinning wildly, and I felt his eyes tracking me as I swallowed the last of it. As soon as it was done, he grabbed the empty flute and set both on his nightstand.

"You sure you don't need to rinse and wash those out first? The dirty dishes aren't going to distract you?"

Tripp continued to grin at me, and for a moment he looked like that twenty-year-old boy again, before he leaned forward, grabbing my chin, and tipping it upward.

"Usually, it would depend on someone's performance. But I think the building could collapse, and nothing could distract me from you."

Before I could respond in any semblance of outrage, his lips were on mine. This kiss was different, too. It wasn't scraping, stolen moments together. It wasn't like the before years. This was the after years, a new world, and maybe we were building a new home together. Each kiss, we're excavating the land we want to live on together. Tripp pulling my sweater over my head, a new brick laid down. My hands snaking up his chest, the foundation is erected. His palms moving down my body, all the way down my legs and leaving me entirely bare; the framing goes up. His breathing was rough in my ear as his grown-up hands grabbed, gripped, and explored every new inch of my skin.

I read it takes seven years for your skin to fully regenerate. This is a whole new body he's touching; one he's never hurt, never left a mark on—the windows and doors are installed. My hands roam down the planes of muscle in his back, finding themselves under his waistband. The flooring goes down. He pulls me up to stand with him, and I push those dumb sweatpants down. The walls encase us.

He lays me back down, gently, reverently, entirely unchanged, and yet dissimilar to the boy I used to know at the same time. The shingles of the roof click together. His hands are all over me; they grip my ribcage, his teeth graze my neck and his lips chart a path across my chest, and those hands move down my stomach to touch me. He catches all my sounds with his lips. Our breathing turned ragged and rough, and Tripp broke his lips away from mine, dark hair falling forward across his forehead as he breathed, suspended over me, melted eyes asking for permission.

"Woah, condom. I don't know where you've been all these years," I whispered, my own breath catching, all too aware that he's touching every part of me.

Tripp's lips quivered into a grin, and he propped himself up on one forearm, the other reaching to rummage in the drawer of the nightstand. He dropped his lips to my earlobe, tugging on it gently.

"Waiting for you."

The front door shuts us in.

CHAPTER TWENTY-EIGHT

Tripp made it a habit of walking around shirtless more often than not. He was across from me now, the muscles of his arms and shoulders popping and always on display. "This is a great picture of me, don't you think?" Tripp leaned over my kitchen island, holding out his phone.

I pursed my lips, snatching his phone to see whatever he was talking about. Photos of us had become quite commonplace over the past two weeks, because there was nothing to report about Noa. One photo was taken of us standing outside a restaurant with Noa, and that was that. I was nowhere near as good at spotting paparazzi as Deacon, and my eyes were closed or my mouth half-open in most of the photos.

In this particular shot, Tripp's sunglasses were pulled down over his eyes, and his arm was slung casually over my shoulders. He was looking down at me, lips curved up mischievously. I looked sort of dumb and baleful if I was being honest. My chin was tipped up at him, and I was pretty sure I was probably seconds from insulting him, but the way the sun hit my eyes, they looked like they were sparkling up at him.

"You look like Edward Cullen in Twilight," I supplied, tossing his phone back at him, and warming both my hands gripped on my mug of coffee.

I was sitting cross-legged on one of my barstools, early morning sunlight spilling across the kitchen, still in the gray Cosabella sleep romper I slept in the night before. Tripp had deigned to put on a pair of sweatpants; it turned out he just wasn't a fan of shirts in the morning.

"Does that make you my lamb?" He asked, continuing to grin at me from across the island.

"What?" I knitted my eyebrows in confusion.

"Twilight. The lion and the lamb?" Tripp continued, a predatory glint shining in his eyes.

He walked around the kitchen island, smiling down at me when he came to stop in front of me.

I bit down on my bottom lip, shaking my head at him before taking another sip of coffee. "Quoting Twilight doesn't do it for me."

Tripp narrowed his eyes at me, hand dropping to my bare shoulder, and began toying with the lacy strap of my pajamas. "What does do it for you?"

"Well, I've been faking all my orgasms so clearly you haven't figured it out, yet," I said, raising my eyebrows and my mug to my lips again at the same time.

Tripp grinned down at me, dropping his hand to the lace front of the romper and tracing where it met my collarbone. "How about you lay back, and I—"

"Absolutely not. I eat on that island."

I popped my head over his shoulder to see Taylor standing in the living room doorway, arms crossed, and lips puckered in disgust. A garment bag was folded over her forearms.

Tripp groaned in frustration, rolling his neck before turning to face her with a tight smile. "Didn't hear you come in, Taylor."

She smiled in that all teeth way she seemed to reserve exclusively for Tripp. "That's because I have a key."

"What dress did you decide on?" I tipped my chin toward the garment bag, ignoring them both and changing the subject.

Their unpleasant banter could go on and on. I leaned my head back against Tripp's chest, shooting her a look and widening my eyes. I watched her exhale, practically snort through her nose, before schooling her features. I had been giving her that look since we were children, and it usually translated to shut the fuck up, or behave.

"I brought four," Taylor said, walking into the kitchen and dropping the garment bag on the island with a flourish before grabbing the coffee mug from my hands. She took a sip before continuing, "As a gift to you. As you are my best friend, I thought I would let you pick whichever dress you think your father would hate more, and I'll wear that."

I slapped my hand to my chest as if I was beyond touched. "You are too generous. But I will gladly take you up on that. God knows what Sabine pulled for me."

Our family weren't her only clients, but she always dropped everything whenever Steven called. Apparently that extended as far as flying to other cities for WH events.

She leaned forward, tipping her head back and forth as she considered with her bottom lip out. "If I had to guess, now that

Noa is on the scene, you're looking at understated, probably black dresses, from conservatively priced designers."

Before I could answer and give thanks for the fact that Sabine's top priority was now ensuring I didn't detract focus from Noa, Tripp's phone began to vibrate against the island counter. I felt him lean over behind me, reaching across to grab the phone and peer at the screen.

Looking over my shoulder, I noticed his eyebrows crease momentarily before he turned to me. "I've gotta take this. I'll be right back."

I nodded, saying nothing but cataloging the way his shoulders seemed to tense as he headed out through the doorway to the garden terrace. A frown pulled at my lips before I turned back to Taylor and popped off the stool to get another mug of coffee. She was still content to drink mine.

"I can't believe you're fucking him," she said, still leaning forward over the island but eyeing me shrewdly.

I narrowed my eyes in deference. My hackles rose, and my skin pricked uncomfortably. It wasn't just that with us, and it never really had been. But no one got it, no one understood, because no one saw what I did. No one saw him laugh so hard that the ever present, infuriating mask slipped off, when we both thought it was so fucking funny someone on a television show got hit in the head. No one heard him speak softly, quietly, lovingly, to his mother about a reality TV show. Those things were just for me.

I rolled my eyes and shook my head, pouring myself another cup before deciding to give her a response, "I'm not just fucking him Taylor. There's more to it, to us, to him, than that. But even if I was, why wouldn't I? Have you seen him?"

Taylor pulled a face, puckering her lips again before peering over my shoulder to watch Tripp's outline through the glass doors. "He does have a particular...je ne sais quoi about him, I suppose. If you're into that sort of thing."

"You're into that sort of thing. I don't think a single person you've dated hasn't been vaguely mysterious in some way. Except my brother. He is an open book and not a particularly dense one at that." I grimaced, hopping back onto my seat.

"Mhm. This is true. But how should I put it?" She pursed her lips again and started snapping her fingers, like whatever she wanted to say was on the tip of her tongue. "Deac really knew how to turn a page."

I pulled my lips back in disgust. "Ew. First, don't mention anything to do with my brother's *skills*, complimentary or otherwise. Second, you're a doctor. You went to med school. You save lives for a living. You can come up with a better metaphor than that."

Taylor grinned at me, drumming her impossibly short fingernails against her chin. "Are you excited to get ready with Steven and Marta today? I personally cannot wait to meet her."

I made a noncommittal noise of disinterest, draining the rest of my coffee before grabbing more. Today was Winchester Holdings'—really Steven's—entrance into Manhattan finance. This dumb charity gala he proposed was happening tonight, and in a bizarre move he requested that Taylor, Noa and I get ready with Marta in his suite at The Carlyle before heading to The New York Public Library where it was being held. I assumed this meant that Sabine was probably dressing Marta, too. We hadn't spoken since our dinner, but Tripp told me he saw her meet Steven at the office once or twice for dinner. The patio door opened behind us, and I swiveled in my seat toward Tripp.

He was twirling his phone almost nervously between his fingers, and the muscles in his jaw twitched. Tripp rolled his shoulders back and shoved the phone in the pocket of his sweatpants. He smiled tightly at me, raising his eyebrows when he came to stand beside me, and his posture seemed to relax slightly, but I watched the muscle feathering away in the corner of his jaw. What was most disturbing to me was his eyes. They were harsh, sharp and frozen all over again after the spring thaw.

"Everything okay?" I asked gently, tipping my head to the side to try and get a better read on him.

"I just have to run home and take care of something. I'll meet you at The Carlyle later." Tripp dropped a brief kiss to the crown of my head before turning toward Taylor and offering a flat goodbye. "Taylor, nice to see you."

My lips parted, bewilderment lighting my features. "The limo is picking us up at—"

"I know," Tripp interrupted, his gaze softening for a moment before I watched the ice inch back across the endless waters of his eyes. He tugged on a strand of my hair that had fallen out of my ponytail. "I'll be there, Chuck."

I nodded, swallowing audibly as I watched his retreating form. The muscles in his exposed back still tense, and I noticed him roll out his shoulders again before disappearing up the staircase; the only evidence he was in the house at all was from the creak of the old staircase. I looked at Taylor, swallowing down a burning sip of coffee to push down the lump starting to rise in my throat, offering her a small shrug.

Her eyes softened, and she reached forward, brushing her fingers across the island in front of me in an invitation before flipping her palm over. I dropped my hand down to hers, and she squeezed one, two, three times.

"Come on, let's figure out what dress is going to piss your father off most."

———

The Empire Suite at The Carlyle no longer belonged to Steven Winchester. It belonged to Sabine. An audible gasp slipped from Taylor's mouth as we walked through the front door to the suite. She quickly covered it by clearing her throat. Turning to me, she scratched the back of her head absentmindedly and raised her eyebrows. There were five racks strewn throughout the room, each bearing their own sign with a name that appeared to be written in golden sharpie.

"What am I looking at?" Taylor hissed from the corner of her mouth.

My eyes widened at the swathes of impossibly vibrant fabric spilling from all the dress bags. It really was an assault to the senses, an impossible clash of colors and types of fabric every which way you looked. I immediately looked toward the gown rack in the middle of the room that bore a giant sign with my name written in fancy gold calligraphy. There was an alarming number of shiny, gold dresses falling from the open bags. My gaze swiveled quickly between the other racks. There was one for Noa, one for Marta, and one for Steven and Deacon for later. At least their's looked to be different options of the exact same tuxedo.

I turned to Taylor, a hopeless sort of grimace pulling on my lips. "My worst nightmare."

Right on cue, Sabine sauntered into the room in her usual all black attire. I wasn't sure why that was okay for her but not for me. The belt of the A.L.C Capri Jumpsuit was tied tight around her waist, and her classic black Louboutins sunk into the carpet as she made her way across the room toward us. Her dark curls were slicked back off her face, and her brown skin was dusted with a simple gold shimmer over her cheekbones, the rest of her skin bare save for a bit of mascara. I felt the corner of my mouth twitch. I would give anything for her to dress me the same way she dressed herself.

"Charlie, Taylor. You're here! Marta and Noa are in the master bath. I'll get you set up there as well." Sabine smiled at us before beginning to make aggressive checks on a clipboard, like she was responsible for ensuring all the guests were styled at the Met Gala. Her eyes narrowed at the garment bag draped over Taylor's arm. "Taylor, you know I'm more than happy to dress you. You're practically a Winchester as it is."

Taylor nodded, smiling politely. "I know the offer is always on the table Sabine, thank you. But as you know I have a very particular sense of style. I really enjoy pulling my own clothes."

"I wish Charlie liked bright, vibrant things as much as you." Sabine beamed at her, reaching out and patting her cheek before turning to me with a pout. "I have a beautiful gold Balmain gown for you, Charlie, but I know the Oscar de la Renta you wore at the engagement party was gold lamé. There's a beautiful tiered floral applique gown for you as well."

"Well, Sabine, you know that Taylor herself is a bright, vibrant thing. I have never claimed to be such," I offered, peering over her shoulder for any evidence of Steven or Deacon. "Where's Steven?"

Sabine frowned, quickly looking down at her clipboard like she might find his whereabouts there. "I think he and your brother went downstairs for breakfast. They don't need to get ready until much later. What's your new boyfriend's name? The handsome one? You never gave me his measurements, so I didn't pull anything for him."

"My last boyfriend was handsome, too," I responded petulantly, earning an elbow to my ribs from Taylor.

The instinctual need to defend David rose in me immediately, and I hadn't even bothered to correct her assumption that Tripp was my boyfriend—we sort of just fell into whatever this was.

"Of course he was." Sabine waved me off. "He's with that little blonde thing now, yes? You two looked lovely together, but the dark, brooding thing that new one has going on really works with your hair and complexion. I really think we should go with the tiered floral Oscar de la Renta—it's as much about how it matches whose arm you're on."

My eyebrows rose, but she had already turned back to ponder the gowns. "That seems a little antiquated, no?"

"It's just a fact, Charlie," Sabine said absentmindedly, wandering back over to the racks and beginning to paw through the gowns hung on the one designated for Noa. "Why don't you two go join Noa and Marta for skin prep? Your father has the people from Kiehl's here to prep your face before makeup and hair come."

"Are you fucking kidding me?" I whispered out of the corner of my mouth to Taylor. "That is absurd and so unnecessary."

Grabbing my wrist, Taylor marched forward across the sitting room and past Sabine who was back in her own little world. "Just relax and enjoy it, Charlie. When was the last time you had a facial?" Taylor tossed me a look over her shoulder. "We can get to know Marta."

"Fun," I said, my voice dripping with sarcasm as I trailed along behind her.

I had no real interest in getting to know any more about Marta than I already did. She worked at Vogue, she was only about ten years older than me, her hair was impossibly bleached, and I was pretty sure she had to be a gold digger. That was four facts too many. Five if you counted that I knew her name.

We rounded the corner into the impossibly large guest bathroom. There were three marble sinks lining the wall with three individual mirrors, all lit up with bulbs around the outside. Noa and Marta were occupying two of the black leather chairs that wouldn't have looked out of place at a high-end hair salon. They were each wrapped in a branded Kiehl's robe. Noa's dark curls were piled impossibly high on her head, and there were gold masks under her eyes. She was propped up, both hands wrapped around a mug of coffee, nodding along at whatever Marta was saying. Her hair looked freshly bleached and was pushed off her face with one of those terry cloth headbands that had bunny ears. Taylor pinched the back of my arm, and I forced a smile on my face as they both turned around.

I found myself wishing with all my heart that Tripp was here with me, to provide a distraction, so I could pretend this woman wasn't interloping in the chair my mother should be sitting in, if we all hadn't made so many mistakes. I saw my mother sitting there for just a moment, hair like mine, eyes like mine. I wondered what it would be like if she was really sitting there instead. What it would be like for me, for Deacon, for my father. But my mother wasn't sitting there. She was nothing but dust in the Graceland cemetery on the north side of Chicago. Marta was sitting there instead, and it wasn't lost on me that I was counting down the hours until I saw Tripp again but for an entirely different reason.

CHAPTER TWENTY-NINE

Sabine had decided on the tiered floral applique gown from Oscar de la Renta in the end. I rolled my shoulders as Taylor zipped up the back of the gown, and I tugged down the long sleeves. The bodice was nude but embroidered with red and pink roses, complete with intricate green leaves and stems, and it gave way to a vibrant red, tiered silk asymmetric bubble hem skirt. I looked like an overly decorated cupcake. Sabine seemed to be favoring Oscar de la Renta tonight, because Noa was wearing a black and sheer floral sequin-embroidered off-the-shoulder gown with long sleeves, an open back and trailing hem. I would have preferred her dress but here I was.

The last I had seen before taking my cupcake monstrosity and disappearing into one of the bathrooms was Marta debating the merits of a black silk halter neck trumpet gown, also by Oscar de la Renta, versus a black Marchesa ruched floral gown with a plunging neckline with some sort of extravagant ruffle on the one shoulder and a flowing skirt.

I wasn't sure if it was in solidarity, or if this was really the dress she would have chosen, but Taylor was wearing a pleated, green one-shoulder lamé Oscar de la Renta dress that hung around her body like a sheet. Her blonde hair had been crimped and braided in various places to give it more volume. She never let Sabine dress her, but she was always fine with whoever she hired for hair and makeup squeezing her in.

Pulling at the floral embroidery around my neck, I flicked my eyes up to look at myself in the mirror. My hair was straightened, even though it wasn't really necessary, parted down the middle and teased at the crown to give it some semblance of volume. There were a pair of giant Autore cultured pearl stud earrings that were weighing down my earlobes to set the entire outfit off. I was pretty sure Steven bought them at an auction years ago.

"She's not that bad," Taylor whispered, patting the zipper of the gown before peering into the mirror and raising her eyes to mine.

She dropped her chin to my shoulder, hands pressing into my arms.

"She's not my mom," I answered quietly in return, blinking rapidly.

"Who could be?" She replied, dropping to press her head against mine.

I rolled my eyes before I could stop myself. "All my mom ever did was paint and embroider and do God knows what in that studio of hers, before she became a vacant shell of a person, Taylor. Don't tell me you have some memories of her that I don't."

Taylor exhaled and pinched the bridge of her nose momentarily before dropping her hand down my arm and threading our fingers together. "She was sick, Charlie. I know you're mad, and I know you miss her. But don't forget how she used to smile, how she used to laugh."

"I don't remember," I forced out stubbornly, shrugging my shoulders, like it was of no consequence to me.

When really, I was crawling through, scraping all the recesses of my mind for the few times I could vaguely recall before her eyes just became a hollow, flat version of mine and Deacon's.

"Are you sure you aren't just mad that you haven't heard back from Tripp today?" She asked, squeezing my hand once, twice, three times.

My stomach tightened uncomfortably. I hadn't heard from Tripp all day and had been fielding questions about him from Marta with vague, nondescript answers while Noa and Taylor exchanged concerned, knowing looks.

"I'm not in the mood for the *I told you so's*. I know you think he's untrustworthy, scum of the earth, etc., etc. He said he would be here, and he knows how important it is to me. How I've been feeling about it. He'll be here, Taylor."

My words did nothing to reassure Taylor, and I think they were more for me than her. Both of our eyes wandered to the clock on the mantelpiece above the fire in the living room. We could see it reflected in the mirror, and I had been tracking the hands as they ticked down all afternoon, unease settling over me like a second skin.

"I wasn't going to say that," Taylor whispered, leaning her head against mine in what was supposed to be a gesture of comfort, but all it did was serve to remind me that he wasn't here. "I just don't want you to be hurt by him again, to be hurt by your own—"

Whatever Taylor was going to say was cut off by a sound that could only belong to Deacon echoing throughout the suite. It was something caught between a groan and a whistle. I grimaced, and a matching look of disgust popped up on Taylor's features.

"I guess that means Deacon has seen Noa." She laughed, squeezing my hand one more time before extracting her fingers and walking out into the sitting area adjacent to the bathroom.

It was kind of sweet in a way, the way he fell all over her and couldn't believe his luck, how beautiful she was each time he saw her. It was just so over the top, like everything else he did. I smoothed the front of my dress unnecessarily, quickly pulling on the embroidered sleeves before turning and following Taylor.

Deacon was on his knees in front of Noa, holding her hands and gazing up at her in a way that simultaneously made me want to punch him and made my heart swell with happiness for him. He was wearing a tailored black Ralph Lauren Purple Label peak lapel tuxedo, and his hair was expertly pushed back off his face. I would have laughed at him—the heir to a multi-billion dollar empire on his knees before someone who was probably considered one of the most beautiful women in the world—but an audible clearing of a throat had my gaze swiveling immediately.

David was leaning against the mantle, hands tucked into the pockets of a navy Zegna wool tux with a black peak lapel. Someone, probably Deacon, had pushed his hair back off his head with just enough styling gel to contain the rogue waves. Stubble peppered his jaw, and his lips were parted slightly. And his eyes, those anything but boring eyes, were on me and only me. His pupils were wide, and he cleared his throat again, bringing a hand up to rub the back of his neck.

I raised my hand and gave him a small wave, mouthing the word "hi," not sure how to exist in this world where we were well and truly no more, where I was with someone who wasn't him, before my eyes roved over every inch of him—categorizing exactly the way his shoulders filled out that jacket, the way the black lapel seemed so stark against the dark navy of the wool, how the pants clung to his muscular thighs before tapering down his calves. I wondered if this is what it was like when people went back to visit their childhood home that no longer belonged to them. If they could feel the house itself, the memories, the love all around them—the ghost of a past life whispering by their skin. Because that's what it was like staring at David. I sniffed gently, wondering if I would be able to smell his cologne from here and catch the scent of the ocean on him.

David exhaled through his nose before his eyes tracked every inch of me in return. I could feel them moving up from where my fingers fluttered uselessly beside me, trailing over the embroidered floral sleeves, to cross my shoulders and down the bodice of the dress, where they lingered on the red silk wrapped around my waist before dropping down the tiered skirt. "You look...indescribable."

My lips parted to utter a tiny thank you when Deacon spoke, shattering whatever thread or precipice David and I were teetering on.

"You know there are other people in the room, right?" Deacon asked dryly, and I whipped around to look at him.

I had forgotten they were even here. They weren't of any consequence to me, not when David was looking at me like that. Deacon was still on his knees in front of Noa, holding her hand, and his eyes swiveling back and forth between David and me. A tiny "O" formed on Noa's lips, but her amber eyes were soft, almost watery as she looked between us. I felt my cheeks burn, and I tugged on my sleeves awkwardly again before looking at Taylor helplessly. Her eyes were glowing, and a small, knowing smirk tugged on her lips.

"Not when she looks like that," David spoke, his words almost impossible to hear before he shook his head. Deacon's mouth fell open, and I wasn't sure what he was about to say, or do, when David continued, "Noa, Taylor, you both look beautiful as always."

"But not indescribable?" Taylor asked, tipping her head and narrowing her eyes at David.

She seemed to have quickly changed sides again. I shot her a look, widening my eyes. She shrugged, no remorse on her features, and she continued to look at David sharply. A heavy silence fell, with Deacon still down on his knees for some unknown reason, looking back and forth between the three of us now. I cleared my own throat, turning abruptly on my heel and moving to the bar built into the wall of the sitting room to pour myself a drink.

"What are you doing here David? No Victoria?" Taylor asked from behind me.

I stared resolutely at the glass I was filling in front of me, hoping no one noticed the way my shoulders tensed at her name. I felt a sour expression forming on my face. Even though I was, sort of, with Tripp, the thought of her with David still turned my stomach.

David cleared his throat for the third time, prompting Deacon to finally speak. "Do you need a glass of water or something?"

"Oh my God, Deacon. How daft are you?" Taylor said derisively. "Also, can you stand up already? I'm growing more disturbed by the sight of you kneeling in front of your fiancée the longer the time goes on."

"Victoria is meeting us there," David said, voice sounding strangled.

I made a show of dropping multiple ice cubes into my crystal glass, knocking all the bottles together as I pulled the vodka from the back, trying to drown out the conversation and pretend that my skin wasn't on fire, that my heart wasn't beating out of my chest because of the way David looked at me. And that at the same time, I wasn't on the precipice of sobbing because Tripp still wasn't here.

"Yes, Deacon. Please stand up." Steven's voice was dry, and I finally turned, bringing my drink to my lips for something to do with my hands.

He was doing up the cufflinks of his jacket. The simple Armani S-Line wool blend black tuxedo had been tailored to fit him, and he looked classically handsome as always. His blue eyes were sharp, assessing the outlandish scene that lay in front of him. Deacon was still on his knees, holding hands with Noa while Taylor, David and I were practically pushed against opposite ends of the room. Marta trailed behind him, having clearly decided on the Marchesa. The ruffles seemed to flutter in an invisible breeze. Her blonde hair was slicked back into a low chignon, setting off her arguably perfect features. Her lips were pillowy and painted a pale pink, and her high cheekbones shimmered with a rose gold highlighter that complimented her eyes. She smiled politely at me, evidently not disturbed by the scene unfolding before her.

"Are you all ready? Taylor, your parents said their car was arriving shortly. David will be riding with you. Charlie, where is Tripp? I told you our limo was arriving at 6:30 sharp, and we were to go together." Steven looked around, blue eyes narrowing like he had only just realized Tripp wasn't there.

His mouth tightened into a thin line as he appraised me, clutching my drink and standing there mutely in this insane dress.

The ornate clock seemed to mock me. Showing me its hands pointing to 6:15. The seconds ticked on, my silence stretching out across the room. I had nothing to say. I didn't know where Tripp was. All of my texts and calls had gone unanswered, my pathetic pleas for him to come save me from this painful hell I was trapped in as I sat beside my father's new girlfriend, hair pulled in every direction and styled into this perfect wig-like sheet it was now.

"He's running late. He said he would meet you all here at 6:30," David interjected, and my eyes shot to him.

A dumb sort of hopefulness rose in me that maybe for reasons unknown, Tripp had entrusted David with that information. That he was coming, that he wasn't abandoning me, that he would be there for me like he promised. That all those moments over the last weeks, where I gave myself to him, where we moved together, panting breaths and laughter following weren't a lie. Like maybe he *was* a grown-up version of the boy I used to know.

My father seemed displeased with the idea of Tripp arriving right on time but said nothing as he finished buttoning up his cufflinks. "We're meant to walk out together when we arrive, Charlie."

"I know," I said quietly, lamely.

He had been impressing the importance of this event, the seriousness of it for two weeks now. We were to appear as a highly functional, well-rounded family who was totally okay with this unwanted new addition he had brought into the fold; and at the same time, my brother and I were responsible for taking the pressure off him.

"I just need to grab my touch-up kit for my makeup. I'll meet you all in the lobby." I turned before any of their gazes could land on me with pity, and I tipped back the rest of my drink, staring at the wall in front of me.

I couldn't hear anything at all. Just a dull murmur behind me. My heart pounded in my ears, and I began stretching my fingers in and out, trying to focus on anything but the utter disappointment, devastation, pressing against me. I was twenty again—abandoned and alone, good enough for no one. I forced a breath through my nose, breathing out in a small oh through my mouth. Tipping my chin back, I looked up at the ceiling, the corners of my vision beginning to blur when I heard the click of a door. I was all alone. Left behind.

"Where is he?" David's voice sounded from behind me, and I whirled around to find him standing in front of me, head cocked to the side and hands shoved in his pockets.

"I don't know," I responded. My voice was small, and I ran my hands down the front of my dress. They stuck to the silk intermittently as sweat that was pooling on my palms snagged against the fabric. "It's fine. I'll walk out alone. It doesn't matter."

David looked at me, his eyebrows knitting together. He pulled a hand from his pocket on instinct and reached toward me. His muscular hand grabbed my own and wrapped around it, stopping me from assaulting the red silk of my dress.

"Charlie. Stop. Stay with me," he whispered again, the heat of his hand against my own causing me to tilt my chin up toward him, to finally look at him.

"This is so fucking embarrassing. Deacon is walking out with his fiancée, even my father is walking out with gold-digging fucking Marta, and I'm alone. The only thing Steven asked of me was to bring a date. I can't even get that right," I hissed, my voice catching in my throat, the tears threatening to spill over and ruin the goddamn rainbow Sabine had painted on my eyelids.

"It matters. If you don't want to walk out alone, if you can't, I'll walk with you." David gently dropped my hand, his thumb pressing down on it before extending his elbow to me.

I eyed his extended elbow, an olive branch I would never earn. "David, there'll be photographers everywhere. People are going to see. Victoria...Tripp...they're going to see."

David's eyes remained impassive as he stood there, an air of maddening patience wrapped around us.

"Let them." His voice was cool, and my mouth popped open about to ask if this was somehow a way of getting back at me, at Tripp. But that would never be who David Kennedy was.

I nodded, barely a tip of my chin and placed my hand in the crook of his elbow. The wool of his jacket was so soft, and my fingers tensed. I could feel the muscle of his forearm through the sleeve. I tipped my chin up to look at him. His jaw was tense, but his eyes swept over me—and there it was. The soft, sparkling honey. The lights of my former home twinkled at me from behind the glass of a window, inviting me back in.

No one said anything when I ducked into the limo, and David followed after me. Deacon looked at me over the glass of champagne he was holding, eyes wide for a moment before his expression changed and his jaw clenched. I saw the moment it clicked behind his eyes; they went from the light, dancing emerald I loved to a waxing, foreboding color that wouldn't have been out of place in a decaying forest. I watched him toss back the rest of his champagne before jerking his chin at David in acknowledgment and reaching out to shake his hand. Steven said nothing, barely sparing us a glance before turning back to Marta. This probably couldn't have turned out better for him. Not only was his family seemingly full, whole, complete—the entire last week the press was littered with photos of Tripp and me. Arriving with David would surely send them all into a flurry.

Deacon yanked open the bar fridge, his jaw continuing to twitch. Noa's delicate fingers were drawing circles on the back of his hand that was gripping his knee in a way that told me he was barely containing whatever explosion lurked under the surface. She looked at me, a curl falling across her face and escaping the messy low bun the rest of her hair was pinned to. Her smile was sad, and I shook my head imperceptibly. Deacon thrust a champagne flute toward me, full beyond the measure propriety would allow, an offering of comfort in one of the ways he knew how. After I reached out to accept it, he gripped my wrist, looking at me in earnest, familial love and hurt, and anger practically bleeding from him.

I tried to smile at him in reassurance, but I felt so dumb, so fucking stupid, it probably looked as strangled as it felt. I fell back against the leather seat, my shoulder brushing David's. He flipped his hand over, palm up, and dropped it on my thigh in offering. Turning to him, he was staring at me intently, and the press of his hand was so warm and became so heavy, I thought I might die if I didn't thread my fingers through his. Tentatively, I dropped my own hand, laying it against his palm. His fingers wrapped around mine protectively, and it was like knocking on the worn wood of a familiar front door.

I said nothing as David inevitably fell into polite conversation with my father and Marta, Deacon still too irritable to contribute much. I peered past David's shoulder, watching the mess of lights through the window until we rolled to a stop in front of the steps of the New York Public Library.

My fingers tensed against David's, and he turned toward me, whispering against my temple in response. "Stay with me."

The steps had been transformed and wouldn't be out of place at a movie premiere. They were lined with red velvet ropes, keeping the alarming amount of press at bay. I saw the train of Taylor's dress moving across the top steps. I knew Steven had timed this out. All guests would have arrived by now, and we were the main event. My father said nothing as the door was opened for us but simply ducked out and offered a hand back for Marta who slid across the leather seat with shocking grace, despite the ruffles of her gown. I was probably going to have to be tugged through the door. Deacon ran a hand over his face, gripping Noa's fingers with the other one. He looked at me softly, his lips forming into a sad sort of smile.

"I'm sorry, Charles," his voice was low, and he reached out to knock my chin as he passed.

Deacon ducked out of the car after our father and Marta, followed by Noa. I heard the shouts for her to look this way or that way starting from the circling photographers.

I exhaled and began fidgeting with my skirts. "I don't even know how I'm going to get out of the car in this fucking thing. It's like a giant cupcake," I muttered, lifting one of the silk tiers of the skirt and inspecting it.

David dipped his head, looking at my hand as I toyed uselessly with the fabric. His hand was still firmly wrapped around mine. He looked back up, eyes dancing like they always used to whenever I was forced into some clothing contraption like this one.

"You don't look anything like a cupcake. You look beautiful, Charlie."

"Do I look *indescribable*?" I raised an eyebrow.

"Always, billion dollar baby." David laughed, the name falling from his tongue like it was nothing.

I stilled, shaking my head. "Please don't...not tonight. I already feel so stupid so fucking dumb for trusting him. I never learn, apparently."

"You're not dumb. You're not stupid." David reached out, grabbing my other hand. He raised them both to his chest, pressing them right above his heart. "You're the most beautiful girl in the world."

"Noa Dahan is on those steps!" I gestured wildly, sending our joined hands over David's shoulder and trying to point toward the library steps. "I don't think your girlfriend would appreciate this."

"Noa Dahan is right there, and she is very pretty. So is Victoria." David nodded, laughter escaping him. "But here you are."

"Stop," I breathed, pressing my forehead to his shoulder. "You let me go, don't pull me back in."

"I'm sorry he did this to you, Charlie." I felt David press his chin to my head. "But how about it? Just me and you, for a few more moments? We can pretend the rest of the world doesn't exist until we walk through those doors. And I promise afterward, I'll let you go."

"Okay," I whispered, nodding and pulling back. Just a few more moments with David.

David tightened his grip on my hand, stepping out of the still-open door, and it was like there was an audible gasp issued from every photographer there, like time stopped and was suspended because somehow everything fell silent, not a single click of a camera. Gathering my dress in my hand, I gently dropped my legs out and raised my face, perfect Winchester teeth on display as a million flashes went off.

––––––––––

It turned out staring at my phone screen all night couldn't make Tripp return any of my calls or texts. I waited all night, making forced and polite conversation with patrons who were dead set on kissing my father's ass, and actively avoiding him and Marta until I finally convinced Deacon, Taylor and Noa to leave with me. I couldn't bring myself to say goodbye to David. Victoria had pulled him away from me promptly after arriving, her features set in such a cold and predatory way that she could have given Taylor a run for her money. But that might have been for the best. I needed to go back to the world where I was a giant idiot, abandoned by Tripp Banks—again.

It was a nice fantasy to exist in with David, for him to pull me out of the car and across the dance floor, keeping me company when I was seconds from breaking. But it was only a fantasy. I was all alone again. Maybe existing with Tripp had all been a fantasy, too.

The town car pulled up the curb in front of my townhouse, Deacon immediately falling silent, ending whatever tirade he had been on because I wasn't paying attention. I slammed the door behind me, much louder than I intended. Tripp was sitting on the steps leading up to my front door, looking at me from behind shuttered eyes. He was twirling his phone in one hand, the other pressing into his thigh. He looked like he was grinding his teeth.

"Where the hell have you been?" I shouted, my voice cracking with a mixture of relief that he wasn't dead in a ditch somewhere and fury over his disappearance. I didn't care that Deacon, Noa and Taylor had followed me out of the car. "Are you alright?"

A muscle in Tripp's jaw twitched, and he shrugged, cocking his head, looking past me at Deacon. "Your brother here to kick my ass?"

Deacon came to stand beside me, placing a firm hand on my shoulder. "I should because you don't even deserve to be breathing the same air as her after the stunt you pulled today. Standing her up at a WH Charity Event? Really? Where the fuck were you?"

"Deacon, go inside and go upstairs or something. Stay out of it!" I barked, stepping out from under his hand and marching past Tripp to unlock my front door with as much dignity as this giant gown would allow.

I pointed through the open doorway, breath heaving as they all marched past me, leaving me out here with Tripp.

Part of me wanted to slam the door in Tripp's face, but he remained seated before finally pushing himself up, stopping just short of walking in the door.

"You've never looked at me like that. Not once," he said, shaking his head and finally stopping the incessant twirling of his phone.

He thrust it at me, and I looked down at it in confusion, until I saw the photo he had zoomed in on. There were two in the article that must have just been run by Page Six. One was of David and me right as we exited the limo, clutching hands, and I was looking up at him with what I could only describe as a reverence. The second photo was of us dancing. He was smiling down at me, hair all askew, and I was looking up at him and my eyes, honest to God, looked like they were twinkling. I shoved it back at him, not needing to read any further to see what the article said.

"Where were you Tripp?" I whispered, crossing my arms in front of me, like I could cradle my heart and keep it from hurting. "Are you okay?" I asked again.

"I had to go back to Boston unexpectedly." His voice was flat, giving nothing away just like his newly frozen eyes.

I wondered if it was the type of ice that you could fall right through if you jumped hard enough, into the freezing cold water that drowned you and sucked all the air out of your lungs.

"Oh!" I threw up my hands before continuing. "Boston in 1850 with no phones? What the fuck Tripp! I was counting on you, you promised, you—"

"After all this, I'm just your friend, aren't I? I was there for you when you were practically a fucking pariah at WH events. You're only with me because you can't be with him, because he doesn't want you, and you're too scared to be alone." Tripp raised his voice and shook his head like he couldn't believe I was hurt by him.

"That's not true—"

Tripp cut me off with a mocking laugh. "Bullshit."

"I'm not lying, Tripp!" I shouted, resisting the urge to stomp my feet.

"You want to know how I know you're lying? It's a lot harder to lie to a liar, and I'm a liar. We're both liars." His eyes were narrowed in on me, and his jaw was grinding back and forth.

"I lied to David by omission," I said uselessly, irritation rising at the way his words dug into my skin, planting themselves in the very marrow of my bones.

"Oh, fuck off, Chuck. If that's what you want to tell yourself. You never cared about me, just admit it."

"You want to talk about people being pieces of shit? You call me CHUCK! That demeaning name your stupid frat brothers gave me. You don't respect me, not really—"

Tripp stepped forward suddenly, shouting and pointing at me. "I call you Chuck, because it's ours. It's something he can't touch."

I let out a scathing laugh, tipping my head back like it was the most preposterous thing I had ever heard. "You know what else is ours? Your inability to be reliable. You PROMISED!"

Tripp's eyes flashed, and his nostrils flared momentarily, the anger giving way to hurt for a moment before he schooled his features again. His voice was deadly when he spoke, "David doesn't want you, Charlie. If he did, he could have you, pretty easily it seems by the way you trail after him like a puppy begging for scraps. It's fucking pathetic. It's—"

"That's enough," Deacon stormed out the still open front door, knocking me aside. I hadn't even looked back to see if they went inside. Maybe they had been standing there the whole time. "You do not speak to my sister like that ever, let alone in her own home. You and her? You're done. Don't even think about breathing in her direction ever again. Go home, Tripp. I'll deal with you Monday."

"No, you won't," Tripp said flatly and shoved his hands into his pockets, his eyes on me for a moment longer. There was something there, lurking just under all that ice, and I felt myself squinting like whatever he was really feeling might be easier to see that way. "I have to move back to Boston. I quit."

I started forward, a hand reaching out toward him instinctively, but I dropped it as Tripp took a measured step backward. "Tripp, what happened?" I asked, softer this time, my eyes searching for any possible clue that would tell me why looking at him was suddenly like looking at the endless expanse of the arctic.

His words burned against my skin, and my heart felt like it had been ravaged, torn apart entirely, which was becoming quite commonplace these days—but I knew there was something wrong here. I was looking at someone I didn't even know and never on his worst day would the person I know speak to me like this.

Tripp looked at me one last time, and his gaze flickered—unfrozen, unthawed—for one brief moment before it shuttered over. "I'll see you around, Charlie." He turned on his heel, hands still shoved in his pockets and walked away from me.

I knew now whatever we were building together wasn't a home, wouldn't ever be a home, but I felt the foundations crumble and fall away beneath me all the same.

CHAPTER THIRTY

Our family used to stay at The Hotel de Paris Monte Carlo every year for the Grand Prix. It was a Winchester tradition. My mother's family had actually made all their money in the auto industry, her great grandfather having made a lucky investment into an engineering firm that went on to create some sort of very important engine, and our parents met at a Grand Prix when they were both fresh from college. And here we were again, short one mother and minus our father, for Deacon's first bachelor party. I was tempted to ask Deacon if it was sentimentality that drove him to this hotel, this event, but I knew it had more to do with the fact that he deemed it opulent enough for the likes of his bachelor party.

I said nothing as I saw the perfectly manicured palm trees that stood in front of the building, with its intricate ivory moldings and spires that wouldn't have looked out of place in Versailles. It was just a lot less gold. I checked my phone out of habit, ignoring the towering ceilings and the smooth wood of the brocade walls while I walked beside Taylor.

I hadn't heard from Tripp since he left WH, left New York, *left me*. Two weeks had gone by without a word. I was mad at him—so fucking mad at him, and myself—but I knew there was something more to it. It kind of made me laugh, how quickly and how spectacularly the whole thing had blown up in our faces. But I missed him. I missed his dumb matching sweat suits and his stupid British reality show, I missed him needling at me constantly. I missed him under my skin, which was where he always liked to be because he was an antagonistic bastard, and I missed him next to me in the mornings—even if only for a brief time.

David and Deacon were walking ahead of us, almost identical in Tom Ford khaki shorts, pastel toned button-ups rolled up their forearms and sunglasses pushed back on their heads, save for the deeper tan of David's skin, hair curling at his neck, and the slightly more broad set of his shoulders. They were within centimeters of the same height, and depending on the way they walked, it was impossible to tell who was taller. There were more people coming than just the four of us, a group of guys they knew from their social circles and business school, who were surely awful. Tripp would have been walking alongside them, but in his move back to Boston, it seemed he also forfeit his invitation.

Taylor's Chloe Linen sandals were slapping loudly on the perfectly lacquered marble floor, her nose scrunched and lips pursed while she typed at an alarmingly fast rate on her phone. I opened my mouth to ask her if she was going to be working all weekend when I saw Deacon spin around, his phone held in front of his face. He continued to walk backward, but he looked up at us, green eyes clouded and eyebrows pulled together.

"I just got an alert that Tripp's father stepped down as president at the bank. Post is taking over in the interim," Deacon called, waggling his phone at me before pocketing it in the back of his shorts. "What's that about? Something's going on with him."

My stomach clenched, and my heart felt like it snagged against the sharp edge of one of my ribs. The warm, unthawed blue of Tripp's eyes flashed behind mine and I blinked, the entirely frigid stare when he sat on my stoop with his phone taking over. The edge of my white Gucci sneaker snagged against the smooth flooring, and without taking her eyes off her phone, Taylor grabbed my arm to stop me from lurching forward.

I cleared my throat. "How would I know? He won't return my texts or calls."

Deacon looked at me, forest eyes wide and dubious. "He that good in bed you're still trying to talk to him after what he did after the gala?"

"Deacon! Jesus. You know it was more than that right? Just shut up about it. It's none of your business," I hissed, staring determinedly over Deacon's shoulder and anywhere but the back of David's head.

"What happened after the gala?" David stopped suddenly, looking over his shoulder at me.

We hadn't spoken since then, either. I made my exit when Victoria was pointing wildly at him in the corner, furious about our grand entrance, and I certainly hadn't called him up to tell him that he had been right about Tripp all along, that everyone had been.

"Oh, they had quite the fight. About you, actually. He called her pathetic and waved photos of the two of you in her face." Deacon glanced sideways at David, his jaw set in irritation, like it bothered him to think about what Tripp had said. Clearly not enough to keep it to himself.

"Deacon!" I half-shouted, my voice a strangled whisper.

My brother's face tightened, and he opened his mouth to speak again when David cut in. "Leave her alone, Deacon. Let them work it out."

David glanced at me quickly, a rueful smile on his lips, and he jerked Deacon's shoulders around and gestured to the concierge desk. I missed him, too. I wasn't quite sure how that could be. How you could hold room in your heart, your soul, for two entirely different people at the same time. But here I was, effectively split in half.

———

The top of my head was starting to get too warm underneath the black leather Ferrari baseball cap Taylor had shoved on my head when we arrived at the Paddock Club. She was wearing a matching one, and our outfits looked almost identical without being planned. Both of us in white cropped t-shirts, whereas the A.L.C. shirt I was wearing was oversized, her MM6 shirt looked like it was painted on, and the same pair of 90s pinch waist Agolde jeans. Her blonde hair was styled in its usual insanely messy wave and was expanding throughout the afternoon, while mine felt like it was growing stringy underneath the hat.

Deacon was gone, off somewhere with Fred Vasser. I was sure it was a favor called in by our father, though Deacon was charming and probably influential enough for the Ferrari Team principal to donate his time and walk a section of the track with him. I had been in this Paddock Club before, as a small child, standing up on the rungs of the balcony, leaning over to see the cars whipping by, one sweaty, small hand clamped on my brother's. I remembered there being a hallway that led between the bar and the restrooms where no one stood to watch the race. I stood there now, halfway between the bar where various celebrities and other figures of importance mingled, drinking out of heavy glasses in their hands.

David came to stand beside me, forearms coming to rest on the rungs. "You look beautiful."

Nothing was happening on the track today. The qualifying race happened tomorrow. His eyes wandered over me, spending too long on the exposed skin of my abdomen. My skin prickled, the ghost of his fingers skimming the waistband of my jeans, pausing on my hip bones.

"I'm wearing jeans and a t-shirt," I rolled my eyes, pushing off the rungs and taking measured steps back from him. The rubber sole of my sneaker hit the wall.

David arched an eyebrow, shrugging. "You know my favorite version of you is this one. Not the little rich girl in the big, pretty dresses. Just you, when your skin is practically bare, and you're just existing as you are."

Pressing back, my shoulders hit the wall through the thin material of my t-shirt. "David...stop saying things like that. It was nice of you, too nice really, to walk out with me at the gala. But it looked like it got you in quite a bit of trouble. I asked you to let me go."

His lips pulled to the side and he walked toward me, somehow seemingly causing the small space between us to stretch and seem endless. The ivory linen Theory short-sleeved button-up tightened around his arms as his posture tensed. "I was a good guy. I was good to you. A good boyfriend. I would have been a good husband."

"Yes," I whispered, now pushing my head back against the wall, the buckle of my hat digging into my skull uncomfortably. "You're still a good man, David."

He shook his head, mouth pressed into a tight line now. He stopped in front of me, tipping his head down, one tendril of hair flopping forward onto his forehead. I could see the lines wrinkling around the sides of his eyes. Aging suited David. My breath hitched when I felt his fingers pull on the hem of my shirt, the back of his hand, not the ghost of it, the real thing, brushing along my stomach ever so lightly.

"A good man doesn't think the things I think. A good man doesn't look at someone else, other than his girlfriend, and spend every waking moment thinking about ripping her clothes off and doing unspeakable things to them. Why do you think that is?"

I shook my head, my hair shifting. His thumb was circling my side, and I couldn't think. "You're confusing me," I breathed, my eyes widening, and my skin sweating as David brought his other hand up to flick the brim of my hat.

In one movement, he lifted it off my head, flipping it backward and down onto his messy hair.

"You confuse me by being in the same city, the same building, let alone the same room, by breathing the same air I do. You confuse me simply by existing. I don't want to be like this, and I can't stop," David said, his breath whispering past my cheek, and I felt his nose brush my ear.

Then, his lips landed there. His hand gripped my side, thumb stroking upward toward my ribcage and his teeth grazed my earlobe. His entire body was just a breath away from mine. I could feel the linen of his shirt against the front of my stomach, the heat of his thighs through the denim of my jeans, and when I inhaled I could smell the faint hint of a cigarette, but what was entirely overwhelming was the smell of sunlight and the ocean. His mouth started to move against my ear, and for a minute I thought he was laying small, tiny kisses there the way he used to, but he was whispering, "You fucking ruined me, Charlie."

His hand dropped from my side and the heat of him being there, pressed up against me, disappeared suddenly as he stepped back. David's lips twitched and he cleared his throat, palming his jaw and rubbing it before flicking his gaze to me one more time and turning to walk away down the hall back toward the bar, shoulders rolling under his shirt and the broad muscles of his back tightening with every step.

I pressed my palm flat to my chest, trying to contain all the pieces of my own ruined heart.

———

A heavy, urgent knock sounded against the wood of the door to my hotel room. I was still wearing the same outfit I had been in all day, my suitcase open in front of me. I barely had time to cross the room when the pounding started again.

I pulled it open, assuming it was my brother and about to tell him he needed another lesson in patience. But David stood in the doorway, looking decidedly disheveled. He was wearing a charcoal suit, having abandoned the more casual clothes he was wearing earlier. His phone was gripped so tightly in his hands all the veins were popping out of his forearm. I usually would have taken a moment to appreciate it—David Kennedy's arms would forever remain my favorite appendage—had it not been for the harsh set of his jaw, and the wildness of his eyes. He thrust the phone at me, running a hand through his hair and shouldering his way into my room.

"What's wrong?" I asked, his phone practically slipping through my fingers.

He jerked his chin in response, pointing at the phone like it had personally done something to offend him. I eyed him warily, flicking my gaze down to the screen. An email from Rebecca was open. Photos from today were embedded in the body of the email. There was one of Taylor and me, identical save for the hair spilling from our hats, holding flutes of champagne and flashing ironic peace signs at one another. Deacon and I shaking hands with Fred Vasseur and Charles Leclerc. The four of us posed by the balcony railing. I looked up, scrunching my nose and pursing my lips. "I don't get it. She's sending you the press photos. This isn't weird, it's pretty—"

"Keep going," David bit out, a manic sort of energy radiating from him as he began to pace across my room, eyes never landing on one thing, constantly rolling his shoulders under the suit jacket.

I looked back down, my thumb brushing up on the screen. And there they were. Photos of us, leaning against the railing in the hallway. Me stepping back, David following. His hand finding the hem of my shirt, his forehead tipping down to mine, David's thighs pressing in between my own—I thrust the phone out, shaking my head and blinking.

"Take it back. I see it. I get it."

He snatched the phone from me, never closing the screen and looking down at the photos again. David pulled the ends of his hair, disgusted at the display on his phone leaking from him.

I peered at them again and cringed. They were blurry—but it was clear who it was. It might have been a bit harder to discern had there not been a series of photos. David flicked the beak of that ridiculous black leather Ferrari logo baseball hat, followed by a frame of him removing it from my head, twisting it upward to settle backward on his wayward hair. David's hand on my waist and his forehead tipped down to mine.

"People might not know it's you. You can't see your face," I whispered, guilt gnawing at my insides.

"It's obviously me, Charlie. Fuck!" David yelled, tossing the phone away from him where it landed on the floor with a clatter. "Rebecca said the photographer and reporter both named me. There's no point in me telling Victoria it wasn't. Pretty sure she would be able to recognize me. This isn't us walking at a formal event for your family business! I'm practically groping you in a fucking public hallway!"

"I'm so sorry, David." I reached out, fingers grazing his shoulder, but he jerked away from my touch.

The words had tumbled from my lips on instinct. I was so used to apologizing it didn't occur to me that maybe it wasn't always on me. Maybe this wasn't my fault.

"Don't. Don't touch me. That's how we got into this mess, isn't it? Touching each other when we shouldn't be?" David looked everywhere but at me. "I need a fucking drink. I'm going down to the bar."

His phone was still sitting there, half under the nightstand beside the bed, the photos face up on the screen seemingly taunting us. I couldn't look as he snatched it from the ground, and then ripped off his suit jacket, swinging the door open. "I'll take care of it, David," I called uselessly, my voice low and hopeless.

He turned to look back at me, his features hard and his jaw clenched. He looked like he was on the precipice of saying something but decided against it, swinging the door open and letting it slam behind him.

I backed away from the door, the noise of it slamming reverberated in my head until my legs hit the bed. Sitting down, I pulled my phone out wanting to be doing anything else but this. I exhaled, drumming my fingers on the glass screen before dialing a number I knew by heart but rarely ever used. My heart dropped when it was answered before the first ring ended.

"Steven Winchester." His voice was clipped, and I barely restrained an eye roll. He had caller ID.

"Hi," I said, my voice cracking and tears threatening to spill over. "I need you to make something go away."

My father answered after a belated silence. "Please don't tell me your brother drunkenly crashed a Formula One racing car or something equally ridiculous."

A stilted laugh escaped me, punctuated with a wet rasp. "No. No, it's something I did. Shocker, right? Uhm. There are some photos of David and me that are going to go to press in a few hours. They were sent to Rebecca, and I'm sure you have a call or email about them. But uhm, I know I'm not a WH employee anymore, but David is and he just...the photos need to go away. I need you to make them go away. No matter the cost, you can take it out of my trust, or I'll write you a check. Just please?"

"Of course I'll make it go away. You're my daughter. I'll take care of it." His voice was low, bordering consoling even. "Does this mean you two are back together?"

"No," I choked out, a sob mixed with a forced laugh. "No. If anything, I think this means he hates me more."

I heard the telltale sound of my father exhaling through his nose, and I could picture him. Sitting in the practically empty office in New York, leaning back in his chair and wondering what kind of karmic monster he had been in another life to be shackled with two idiot children. "I'll let you know when it's taken care of. For what it's worth, Charlie, I don't think there's anything that you could do to make that boy hate you."

CHAPTER THIRTY-ONE

David was swirling a glass of what I assumed to be stupidly expensive scotch, leaning over the padded cognac leather of the hotel bar. His charcoal suit jacket was draped over the matching leather barstool, and he had unbuttoned the neck of his white shirt, the sleeves rolled up to complete the look of irritation and carelessness. I could picture him storming down here, practically ripping the buttons of his shirt open in frustration and throwing himself down. But no matter his anger, David would have been polite when he asked for his drink.

I dropped into an empty seat beside him, pushing my phone across the polished wood of the bar. A text message from my father was open on the screen. It read three words, but it was all he needed to see.

Steven: Taken care of.

David looked down at the phone, nostrils flaring before he shook his head. He dropped his glass, staring resolutely ahead. "What's this?" He asked, his jaw contracting.

David exhaled sharply again, grabbing the scotch and emptying it.

My voice was low. "I took care of it. I said I would."

There was no point masking it now, but I whispered like anyone could be listening. Half the people in the bar probably saw us pawing at each other in the hallway earlier.

"Yeah, so did I." David raised his eyebrows, nodding at the bartender who slid another too full glass of scotch across the bar to him. "She broke up with me about fifteen minutes ago."

"You told her?" I asked, disbelief coloring my words. "David, I took care of it. I told you I would. It's like it never even happened."

David turned to me, his lips pulled back to reveal his teeth and his eyebrows knitted together incredulously. "Was I supposed to just lie to her? I'm not you, Charlie."

I blinked, the words harsh and biting. But they were true. I had lied to him, to his face, whether by omission or not. "I *am* sorry David. What will it take to make you believe that?" I asked, my voice barely audible. Because I was sorry, and I had been sorry. I was losing count of how many times I apologized only for him to throw it back in my face. "You're confusing me, too, you know that, right? You tell me you can't forgive me, that you won't forgive me...and then you do all these things. You say all these things. You tell my father and brother I'm the love of your life. You were mad I was with Tripp, and I would be tempted to let that go if I wasn't so sure you would be mad about me being with *anyone*. You said you would let me go, and then you say and do things like walking out with me to the gala, and today, you're the one who pushed me up against that wall!"

David was looking back at the bar, seemingly staring at his reflection in the glass wall barely visible behind the vast array of liquor bottles. "I was on thin ice anyway. She wasn't too thrilled about those photos in Page Six. It was only a matter of time before she ended it."

"That's not what I meant—" I started, but David cut me off with a look, draining the rest of his glass.

"I never thought I would utter these words, but I need you to not be anywhere near me right now, Charlie," he muttered, pushing his glass across the bar.

My eyebrows narrowed, anger at his dismissal causing my mouth to pop open, but David stood, grabbed his jacket and turned, walking away from me again as easily as breathing.

———————

I found Taylor where I left her, in the restroom connecting the two bedrooms of our suite. She paused her endless step nighttime skin routine, arms crossed at her chest, and her face giving nothing away, save for a slight downward pull to her mouth, as I recounted what happened between David and me.

Taylor exhaled sharply through her nose, pinching the bridge before closing her eyes in apparent frustration. Her hair was pushed back off her face with a giant black Prada terry cloth headband. It was probably for everyday wear, but she had clearly incorporated it into her skincare routine.

The bathroom countertop was littered with products that were part of her pre-bed skin regimen. I could recite Taylor's skincare steps with my eyes closed. A giant tub of La Prairie Skin Caviar was sitting open, so I knew that to mean she was almost done and about to slather her face and neck with it.

She opened her eyes again, narrowing them at me before loading her hand up with generous amounts of the cream. I watched as she began to slap it on her skin, all her movements jilted and agitated.

"I'm sorry, did I interrupt your quiet time? I was trying to tell you that—" I started, but Taylor held up a palm to silence me.

"Oh, I heard you. Steven bailed you out, and you somehow remain shocked that David was still mad at you. Offended even. The audacity of that man to suggest he didn't want to lie to his girlfriend like you lied to him!" Taylor shrieked, but somehow not breaking from her routine as she began to massage the cream into her neck.

My mouth parted. I could count on one hand how many fights Taylor and I had in our adult life. As adolescents and teenagers, we had stupid fights occasionally, but none of any significance since entering adulthood. I couldn't even think of anything to say and stood there, hands open uselessly at my sides while she moved on to aggressively slap the moisturizer to her forehead.

"Charlie, I'm going to level with you, and you're not going to like it. But you're going to listen. Got it? Good." Taylor slammed the lid back onto the tub of lotion before turning to me and crossing her arms over her silk green pinstriped Morgan Lane pajamas. "You keep saying David was your home. All this time, that story has never changed. And then suddenly, when he couldn't forgive you, because you CHEATED ON HIM, by the way, you were building a home with Tripp. And that was fine with me, because he made you laugh and you seemed happy for the brief snippet of time you were together, but somehow now, at your brother's bachelor party, you've managed to steamroll David's relationship? I get it, he's in the wrong here. You're a free agent, and he cornered you. But come on!"

"Taylor—" I began, shaking my head slowly, but she made a zip-it motion with her fingers and continued on.

"This notion, this idea that you keep wanting to find homes in other people's souls, that's all well and good, and it's beautiful to want to build a life with someone, but you need to stop looking for home and love in places that aren't *you*." I watched in a sort of abject horror as Taylor pulled off her ridiculous headband and threw it onto the countertop. "First it was London, then it was David, then you ran away again, then it was New York, and then it was Tripp, but it's never been *you*."

My eyes burned, and I started to blink, willing the tears not to fall, because I didn't want to give her the satisfaction of knowing she was right. Because she was. Every single thing she was saying was true, and that realization settled against me like a second skin that was too tight and didn't fit properly. I couldn't think of anything to say, so she continued.

"Tripp was right, you know. You're scared of being alone, aren't you? I don't know who told you that you weren't good enough. But this is getting to be absolutely absurd."

"So, what do you suggest I do?" I raised my hands in question, my words choked with tears and irritation flaring in my chest. "Do all these facts negate the one where I love David? Am I supposed to stop loving him because oh so wise Taylor Breen says I can't be alone?"

"Jesus Charlie!" Taylor turned to me, a mirthless sort of expression marring her otherwise beautiful face. She started throwing her various products into her giant Smythson Vanity Case that went everywhere with her. "This isn't about me. I'm not even saying any of this with judgment! You could kill someone and I wouldn't blink an eye. I'd help you burn the body, I know all sorts of ways to destroy DNA. I'm saying that you need to look in the fucking mirror and realize you are the cause of all of your problems. Come stand in front of this mirror right now and tell me one thing you love about yourself, go on. I'm serious."

I watched with disdain and an ever-growing grimace as Taylor began to tap her foot exaggeratedly waiting for me to throw myself in front of the mirror in whatever self-love exercise this was. "What sort of tough love speech is this? Seems like you've been saving this one up for a while, Taylor. I'm not going to play along."

She rolled her eyes and shook her head at me, a snort escaping her little ski slope nose that was infuriating me to no end at that moment. "I'm saying this because I love you. And I think you deserve to forgive yourself for whatever it is you think you did wrong when you slept with Tripp after your mother died. That's what started all this isn't it? Your mom left this world, and she left *you*. You were young and your brain was still maturing, and you were grieving, Charlie. There's no right way to grieve, and it doesn't make you a bad person if you fell into bed and had consensual sex with someone to distract yourself. You didn't spit on her grave."

A sob was forcing its way up my throat, my skin felt too hot and my clothes were too tight. Everything Taylor said hurt. Hurt me, hurt my heart, and my soul. But it was all true. Every single thing. I wasn't sure I liked myself very much at all.

"I'm going to bed," Taylor said, her words soft now, and I watched through blurred vision as she pulled open the door that separated our bedrooms. "You know where to find me."

I stood, rooted to the spot, hot tears pouring down my face, and I waited until I heard the noises of Taylor's sound machine starting faintly through the door. She couldn't fall asleep without the sounds of whales. It was one of the reasons we rarely shared a room. I padded across the plush carpet to the cold marble tile of the bathroom. The vanity lights surrounding the mirror were still flicked on from Taylor's skincare ministrations.

Inhaling deeply, I raised my gaze up to my reflection. My cheeks were blotchy from crying, and my eyes were already puffy and bloodshot. I had seen better days, but I looked anyway. Tucking my hair behind my ears, I inhaled again, sucking as much air down into my lungs as I could before I started. My voice was so quiet, and so small, but that was okay, because it was just for me.

"I like my eyes. I like that I share them with my brother."

———————

Strips of moonlight illuminated the bedding that lay balled up beside Taylor. Her blonde hair fanned over her face, and her chest rose and fell in a steady rhythm. I watched the freckles smattering her nose and cheeks grow lighter or darker depending on the way the moon shone through the curtains. A smile pulled across my face as I thought of her, bent over a body with a scalpel, all precise movements and so different from the soft, sleepy version of the person in front of me that I loved with my whole soul.

I knew she preferred to sleep alone, and her stupid whale sounds were still coming from the sound machine, and that she probably didn't want to talk to me right now, but I pulled back the covers and crawled in bed beside her. Her eyelids twitched, and then she squinted, opening one eye halfway.

"You were right," I whispered, laying my head down on the pillow, mouth pulling in a sort of resigned smile.

"I know," she answered softly, both of her brown eyes on me now.

She pulled the sheets up to her neck, leaving only her tiny fingers and cut-to-the quick fingernails exposed. She once told me her tiny hands were part of what made her such a good surgeon.

"I needed that," I conceded, and something like triumph flashed in her too sleepy eyes. "I picked the first thing I like about myself. I like my eyes, and I like that I share them with Deacon."

"Why did you have to pick something you shared with Deacon?" She muttered, giving me another small smile before letting her eyes close again.

I snorted, watching as all those sharp edges to her face instantly softened again when her eyes closed and sleep pulled at her. "Well, I figured he loves himself enough for the both of us, maybe by including him some of it would start to rub off on me."

Taylor smiled, her still closed eyes, a small snort of air escaping her nose. "I'm glad you picked something, Charlie. It's a start."

The sound of shattering glass came from beyond the door in the hallway, followed by the very distinct sound of Deacon's drunken laughter. Taylor's eyes shot open and immediately narrowed. She started to throw back the covers, but I shook my head. "I'll deal with it. I'm sure it's nothing a Winchester can't afford to replace."

I cringed as I threw back the covers and crossed the room, really hoping my brother and his band of idiots hadn't smashed any of the vases lining the hallway. I was pretty certain I had spotted at least one 19th century vase out there. Throwing open the door, I stepped into the hallway, an angry admonishment for Deacon ready and expecting to see him being dragged to his room, because he was too drunk to walk.

But Deacon had an arm around David, who was doubled over in what was clearly beyond intoxicated laughter. My eyes widened and my mouth pulled down when I spotted shattered pottery at their feet.

"What the hell is happening out here?" I hissed, crossing my arms and trying to look anywhere but at David.

Deacon turned to me, a laugh dying in his throat. His cheeks were red and his green eyes glassy. The buttons of his shirt were undone and his hair was falling every which way. It didn't look like he was far off from David's state.

"Uh oh, fun's over David," he said in an annoying stage whisper. "Sorry, Charles, didn't mean to wake you. I was just helping David to his room."

"Mhm. Clearly he needs the assistance," I said flatly, my heart collapsing at the sight of him.

Had I done this to him? Steamrolled him in the exact same way I had back in Chicago? I asked him to let me go, but had I actually done him the same courtesy?

David looked up, his mouth still pulled back in laughter. His eyes were bloodshot and glassy, too. His hair was a mess, and not in the way I usually liked how it looked when the waves were untamed. "I think we're in trouble," David said, doubling over in laughter again. "Did you know she cheated on me? I made it all the way to twenty-nine without that happening."

"I know, and so does everyone else. You told the whole fucking restaurant," Deacon muttered, looking up at me with glazed over eyes and a sort of apologetic smile. "Let's get you to bed before you make this any worse."

I crossed my arms, half-hugging myself in an attempt to provide a small measure of comfort. Tipping my head, I looked at the way David was laughing, hunched over and so obviously drunk out of his mind, all I could think about was what Taylor said. How right she was. All of this destruction left in my wake, because I was looking for love everywhere but in my own heart. "I'll put him to bed. Go back downstairs and enjoy yourself, Deac."

"You sure?" Deacon looked up at me, eyebrows raising as he practically dragged David toward his hotel room door.

David dropped his head to the doorframe while Deacon pawed through his pockets to find his room key.

I nodded, stepping forward to grab the key and open the door. "Just get him to the bed. I'll make sure he has water and a bowl to puke in. He'll surely need it."

I moved into the suite, ignoring the continued laughter and schoolgirl giggling coming from the two of them. I started pilfering through the mini fridge for water to leave on his bedside table. I turned just as Deacon dropped David unceremoniously onto his side, which somehow resulted in the two of them laughing even more.

"Okay, night night David. Sleep it off, and I'll see you tomorrow," Deacon choked out through laughter, untangling himself from David. He turned to me, his eyes staying closed for too long, and he threw his arms around me. "I'll go to bed soon, don't worry, Charles. Just going to have one more drink."

"No Hydra-V to bail you out tomorrow morning, whatever are you going to do?" I rolled my eyes, hugging him back briefly, and my nose crinkled. He reeked of booze and cigarette smoke.

"Money talks, Charlie. Never fear." Deacon pulled away and raised his eyebrows at me before casting one more appraising look at David and turning to leave the room.

David was lying on his side, one hand rubbing his temple like a headache was already setting in. I gently popped the cap off the water bottle I pulled from the mini fridge and set it beside him on the mahogany nightstand. "You're probably going to want to drink that and more where that came from." I gave David a small smile, turning to leave the room when the familiar grip of his fingers landed on my wrist.

I looked back over at him, his hair plastered to his forehead and all wrong. David exhaled, puffing out his cheeks before looking up at me with a solemn expression on his face, and those eyes I loved so much looking so sad. "You cheated on me," he said flatly.

"Yes," I nodded, closing my eyes briefly before forcing myself to look at him, the consequences of my actions. The consequences of not loving myself enough. "I cheated on you, David."

"And today, any other day really...I would have cheated on Victoria with you," he continued, his eyes glassy unable to focus on one thing. "I've been a terrible boyfriend to her since you showed back up in my life. That's on me. But that's not who I am, Charlie."

I shook my head, lips quivering and my voice sad. "No, it's not."

"I think you're the worst thing that's ever happened to me. I wish I could hate you," David breathed, finally dropping my wrist and rolling onto his back. A groan of frustration left him as he began to scrub his face with his hands.

I nodded, weary acceptance settling over me. "Roll back over on your side, David. I don't need you choking on your vomit in your sleep."

I could have cried; I could have raged. But it wouldn't have mattered, because the facts were simple at the end of the day: I would never think I was good enough for anyone until I was good enough for myself. The temptation to fall at my feet and to grovel for him, for this love of my life was there. But I had a more important relationship I needed to be working on.

I turned, forcing myself to stare straight ahead, to keep my lips clamped shut so the sob that was clawing at my throat wouldn't escape, to keep walking. To leave this room. I stayed quiet until I crossed the hallway and crawled back into bed with Taylor, where she sleepily extended a hand to me. I sobbed into the pillow until moonlight shifted to the first rays of dawn. Sobbed for David, for Tripp, for my mother, and for me.

I wasn't doing a very good job of focusing on my own self-love, not when I could hear David's words over and over again in my head, and all I wanted was for him to forgive me. But that was going to have to be okay. I picked one thing I loved about myself today. I could try for two tomorrow.

CHAPTER THIRTY-TWO

I hesitated in front of the door to my father's suite, fist raised and ready to knock. There was a laughable sense of irony hanging around me, déjà vu maybe; the last time I confronted my father after a WH event, it hadn't gone well. And this was doubled down with me needing him to bail out David and me. But Deacon and I had been summoned for breakfast the Sunday after our return from Monaco.

My eyes were rimmed red and a headache pounded behind my temples. I hadn't been sleeping well. David's words echoed in my ears, but they were eclipsed by Taylor's. Those had somehow become the most important ones. Deacon claimed he was still hungover, having woken up with a headache and said he needed an IV drip stat before he could make it to breakfast with Steven. So, I was standing here alone. I debated waiting for him but decided it would be better to get the inevitable Steven Winchester beratement out of the way.

Exhaling a puff of air, I knocked quietly. My father's voice answered immediately, somewhat muffled behind the ornately carved door. I hesitated a moment longer before turning the knob and peeking my head around the corner, not really wanting to see my father and Marta sitting there after a night spent together in his stupidly lavish suite.

But it was just him, sitting around a table that was clearly prepared by room service attendants. He was pouring over a copy of the New York Times, still wearing a tailored button-up shirt, even though it was Sunday. He looked up at me, frowning as he took in my eyes and general appearance.

"Where's your brother?" He asked, folding his paper neatly before reaching forward to pour himself coffee from the carafe steaming on the table.

"Hungover still. He says he needs some IV ministration before he can join us." I raised my eyebrows and dropped into the empty chair across from him. "Where's Marta?"

"At home. I wanted to spend some time with you two before I head back to Chicago. Ash needs me back in the office," he supplied, leaning back in his chair and appraising me over his steaming coffee.

I furrowed my brows. That sounded like an excuse. Ash could probably run WH with his eyes closed at this point. "Well, you get one-half of the set."

My father took a measured sip before responding. "I received an interesting phone call from Tripp Banks this morning. I hadn't heard from him since he let me know he was resigning."

"Ah," I leaned forward, grabbing the open bottle of Dom Perignon and pouring a glass, topping it up with what I was pretty certain was freshly squeezed orange juice. "The second member of your leadership team I've driven away."

My father's voice was uncharacteristically soft. "Tripp had reasons for going back to Boston that have nothing to do with you, Charlie."

My stomach twisted, and I imagined Tripp's eyes from the night after the gala. I knew there was something wrong, something foreign and off. "Is he okay?"

"I think he will be, in time. He needed help with something...delicate." I watched as he reached across the table, mimicking my movements, and pouring himself a glass.

I wanted to ask more; I was dying to ask more. I was so mad, so embarrassed, but I cared for Tripp in ways I was only beginning to understand.

My father paused, taking a sip of the champagne before adding a tiny splash of orange juice.

"Your brother told me you two had quite the fight after the gala."

I coughed, choking on the sip I had taken. "When did Deacon have time to relay that information to you?"

"He also told me you turned down an offer from your supervisor to join her at Oxford."

My mouth fell open. Fucking Deacon. "Does he have nothing better to do than gossip about me? Surely, that's not what you pay him for."

"Your brother has a big mouth," he said dryly, leveling me a look that I couldn't really decipher. "That's one of the best schools in the world, Charlie. That seems like something you would have jumped on, once upon a time."

"I'm not taking it. Feels a bit like running, doesn't it?" I asked quietly, staring back at him.

I was pretty sure this was the longest time we had looked directly at one another, spent time just the two of us, in who knew how long. But I could feel it, the time and the expanse of years stretching out between us as we stared at one another.

"Running implies you don't have a choice. I'll give you one. I'd like you to come back to Winchester Holdings. There's a lot you could do here, locally even. I looked into that organization you chose for your gala donation. They do good work. You did good work for me." The corners of his eyes crinkled with worry, like he was bracing himself for an answer he didn't want.

My mouth dried out, and I continued to stare at my father, a man I barely knew anymore. Here he was offering up all I had ever wanted, even though I pretended otherwise. His approval, his love in the only way he knew how to show it. But for some reason, all I could picture was how he used to look at my mother, long before she got too sad to smile. "When was the last time you said her name?"

He swallowed uncomfortably, finally dropping his eyes. I waited as he swirled the champagne in the intricate crystal flute uselessly. "Claire."

I closed my eyes, squeezing them shut against the onslaught of tears pressing against them. My mother's name tumbling from my father's lips, the acknowledgment of her existence; that she had been a living, breathing person with a beating heart once upon a time. I felt heavy and light all at once, but as I exhaled, my shoulders slumped—the muscles seemingly loose after all these years.

"Claire," I repeated gently, looking back up at him through blurred eyes.

"You tried, Charlie. When you were younger. I'm sorry for not honoring that. You tried to keep her alive, keep our family together." His voice cracked, and if I wasn't mistaken, his blue eyes looked lined with tears. "I know you and your brother toss blame back and forth about what happened to her, how you've both chosen to grieve. But you know, if there is anyone to blame, it's me. And maybe that's why I've put so much distance between us—my own shame. I was too busy to notice her slipping away until it was too late. Her eyes, the way they used to sparkle. You look so much like her, you know? You remind me of her."

My father cleared his throat and rolled his shoulders back. His mouth popped open and closed in quick succession, like he was weighing his next words. "She made me promise that I wouldn't be hard on you, she could tell even when you were little, that this," he gestured around at the opulence surrounding us, and everything that went along with it before continuing, "you were both too good for this world. I should have listened, really listened to her. There was a veiled goodbye there, and I chose not to hear it. And then she left us, and you left for London, chased away by my inability to be there for you, and my worst fears were happening all over again."

And there they were. All the words I had ever wanted to hear from him, the acknowledgment, the breath of life back into the lungs of my mother's ghost. They settled around me, tucking me in like a parent might a child, pulling the covers all the way up to their chin. I waited for them to fix everything. To fill all the holes and plaster over the cracks of my heart, my soul. I felt them filling them up, some part way, some all the way. But the final touches, the final plaster and paint over top of them, those were mine to make.

The well of tears spilled over, tracking down my face in pathways that were surely becoming familiar. A choked sob escaped from my lips, and I could see the blurred outline of my father lurch forward instinctively before settling back down into his seat. I snorted a laugh through it all. Physical touch was still too far off for him, but the vulnerability in his words were giant steps for Steven Winchester.

He cleared his throat, clearly uncomfortable with the silence. "So, will you come back? Consider it at least?"

I laughed again, wiping at my eyes, and shaking my head. This offering, this approval, this seeming forgiveness, was all I thought I had ever wanted. The tightrope I had walked my entire life between wanting something for myself and wanting him to see me, to understand me. There was a time when I probably would have fallen to the floor in thanks, but the idea of returning to WH left me hollow. It wasn't what excited me, and it wasn't what I wanted.

"Thank you very much for the offer, but no thank you. Not right now. Maybe after I'm done with school."

My father nodded, the ghost of an approving smile twitching across his features before it was gone. He flipped open his paper again, casually raising the champagne to his mouth. "Should we catch a play before I leave this week?"

Another bizarre laugh rose on my lips, and I found myself nodding when the door was thrown open.

Deacon's hair was disheveled, and he was wearing a crumpled button down. Sunglasses were shielding his eyes, and he pushed them up, green eyes darting back and forth between the two of us. My face was wet with tears, and I was caught between laughter and sobs, with our father having disappeared behind the Sunday Times.

"What's going on here? Is everything okay?" He asked, narrowing his eyes at our father like he was ready to jump to my defense.

I held up my hand and wiped my eyes one last time before reaching forward to pour another drink. "Everything's fine, I'm just catching up with Dad."

The word felt heavy on my tongue. I couldn't remember the last time it was used to form the syllables that made up that word.

Our father's gaze lifted behind the paper, and he jerked his head, sort of a nod, sort of in surprise, a very Steven Winchester gesture that meant acknowledgment. He heard me call him *Dad* again, and he knew what that meant.

Smiling, he said, "There's nothing going on, Deacon. I'm enjoying breakfast with my daughter. Or, I was, until you interrupted. You look like you've seen better days."

Deacon gave me a sideways glance, eyes wild before a mischievous grin slid into place, and he dropped down into the available chair with a flourish. He dropped his sunglasses back to cover his eyes. "Charlie, pour me a mimosa. My IV hasn't set in yet."

"Pour it yourself. Unless you usually have someone on staff pour your drinks?" I rolled my eyes at him, leaning back in my chair, shoulders still loose and at ease. I couldn't feel any tension in my muscles at all, in fact.

"Jesus Christ, I'll pour it," our father muttered, snatching the bottle and offering the drink to Deacon, who accepted it before dramatically slumping back in his chair, issuing the occasional moan.

Our father disappeared behind the paper again, the only sound coming from him was the occasional flick of a page. But I found I didn't mind. I closed my eyes, relishing the first time our silence was comfortable.

CHAPTER THIRTY-THREE

My living room was a mess of half-packed boxes and folded cardboard waiting to be filled. Swirling my wine glass, I thumbed through the Oxford course catalog absentmindedly. Dr. Batra had sent me over what seemed to be an ever-growing list of readings she wanted me to complete that were authored by her new colleagues. But I found myself tracing the photos of the buildings with my fingertips and looking forward to it. It didn't feel like running; it was my choice. I tapped the wine glass to my teeth before taking a small sip and flicking the page to read a specific description for an economics seminar.

Rain dotted the windows, and I could faintly hear it trickling down the panes of glass over the low hum of music filtering through the sound system in the living room. It could have been a movie at that moment—the lost daughter finally reconciles with her father, gets his approval but makes the best choice for her in the end, finally at peace; the war with herself is over. And I did feel at peace, comfortable in my own mind and my own body, comfortable with my choices. I would have felt bad about all the casualties of the war along the way to get me here, but I couldn't bring myself to. I deserved to forgive myself.

The chime of the doorbell rang, and my eyes flicked up. From where I was sitting, I could see the front door just down the hallway. I frowned, taking another sip of my wine before setting it on the coffee table in front of me and letting the course catalog drop onto the couch. My feet moved across the worn hardwood floor, the creaks echoing throughout the house. I would miss this house. Fumbling with the heavy lock, I peered through a small opening in the door before pulling it all the way open.

David's hair was plastered to his face, and raindrops fell freely down his jaw. The sleeves of his dark sweater were pushed up on his forearms, and his hand was raised in a fist, like he was going to pound on the door if I hadn't opened it. He pushed his hair off his face before dropping his hand where it fluttered uselessly by his side. I cocked my head, noticing the tense line of his jaw and the way he kept clenching his fingers into fists. Unwavering, unflappably composed David Kennedy seemed nervous.

"You look beautiful," he breathed, darkened eyes roaming me.

A twinge of self-consciousness rose, and I looked down, tempted to cross my arms over the lacy top of the La Perla set from Noa. David teasing me about it at Deacon's engagement felt like a lifetime ago, like looking across an endless expanse. My skin was bare and my hair hung in a sheet around my face. There was nothing extraordinary about how I looked. My heart made a small jump at his words, but not the same way it would have torn itself apart against my ribcage in an attempt to get to him. The last words he spoke to me rang in my ear. Part of me wondered if he was right—I was probably the worst thing that happened to a lot of people. Including myself. But that was okay. I forgave myself.

"What I said to you...I didn't mean it. I don't wish I could hate you." David's voice was low when he spoke again. A pained look was etched into his features. "You're not the worst thing that's ever happened to me. You're the only thing that's ever mattered."

I opened my mouth, and there were a million words lingering on my lips. I didn't know where to land, but then David was there, right in front of me. Eyes dark, he tipped his head down, his restless hands coming to grip my chin. And then his lips were on mine. They were warm, tasting like rainwater, like home, and all I could smell was the ocean.

He pulled back before I even really had a chance to kiss him in return. "You've made mistakes. But so have I. Colossal, unforgivable mistakes. I should have stayed. I should have fought for you the way you fought for me. I should have shown you that there was nothing you could have done to drive me away. That there wasn't a single part of you I didn't love, that wasn't perfect. Letting you go, not being able to get past my own pride, because that's really what it was about at the end of the day, Charlie. That's the biggest one of all."

I crossed my arms, the rain starting to cause my hair to stick to the sides of my face. "Do you want to come in then?"

I turned on the ball of my foot, walking down the hallway before he had a chance to respond, but I heard the telltale click of the door. "Wine?" I called over my shoulder, already walking to the kitchen to grab another glass and the open bottle from the fridge.

"Sure," David answered, stopping in my living room. I looked up at him from where I was standing in the kitchen, filling up the glass. "So, you're going?"

"I am," I said, softly but confidently. "You didn't come here to ask me to stay, did you?"

David grinned, shaking his head. "I'd never do that to you, billion dollar baby. But I couldn't let you leave without telling you, letting you know I love you. That I'm sorry."

"Good, because I wouldn't stay for you," I said, my voice wavering.

I wasn't sure that I had the resolve to say no if he actually came out and said it. I walked forward, handing him the glass of wine. Our fingers brushed, and I felt the familiar niggling of that shock running through me. I folded my legs underneath me and sat back down on the couch. I watched David pick up the Oxford course catalog, eyes skating over it before dropping it on the coffee table.

"I wouldn't expect you to." David sat down beside me, his eyes never leaving mine. And there they were, the best stars in any sky—sparkling, all melted, warm honey; the lights left on in the window of your home after a long trip away. "I meant what I said. The mistakes aren't just ones you made. I own some of these fractured pieces, too."

"Thank you for saying that," I whispered, and I meant it. I had spent so much time blaming myself that it never occurred to me I was holding onto pieces that maybe didn't belong to me, that he should have fought for us the way I tried to. "But before you go throwing yourself at my feet. Things are different now. I need you to know...I slept with Tripp. You know we were...sort of together, for a very brief time before it imploded."

David nodded, eyebrows creasing and a frown stretching across his lips. "I know. I'm sorry it turned out the way it did."

"Does that change things for you? Your feelings?" I asked tentatively, unsure what answer would be easier to handle.

"No," David breathed. "You're in my blood, billion dollar baby. In my bones. I couldn't dig you out now even if I wanted to."

I nodded, taking a sip of my wine and relishing the way it burned my throat. We sat in silence for a moment longer, the raindrops trickling down the windows and the low din of the radio still in the background.

David swallowed, setting his wine glass down before turning to me and grabbing my feet onto his lap. My heart stumbled a bit, remembering all the times we sat just like this, in a different life, in a different city. "Does that change things for you?" David asked, his mouth twitching at the corner.

I paused, taking another drink before shaking my head. "No, I'll always be in love with you, David. Feelings for someone else, no matter how heavy, how complicated they were, can't change that. You're untouchable. Nothing could carve your place out of my heart. The whole thing belongs to you."

A grin stretched across his face, and he ran a hand through his hair before he pulled on my legs, bringing me forward and practically sloshing my wine everywhere. "This is La Perla, David!" I squawked jokingly, but my breath caught when I realized how close our faces were. I could feel the whispers of David's breathing against my cheeks.

"You're leaving," he repeated, dropping his forehead to mine and pressing his lips to the bridge of my nose. I nodded against them. "Can I stay here tonight? One last time?"

I nodded again, pushing off him to down the rest of my wine. Reaching out, I tentatively laced my fingers through David's, eyelids fluttering closed immediately at the warmth, the familiarity of them. David's lips brushed against my jaw, my earlobe, down the column of my neck before he raised them to meet mine in a featherlight touch. It was another kiss of permission, a knock on the door of your home, asking to come in. I nodded softly, swinging the door wide open when my tongue met his. This home had been shuttered, abandoned, but when I opened the door, I realized it had been standing all along. Dust covers over the furniture, waiting to be torn off, blinds and shutters ready to be opened for light to stream in. The foundations of this home would never fall down. This home would stand while I built another inside my own heart.

I was lying on my back, head turned and eyes angled toward the little bit of city light I could see from my bedroom windows. I could feel David beside me, his body curved toward mine, and his head propped up on his hand.

"It always made me...not sick. But...it made me something," he whispered, almost quieter than the vague hum of the city rising up around us.

I turned myself over, so I was facing him. I was just a finger brush away from his face. That beautiful face. "What made you sick?"

"Tripp. The fact that...you were his before you were ever mine." David's voice was nothing more than a whisper.

He leaned forward, hair flopping forward, and he pressed his forehead to mine, his hand coming to rest against my bare hip.

"I'm not sure I've ever really been anyone's, David, not when I've never even really been mine," I offered truthfully.

Like a magnet, my hands snaked their way up his chest to run through his hair. He sighed almost imperceptibly and leaned into my hand, honey eyes closing briefly.

"Did I make you feel small?" David asked, his breath turning ragged. "You say that you never deserved me. You didn't feel like you could tell me when you made a mistake, and I contributed to that, didn't I? Made you feel like you couldn't be honest with me? You know I said it was pride, the only thing that kept me from you, but I think it was guilt, too."

"I think so," I closed my eyes briefly, twisting his soft hair between my fingers. "Sometimes I felt...I don't know, infantile around you. I felt like you were just this fully grown up, functional person, stratospheres ahead of me in life. I don't think you did it intentionally. But you just seemed so big, so all encompassing. You were my whole heart. My whole body. My entire life. My entire world and..."

"You put me on a pedestal. But I did nothing to step down from it." David's voice was rough, his fingers tense against my hip. He pressed his lips to each of my cheeks before continuing. "You're not small, Charlie. You're the universe that I'm just fucking lucky to exist in."

I breathed, pressing my forehead into his and fingers tracing his shoulders, down to his collarbone and up his neck to his jaw. A small groan sounded in his throat, and I felt his lips part against my cheeks. "I was so scared you'd leave me, leave me like everyone else left me. So scared you'd figure out I was just this person so easy to forget and leave behind. I've waited years for my father to love me, to accept me. I could never figure it out—why no one seemed to love me enough to stay. And I loved you so much, and you saw me.

It just never occurred to me that I should have been falling in love with myself at the same time I was falling in love with you."

My voice was barely audible, and David said nothing. He gripped my hip in his hand, warmth from his fingers.

"I didn't even realize I didn't love myself. Not the way I'm supposed to. Not the way I deserve. I spent so much time wondering if maybe I was different, maybe my mom would have stayed. That if I had been different...if we had all been different back then, things would be so different now. That we'd be the family I wanted, that I thought we should be. I was trying to put pieces in a puzzle that no longer fit. I don't know who I would have been, who my dad would have been, who Deacon would have been, if she hadn't killed herself. I've been grieving something I was never going to have and just trying to shove myself anywhere I might possibly fit. I don't even think I know who I am."

David's lips brushed mine, and my heart stumbled over itself as I tightened my fingers on his face. It would be so, so easy to give in. To fall into him and pretend none of this happened.

"You fit in my head, Charlie. You always will. I wish just my love was enough. That I could make you love yourself the way you deserve to be loved. I'd do so many things so fucking differently. I'd never let you go again. But I'll be here in your corner the entire time you're figuring this out, loving yourself the way you deserve, forgiving yourself. I just want you to be happy. No matter how long it takes. And if when you do, I still fit for you—still make sense for you, give me a call, and we can see if *we* still fit."

I leaned forward, pressing my mouth against David's in urgency, and I pressed my eyes closed to stop the flow of tears. A sob crept up my throat.

David pulled back, forehead still pressed against mine. He removed his hand from my hip and placed it firmly around the back of my neck. "You deserve everything and more. Go, find yourself. Be who you were always meant to be—with or without me."

Our lips met through my tears and his trademark easy grin, kisses giving way to ragged breathing and teeth scraping final stolen moments against skin, gasps and moans caught in both our throats from our bodies moving together in the way that only happens when you've mapped someone's entire being, when you know who they are better than you know yourself. We stayed together like that—touching and loving and entirely wrapped up in one another until the sunlight began to stretch across the sheets of my bed. And there it was laid bare in my mind, what life could have been like with David or Tripp. But they had both hurt me, and I had hurt them. I knew they both deserved better, but for the very first time, I knew that I deserved better, too.

―――――――

In another Steven Winchester offering, the only way he really knew how, he insisted I use the jet for my move. It resulted in one of the most normal family arguments we could possibly have, with Deacon weighing in at one point and saying that I didn't deserve the jet, because I didn't appreciate it, nor did I appreciate the finer things in life, so my trust should probably just be directed toward him as well.

Dr. Batra had laughed hysterically when she asked for my flight information, but here I was, sitting in the back of a town car with nothing but my ancient Louis Vuitton Keepall from Taylor, because my father had all my things sent ahead of time, pulling up to the private airstrip at Teterboro. Guillaume was standing there with an overly large sign that had to be a joke, reading Ms. Winchester. I offered my thanks to the driver before shouldering my bag and stepping out of the car. I shut the door behind me, offering Guillaume a wave.

"Chuck."

I whirled around, eyes wide and heart plummeting in my chest. Tripp was slamming the door of a car I didn't recognize, but I assumed belonged to him. His hair was disheveled, and he appeared to have given up shaving, more than a thick lining of stubble grown across his face. It was the second-most casual I had ever seen him, nothing but a plain white t-shirt and a pair of Tom Ford khakis. His eyes were still frozen and looked borderline hollow now, and the lines around them more pronounced.

"Are you okay?" I asked softly, immediately stepping toward him and wrapping my arms around him.

He groaned, almost in relief, pulling me tightly against him in return.

"Better now," he said roughly, pressing his cheek to the top of my head. "I didn't have a choice. I can't say more than that but—"

I pulled back, grabbing his hands with mine. "I know. I know that. Despite what everyone else thinks, I know you wouldn't hurt me like that on purpose. It doesn't mean I'm not furious, not embarrassed. But I know something's going on. You're not a bad person, no matter how much you might pretend to be."

Tripp's features collapsed, and he ran a hand over his face, like he could scrub whatever it was away. "Don't go. You're leaving because of what I did. You asked me to be there for you, and then I wasn't. I fucked up, Charlie. Colossally. But please, stay. Hear me out."

"Tripp, I have to go," I said, taking a measured step back and surveying him.

"No, you don't," he gestured behind me, to where Guillaume was standing in front of the jet. "You have access to a private jet. You can leave whenever you want."

"I'm choosing to go," I whispered, tipping my head and reaching out for his hand.

He jerked backward and left mine there to hang uselessly.

"If Kennedy asked you to stay, you would. You're leaving because of me," Tripp said stubbornly, his jaw set in a firm line.

I shook my head, puffing out my cheeks and exhaling before reaching out and firmly grabbing his hand. "That's not true, Tripp. And there's a difference. David wouldn't ask me to stay. I've never felt like I was good enough for anyone. My mother, you, David. I need to feel good enough for myself. *This* is what I want. The only person I'm leaving for is me."

Tripp's fingers tightened around mine, a plea forming on his lips, but I shook my head and spoke again. "You're a better person than you pretend to be. And you were right. You *are* my friend, but it's always been more than that, too. I like what I see when I look at you, but I have to leave. It's not about you."

"It feels pretty fucking personal," Tripp said, disdain lacing his words.

"It's not. It's not about you, I promise," I whispered, searching his face desperately for any sort of answer. "Tripp, is everything okay? Your dad stepped down at the bank...please, you can tell me anything. What's going on?"

"What do you care? You're leaving," Tripp scoffed, trying to pull his hand away from me, but I kept hold of it.

"Please don't do this. I told you, it's not about you."

His jaw popped, and he looked like he was about to argue, but I shook my head again, squeezing his fingers once before bringing my hand to his chest and popping up on my toes to brush my lips against his cheek. Tripp stepped backward, taking a measured breath and closing his eyes before they opened, as frozen and as hard as ever. He gave a jerk of his head, turning back toward his car and shoving his hands in his pockets.

I closed my eyes, rubbing absentmindedly against my chest. It hurt my heart. Leaving David, leaving him, but I wasn't twenty years old anymore, clutching to a boy for salvation in my darkest moment.

I turned, offering Guillaume a small nod and smile, and started up the steps to the jet. I wasn't twenty-seven, either, clutching to one word of hope offered to me by someone I never felt good enough for. I dropped down in the ridiculous leather seat, not looking out the window but leaning my head back and closing my eyes. I was twenty-nine, and I was free.

Did you really think the story ended here? Charlie might just be finding herself...but there are a lot of players left on the board. On the next page, find the exclusive sneak peek to the third book in The Rich Girl Series, Found Girl, coming 2024.

FOUND GIRL

JANUARY 2024

FOUND GIRL

I was dreaming. It was a great dream. It was one of those dreams where all the pieces of my life fit with no sharp edges, nothing jutting out to poke me. They all softly clicked together, melding seamlessly. It might have been a boring dream to most people, but it was my best dream. The one where I lived with myself, made a home in this body made of muscle tissue and ligaments. This body that had chocolate hair and forest eyes, just like my brother, my favorite human in the world. Features I was proud to share with him. Features that came from the mix of our parents' genetics, both our mother and our father. This body that had hurt people but hadn't hurt anyone as much as I had hurt my own heart.

I am at home now, though. At home in this body, in this dream. It was a great dream. And then the phone rang.

I groaned, smacking my hand against my pillow uselessly, because there was only one person in my life who couldn't ever seem to remember the time difference. I popped an eye open, my hand ineffectually fumbling for my phone and propping it up to reveal my brother's name, along with a photo of him back in prep school I was particularly fond of. He had too much baby fat on his cheeks and couldn't grow a beard to save his life. But he was perfect.

"Deacon, it's three in the morning," I said, through closed eyes and a mouth that felt like sandpaper. "I'm not flying back to New York because the alterations on your tux for the rehearsal dinner weren't right. *Again*. It's an egregious waste of jet fuel."

"Charlie. You need to come home. It's, uh, it's dad. You have to come back."

I wasn't dreaming anymore. I was wide awake, and there was a new, sharp edge of life poking at me. This one jutted right through my heart.

ACKNOWLEDGEMENTS

Here we are again.

First and foremost, thank you for getting here—for sticking with Charlie when she was lost, for dealing with Deacon's irreverence, while David worked through his own issues, and while Tripp (sort of) became a likable human again. Taylor, of course, remains the only sensible one in the bunch, despite her penchant for shiny, expensive things. I think Noa might be too kind for all of them but more on that later.

But these books, and these characters, wouldn't be what they are without so many people. They wouldn't be even half of what they are without Krys and imPRESS Millennial Books. Krys, thank you for being the best publisher, editor, and friend. I'm so happy to know you.

To my beta and ARC readers, you're so important to me, and I am forever thankful for your time and your thoughtfulness.

Benjamin, you've spent almost as much time with these characters as I have. Your belief in them (and me), has never waivered. Thank you for always being the steadfast ship in my hurricane. You're my best friend, and I love you.

I have an endless list of friends who have supported me and this book, and for that I consider myself endlessly lucky. Thank you all for listening to me when I wouldn't shut up, for lifting me up when I didn't believe in myself, and for always celebrating these accomplishments with me.

Finally, to my Mom, for being who she is, and her enduring commitment to this series being a murder mystery. I'm sorry, it's not, but maybe I'll write one for you one day.

It's hard to believe I'm here—looking at writing the final book, at least in Charlie's story. Rich Girl was originally going to be a standalone with a very morally ambiguous ending, and then it was going to be a duology, ending at Lost Girl, but I love writing these characters and this world so much—and if I'm being honest, it's not just Charlie that needs some healing (looking at you, Deacon). I can't wait to spend more time with all of them, and I hope you can't, either. Charlie might be found, but I'm not sure anyone else is.

See you in January.

Ingram Content Group UK Ltd.
Milton Keynes UK
UKHW011614210623
423807UK00004B/194

9 781778 248337